The Betrayed

The Betrayed

A Novel of the Gifted

LISA T. BERGREN

BERKLEY BOOKS, NEW YORK

THE BERKLEY PUBLISHING GROUP
Published by the Penguin Group
Penguin Group (USA) Inc.
375 Hudson Street, New York, New York 10014, USA
Penguin Group (Canada), 90 Eglinton Avenue East, Suite 700, Toronto, Ontario M4P 2Y3, Canada
(a division of Pearson Penguin Canada Inc.)
Penguin Books Ltd., 80 Strand, London WC2R 0RL, England
Penguin Group Ireland, 25 St. Stephen's Green, Dublin 2, Ireland (a division of Penguin Books Ltd.)
Penguin Group (Australia), 250 Camberwell Road, Camberwell, Victoria 3124, Australia
(a division of Pearson Australia Group Pty. Ltd.)
Penguin Books India Pvt. Ltd., 11 Community Centre, Panchsheel Park, New Delhi—110 017, India
Penguin Group (NZ), 67 Apollo Drive, Rosedale, North Shore 0745, Auckland, New Zealand
(a division of Pearson New Zealand Ltd.)
Penguin Books (South Africa) (Pty.) Ltd., 24 Sturdee Avenue, Rosebank, Johannesburg 2196, South Africa

Penguin Books Ltd., Registered Offices: 80 Strand, London WC2R 0RL, England

This book is an original publication of The Berkley Publishing Group.

Copyright © 2007 by Lisa T. Bergren.
"Readers Guide" by Lisa T. Bergren and "An Interview with Lisa T. Bergren" copyright © 2007 by Lisa T. Bergren.
Interior map created and provided by Lisa T. Bergren.
Interior text design by Tiffany Estreicher.

Scripture quotations are taken from the Holy Bible, New International Version. Copyright © 1973, 1978, 1984 International Bible Society. Used by permission of Zondervan Bible Publishers.

FIRST EDITION: September 2007

Library of Congress Cataloging-in-Publication Data

Bergren, Lisa Tawn.
  The betrayed : a novel of the Gifted / Lisa T. Bergren.—1st ed.
    p. cm.
  ISBN 978-0-425-21708-5
  1. Aristocracy (Social class)—Fiction. 2. Siena (City-state)—Fiction. 3. Italy—Fiction. I. Title.

PS3552.E71938B48 2007
813'.54—dc22   2007017476

PRINTED IN THE UNITED STATES OF AMERICA

10 9 8 7 6 5 4 3 2 1

To Rebecca, dearest of friends and sisters.
Thank you for remaining true through it all.
I love you.

COUNTS
OF SAVOY

VISCONTI
FAMILY

PATRIARCHATE
OF TRENT

DELLA SCALA FAMILY

PATRIARCHATE
OF AQUILEIA

REPUBLIC OF VENICE

GONZAGA FAMILY

ESTENSE FAMILY

REPUBLIC OF FLORENCE

Como

Milano

Verona

Venezia

MARQUISATE
OF SALUZZO

REPUBLIC
OF GENOA

REPUBLIC
OF PISA

REPUBLIC
OF SIENA

Firenze

PAPAL
STATES

Siena

• Roma

KINGDOM
OF NAPLES

Napoli

ITALIA c. 1350

KINGDOM
OF SICILY

The Betrayed

THE HUNTED
Siena

CHAPTER ONE

October, The Year of Our Lord 1340

"Sɪʀ, we have brought the one you seek," the wiry man said from a dark hallway.

"Good. Bring her in," Vincenzo said. He glanced toward the man beside him, Abramo Amidei, staring out the window, apparently deep in thought. Or preparing for this . . .

A small, elderly woman arrived, flanked by two large guards.

Vincenzo descended the two steps downward and looked her over. Here was the last one to be questioned—the last one touched by Daria d'Angelo, healed by her. He and Abramo had wrung every detail they could from each of those healed by the "Duchess"—a title more granted out of honor than true. There had been far more than Vincenzo had realized, and each gave them more insight into Lady Daria's life with her new companions.

The city dwellers called this one Old Woman Parmo, in that there were few who reached their gray and wrinkled years, and yet she had the spirit of one who could still take on another in battle. Old eyes, rimmed in wrinkles and understanding, met his own. "Baron del Buco," she said in greeting. She did not fear. She only waited.

As with the others they had questioned, Vincenzo recognized something of Daria within this one. There was a common strength within them all. Daria had healed her. Given her height and vitality again. Vincenzo had seen this old woman himself in the marketplace, done business with her. For decades she had sold cloth, so bent over that she could not meet her customer's eye. Now here she was, before him, upright. . . . What power was that? That Daria, Daria d'Angelo, *his* Daria could do this?

Old Woman Parmo met his gaze unflinchingly, as if she already knew he had turned against Daria. Suddenly, Vincenzo's master, Lord Abramo Amidei, turned from the window and descended the stairs. With one broad stroke, he took the old woman by the neck, rushed her to the wall, slammed her against it, and held her there, struggling to breathe. "Where?" he asked between gritted teeth. "Where have they gone?"

"Who?" she said, through strangled breaths. She glanced toward Vincenzo, as if holding hope that he might assist her, and he shifted uncomfortably.

Amidei leaned closer. "You know well of whom I speak. Tell me." He leaned harder into his grip, lifting her a little higher. Her lips became blue as she desperately clawed at his big hands.

"I . . . know . . . not."

Abramo stared at her for several long moments, as if she were no more than a bug on the wall, about to be squashed. They all could hear two young men in the streets, banging on the front door of Amidei's home, shouting demands, calling for the magistrate.

Abramo released Old Woman Parmo suddenly, allowing her to drop to the floor.

Vincenzo held back, although his instinct was to rush to the old woman, assist her up. But she was not to be touched. She was not for him, not for Amidei, therefore. . . . Still, he was moved to speak. "We ought to release her. She knows nothing, Abramo."

Abramo turned upon her, writhing on the cold stone floor, still trying to catch her breath. He saw what Vincenzo saw—knees, hips, back that moved like a young woman's, not like the woman who had long suffered from rheumatism. Looking away as if in disgust for a moment, Abramo turned, bent, and grabbed her arm, hauling her upward and forward. "Very well, then, old woman. You cannot tell us where they went. But you shall tell us everything you've learned."

Laguna, Northern Italia

"I do not understand," Gianni said, looking out to the lone fisherman off their island. "He has brought in his catch. Who does he think he fools, tossing and pulling on that net?"

It was late afternoon, and his knights, Basilio and Rune, stood beside him along with Hasani, Lady Daria d'Angelo's guardian and companion. They stared out to the lone fisherman. It was the same each morning. The fisherman arrived, hauled in his catch of mullet, left for Venezia, and then returned a few hours later, still fishing and yet catching nothing every afternoon, until sunset, for two days now.

"He watches us," Father Piero said, drawing near them.

"That much is obvious," Gianni scoffed, looking down at the much smaller man. "But is he friend or foe?"

They watched the big man in the small boat a while longer. "Go and fetch Tessa," Gianni said to Rune, his eyes remaining trained on the man. "She will tell us if we need fret or not."

"You still believe we are safe? Or do you believe we have been discovered?" Basilio said as Rune left.

"I know not. Tessa will."

⚓ ⚓ ⚓

THE banging on the door continued until Abramo threw it open abruptly.

"You wished to speak to me?" he said to the two young men who stood there, fear etched upon their faces.

"Nay, m'lord," the slender man said, bowing a couple of times in nervousness, obviously surprised to see him at the door. "I only wished to . . . see my grandmother home."

"And so you may," Abramo said. He gestured down the street. "Allow us to see to your safety."

"That is not necessary, m'lord," the boy tried.

"Please. It is no trouble whatsoever. An afternoon walk," he said, thumping his chest. "I always find it bracing. Don't you agree, Baron?"

"Absolutely," Vincenzo returned.

"There you have it, boy," Abramo said, turning the young man forward with a little toss toward his guards.

Abramo and Vincenzo took the lead down the street, with two guards behind them hauling along the old woman. Four others took the grandson and his friend who had banged upon Abramo Amidei's door.

The crowds split before them, cascading on either side like the wake from a boat, no eye meeting theirs. As they walked, Vincenzo thought about Daria, about how she had lied to him, refused to bring him into her confidence, failed to share with him what was happening to her as it occurred. She had taken another path . . . it was as if he could see them on the side of a steep mountain, he on one trail, she on another. But she had chosen wrongly. As hard as this was, she must be brought around to his way of thinking, Abramo's way of thinking. This was their destiny . . . power. Strength. Passion.

They had once been like family; Daria had called him Uncle. But death had destroyed them. The death of Daria's parents, the death of her handfasting to her beloved, Marco, and their future. For Vincenzo, it had been the death of Tatiana, his third wife, pregnant at last with an heir, and then the death of his trust of Daria. That she had not confided in him, allowed him to guide her in this, enraged him for a time. Now he only felt an empty hollow within his chest when he thought of her. He wanted her with him again, beside them, making him feel alive again, whole. Abramo wanted her and hers. Together, they would leave suffering behind, cheat death, rule life.

Could she not see that his was the way to hope? Dimly, he could see her in Il Campo on that last night, tears streaming down her lovely face, a hand reaching out to him. Light surrounded her, a holy glow, her hair lifting in the wind, her eyes awash in pleading. It was as if time slowed down to a crawl, and he could see each moment with such clarity! So much was unspoken, and yet he knew what she offered—beauty, love, peace, courage. But it would take some time, work . . .

He had no time. The years were quickly advancing upon him. Now was the time to seize what was his, not wait on Daria's way. He remembered little else, other than the decision not to reach out to her when she beckoned. This was his path. This. Amidei's path. It was harsh at times, but the power made his heart surge with glory, strength. And it was immediate. Already, in taking Amidei's road, adopting his ways as doctrine, Vincenzo had doubled his wealth and holdings, lost most nights in the arms of beautiful women and other pleasures, and over the months, watched the Nine of Siena, those who held political power, cower before them. Together, Lord Abramo Amidei and Baron Vincenzo del Buco owned Siena.

They arrived at the old warehouse and reluctantly the boy turned the key in the large door, nervously nodding to them. "Thank you, my lords, for seeing us home. We will be well on our own from here."

"That is yet to be determined," Abramo said lowly. He turned the boy and shoved him through the door, into the dark warehouse. "Light some of those lamps," he said to his guards. He turned and leaned in close to the boy's friend who had accompanied him to the Amidei door. "Do not let me catch sight of you ever again," he said slowly, enunciating every word. "Do not call for help, or I shall hunt down each and every one in your family. Run home, boy. Run."

The boy's eyes grew larger and larger and with one quick, apologetic glance at the Parmo boy, he did as he had been told.

Abramo advanced upon the old woman's grandson and she cried out. The boy tried to hold his ground, fight back, but Abramo was much stronger, much larger. The boy was the key to getting to his grandmother. It was always easy, so easy, to play upon emotions. Love. It was a weakness.

Abramo turned the boy's arm around behind him and forced him to a pile of carpets. He looked upward. Good, strong beams crossed beneath the steepled roofline. "Fetch a rope and fashion a noose," he said to a guard.

Old Woman Parmo cried out, bringing one hand to her mouth, another to her forehead.

The boy dared to try to look at him from the corner of his eye. He was a strong one, this. "We know not where they went. It's been months . . . we haven't seen them!"

"I believe you speak the truth," Abramo said, handing him off to his guards. "But you know what transpired while they were here. I want to know all of it. What happened to your grandmother? How did they discover you? How did the Duchess heal her? What words were exchanged? I want every word, every moment you can remember, or I shall have your life."

"We shall not betray the Duchess," the boy said, the glint of manhood in his eyes. "You are plainly her enemies."

Abramo raised his hand and a guard slipped a noose over the boy's neck and tightened it. Another guard drew in the slack.

The grandmother cried out, "Stop! Stop!"

Abramo gestured again and the guard ceased the upward momentum of the rope. "You are willing to tell me what you know, woman?"

She nodded through her tears and watched as the noose slackened around her grandson's neck.

"Catch your breath, woman," Abramo said soothingly, taking her arm and leading her away a few paces. He sighed, as if weary. "Duchess d'Angelo obviously has uncommon gifts. She undoubtedly told you to tell no one about them. But we are not the lady's enemy, as your grandson believes. You two are merely trying to be faithful to your word. We respect that," he said with a winsome look, tossing his hands to either side. He gestured toward Vincenzo. "That man is the Duchess's trusted advisor and friend. Surely you've seen them together many a time. We fear for the lady's life, thus the necessity for our extreme actions. She left Siena under very mysterious circumstances. It is most urgent we find her, and find her quickly. You know yourself of her extensive business and holdings here." He paused to laugh under his breath. "You know who she left in charge? An artist! Things are in disarray for the Duchess. We must get word to her at once. She stands to lose everything."

Old, wise eyes followed him intently. But instead of falling toward Abramo's soothing charms as Vincenzo had seen so many do, she was edging away, visibly leaning back from him.

It was only a moment later that Abramo saw it too. He sat down on a pile of carpets as she stood against the warehouse wall, staring toward her grandson as if she were saying good-bye. Abramo rose immediately, slicing their glance with his torso.

"Tell me. Tell me everything you know." His tone had returned to cold stone. He stared at her while lifting his hand. All the old woman could see was the rope again becoming taut above Abramo's shoulder, could hear her grandson strangling.

"No. No, m'lord. Don't do this. You ask the impossible! I cannot! Not after all the lady did for me . . ."

He raised his hand again, furious eyes upon her. Now she could see her grandson's feet kicking out on either side.

"Please!" she said, hand over her heart. "Please!" She panted in desperation, shaking her head. Several moments passed. She wept, trying valiantly to hold on, failing. "All right! Release him, release him," she said through her tears. As the boy's body slumped to the ground, she turned to the wall and gave in to sobs, furious at herself for betraying her lady, unsure of what else she could do.

Abramo gave her a moment and then handed her a handkerchief. "Turn and tell me, woman," he said in a tone that belied the ferocity of his words. "If you pause for but a breath again, I will haul him to your rafters myself and leave the rope so high that you cannot cut him down for hours."

ぐ ぐ ぐ

"WE must move into Venezia, m'lady," Gianni said, pacing behind her.

They had taken up residence on a tiny island off Venezia, once a town, now inhabited only by the skeleton of a chapel, ruined by fire, and several families who raised vegetables and fished to feed the city. The gardens were now mostly turned over, about to release their last crop of squash and zucchini.

"Why not winter here?" Daria said, staring out a window to the sea.

She felt safe here. He understood that. But nowhere was truly safe. And here, on this tiny island, their only escape route would be to the sea. If the time came, he wanted the choice of either land or water. Their only course was forward. Their only hope was forward. "We've been here for better than two months. It is time we take our next steps, discover where the Lord is taking us."

"I thought he had brought us here," she said, looking only to Piero.

"He did," the priest put in. "We were to catch our breath, regain our strength. And we have done so. I agree with Gianni. It is time to move inland, to Venezia. We came here for a reason. Let us be about it."

Gianni moved around so that he was between her and the window. "I have found a small palazzo, m'lady. It is off the Grand Canal, the old residence of a Turkish trader. There is a warehouse on the canal level, and a floor above that. Eight, nine rooms. Two turrets, which could serve us well. It is not as nice as your home in Siena, but it is suitable. And it is for rent. I have secured it for six months' time."

She sighed and looked at the rough-hewn table beneath her hand. Gianni noticed she appeared weary. She had been through much in these months, his lady. "Very well," she said. "But before we become absorbed in city life and winter is fully upon us," she said in a voice nearly as low as a whisper, "there is something we must do."

Gianni found himself bracing as her large brown eyelashes lifted and her eyes met his. "And that is, m'lady?"

"The island of lepers. I must go there. And soon."

Gianni drew back and looked to Piero, who did not react, and then to Hasani, in the corner, who as always, seemed to have anticipated just this. Gianni shook his head. "No, Daria. Not there. Lepers! God could not be calling you there. There are hundreds upon that island. Hundreds!"

A small smile pulled at the corners of her cheeks. "Yes," she said. "Hundreds." She rose, more light and life in her eyes than there had been in some time. "We shall need to pack food. Water." She turned to Rune and Basilio, at once every inch the regal lady of Siena. "You must obtain a finely woven silk veiling. Several bolts of it. They need it for protection from the sun, and woolens to battle against the winter ahead. A hundred pair of sandals or boots. No doubt they've been left with no protection for their feet. And I need several bottles of a special oil . . ." She turned away with the knights, instructing them further.

Gianni shook his head, half in exasperation, half in glory to see the light in his lady's eyes return.

"We'll leave as soon as all is in order," she said, turning to face Gianni from across the room. "And then, master Gianni, you shall take us to our new home in Venezia."

ය ය ය

ABRAMO fingered the tapestry and lifted it closer, observing the delicate weave and detail. An old altar cloth, and at the lower right corner, a woman who bore an uncanny resemblance to Daria d'Angelo. "Fascinating, this trail of clues they have discovered," he mused. He pulled the large tapestry loose from the wall and flipped it, laying it upon a stack of linens nearby. He backed up several paces, arms crossed, and studied the image, visible among the crossed threads of the backside—a peacock, in the lower left corner. Above it, spreading across the wide expanse, towered a threatening dragon. Abramo let loose a deep, guttural laugh, arms spread wide. "Yes, yes, so my little peacock knew that I was coming."

He whirled and paced back and forth. "The Gifted are a worthy and entertaining conquest." He turned bright eyes upon Vincenzo. "This is good," he said, clapping him on the shoulder. "Good!"

"I confess it is difficult for me to see it that way," Vincenzo said. "Finding these clues only strengthens their thought that they are on some divine path. It gives them power. How is it good for us?"

Abramo waved his head back and forth. "Well, I admit, it does complicate things. But do you know how long, how long, Vincenzo, it has been since I have had a true challenge? I still consider your little Daria my greatest conquest. We must bring her and hers to our side. Many a soldier has lost a battle, but gone on to see a war won. The key is to change tactics, now. You tried to woo her, bring her along through friendly tactics, reason. You can see for yourself," he said, gesturing toward Old Woman Parmo, cradling her grandson in her arms, who still labored to breathe, "that sometimes alternate methods are needed."

He leaned closer, speaking across Vincenzo's shoulder now. "You appealed to the Duchess out of love, out of loyalty, friendship, and familial ties, good God man, even as her co-consul of the guild, and she denied you. But mark my words: We shall see your Daria, Sir Gianni, even the priest, submit."

"How? How do you intend to do that?" Vincenzo whispered, still staring at the old woman, rocking her grandson back and forth, willing him to keep breathing.

"The same way I forced the old woman to talk to me," Abramo said, a smile curving his lips. "We shall make them suffer—and exploit their greatest weaknesses."

"Weaknesses?"

"Come now, Vincenzo. You are quicker than that. Where is each of us the weakest? Where we are most tender, of course. The things, the people we hold most dear. Our values. Or mayhap," he said, pausing to stare out a high, narrow window, "through what they perceive is their divine call. Yes," he said with a pleased grin. "Yes. We shall find their weaknesses, every one of them. And through those slices in their armor we shall worry a hole that becomes a gap that becomes a chasm. And then, there, Vincenzo, we shall have them."

CHAPTER TWO

"THIS is insanity," Gianni said to Father Piero, staring at his lady, standing regally, at the front of the boat.

"Our friend is back," Vito said, nodding to the fisherman in the distance.

"Tessa . . ." Gianni began.

The child shook her head. "All is well. I think he may be a friend."

"What? We know him?"

Tessa shook her head. "I . . . I am uncertain."

Gianni looked hard at her. "But you are certain that he does not intend to do us harm."

"Yes."

"He could still be a spy," Ugo said. "He doesn't intend to do harm to us himself, but he could harm us by his watching."

"Cease," Daria said, over her shoulder. "All of you. Father Piero, will you lead us in a prayer? We are nearly there."

All eyes went to the long island, several miles off Venezia. They could see figures roving the shore, watching their approach.

Father Piero raised his arms as if sheltering all of them, bowed his head, and closed his eyes. "Lord God, we ask for your protection. Keep us from the illness, Father. Work through Daria, through all of us to bring healing and light. In Christ's holy name, amen."

More and more gathered on shore, anticipating their arrival. "They think we're bringing food, like the monks," Basilio said.

"They are hungry for much," Daria said, closing her eyes and lifting her face to the sun now rising high in the sky above the island.

"Is that the word of healing you bring to them, daughter?" Piero asked softly.

Tessa was nodding. "Yes. They are so hungry, so hungry . . ."

"So hungry they will have *us* to break their fast," Vito quipped lowly.

ᖬ ᖬ ᖬ

ABRAMO and Vincenzo were in the villa gardens several days after their interview with Old Woman Parmo when word arrived at last.

A maid came in, gave a brief curtsey, and said, "M'lord. You have a messenger from the Vaticana a Roma."

Vincenzo and Abramo shared a look, and each sat up a bit straighter. "See him in," Abramo said, "and fetch some more wine and bread."

In moments, the rider entered the gardens, a scrawny man in his middling years, pulling off his gloves as he made his way between the rose bushes. He bowed his head. "M'lord, I have brought you word of the knight Gianni de Capezzana and his lady, Daria d'Angelo."

"Come, come," Abramo said, gesturing toward the empty chair across from him. The maid brought the wine and bread and immediately departed. They watched patiently as the rider stuffed a piece of bread down his mouth and hurriedly guzzled a glass of wine without pause.

Vincenzo could see Abramo swallow his distaste. But he was infinitely patient. Vincenzo had already learned much from Amidei in how to wait for the right time to act—in closing a deal, discovering new means of increasing wealth, or bedding a woman.

"Word came to the cardinal, just as you hoped it would."

"Go on."

"The story is of a female healer in or near Venezia. She healed a crippled child on a remote island. She was accompanied by at least four knights and a priest, as well as a young girl."

"Venezia? Venezia. Of course." He looked across the garden to the light playing on the water of a still fountain. "I would give a pouch of gold to know what sent them scurrying northward."

"Mayhap they only knew we would give chase. Venezia is a city that one can easily escape within," Vincenzo offered.

"Indeed," Abramo said with a sigh. He looked to the messenger. "What did the cardinal do with this information?"

"He immediately packed and departed the same day as I."

Abramo rose and gestured toward the messenger to complete his meal. "Your award will await you in the kitchen," he said. "Come, Vincenzo." As they entered the house, he tossed a bag of coins upon a table that could be seen from the courtyard. They continued walking, down a hallway now, and he paused to say to a knight, "See to it that that man does not leave our gardens alive. Dispose of his body in the night, and be certain no one sees you do it."

"Yes, m'lord," the man said. "It shall be done."

Abramo turned to Vincenzo. "Venezia in the autumn and winter can be quite lovely but rather cold. You must go home and prepare, pack. We have a trip ahead of us."

Vincenzo smiled. "Anything in particular that you wish for me to bring?"

"In fact, there is. Master Marco Adimari."

"Marco?" Vincenzo felt his grin fade into a frown. "Why Marco?"

Abramo paced before him, finger tapping his chin. "You've said they shared a great passion. Seeing him in Venezia, where she least expects to see him, will throw Daria off balance. We will use him for some good work on our behalf."

"But Daria neither trusts nor cares for Marco any longer."

"Nay?" Doubt flooded Abramo's eyes. "Once a woman loves deeply, it is my experience that a part of her always loves. It is a weakness in the Duchess's armor. And we are seeking every chink in the armor we can find, are we not? Both you and Marco will be of use because of this."

Vincenzo gave him a tiny, reluctant nod. "Marco's child is due in the spring. I do not know if I can entice him to come along."

"Of course you can, Vincenzo. He looks to you for guidance; I've seen it myself." Abramo gave a tiny shrug. "Very well. We can wait to find the Gifted before we bring him north. It may very well take time to rout them out. But go to him, now. Tell him you are about your business in Venezia that he'll wish a part of"—he paused until Vincenzo met his gaze and nodded—"Yes, you shall see to your business in Venezia as well as our joint interest in the Gifted. Once there, we will seal your agreement with Lord Frangelico and his maritime partners on behalf of the guild. It is a new era for the house of Baron del Buco."

Vincenzo paced, chin in hand, thinking of all that had transpired within the last few months—of Daria's broken handfast with Marco Adimari and her journey to Roma, where she met up with that cursed priest. About her stubborn, adamant refusal to see how a partnership with Frangelico would increase their joint wealth threefold, how her new ties to the Gifted had pulled her attention from even the guild, the business he had labored to build beside Daria's father, and then Daria herself.

Foolish, foolish woman! No other woman had such prestige and power. Briefly, he allowed himself to think of her gift of healing, of this latest story of a child healed . . . of Old Woman Parmo. And yet she had refused to heal his beloved, pregnant wife, Tatiana, save her and their tiny baby, so dearly wanted, so dearly needed. A shiver of rage raced through him. He glanced up at Abramo. "What of Daria and the guild?"

"Things are progressing as planned. Ambrogio has made a number of gaffes that have cost him credit among the guild council. A movement has begun already to oust him from Daria's seat as your co-consul and make you sole consul. In fact, I expect it to happen this night."

"Excellent, excellent." When had Abramo planned to share this information with him? He'd clearly known of it for days. Timing. Abramo always watched for the perfect time to do anything—like a chess player in no rush to finish the game.

"As for the Duchess, it is my hope that we can sway her from her current path and bring her home. She belongs here. With you, Vincenzo. We'll make her face her losses—the guild and all that her father struggled with you to attain. Add Marco in an intimate, surprising setting, and old wounds will be relived and who will she look to? Her old mentor and confidant, the baron," he said, gesturing toward Vincenzo. "And without her, the others will be easier to bring down. In fact, if we take down any of them, I believe the rest will fall. That is our call, my friend. To create chinks in the armor, chinks in the armor."

⚓ ⚓ ⚓

DARIA was prepared, somewhat, for the sight of the lepers. What she did not anticipate was the smell, the rank smell of rotting flesh. There were hundreds here upon this island, all in various states of undress, all with open sores that covered scalps, leaving only bloody flesh where there once was hair, some with disfigured noses and eyes due to infection and the waste of the disease. There were old women and small children. Mothers with babes at their breast. Curiously, there were few young men. Had they somehow escaped this island, or died trying?

They amassed on the short hillside, waving wooden clappers or clanging bells, as demanded by the city and clergy, desperately trying to do as they had been told, desperately trying to avoid anything that would keep them from help. Daria had seen the ceremonies herself; the rites of separation from community, the sentencing of isolation.

"*Quicumque ergo maculatus fuerit lepra et separatus ad arbitrium sacerdotis . . .*" Piero muttered.

Defiled, unclean. Daria silently continued from Leviticus, gazing about. *As long as he has the infection he remains unclean. He must live alone; he must live outside the camp.*

Daria wept as she walked between each bank of the ill, wept at the starvation she saw within their eyes more than across their narrow frames. She had seen this disease before. Knew that numbness and paralysis led to injury that led to infection that led to loss of toes or fingers or even eyes. They paused about fifty feet up from the beach and Daria scanned from one side to the other, searching for the one she came to heal. Some had only a single reddish spot on their scalp. Others were so incapacitated, so taken by the paralysis, that their hands were like claws, useless before them. Oh, if only they were all to be healed!

"Daria, whom do you seek?" Piero said softly, at her ear.

⚓ ⚓ ⚓

THE group was edging closer to the Gifted, all of them asking for money, for food, for bandages, for help.

Gianni unsheathed his sword and the other men did the same, menacing them backward. "Father Piero," he began.

He knew the edge in the knight's voice. There were many here with little to fear in death. The Gifted could be overrun, overtaken, despite the knights and their weapons, their clothing stripped from their bodies, even killed and eaten. These were a desperate people.

"M'lady," Tessa said in a high pitch, pushing toward Daria as an old woman reached to touch her fine dress.

"Duchess!" cried Vito, raising his sword high when a man reached for her. The crowd drew back with a weary gasp.

"Nay!" Piero and Daria shouted, both whirling. Vito pulled back his sword, just before striking an advancing old man.

This place was filled with the devastated, the hollow. Piero hadn't felt so overwhelmed since . . . the day in the marketplace, back at home, in Siena. The day Daria had preached of love and ultimate healing. He glanced at her; she was clearly overcome, with the same look of longing upon her face that always came upon her when she was about to ask her Lord to heal.

Hasani drew near, then, beside her. Piero studied Daria's tall, black companion, his steps sure, as if he knew what they were to do. Piero had seen it before in the man. Hasani took her hand in his and reached out to the nearest child with his other, covering the boy's matted hair with his long, black fingers. He smiled down at the boy with sorrow, as if he knew the child's pain, and the child looked up to him with such shock and overwhelmed pleasure at the sensation of touch that the entire group seemed to hold their breath.

Tears cascaded down Daria's face and, resolutely, she reached out and pulled the boy into her arms. Perhaps three, he gazed up at her in wonder. This was the one, the one they had come to heal.

"My friends, my friends," she said, breaking away from the boy's glance only to look about her. "You have suffered much here. I am so sorry for your pain. You are ill and hungry and longing for home. But we are here to tell you of the bread of life. We are here to tell you about the food that fills and keeps on filling. We are here to tell you of ultimate healing."

The crowd surged around them as others arrived from the other side, all trying to see. "I don't like this," Gianni said in a low voice to his knights.

"We have the western flank," Rune said, nodding to Basilio, swords sheathed but hands up in warning.

"We have the north," Vito and Ugo said.

Hasani lifted his chin from the south.

"And I have the east," Gianni said. "But I think we need a way to make these people beholden to us, and quickly."

"We are on defense," Piero said quietly from beside Daria and Tessa. "We must appear as if we trust them, that we are only here to provide aid. Quickly, Basilio and Ugo, go to the ship and bring up the chests full of veiling, sandals, and salve."

"We are here to help you," the priest shouted to the crowd, moving closer to the lepers. "The lady has brought blankets to warm you, veils and hats to protect you from the sun, sandals for your feet, pumice stones for your calluses, salve for your sores! Food, fresh water, fresh bandages."

The crowd stood, unmoving, eyes still upon Daria.

"Father Piero," Daria said, "speak to them the words that are in your heart. Bring them truth and wisdom while I bring this child healing."

He eyed her for a moment and then walked deeper among the lepers. He raised his hands. "Our Lord knew what it meant to be an outcast. He was betrayed by his enemies, but worse, his friends as well. Many of you have suffered much." He paused to touch a man on the shoulder and a woman on the face. "Some of you are not long for this world. You feel forgotten and barred from your very homes." And as he passed, speaking words of hope and healing to his open-air congregation, each fell to his or her knees, praying and crying. How long? How long had it been since someone touched them? Reached out to them? Where were his Christian brothers and sisters? Why were these people abandoned? Forgotten?

He thought of his years in Roma, as abbot where Daria had come to rest and recuperate from her heartbreak. Had his years been wasted there? Certainly not. Time of prayer and ministering to those who came to him were what God had wanted him to do at the time. And it was there that God had placed him so that he could begin gathering the Gifted, at just the right time, gather them together to do as the Lord led. There was a time in any man's life to stay, be still, rest, learn. And there was a time to go, move out, apply what one had learned. Piero ground his teeth as he stood and studied the people about him, searching for the right words.

"We are here for the One who said, '*Caeci vident claudi ambulant leprosi mundantur surdi audiunt mortui resurgunt pauperes evangelizantus.* The blind receive sight, the lame walk, those who have leprosy are cured, the deaf hear, the dead are raised, and the good news is preached to the poor.' " The crowd gasped and stumbled away a pace, recognizing that the priest had dared to translate the Holy Scriptures into their common tongue. But they did not go far, hungrily listening for more, eyes glazed in wonder.

"Blessed is the man who is not ensnared by doubt or discouragement. Hear me, brothers and sisters, *hear me.* Let my words fall upon your ears and enter in, like rain upon dry, cracked soil. There is nothing you have done or can do that will separate you from the love of our Messiah. And he will see each one of you to complete healing, in either this life or the next."

Piero took another step, knelt beside a little girl, and spoke to all around him—of suffering, of sin, of a Savior. They listened, most with lifeless, uninterested eyes, but they did not turn away. Were they hearing the sacred words? He touched one and then another. Some shied away. Others leaned into his touch and closed their eyes as if wishing to memorize the sensation.

Jesus had dared to touch a leper. Piero prayed for his strength now, for Daria, leaning over the boy, higher up on the hill, pouring holy oil upon him. He studied them for a moment and Tessa met his gaze, smiling for the first time since they had arrived. And in that desolate, forsaken place, Piero knew again the meaning of light within the darkness.

ൟ ൟ ൟ

CARDINAL Boeri watched as the sails snapped full with a crisp autumn wind and the coast of Italia moved by. In another day, they would arrive, and he could once again track the Gifted's progress, observe, keep them within reach. Gianni de Capezzana's promised letters had long since ceased coming, his allegiances to the Gifted now obviously outweighing any previous devotion he had once felt toward the Vaticana a Roma. The cardinal waved away a guard and Bishop di Mino, signaling his desire to be alone. He leaned down to rest his forearms on the edge of the ship's rail, remembering Gianni's years of service as captain of the Vaticana guard, his constant protection, his unfailing intention to destroy their common enemy—of late, the Sorcerer that had drawn Gianni away and killed all the captain's men about him. Indeed, Gianni had narrowly cheated death himself. Had it not been for God and the healer—that d'Angelo woman—he certainly would have been buried alongside the others.

And yet God clearly had something else in store for Gianni. And in turn, with his ties to the Vaticana, Gianni would undoubtedly return to the cardinal's side and the Vaticana a Roma would find favor and blessing as well. The powers at work here were beyond the powers of men. For all the blustering of the interlopers of Avignon, none could come against the will of God himself. Boeri knew the ancient letter's words by heart. The Gifted's role was to bring Christ to humanity, as Christ brought God to humanity, through the power of Holy Spirit. The Holy Spirit . . . present to remind God's chosen of their access, the open gate between humanity and the holy.

When the time was right, it was imperative that the Vaticana a Roma own the Gifted, control them, or sequester them. This could be just the source he needed to seize power back from Avignon, the fodder he needed to win approval. The world revolved around public opinion and sway, and it was no different here.

He must win the Gifted to his side, convince them that he was on theirs. Win the nobles by giving them access to the Gifted's fantastic gifts, preying upon their insatiable need to be near anything beyond themselves. Win the people through uncommon means among the common, through events like Lady Daria's healing in Siena's marketplace. And ultimately win the Church—bringing her back to her rightful home in Roma.

They would applaud him, all of them. God had given him this, this vision. Mayhap he would even be considered among cardinals as the next successor to the holy throne. But all Cardinal Boeri knew was this: he must find the Gifted and insert himself, when the timing was right. They must become more beholden to him than they were to their quest— their fruitless search for the next segment of the letter that already lay securely stowed, in his cabin.

They were lost, without these pages, seeking their cause, their mission.

And he intended to show them the way . . .

CHAPTER THREE

DARIA covered the child's sores with her hands, and the child remained motionless, watching her through wide, bloodshot eyes. But there was a peace about him, a stillness she had not seen in many others beyond those of the Gifted.

Tessa knelt beside her and gasped as Daria's hand left one of the child's sores on the boy's chest and moved on to one at his mouth. "M'lady, you are doing it, you are doing it!"

"Nay, my Tessa. God is doing it. You are witnessing the holy. He is present. It is he who acts. Join me in praying for this child's healing. It was for him that we came."

"Is he one of us?"

"I know not. Is he?"

Tessa screwed up her face and tentatively reached out to hold the boy's hand. After a moment, she rose again, and shook her head. "Nay. He is good and true, but not one of the Gifted."

"Nay, but he is," Daria said, cradling the cheek that now no longer carried a sore. "He has just been given a great gift, has he not?"

The people, mollified in the face of Piero's mesmerizing and inspirational words, cried out, seeing the child's clear skin. "A healer! She's a healer!"

"Come! Come quickly!"

"She has come! Our Lady has come to heal us!"

"Daria," Gianni said, with a grunt, pushing back with full force against the crowd.

"M'lady!" cried Rune, through gritted teeth.

"Not faring so well here, either!" cried Vito.

"Just a few moments longer, gentlemen," Daria said, her eyes still upon the boy and the sores on his leg. "Just a few moments longer . . ."

She closed her eyes, filtering out the words and cries all about her, the swell of bodies waving toward them and then pushed away . . . "Father, heal this child. Bring him total healing. Drive out this leprosy, Lord Jesus. Let it not savage his body any longer. Drive it out from within and close the sores behind it. Leave him free to live and breathe and tell others of this miracle." She could see the boy, fully healed, well fed, growing to manhood, of the power of his story and how it would draw others, others who would know the Healer of healers.

She opened her eyes. Hasani greeted her with an uncommon grin. The child would grow up to teach and preach and heal and love . . . she could see it all, somehow, in Hasani's eyes, because he knew it too. And he had known this was the child, this was the one to whom they had been sent.

Tessa pulled on her arm, but Daria only had eyes for her oldest friend, her silent guardian. "You," Daria breathed in understanding. "Hasani, you are the one among us."

"What?" Piero asked, looking from lady to man. But then he knew too. They had long been anticipating one gifted with visions, and here he was, already with them! "Hasani, you are our seer? Why did you not tell us?"

Hasani, largely mute since childhood when a slaver cut out his tongue, said nothing, but his eyebrows lowered in consternation.

The boy rose between them all, studying his arms, feeling his face for the wound that once was there. "Clean!" he screamed. "I am clean! **Clean!**"

It was then that the crowd surged from all directions, falling upon them in a mad, swirling mass. Ugo and Basilio dropped their chests of blankets and tried to fight their way up to the others, but they were cut off.

The knights were overpowered at once, lacking momentum. Some among the crowd fought back with them, shouting out words of defense, but the majority was against them, all desperate to get to the healer, the healer, the healer. The men backed up to surround Daria, Tessa, and the priest, but it was not long before they were pulled apart.

Hasani gave her a tender look, one that said she should not worry, before he was pulled away and disappeared among the people. Piero was shouting out Scripture desperately, trying to gain an upper hand again. Gianni fought off one man and then another who reached for Daria and Tessa, but then was pulled from them by four men.

"The healer! The healer! The healer!" cried a man. "We have our healer!" He was a large man, strong, mayhap not long on this isle of lepers. He looked as if he had just been dumped from a passing ship, a ship with a well-fed crew.

Two others grabbed her arms, surprisingly strong. The large man looked her up and down and then deep into her eyes. "What magic do you carry, witch? What amulet?" He reached to her undergown and pulled it apart, ripping it at the neck and downward.

"Stop!" Daria yelled.

"Daria!" Gianni shouted, pulling away from two men and nearly succeeding in escaping.

The man grabbed her hair to still her and then reached for her necklace chain, pulling out a large crucifix from the folds of cloth. With a grimace of disgust, he ripped the chain from her neck, cutting her as he did so, held the crucifix high, and showed it to his comrades. "She carries this as her magic. We've all seen what it can do." He leaned closer to Daria. "Nothing."

"You're mistaken," Daria said. "It is not the crucifix that heals—but who it symbolizes. It is only because of the risen Lord that I was able to heal that boy. Healing comes from Christ and the Holy Spirit."

The man studied her for a moment and then knelt before her. He ripped his shirt open, slowly pulling off the sleeves, pulling it over his neck, and letting it go in the wind. It gathered in a clump on the rocks, but his arms remained outstretched. He turned, so she could see his naked back. "If you speak the truth, then heal me."

Daria's eyes roamed over his brown skin, mottled with sore after seeping sore. She searched her heart, yearning for approval to do this, to heal here, heal now, but she sensed no approval from her Lord.

It was a way out. If she could just heal this one man, they could gain some time to find their way out of this mess.

I have prepared a way for you.

Just one. If she could only show them that this was the way . . .

I am the way and the truth and the life.

Could he not see? Why not this one? This was the way! If they could prove that they were the Gifted—

I am the Way.

Daria stilled at last from her inner argument and looked about the crowd. That was when she saw the man on the hill, making his way down to them.

Her captor grabbed her hand then, and pulled her attention back to him. He yanked her to her knees to face him. "What? What is it? So you do not have the magic after all? Or do you not choose to heal me?"

"You have lost your way," she said, panting with sudden, inner understanding now. "God sent us to this island to heal the child, because he was an innocent among you."

She flung off the man's hand and rose. "You all must choose. My brothers! My sisters, if you hunger for healing, you must choose the Way! You must confess your sins and ask for the Savior to heal you." Many in the crowd fell to their knees, heads bowed or faces lifted up in prayer. Most formed a human chain, with one hand upon another's shoulder to another's hand to another's back, but still a crowd menaced Daria.

"Kill her," the big man muttered, turning away from her.

Tessa screamed and the men shouted as the others moved in upon Daria.

"You are the way, the truth and the life, my Lord, Jesus. There is no other. You are the way and the truth and the—"

Her words broke off as hands reached to rip at her clothes, pull at her hair. She closed her eyes, wanting only to see the wounded body of Christ on the necklace. If she was to die, if here was where it would all end, all she wanted to see was her Savior . . .

"Cease! Now! *You shall cease now,*" said a thunderous voice.

Hands abruptly dropped from Daria, and she could feel the breeze on her face once again. Tears of relief came then, and slowly she opened her eyes. Those who were not in prayer moved away from her, down the hillside, and away, apparently fearing the large, broad-shouldered man as big as the one who had taken her crucifix. Others still held her knights at bay. Daria looked again to the stranger. He was about sixty, as tanned and muscular as the local fishermen, similar to Gianni in stature. Both of his arms were up, fingers spread out and held out toward the lepers en masse.

"Release them, my friends," he demanded, and immediately, the knights were released.

"They brought you gifts. Return their belongings," he said. "All of it." Swords and shirts and even Daria's necklace were handed over.

The knights, Basilio and Ugo, ran to rejoin the group, swords drawn, ready for another charge. But the strange old man still seemed to hold the crowd at bay. "They came to heal one among you! You would do well to consider their words. By the Christ's wounds, you are healed. You suffer nothing more than what he suffered among us. Through him, you will find ultimate healing, either on this side, or in heaven. Do not give in to the dark! Do not give in to the dark!"

The man, with strange blue eyes, surely a remnant of Germanic invaders, looked in Daria's direction. "Your task is not complete, m'lady."

Daria began to contradict him, but then paused, feeling the check within her heart. Her eyes shifted to the group of lepers who had continued to pray as they had been told. The small boy she had healed hovered near a woman, undoubtedly his mother.

"M'lady," the man said, offering his left hand.

"Daria," Gianni said in warning.

"Nay. It is all right," she said, never letting her eyes leave the stranger. There was peace within those eyes, a heavenly assuredness. She placed her right hand in his and he led her down a short path to the group of those huddled in prayer.

He waited for her to look from the pitiful mass, still on their knees, aching in need and misery, to him again. "He is here," the man whispered. "Our Lord. You have given of your gift this day, but there is more to be done. Pray, m'lady. Believe."

Slowly, he pulled her hand to rest on the young mother's head. He did the same. "Pray, m'lady," he repeated urgently.

Daria, weary already from the boy's healing, closed her eyes and willed strength and belief into her words, her heart, her mind. The stranger's hand covered hers and he whispered a prayer, barely audible.

Daria formed words in her mouth, words that were becoming more comfortable and known. "In the holy and strong name of Jesus Christ, we ask, Father, for healing—"

She cried out, feeling the hot wave wash through her and out. She stumbled backward.

"Daria!" Gianni cried, rushing to her side, holding her up from falling.

But she could only stare forward, at the group of lepers who had held together, who had done as they had bid, remaining in prayer, praying for a miracle of healing.

Eyes were no longer bloodshot, already clear. Wounds and sores appeared sealed, as if weeks into healing rather than seconds; hands curled in paralysis were straight. Anyone who had touched another who had touched another who had touched the young mother, was clean, healed, whole.

Daria let out a breathy laugh of wonder. The stranger glanced over his shoulder at her and Gianni and smiled as well. "*Now* your task is complete, m'lady."

He turned to walk back up the hill, away from her, staring at the group of healed lepers. "Come, my friends," he said to the crowd. "My ship is laden with fresh fish for all of you. We will feed you, find you suitable clothing, and then return you to your homes."

And the people followed him, as docile as if they were sheep following their shepherd. The stranger turned at the crest of the hill and eyed each of the Gifted, as if committing their images to memory, and then turned to trudge behind the rest.

ઠ ઠ ઠ

"WHO was that man?" asked Ugo that night, around their fire.

"A fisherman. Someone who has obviously been feeding those people for some time. That was why they respected him, did as he said."

"The Duchess keeps us in fine slop and look how devoted we are to her," Vito said.

Daria smiled, picking up a spoon full of porridge and letting it drip to her trencher. "I'm afraid the house of d'Angelo has seen better eatings than this."

"Ah, but tomorrow, we again are in a house. In a city, near all sorts of foodstuffs. We shall have fine eatings tomorrow," Basilio said.

"And the next day," Ugo said.

"And the next!" cried Vito. All the men gave a cheer.

"All I can think is that that man stepped in at just the right time," Piero said, eyeing Hasani. "It was more than provision that forced their respect."

"It was not only I who healed them," Daria said quietly. "That man was a great part of it."

Piero nodded, stirring the fire with a stick. He eyed Hasani. "You knew he was coming, didn't you?"

Hasani kept his eyes to his porridge and kept eating.

"Hasani?"

"What is this?" Gianni said. "How could Hasani have known?"

All spoons gradually stilled while Hasani scraped the last of his meal into his mouth. He set aside the trencher and then looked each of them in the eye, sighed, and rose, walking to his tent.

Gianni raised a hand to silence the inevitable comment from Vito. Hasani threw back the flap of his tent and came back to the fire. He opened a leather satchel and slid out a thick pile of papers.

Piero held out his hand and shuffled through them, pausing at one, racing through a few more, then pausing at another. At last he stopped and turned a paper around.

It was an illustration of Daria, on a beach, hair free and whipping in the wind, a man holding her on either side. Another knelt before her, arms outstretched, and each arm was covered in sores.

"The leper, the leper who menaced her," Gianni said in barely more than a whisper, rising to take the paper from the priest. He stared hard at Hasani and then back at the paper. It was then that he saw the figure— a broad, short man, with arms upraised, coming near the crowd. Several faces in the back turned toward him.

"You saw it all," Gianni said in a whisper. "You knew it would happen. You are our seer."

Hasani took his fist and clapped it to his chest, ducking his head once.

"He's a seer?" Ugo said. "You mean he has the visions?"

"We've been expecting him," Piero said. "He is one of us. One of the foretold Gifted. And he was right here with us all the time."

"So," Vito said. "If Hasani is our man of visions, just who was that who saved us all upon the beach?"

ॐ ॐ ॐ

HE came to the house, unannounced, surprising Ambrogio into his sur-coat and to his feet. It has been years since he had spoken to the baron, since the days when Vincenzo had begun to court Tatiana. During each of the council meetings Ambrogio had attended, Vincenzo had ignored him as if he was invisible and Ambrogio had remained mute.

But that was now clearly about to change. Vincenzo strode into the solarium, followed by Agata, who awkwardly announced the baron to Ambrogio.

Vincenzo passed the young painter and went straight to the window, looking down to the gardens. "What was she thinking, leaving you in charge?"

Ambrogio threw up his hands, pursed his lips, and shook his head back and forth. "I know not. I am an artist, not a man with a head for business."

Vincenzo blew out a breath of exasperation. "Exactly right. Although Aldo Scioria is a fine steward, he cannot make you into a true consul. I have made a motion to remove you as co-consul."

"A wise move, Baron, and one Lady Daria anticipated. She only wishes to keep her seat on the guild council."

Vincenzo narrowed his eyes in his direction. "If she gave you such instruction, she must have anticipated a long absence."

"Nay, nay," Ambrogio waffled, wishing he had remained silent. "I stand in her stead for but a short time."

"As you wished to stand in mine?" Vincenzo pushed away from the window and circled around Ambrogio to the other side.

"Baron, I never wished to stand in—"

"Mine? Was it not what made you try to persuade my Tatiana to run away with you, on the very eve of our betrothal?"

Ambrogio swallowed hard and then stood to his full height, a few inches shorter than Vincenzo. But he held the baron's gaze unwaveringly. He was long used to overbearing nobles. "I felt you were mismatched, that she was making a mistake, you both . . . It was not a desire to stand in your stead."

Vincenzo lowered his gaze to meet Ambrogio's. "And yet you loathed me so much that you would make a move against me?"

"Nay. Baron, it was only that she was so young and . . ."

"I was so old?"

Ambrogio sighed. He thought of the boy Tatiana had loved, who would have been her husband into their years of stooped shoulders and age spots . . . it had not been that she was *not* meant for Vincenzo, only that she had been clearly meant for another. As Daria had always been meant for Marco.

But now all that mattered not. Tatiana was dead. Her widower stood before him, still raw and grieving. And now Ambrogio stood between Vincenzo and Daria, the only other woman Baron del Buco had ever truly loved in his lifetime. "I understand," Ambrogio said at last. "I have caused you pain. And for that I am terribly sorry—"

"Then tell me," Vincenzo growled. "Tell me where Daria has gone."

Ambrogio studied him, saw the shift in his features and eyes. "I cannot. You do not think she would tell you her location if she so wished?"

Vincenzo slapped him suddenly then, so hard it turned him to one side. "Tell me. I will know where Daria went."

Ambrogio looked at him with sad eyes. "I cannot."

Vincenzo slammed a fist into his belly, surprising him again.

Beata coughed awkwardly from the doorway, wringing her hands in worry as she anxiously eyed Ambrogio. "Baron, master Ambrogio, Sir Amidei is here to join you." She said the words more as warning than introduction.

Vincenzo turned toward Abramo. Lord Amidei slowly removed his gloves, pulling off one finger and then the next; he then dismissed Beata, laying a calming hand on her shoulder and speaking a few quiet words to her. He waited for Ambrogio to meet his gaze when she departed. "Come now, friend. Tell us where the Duchess has gone so we might see to her welfare. She could be in trouble, so long away from her own."

Ambrogio stood up with some effort and straightened his coat, trying for a measure of composure. "I know not where she is."

"Come now," Abramo said, walking to the window and pausing beside Ambrogio. "Daria is a businesswoman. She would not leave you in her stead for this long and not even tell you how to send word to her."

"She must be intent on returning soon."

"Any day?"

"I can only pray it is so. Now if you will excuse me, gentlemen, I must see to my work down at the palazzo." He took a step, but Abramo sidled left to stand in front of him. He stared at him until the smaller Ambrogio was forced to look up.

"You think we do not know where Daria and her precious Gifted have gone?"

"Gifted? What are you—"

"You think," he said, edging forward, making Ambrogio take a step back, "that I do not have the connections it takes to find anyone I wish?"

"Nay, my lord, I—"

"You think that you are fit to sit and do business with a man such as the baron? With me?"

"Lady Daria believed it," said a voice from the door. Aldo. It was the old, stooped servant who had come to his defense. "I have the documentation right here," he said, lifting the parchment.

Abramo turned away to quietly confer with Vincenzo. Vincenzo's eyebrows lifted in surprise, and then he reached for his overcoat. "We will finish our business on another occasion," Vincenzo said to Ambrogio with a slight smile of victory. "Abramo tells me that we have business to the north. *A* Venezia . . ."

He watched as Ambrogio faltered, eyes widening before he caught himself, and then both Abramo and Vincenzo grinned. "We are on the right trail, Abramo," Vincenzo said over his shoulder, still staring at Ambrogio. "The Gifted *are* in Venezia."

db db db

VINCENZO went to the bow of the ship and raised his face to the wind. They were on their way at last. They would reach Venezia in but a day, maybe two, depending upon the winds. By making their way to Italia's eastern coast and traveling the rest of the way by sea, they would save days of overland travel. He sensed when Abramo drew near, but purposefully stayed in silence for a while.

Several long moments passed, each staring out to the sea, a deep turquoise green in the early evening light. "It bothers you that Ambrogio would not confide Daria's location?"

"My history with the man runs long," Vincenzo said. "It is but one of many grievances I have with the man."

"Say the word and I'll have him destroyed. He will never paint again."

Vincenzo paused. "Nay. If we are to bring Daria along, we cannot harm those she loves. It will merely turn her further against us."

"Sometimes it is a catalyst. Think of Old Woman Parmo and her grandson." They watched as the ship crested a wave and then another, feeling the sway of the ocean beneath their feet. "We know that the Duchess and her troop have been sighted near Venezia. We will seek them out, then take them down, one by one, leaving none but Daria standing, but even Daria will be uneasy upon her feet. She will look to you for guidance. And so it will begin. You will see victory in this."

"I am counting on it, m'lord," Vincenzo said. He turned then. He felt a bit queasy upon the roiling seas, and unsteadily made his way back to his cabin. He paused for a moment before he went belowdecks, feeling an unaccountable longing for his wife, for Daria, for feminine comfort.

Mayhap Abramo was right . . . mayhap they would find Daria and all would be restored to him. Marco and Daria and the guild and all that was right and true. But something was amiss, something odd in the sea air, flowing across the decks. For the hundredth time he tried to remember the details of that last night, when Daria left Siena.

If only, if only. Why was it that his life was crisscrossed with if-onlys? He was tired, so tired. He must rest.

He stumbled and lurched his way down the steep stairs. It was an odd feeling, for a man of the land to abide deep within the sea. But sleep called to him. All would feel better in the morning. He was sure of it.

ॐ ॐ ॐ

"Pack a bag for me," Ambrogio said to Beata.

"But master, where are you going?"

"I must warn Daria. She left me in charge. And all appears lost. Her position within the guild, her relationship with Vincenzo. Worse, Amidei and Baron del Buco may already be on their way to Venezia. I'm certain they intend to do our people harm. Daria must be warned."

Aldo looked at him steadily as he entered the room, hearing Ambrogio's last words. "You think she is not well aware that he is coming? This is a chase, a deadly chase, sir. She left you here, where you could watch out for what is hers. She needs you here."

Ambrogio paced, running a hand through his hair. "But all is lost, Aldo," he cried. "I cannot hold her position as co-consul! Vincenzo has already made a movement within the courts to have me removed, and I can hardly find a reason to turn him aside! I am an artist! An artist! What was Daria thinking, placing me in her stead?"

Aldo moved slowly forward, pausing to speak over his shoulder. "She was thinking you are strong within. And that you know people of power, how they think, how they move. She was thinking that you were her best hope to hold some portion of her position, here, in her stead."

Ambrogio turned to the window and leaned on his elbows, cradling his head in his hands. "Then she was a fool," he said at last. "I've always been a sorry Rossellino and now I'm an even sorrier d'Angelo." He turned to look at Daria's servant, a man who had served this household for longer than Daria had been alive. Would he bring her house down? Would he utterly fail here?

"She knew," Aldo said, coming closer to clasp him on the shoulder. "Lady Daria knew exactly who you were, who you are today, who you will be tomorrow. She chose you. Take strength in that, man. She didn't truly believe anyone could hold her seat as co-consul. All she hoped was that you would keep her seat on the guild council. You will find a way to do that. Despite what it looks like today, it will look better on the morrow, master. I promise."

"And the lady? Who will warn her?"

"She knows. She knows he will give chase. We must pray for their protection, and that the peacock stays ahead of the dragon."

Chapter Four

It was only after they had settled in the house off the canal named Rio de San Villo, brought in their meager belongings and cases and found each of their rooms, made arrangements for food deliveries—and then basic furnishings—that Daria permitted herself to go to the windows, opening the shutters to the evening sky, and looked to the east, to the Giudecca and beyond.

"They will not be long in coming," Father Piero said over her shoulder. "Light always calls to dark."

Hasani stepped forward with the priest to join her at the balcony, and with one look, Daria knew he agreed.

She looked down to the canal beneath her, to barges loaded with crates, en route to the pier where they would be exchanged for others—or for a bag of coins. "You think that now that we are visible, here in the city, that we will be found."

Silence greeted her.

"And yet you encouraged me to make this move."

Several long moments passed. "Sometimes, the only way to make one's way through things is through," Piero said.

Hasani made a motion for *rush*.

"We must make haste," Daria said.

Both nodded in response.

"So," she said, looking at her interlaced fingers, then beyond them to the dockworkers. "Where do we go from here? How do we go about this quest for our letter?"

Hasani motioned her inward and spread out a large drawing on the ground. In the center was a mosaic of two peacocks drinking from an urn. On seven sides of the mosaic drawing were seven separate churches. Basilio and Rune joined them then, as did Gianni and Tessa.

"What is this?" Tessa asked, kneeling beside the drawing in wonder.

"A map of some sort, I believe," Piero said, sounding as if he were lost in thought. He knelt to get a closer look.

"We have seen two of these," Daria said, waving to the two familiar sanctuaries.

"That is Sant' Elena and San Giacometto," Basilio said. "We passed by them as we came into Venezia and in the marketplace." He eyed the map. "This is Santa Maria e San Donato, this is Santa Maria Assunta— on Murano and Torcello. I know where the others are too. All except for this one."

They all looked to the last one he gestured toward. It was a simple but strong church, with what appeared to be a monastery attached. "We shall find it, m'lady. It shan't take long," Rune said.

"I think," Piero said, rising on stiff legs to stand upright, "we ought to send out word that we are in search of ancient artifacts . . . anything that contains the lady's coat of arms, namely, the peacock." He met her searching gaze. "It is in everything we've found to date—the frescoes at the old Byzantine church, in the catacombs, the tapestry, the letter itself. There is something within the mosaics, these churches, we are to discover."

"The peacock," Daria agreed. "Yes. We shall make it known that we are seeking heirlooms related to the house of d'Angelo. In case there is something beyond the mosaics, other clues we are to discover."

Hasani sucked in his breath.

"What of it?" Daria asked airily. "If the dark is coming, let him know that we fear him not. We can be as wise as he, making ready for his approach. We will not be caught unaware again. And this is a city famed for justice. What grounds does Amidei or Vincenzo have to take us in hand?"

"Tread carefully," Piero said. "It is also a city famed for her complex politics. It will be best for us if we can stay on the outskirts of those who hold sway here. Religious or government alike."

ɕ ɕ ɕ

BISHOP di Mino and two stewards led the way into the grand palazzo that belonged to the doge, the duke of Venezia. Servants greeted them with deep bows, eyeing Cardinal Boeri's fine red robe and cap. For centuries the doges of Venezia had been at odds with the Church and had spent entire decades excommunicated—extending at times to all Venetians— a fact that was never far from the minds of the faithful. At the moment, the doge was in decent stead with the Church, having solid ties to the princes of France, but fear still lingered in their eyes. Only the Venetians' fierce independence and pride, and their own cadre of independent churchmen—who assured them they would find their way to heaven— kept them from begging at the pope's false Vaticana de Avignon. "Let us be excommunicated, then," said one previous doge of a previous pope. "I would rather be in hell than in heaven with one such as him." And after decades of such an uneasy history, a periodic alliance grew. As always, power served as the common denominator.

Their small group was led through the open courtyard of the palazzo, paused at a well to drink their fill of clean, cold water from a deep cistern, and then moved into a waiting room with high ceilings and a roaring fire. The figures of two naked slaves held up a massive mantel of black onyx. Luxurious fabrics lined the walls, and large, ornately carved chairs beckoned Cardinal Boeri's weary body. The doge's palazzo was famed for its beauty and, with the monstrous basilica of San Marco as the doge's private chapel, its image was widely duplicated and circled the world. And there was a rumor that the doge wanted to built a new, larger, and more ornate palazzo still.

The servants departed and the churchmen waited for more than an hour to be seen. At last, the servants returned and led them through one chamber and then the next, finally arriving in the chambers of the Twelve. The Twelve were Venezia's governing force who kept an eye on the doge and his decisions, created just a decade before when an errant faction of noblemen tried to kill the doge and take his place. Cardinal Boeri knew that behind these Twelve, among the curving and tight streets of Venezia, were the One Hundred and Twenty, noblemen who all had opportunity to vote on Venezia's most critical decisions—of finance and political gain. It was a messy way of governing, but gave many voice. It was part of the reason that Venezia was one of the most political cities in the world.

The doge looked up from sheets of parchment and smiled slightly. He signed his name to the document with quill and ink even as he spoke to the cardinal. "Your Eminence," he said with a slight nod, "to what do I owe this pleasure of your company?"

Cardinal Boeri swallowed hard against the bitter gall that rose in his throat. The doge well knew that his proper place was at the cardinal's feet, kissing his ring. That was what was expected in all civilized states. But Boeri needed him. And the doge would soon need him as well. "I have come to offer you goodwill and the grace of the holy Church *a* Roma. It is my fervent desire, Doge, that we might work together to accomplish something new and worthy, something that will benefit us both."

The doge rose slowly, regally, pulled back his robe and stepped forward, then off his dais. He crossed the wide expanse of marble floor and took the cardinal's hands in his own, but did not bow to kiss his ring. "A churchman who comes and speaks of mutual benefit is a churchman with whom I can get along. Come, my dear cardinal, let us retire to my private quarters and you can speak plainly."

⚓ ⚓ ⚓

"CAPTAIN!" Vito shouted, waving his hand above the crowds across the canal. "Captain!"

Gianni waved back to him and he turned to Daria, Hasani, and Piero, who were completing an arrangement with a butcher to deliver fresh meat each day to their house across the canal. It was proving beneficial to them to have Basilio and Rune—men who knew this labyrinth of a city well—among them. This last arrangement would keep them in fresh food for as long as they remained in the city, through the winter ahead, if necessary. "Let's wait for Vito over there," Gianni said. "He has someone with him." The group made their way across a *campo* to the centered well, tossing a couple of small coins into a man's jar beside it. He immediately drew the water upward and each bent to take a drink from the bucket and metal scoop.

"If the Venetians can make sweet, clean water from the salt, surely we can find other fantastic things among them," Gianni said, handing Piero the scoop.

"We shall see," Piero said, turning to Vito and his companion.

Vito introduced the man, Giuseppe, a Murano mosaic artist working in San Marco. "He has quite the tale to tell," Vito said. He drew them away from the well, away from prying ears. The group circled, heads to the center, and the artist shifted uneasily under their intense gaze. "Go on, man. It is fine. Tell them of the legend. Tell it as you told me and we will see you compensated for your labor of storytelling."

Giuseppe was perhaps thirty years of age, but slender and already stooped from decades of work on mosaics. He squinted as if he could not see well. It was the mark of any mosaic artist. Often, they began as a child apprentice. But the close work in dark quarters soon robbed them of both stature and sight. "Giuseppe, my son," Piero said. "Please, we must make haste. Tell us all you know."

Giuseppe gave him a slight shrug and raised one eyebrow. "I belong to the Arte Mosaica, and in our guild, in our *scuola,* this tale has been passed down for centuries."

"Go on," Piero said, chin in hand.

"It is said that Apollos, follower of Santo Paulo, was a man of Alexandria. It was they who first adopted the art of working in glass, after the Mesopotamians. For a hundred years the Romans created fine glass works, adopting the technique of the Egyptians. For a time, some was even made here, in the basin, until the art was lost. It took us several centuries to recapture the art."

"What of your mosaic tiles in churches from that time?"

"Imported, in large measure, from Alexandria."

"Proceed."

"It was said that Apollos was a great admirer of Santo Paulo and studied his teachings incessantly, preaching them himself, far and wide. He was a scholar, and one night he was granted a vision."

Daria's eyes slid to Hasani.

"He is said to have known that the Church's home would one day be moved from Constantinople and rest in Roma, then be moved again. So he commissioned a great glass map. It was meant to be ever growing, a map of Christendom."

"And?" Gianni asked.

"Such a map was too large to cast together, so it was done in segments, the first pieces memorializing each of the places Santo Paulo traveled to and marked by the principal churches in each land."

Gianni frowned and shook his head. "A glass map? Certainly it was not destined for longevity."

Giuseppe raised his eyebrow again and nodded. "Nay. But still it was cast and put together in Constantinople. It is said that the Nicene Council had it before them on the table as they met."

Gianni glanced at Piero. "Have you ever heard of it, Father?"

"Nay."

"Neither have I, even with all my travels with the cardinal. Giuseppe, why tell us this story? What does it have to do with us?"

"Your friend came to me, seeking churches with mosaic peacocks."

"Indeed."

"Venezia has long collected and protected her relics. We have gone and plundered, but few have taken what has become ours," he said proudly. "At the same time our men obtained the relics of the blessed Santo Marco in Alexandria, they were also given seven urns as a gift from a holy man there. On each of the urns was etched a peacock, the symbol of eternal life. The Venetians were told to place one under the floor of each of their principal churches in their land. Within were remnants of Apollos's famous glass map. It was said that they were to remain beneath the principal churches until the 'day of enlightenment.' "

"Which meant . . ." Gianni led.

"I know not, I know not," lamented the tradesman, lifting his hands and raising his eyebrow again. "I can only tell you what has been passed down among the guild for generations. It was said that those glass pieces would ensure that our land would forever be a part of God's own history, even Christendom as a whole."

The group stared at the man, trying to absorb it all.

"It could be nothing more than legend," Gianni said.

"Nay, I have seen one of the urns myself," Giuseppe returned. "I believe the legend as truth."

"You're telling us that there is an urn beneath San Marco?"

"*Si.* You can see it hanging from the ceiling of the crypt of San Marco. According to legend, the other six reside in our principal churches of the Rialto, Murano, and Torcello. A seventh was unfortunately lost over the centuries."

Hasani pulled his map from the folds of his robe and unfolded just enough to show the artist the sketch of the church that no one could seem to identify.

The artist squinted at it and held it closer to his eyes. "That is the old San Giorgio Maggiore, on the point back there," he said, gesturing in the direction of the lagoon. "An earthquake took it down more than a hundred years past."

"Bah. I've seen that. It's naught but crumbled walls," Basilio said, silently telling them there was surely nothing still there.

"Giuseppe, my son, you have been more than helpful to us. Thank you for passing down such a sacred and celebrated legend. The lady has given me this," he paused to hand the man a small sack of coin, "as thanks. Might we call upon you for further assistance if we have need of it?"

Giuseppe's eyes had not left the sack in his hand. "At any moment, Father. Night or day." A shadow passed over his face. "And yet I am bound by the sacred trust of my *scuola* never to harm one of our churches. You do not mean to plunder?"

"Nay. We are not here to destroy or pilfer." He drew closer to the artist. "But we may well be of the legend ourselves. We are dedicated to the cause of Christendom, the life of the Church. We may well be part of bringing 'the day of enlightenment.' "

Giuseppe studied the priest, his face growing more pale. He quickly glanced at the others. "You were brought here, to Venezia, on a mission?"

"We are following God's own lead. As Vito told you, we have found many artistic representations of the peacock, in frescoes, in tapestries. All have led us here, to your city. The lady, Giuseppe," Piero said, gesturing to Daria, "see her family crest?"

Daria opened the flap of her robe to show a tiny red peacock on a white background.

Giuseppe gasped. "It is true, then."

"Indeed."

"But if the urns, the map was left for you, you will take it?"

"If necessary," said the priest. "But we will leave no damage behind. Your churches will be left whole."

Giuseppe was frowning. "My guild, my *scuola*," he said, shaking his head. "If they discovered I had led you to the treasures . . . I could be punished. Cast out. The doge . . ." He shivered.

Gianni stepped forward and waited until the artist looked him in the eye. "Search your heart, man. Look each of us in the eye. And the Lord will show you that we are doing only what we must, not what we would like to do. We have left our vocations, our homes behind, to follow this mission. You must remain quiet. It is imperative that no one know that we are about. God will make it known, in his timing. It cannot be ours."

"Will you pray over it?" Piero asked. "I, too, believe that God will confirm our words within your heart. This eve, go to your church and light a candle, pray over your concerns."

"I shall," he said, the hint of a dare in his eye.

"Good, good. Then go in peace, my son," Piero said, making the sign of the cross over the man's head. The man crossed himself and departed back in the direction of San Marco, a bit dazed in expression.

"San Giorgio—all her most precious artifacts have surely been taken, salvaged," Rune said immediately.

"There is no way that they would leave behind the urn. Church valuables are always removed—reused in new sanctuaries," Basilio agreed.

"You never heard of this glass map legend, the urns, while you lived here?" Gianni said.

Basilio and Rune shook their heads. "It is possibly a guild fable," Basilio said. "Something to occupy their minds."

Hasani gestured toward them, already making his way to the canal and their boat.

"You and Rune stay with Tessa," Gianni said to Basilio. "We'll see if the old lady is as decrepit and lost as you believe."

CHAPTER FIVE

FEW observed as they tied their small boat to an ancient dock on the isle near the Giudecca and made their way over rickety boards to the abandoned shore. Gianni held Daria's hand, picking their way across giant boulders, down a small hill and then up the next. The rest of their party had paused ahead of them, staring down to the lagoon.

They parted for Daria and Gianni as they neared. Daria gasped when she saw it. The walls of the church were clearly visible, but it was as if the walls were peeled back, like the skin from fruit. Her original rectangle was now wide at the top, where her altar would have been.

"It's like a giant decided to go in," Ugo said.

"From the back. And then chose to make a bath inside," Vito added.

The waters from the lagoon had indeed entered the church's remains, as if the sea sought to claim her, suck her into the depths. Aqua waters lapped at brick walls, both from the outside and inside too. The party made their way down the boulders and into the old church. Daria doubtfully looked to Hasani. "We're to find a mosaic here?"

He did not answer her. He merely clung to the walls and stared into the depths beneath them as if searching. Golden squares—possibly once part of an elaborate mosaic in San Giorgio, glittered from among the rocks. As her eyes adjusted, Daria could see other colors too—dark lapis, honey-colored amber, russet red. But nothing solid.

Daria made her way forward and paused to look about, hoping to find something obvious. The walls were only chest high, the rest having fallen into the sea. Marble pillars, once salvaged from Byzantine churches on the mainland, had again been salvaged for other buildings within Venezia—only their matching bases could be seen in the depths. A few traces of her original frescoes were visible at the upper edge, but none of those could be made out. Mostly, it was raw, decomposing brick.

Daria turned to study her group again, and noticed that Hasani had taken off his sandals and waded into the water. "Hasani?"

He ignored her, staring ahead into the water. Vito and Ugo rushed to the waters that filled the ancient church, staring down in the direction he headed. "There!" Vito cried. "I see it too!"

 conj conj conj

CARDINAL Boeri and his entourage entered the marina off Torcello, planning to pay his respects to the bishop and gain proper introduction to the bishops of Murano, Burano, and finally, the Rialto, as was customary. One did not simply rush into the court of the doge. Unless, of course, one was Cardinal Boeri de Roma. Things had gone well, quite well, with the doge, and he was to return as the doge's guest in but a week. Now he had to backtrack and lay a foundation with the churchmen *a* Venezia.

Torcello—as the island with the oldest established city and church—had been the birthplace of Venezia, which was steadily building to her southwest, on the larger lagoon islands of the Rialto, leaving Torcello to combat silting canals, malaria, and the dwindling remains of a population. But the church there remained, fighting to hold on to a measure of influence and power from afar.

Venezia was a boisterous, busy city, as complex as Roma. Her power was in the hands of the doge and other politicians, not in holy men of the Church. Despite all their positioning, they had no choice but to capitulate to those in political power. The Church was like an old dog with no teeth. No power. No respect. The cardinal turned to spit, a foul taste in his mouth at the thought of it. It reminded him far too much of the papacy in Avignon, held by men who were more swayed by princes and power than by the Prince of Peace. But it was the way of the world, it seemed, and his task was to master this world in order to set it straight. He had long frequented the worlds of noblemen and ladies, doting upon them, plying them with honor in exchange for funds for his disintegrating *Vaticana a Roma*. He was at ease at their tables and in their solariums. Among them, he and Gianni had hunted the face of the dark, witch and warlock, heretics, routing them out, remaining vigilant. His experience would serve him well here.

Here, here in Venezia, where politics and the religious still interfaced, the cardinal would begin to lay the foundation for the changes to come. He would find a way to promise the end of papal interdicts against the doge and the Venetians every time the doge made a decision that angered the false pope. He would promise peace and compromise, and win the maritime power to his cause.

Venezia. It was good that the Lord had brought the Gifted here.

For here, he would set all upon a righteous path.

ళ ళ ళ

"What is it?" Daria cried. "What?"

Gianni took her hand and hurried her to one side of the water, down across from the others. That's when she saw it too . . . a bit of tiled mosaic flooring, underneath another giant slab of rock. Not a lot was visible, since most of it was covered by the rock or bright green, swaying moss. But there was no mistaking the red, blue, and green eye of a peacock feather.

Gianni motioned to Vito, the stronger swimmer between the brothers, and both bent to pull their boots off. They waded into the water, wincing from the cold. Hasani was already chest deep. Without pause, he took a breath and went down to the rock. But as strong as he was, he could not move it alone.

He came to the surface and caught his breath; then, on Gianni's count, all three submerged. They moved the boulder a bit, then came up again. "We'll need you, Ugo. You too, Father."

"I can help," Daria said.

"Nay, m'lady. I think the five of us can get it. Not that I wouldn't pay to see you try," Gianni said, tossing her a grin.

"I'll have you know I'm a very good swimmer," Daria said, crossing her arms. "Much better than Ugo."

"Hey!" the young man cried out indignantly. "I'm surely better than our padre, here."

"Don't be so certain," Piero said, tiptoeing into the water and then resolutely walking in, his robes flowing about him.

On the count of three, the five of them submerged. Long seconds passed, and Daria found that she was holding her breath with them. They had stirred up too much silt at the bottom—she could not see a thing.

They popped up then, first Vito and the priest, then the other three. "Did you get it?" Daria said, kneeling. Judging by their pleased smiles, they had made some progress.

"We got the rock moved, m'lady," Ugo said. "Wait a moment." The water cleared a bit as they paused. "Look there. Most of two entire peacocks and a disc between them."

Daria shook her head in shocked disbelief.

"I think we can bring up the entire slab," Vito said. "Keep it intact."

"I know not," Gianni said. "I grabbed one corner and the mortar disintegrated in my hands." He raised a bloody palm. "The edges of the mosaic tiles are still sharp."

"We have to try," Daria said. "Why else were we led here, if not to discover this?"

"Mayhap it's simply a sign," Gianni said. "Encouragement that we are, indeed, to be here in Venezia."

"I don't think so," Piero said. "Let's go down again, try to dig underneath the slab and bring up a layer that isn't just mortar."

None of the men looked particularly confident in his plan, but they all nodded in agreement to try. On another count of three, they all disappeared again, leaving Daria to once again hold her breath in solidarity and hope.

"I think we have it," Gianni said, when he and his companions emerged again.

Vito emerged and whooped in celebration. "I think that plan will work!"

"One more dive," Ugo said.

"It will weigh us down," Gianni said. "We'll need to walk it up a few feet so all of our heads will be above water and we don't have to release any portion."

They all panted, trying to catch their breath, shivering in the cold, and agreed on the plan. Then they all descended again. Thirty seconds, then forty.

First Ugo emerged from the fog of silty water, then Gianni. Piero, Vito, and Hasani emerged as one, holding the other side. Daria scrambled over the rocks, trying to move ahead of them, to see what they had between them.

It was beautiful. Two perfect peacocks, tail feathers of purple porphyry and blue lapis, and red and amber, a hand-sized green circle between their heads, above the urn they drank from—

"Captain," Vito said, his voice cracking in warning.

Daria glanced down sharply and saw the tiles collapsing into a cloud of dust where Vito's hands were—

"Oh no," Piero said, the same thing happening on his edge . . .

"No," Daria cried. *No, no, no!*

"Grab over there," Gianni said through gritted teeth. "Vito, over—"

But his own edge was disintegrating as well. They moved forward from their outer edges as if in a dance, all moving forward by inches, each madly trying to grab an edge, get under it, keep a hold on the artifact. The water surged with silt, circling mosaic tiles—before they sank to the sea floor—and blood from their cut hands.

"Over here!" Daria cried, reaching out to them, wading in, boots and all. "Bring it here!"

But by the time they were thigh deep, all that was left of the mosaic was the round disc and a clump of mortar about it that made it look like a rough vessel. For a moment, Daria thought they had lost every bit of the stone. Hot disappointment stole her breath. She had been so sure . . .

It was then she saw Hasani grinning. He held the green disk and clump of mortar in his hands. Curious, Daria took a step forward. Hasani bent to grab a loose stone from the waters and began scraping. More of the mortar fell away into the water. The men crowded around him, all trying to see, but Hasani walked forward, out of the sea and to Daria. He handed her the vessel, and she gasped at the weight of it.

The men gathered around her and she took Hasani's loose stone, continuing to scrape off mortar from one side and then the other. It was cylindrical, the diameter of a small melon, with the top disk that was once a part of the mosaic floor forming a lid. And covering three sides, a peacock edged his nose upward as if to drink.

"Open it, m'lady," Gianni urged.

"Nay," Piero said, holding out his hand to stop her. "There is a wax seal that holds disk to cylinder. Let us take it back to the manor and use a proper tool, take it apart gently rather than prying it apart here, on the rocks."

Daria sighed. It was difficult to wait. They all were anxious to see what could be inside. But she recognized the wisdom of Piero's words and nodded her assent.

The group made their way to their barge, off the island and back to the edge of Venezia, drawing odd, long looks from passersby at the sight of their dripping clothes.

"Neighbor!" called out one as they passed. "The idea is to stay out of the canal, not swim in it."

"Ahh," Vito called out, as if that fact had eluded him. "We are people of a dry city, Siena. It will take us a bit to become accustomed to so much water."

The jeering man laughed and turned to make another derogatory comment to his cohorts, who all laughed uproariously and stared back in Daria's direction.

"We draw too much attention to ourselves," Gianni murmured to Daria.

"They are idly curious. We are the newcomers. Their interest shall wane."

"I hope so."

They reached the mansion, pulled up near the rail, and entered through two gates that opened on the water. Many Venetian homes had a warehouse on the bottom floor, at the water's edge, to facilitate easy unloading and loading of goods and cargo. Venezia was a massive trading town, with something from every edge of civilization to be found, purchased, bartered, or sold.

Once inside, Daria turned. "Into dry clothes, all of you. We shall meet in the dining hall and open it together as soon as we're all assembled."

Everyone split off without complaint, eager to get out of clinging trousers and sticky shirts. Daria went up to her quarters on the third floor and pulled off her wet boots and changed her overdress. She felt like a child at Michaelmas, anticipating a gift. Eagerly, she rushed back down to the dining hall. Tessa was there, obviously having gained word of the treasure.

Others rushed into the room, Vito and Ugo tussling like boys, Ugo in a headlock as they rounded a corner. "Gentlemen, gentlemen!" Gianni called out.

They immediately snapped to order, quieting and drawing near the table up on the dais, where Daria stood waiting.

Piero arrived with several knives, a bronze sanding rod, and a delicate iron pick, and sat directly across from her. With a grin around the table at all the waiting faces, he gingerly picked up the cylinder and began picking away at the wax. The first section gave way easily, crumbling, and his brow furrowed in fear. Whatever was inside had surely been stewing in seawater for centuries.

They all held their breath until Vito gasped like a court jester, making them all laugh and breaking some of the tension. Piero continued picking away at the wax, taking out big chunks at a time now. He set aside his tool and tried to take the lid off the cylinder, frowned when it remained stuck, and then pulled it closer to a candle's flame. He picked up his tool and dug a bit more.

The lid made an audible *pop,* startling him, and the lid began to slide—

"Take care!" Daria cried.

Ugo thrust out his hands as if he meant to catch it.

"It is all right, it is all right," Piero said, taking the lid, nearly too large for him to grasp with one hand. He gave them all a mischievous look, pausing for effect.

"Open it, Father!" Tessa cried. "Open it."

He wiggled his eyebrows at her and then took the lid fully from the cylinder, placing it on the table. They all edged in to see.

Inside was an object, wrapped in yellowed linens. "Completely dry," Piero said in a whisper, pulling it out.

It was about five inches long and four across. Piero began unwrapping the object, winding the strip around his hand as he went.

"What is it?" Ugo asked.

"I do not know," Piero said. "But we shall soon find out."

ಶ ಶ ಶ

"What of the state of your people, Bishop Carpaccio?" Cardinal Boeri asked the tall man who leered after the maidservant departing with their serving trenchers. Boeri narrowed his eyes so that the bishop would know his indiscretion had been observed.

"What of them?" the bishop asked absently, stabbing his last bit of bread with the tip of his knife and stuffing it in his mouth. He had been left behind in the politics of Church hierarchy, abandoned to this disintegrating outpost as Venezia moved toward the Rialto. "I have but three hundred left here." He waved his hand upward and then out. "But I get my fair share of pilgrims. All wish to come to Venezia's birthplace, Torcello, to pray before the altar and the saint's relics." He wiped his mouth and studied Cardinal Boeri, still chewing. "There was an interesting story last week."

"Oh? Of what?"

"A healer on the isle of lepers, of all things. The gossip goes that it was a woman, accompanied by knights, and a priest."

"You believe it true?"

"I know a man who has seen more than fifteen healed lepers. They were cleared by the doge's own physician and allowed entry to Venezia again."

"Praise be to God," the cardinal intoned. He well knew this story, of course; the doge's palazzo was rife with gossip. But the public nature of this healing was a cause for consternation, a potential pitfall. Too many instances like this and word would spread; reports might even be sent to Avignon.

"You have always taken an interest in such things, have you not, Cardinal?" the bishop asked, leaning back in his chair and studying him.

"I have considered it part of my vocation to seek out those of the dark and bring them to justice," Boeri said.

"Hunt them down and kill them. Isn't that more like it?" Bishop Carpaccio asked, leaning forward, elbows on the table. The bishop was feeling his wine. Boeri listened to the bishop prattle on about the strange occurrence, the odd group, the female healer. His eyes glistened with interest as he spoke of her. "Mayhap we should find them. Bring them here. So that you might question them and make certain they are not witch nor warlock."

Cardinal Boeri studied him. "That will not be necessary, Bishop. But thank you for your concern."

The cardinal appreciated the fact that the Gifted seemed to be gaining strength. If their gifting became more prominent, obvious, it would aid his process of securing their strength for his own goals. But it was time to find them and entice them to work alongside him. The precious letter he carried with him would be of undeniable interest to them. Unless they had an entire copy, already knew where they were to go, what they were to do. But that was impossible. Wasn't it?

There were others who knew of the Gifted. He was sure of it. Over the decades of his years, he had heard men whisper of it in quiet scriptoriums and ancient libraries. He had chased hints and suggestions as far as Alexandria and Constantinople. He had never seen another page of the letter, but there were enough rumors to make him believe they still existed.

The priest, Piero. He had a portion. And given the Sorcerer's vehement attack upon the Gifted in Siena, his assault upon them right before Boeri's very own knights de Vaticana, his final attempt during tournament . . . yes, the Sorcerer knew them for what they were too.

Enemies of the dark.

And therefore the cardinal's ultimate accomplices.

Yet judging from Gianni's earlier missives, they had uncovered neither the Sorcerer's identity nor their ultimate mission. Boeri yearned for further information. But he would bide his time, make sure Gianni had cause to seek him out when their paths crossed in Venezia. They would reforge their long friendship and Gianni would put his trust in him—and persuade the rest of the Gifted to do so as well. They could not survive much longer without a Church father to shelter them from the coming storm. If it all came together quickly, they could head together to Avignon before snows blocked the mountain passes to the north.

With Providence on his side, he could return to Roma with the people's support, from Avignon to Roma, demons properly corralled, miracles abounding that would hold up under the most strict of Dominican examination. Upon death, they would all be declared saints. The doge and the world's princes would be brought to their knees before them.

It would all play out in divine order. He would see to it.

Why else would God have placed him here, now?

⚓ ⚓ ⚓

Tessa abruptly left the table and went to a window, staring soberly outward, but Daria barely noticed. Gianni studied the girl, noting her delicate eyebrows knitting together in a frown, wondering what could have distracted her at this moment, this incredible moment. Resolving to find out what ailed her later, he turned back to the priest, who removed the cloth from the object as gently as a nurse with a babe.

Everyone in the group was again holding their breath. It was as if the very air about them had become heavy, laden with anticipation.

And then it emerged—the object inside. Glass. Filling the small priest's hand in a gentle oblong shape, blue-green in tone, thick, barely transparent, with a delicate line of liquid gold, rubbed off in places, but a clear line . . . he turned it over in his hand, fingering small metal prongs.

"What is it?" Gianni asked.

Father Piero frowned and turned it over again. Then he gave his head a small shake, raising one brow. "See for yourself." He held it up for all to see, turning it over slowly.

They all leaned forward. It was a little over four inches long, bubbling in places, archaic in comparison to the work of glass artisans of the day.

" 'Tis ancient," Daria whispered. "Could it be that the legend is true? That this is a portion of Apollos's map?"

All eyes went to Daria for a moment, then back to the object.

"It is undeniably ancient," Gianni said. "I have never seen anything like it."

All remained silent a moment. Piero rose and paced, one finger to his lips, one hand still holding the glass piece.

"It was the Venetians who brought glass to the peninsula," Basilio said. "Right?"

"Nay," Piero said. "Our mosaic artist was correct. The art of glass-making has come and gone for centuries. As a young man in Constantinople, I once was given a glimpse of the cardinal's glass collection. He had several vases that he claimed were from Alexandria."

"Egyptian?" Gianni said, casting a doleful look the priest's way.

Daria reached for the object, studied it for but a moment, and then let her eyes slide slowly to Hasani. Gianni followed her gaze to the tall black man and noted his shared expression of recognition. "Daria? Hasani?" Gianni asked. "You have seen this object before?"

All eyes were on the freed man as he took the glass object from Daria and held it to the candlelight. His large black eyes ran across it, from one side to the other and back again. Then he looked each of them in the eyes and pulled his head in the direction of his quarters.

They all followed behind him, an odd grouping, in Gianni's opinion. Their lady, Daria d'Angelo; her freed slave, Hasani; her chaplain, Father Piero; Tessa; and five knights—the brothers Ugo and Vito, then Basilio and Rune, and himself. They were an odd grouping, yes, but Gianni felt the fiercest devotion to them all . . . something that surpassed even what he had experienced as a knight de Vaticana de Roma. Never had he thought he would leave the service of the Church and Cardinal Boeri, but God had definitely brought him here, to these people. His people.

They gathered in the large room that housed all the men of their motley group, over by the desk where Hasani toiled at odd hours. As before, the man secretly rifled through a pile of sketches, searching for the one he had to show them.

"Saints above," Vito said, "Hasani, man, why do you not simply show them all to us right now? If 'tis visions you have, ought we not be in on them now? Could they not serve as warning for us?"

Hasani paused, staring downward as if he were now hesitant to show the group even one.

"Leave him be," Father Piero interceded. "There is a proper time and place to share visions with us. We must trust Hasani to do so when he is led to do so. He already bears a burden of foreknowledge that none of us would truly care to carry ourselves."

With that, Hasani pulled a large piece of parchment from the stack and laid it on the straw tick beside the desk. They all circled around again, some of them staring at it upside-down. In the lower portion of the parchment was a drawing of a magnificent church—"San Marco," Piero mused quietly, fingers brushing over it as if he could touch the ancient church itself—and stretching up from it was a map of Italia. It was the land to their north, extending to the mountains and the lands belonging to the Franks. Yet there were lines crossing the map as if marking borders or boundaries of kingdoms long lost.

Piero leaned down and placed the glass over one portion of the sketch near San Marco, and then pulled it aside. He covered it again, and pulled it aside, then repeated the action once more.

Many of them crossed themselves. Piero went to his knees in prayer.

Hasani turned away, walking to the window. Daria looked to Gianni, wonder in her eyes.

Because in shape, the piece was a perfect match.

Piero leaned closer and traced the delicate gold line on the glass. "This is our map," he said, looking about them. "Our map. We collect the other six pieces, and we shall be certain of where the Lord is leading us next. We shall not be long of this city. We are to find what we are to find and move on. Quickly." He eyed Hasani. "We must not be captured."

Gianni straightened. "Captured. By whom?"

Piero straightened as well, a much smaller man in stature but still strong in manner. "The dark. They are nearing us again. We must remain ahead of them."

"Father, if there is something we should know . . ." Gianni began, looking from the priest to Hasani.

"Nay. It is not the time," Piero said, even as Hasani gathered his drawings and rose, dismissing them all.

CHAPTER SIX

"HOIST more sail, man," Abramo said. "We need to make better time than this."

"Sir," the captain said, "we have her at all the sail she can handle. We risk capsizing if we hoist but one more."

Abramo stared hard at the man and then up to the three sails aloft. He looked down to his feet, and only when he judged the captain's opinion sound did he turn away and walk to the lee rail.

Vincenzo joined him there. "What is it? Why such haste, now?"

"I dislike travel. I want to either be doing something that furthers my goals or be in charge. I am unused to standing back and watching. That is why I've developed business interests from Venezia a Roma. Something for me to do at each stop. This traveling by sea . . . It leaves me restless."

He strode off then and Vincenzo assumed his position at the rail, staring out to the azure seas. A few more hours, and they would be in Venezia. Then the hunt would be on, to find Daria before she did any more damage, before their relationship was beyond retrieval.

Vincenzo thought of the letter that Abramo had shown him in Siena, a portion of the same letter that had started Daria on this errant path in the first place. And she had made a dangerous enemy in Abramo Amidei. He had seen what Abramo did with his enemies—he either brought them to his side or destroyed them. Surely Daria would be no different.

Vincenzo looked up to the sails that fluttered and popped full in the wind, bearing their load. He remembered Tatiana's hair, blowing about in the breeze, covering her beautiful eyes until she pulled it back in irritation. That was a good night, a night before she took to her bed and didn't rise for but the bare requirement again.

He closed his eyes, feeling the wind across his cheeks and lashes. Daria had been untruthful with him. She had kept vital secrets to which he should have been privy. But she was young; a mistake had been made.

He had lost Tatiana. He could not, would not, forever lose Daria.

He opened his eyes and watched the sails again. "Blow wind, blow," he whispered.

༒ ༒ ༒

Two days later, Abramo Amidei and his entourage moved into a palazzo two blocks inland from the Grand Canal, or the "Canalazzo" as the Venetians called it, on the main island. He immediately set out to both further his business interests and find the Gifted. He sent his *secretario* to set up meetings with merchants and tradesmen, arranging for a great feast at the palazzo in a week's time, and a private assembly with the doge.

"Is there no city that you don't manage as easily as you do your own, Abramo?" Vincenzo asked.

"The world is my home," Abramo said with a smile, then picked up a sheaf of papers and turned to confer with another underling.

Vincenzo sank into a luxurious, overstuffed divan that smelled of must and moisture. He looked about the cavernous room on the third floor of the palazzo, what they called the third *piano* in Venezia, the room in which everyone entertained. The building did not have the fine detail of Toscana's villas and mansions, but it was more than sufficient by Venetian standards. And it was certainly large enough—not so large to attract the ire of the local men of power, but big enough to command instant respect . . . as well as hold the feasts for which Abramo was famous.

Once again, Vincenzo marveled at the subtleties of Abramo's work. It was, indeed, how he moved into a city, slipping in, almost unnoticed, but impossible to miss for long. He was like the crocodiles of the Nile that Vincenzo had read about as a child, rising just enough to get a good look at his prey, sinking underwater for as long as a day, then resurfacing with a ferocious attack that no one expected. It was brilliant, really.

The underling moved off. Men carried in trunks and furniture, and Abramo pointed to where he wanted them in distracted fashion, his eyes still on the papers in his hands.

Vincenzo rose and walked to the tall, Turkish-inspired windows that lined the street side of the palazzo. Some had thick, rippled rounds of glass. Others were open to the water, with nothing but a shutter to keep out the autumnal chill. He stood beside one, letting the cool breeze wash over his face, smelling the now-familiar odors of tar and fish. After several days at sea, it felt odd to be indoors. When he sat, he could still feel the crest and fall of the water.

He sensed when Abramo ceased his work and came to stand beside him. After a time of shared silence, Vincenzo spoke: "So it is here that we will cross paths with the Gifted again?"

"That is my intention, yes," he said.

Vincenzo let that sit for a long moment. "How is it that you plan to capture them here? They escaped us in Siena."

Abramo brought his hand to his chin and stared thoughtfully outward. "I do have a plan, Vincenzo. Trust me."

"To capture or kill?"

Abramo let out a small laugh. "Oh no, these people are of much more use to us alive than dead. It is our charge to find a way to reach them, show them what we have to offer. They are misguided. But our neighbors are gaining in power. They must be brought to us soon."

Vincenzo eyed him sharply. "They are right here? In Venezia?"

"Oh yes, most certainly."

Vincenzo's mouth was suddenly very dry. Daria? Here? It had been what? Two, three months since he had seen her? What did she remember of that night, that night that was so dim in his own memory?

"I say it again. Trust me, my friend," Abramo said. He turned toward Vincenzo. "Do you trust me, man?"

"With my life, Master."

"Excellent. Our road before us will undoubtedly become a bit tricky. I will rely on your loyalty. And you will again be sorely tested when the Duchess resurfaces."

Vincenzo nodded. "What makes you so certain that they are here? That they are stronger?"

Abramo turned his face to the window again and closed his eyes. "Close your eyes, Vincenzo," he said in a whisper. "Feel the breeze upon your face, listen to what she has to tell you."

Vincenzo did as instructed, but he felt nothing but ocean breeze, heard nothing but the shouts of men on docks below.

"Concentrate, my friend," Abramo said lowly. "Listen. Reach out for Daria first. She will be easiest for you to sense."

Vincenzo waited, waited, waited . . . and then he saw her, as clearly as in a dream.

"Ah, yes," Abramo said so quietly it was almost a moan. "They are here. And soon, they will know we are here too."

ർ ർ ർ

"Tessa, what distracts you so?" Daria called out to the girl at the window.

She did not wait for the child to answer, too absorbed in studying the glass piece. "So if that's a match, we shall find six others like it," Daria said.

"It's a thought," Vito said. "But how many churches do you know that are partially submerged, with a treasure waiting to be picked up?"

"Vito," Gianni said in warning, not liking the man's lack of respect.

"Beggin' your pardon, m'lady," Vito said, ducking his head.

"Nay, it is all right," Daria said, pacing. "God will show us. Lead us to them. Make a way in those other churches."

"We are on a path he has ordained. We simply must ask him to show us," Piero said.

Daria picked up the glass piece and turned it over again in her hands. "These curious metal prongs—what do you think they are for?"

"The glassmaker's mold?" Gianni asked.

"Or a means to attach them to the other pieces," Piero said, reaching for it again. He studied it for a long moment and then looked back to Hasani's drawing. "They are all here, here in Venezia. We must find them, and guard them with our lives. When we have all seven, we are to follow the path, as the map indicates."

"Map?" Vito asked blankly.

"This gold line," Piero said, pointing it out. "I am not a man who wagers, but I would bet that the others will match up and show us the way."

"And then?" Vito persisted. "We bring in the entire 'day of enlightenment,' as our friend the mosaic artist suggested? Seems a bit much for such a group as we."

"I know not!" Piero burst out in exasperation. "Do we not have enough before us without asking questions before their time?"

Vito's eyebrows shot up in surprise at the priest's uncharacteristic irritation. He smiled. "All right, all right, Father. Keep your robes on."

Gianni looked to the other knights. "Basilio, Rune. This was once your home; go see what you can discover about churches in the area and any symbol of the peacock." They nodded and immediately rose to exit. "Gentlemen," he called to them, waiting for them to pause and look him in the eye. "Quietly. Do this quietly. It is imperative we do not arouse suspicion or attention."

Satisfied with their look of understanding, he turned to the other men. "Vito, please take up a position on the roof. Hasani, when you're ready, if you could go to the door . . ."

Father Piero studied him. "You are alarmed?"

"Yes. And nay." He looked at Daria, then Tessa, who was still staring out the window. He remembered her distraction now, even as the glass piece was unwrapped. Drawing near, he reached out and laid a gentle hand on the girl's shoulder. She jumped.

"Tessa, forgive me. I did not mean to startle you . . ." He paused, noticing the tears in her eyes. This was what had set him on edge, brought his task of protecting the lady and this group to mind so abruptly. Fear.

"Tessa," he said, making her face him, look him in the eye. "What is it?"

She swallowed hard, bringing her chin up, trying to be courageous, obviously losing the battle. "They are here."

Gianni moved her behind him, looking quickly out the window as if an arrow might plunge through at any moment. "Who are here, Tessa?" he asked softly, twisting to see her.

But with one more look into the girl's face, he knew.

Father Piero and Hasani, even Daria, appeared unsurprised. "I knew this would happen, m'lady," Gianni said, shaking his head. "It was why I did not wish you to heal the lepers."

"I could not say no to our Lord, Gianni," Daria said. "And had we not moved that day, we would not have encountered the fisherman—he's obviously one of us."

Gianni let out a growl of frustration and threw his hands out. "Of course not. But what am I to do with such a task? How am I to keep you all safe? How do we follow this path and remain alive?"

Piero covered the distance between them and laid a hand on his shoulder. "Gianni, my son. Your gift is faith. Do not forget that. It is your strength, your shield. God is our protector. If this cause is just, if we remain brave and true, our Lord will make a way for us."

Brooding, Gianni again looked out to the water below.

"It is a big city," Daria said. "There are thousands here. We shall blend in."

"Forgive me, m'lady, but we are hardly without presence. We've just moved into one of the larger homes in Venezia. Female merchants are few and far between, especially one so devout that she travels with her own chaplain, nor one successful enough to hire a retinue of guards. Trust me, word such as this travels fast. And it will not take long for those who hunt us to connect stories of the isle of lepers to this mansion."

"Then we must earnestly seek God's direction," Piero said.

"And move quickly to where he leads," Daria added.

ᘉ ᘉ ᘉ

"You have heard that our very own healer is here, here in Venezia, have you not?" Lord Frangelico said, as they sat back in Abramo's deep chairs and drank fine Toscana wine in celebration of their new deal.

Abramo tapped his glass idly, remarkable in his control. "Healer?" he asked as if he didn't care about the answer.

"Ah yes," Frangelico said, leaning forward with a grin, eager to share his ripe story, something Abramo was not already aware of, something he could use. Vincenzo had seen it time and time again—people clamored to Abramo's side, eager to share anything that might buy a portion of Lord Amidei's grace.

But Abramo was careful, always so careful, never to give away what something meant to him. "Always keep them guessing, feeling indebted, Vincenzo," he had told him not long ago. "Debt is power."

Curious, he sat back to watch Abramo work, desperately shoving his own interest aside. So Abramo had been right; Daria was here in Venezia.

Frangelico dived in without further encouragement. "The story goes that a lady—" he paused meaningfully—"goes to the isle of lepers, surrounded by a guard of twenty men and preceded by six slaves and four holy men."

"Twenty men. Six slaves and four holy men," Abramo said in flat disbelief, raising one brow.

Frangelico lifted one shoulder. "You know the masses as well as I. The tale may have grown with each day."

"How long ago?" Abramo asked, the one question he would let slip.

"Four, maybe five days." Frangelico moved forward, to the edge of his chair. "Yet it is as grand a tale as the Siena marketplace healing."

This time, Abramo remained conspicuously unmoving.

"Well, nearly so," Frangelico hedged. "The lady arrives on the island and looks about. The people come to anyone who dares near, begging. It is rather foolhardy to even near their shore, as I hear tell it. One's clothes are liable to be stripped from one's back."

He paused, making certain both of them watched him with adequate interest. "And so they move forward, speaking to the people." Every man, woman, and child capable of moving pushes toward her, asking her to rescue them, feed them, help them. She finds the boy she seeks, and as soon as she touches him—*as soon as she touches him*—he is healed. What is more . . . She turns around to a group who are praying, and they're so tight, it's as if they're a chain. She touched one—but all in that group were healed at once."

Vincenzo coughed. He could not resist. "Everyone? Everyone in that group?"

"Everyone," Frangelico said with a grin, taking a long sip of his wine and then settling back.

"And this has been authenticated by whom?"

"The minister of public health himself reports it to me, two nights past," Frangelico said, his eyes on Abramo. He wanted Lord Amidei to note his reach and power. "He removed the healed people from the isle himself. With a retinue of guards, of course."

"What was it truly, four, five people?" Vincenzo pressed. Abramo shot him a look of irritation, but he pretended to not see it.

"More toward fourteen or fifteen," Frangelico said. "The minister swears it is true—"

"Come," Abramo said, rising suddenly. "I think we should leave our idle gossip and summon more feastings to properly celebrate our new partnership."

Both men rose with him. "Of course, of course," Lord Frangelico said. "Let me go and send my man home to my wife to give her word of my extended absence."

"Better yet," Abramo said, "Send for her. Bring any of your household. A palazzo is meant to be shared, is it not?"

"Indeed," the man said, an arrow of sorrow shooting across his face. Vincenzo recognized that expression—the man had no choice but to accept Abramo's invitation, but he had had other thoughts on his mind . . . a night of frivolity and Venetian girls, mayhap?

The round man exited the room, and Abramo's face, alight in smiles, immediately furrowed in a frown. He strode back to Vincenzo and Vincenzo braced, as if for an invading army's claw over a castle wall.

"Have I taught you nothing?" Abramo asked, inches from his face.

"On the contrary, Lord Amidei, you have taught me much."

"And yet you insist on asking questions when I deliberately remain silent?"

"Forgive me, m'lord. Curiosity won out." He dared to stare back into Abramo's dark eyes. He must be subservient, but strong, if he was to hold Abramo's respect and interest.

Abramo broke into a sudden smile. "She is a vixen, this one, is she not?" he asked, clapping Vincenzo on the shoulder and moving past him, back to his desk. Vincenzo dared to take a breath and turned toward him.

Abramo sat down heavily in his chair and studied the wine in his glass as he swirled it. "She is worthy," he said.

"Yes, m'lord."

Amidei rose and slowly rejoined him by the window, staring outward as Vincenzo looked in the other direction. "She remains important to you."

"Indeed."

"Tell me, Baron. If I asked it of you, would you give her to me?"

Vincenzo coughed. "Give her to you? She is not mine to give."

"And yet if she were. If I asked it."

A long silence stretched between them.

"Baron del Buco."

Vincenzo turned to him. "If you asked it, m'lord. If she were willing."

"And if she were not?"

Vincenzo took a breath. "If you asked it, Master."

Abramo eyed him for a long moment. "Good, my friend. Good."

ↄ ↄ ↄ

LATER that evening, after the rather formal, traditional dinner concluded and Abramo invited Frangelico back for less urbane festivities the following eve to further celebrate the new agreement between Siena's woolen guild and one of Venezia's most vital sea merchants, Abramo led Vincenzo back to the second *piano* and into his quarters. Five women lounged about the room in various states of undress, hair down and flowing over naked shoulders. Each had a bottle of wine and two goblets before her, as well as a plateful of fruit.

Vincenzo supposed he ought to have become more used to this—Abramo's ability to summon the most choice of young women in a city and bring them into his home to service them, but it still caught him off guard. He thought of his favorite woman in Siena, whom they had left behind, and the mysteries of the cave. It stirred him, made him hungry for her. Hungry for more.

Abramo clasped his shoulder and grinned. "You did not think that while I am making our new friend Frangelico wait, I would do the same to you? Nay. A man has needs. And my closest men are always seen to first. Remember that. But first—come here. I must show you something in the letter." Reluctantly, Vincenzo followed his friend to the desk, tearing his eyes away from two who appeared to be sisters, boldly meeting his gaze.

He fought to bring his attention back to the portion of the letter that Abramo had given him but a glimpse of in Siena, the letter with gilt illumination that clearly depicted Daria, Piero, and Gianni—the Gifted—in combat with a sea monster. Abramo gestured to the illumination in the margins and said in a hushed voice, not loud enough to reach the women, "If we are the sea monster . . ."

"Then we are on attack."

Abramo let that settle. "Here, in their left hands, is some sort of object. See?" He pushed aside the first sheet to show the second and third. "Each of them carries one." He tapped the ancient parchment and rose.

Vincenzo bent closer to the parchment and studied it. In the woman's hand—Daria?—was a blue and brown object. They all appeared to be identical in size but different in shape and color. Each faced the sea monster. Each held the strange objects in their left hands as if they were a sword, and in their right hands, carried a shield decorated with a cross.

Abramo was again beside him. He tapped the picture. "It is these objects they seek here, I'm sure of it. We must intercept them, or take them from them, impede their progress by whatever means necessary. Rout them out before we are forced to attack. We change the course of history, here. Now."

Vincenzo rose. "Why? Why not ignore them?"

Abramo's eyes narrowed. "Because, Baron, they are our enemy. You see it here. Do you not?"

Vincenzo's eyes fell back to the illumination.

"They are strong together, mayhap growing stronger. But look to the sea monster. He has three times the girth, the strength. They are no match for him, and yet still they dare face him. And what do you suppose our new agreement with Frangelico gains us?"

"Strength," Vincenzo said in little more than a whisper, putting it together. He had wondered what Abramo would gain from uniting the Sienese woolen guild with Frangelico. There was little financial gain for him in it. But it was this—power. Brokering the deal kept him a part of both Frangelico's and Vincenzo's world, indebting them both to him. He met Abramo's stare.

"It is here that we must win the Gifted to our side or conquer them. Here. In Venezia. We will work to find them, capture them, use political clout if necessary." He circled Vincenzo slowly. "A night in a dungeon would be eye-opening to the Duchess, I imagine. She thinks she is strong, but she has never really suffered physically, has she?"

"Nay," Vincenzo said, his hands clenching at his side. But he had promised, promised Abramo that he would give him Daria if he asked. Surely he would not—

"Good," Abramo said. A small smile lifted the corners of his lips, and he nodded slightly. "Very good. We must find other methods of reaching them, find each weakness and exploit it, tear them apart. You, my friend—you still have a tender place in the Duchess's heart, despite all that's transpired. You may give us entrée to her. The knight—he undoubtedly feels some guilt in leaving his post with the Church. We can use that. The freed man—I know several slavers who would delight in taking him back to the far reaches of their territory in chains. The priest, he is more difficult. I must give him further consideration. Two of Daria's knights used to be in the employ of one of my friends here in Venezia. He could recall a certain grievance he had with them, giving the doge cause to bring them before him, imprison them. The child—there are myriad ways I can get to her, but it must be from a direction she never anticipates . . . And she is already dear to the Duchess, I could use her as well . . . Yes, yes," he said, now smiling more broadly.

He leaned forward to tap Vincenzo on the chest. "Fear. And chaos. A taste of pain—of the heart or of the body. Elements of our dark powers over which we hold sway. That is what we will sow into the Gifted's lives. And they will eventually come to us, conquered. Vanquished."

"And if they escape?" Vincenzo asked over his shoulder as Abramo went to three of the women and lifted a goblet to his lips.

Abramo smiled again. "Let them try. If they succeed in escaping Venezia, they will have a sea monster or two with which to contend."

Vincenzo leaned down to the illumination again, studying the sea monster. Of course. If the Gifted left Venezia's shore, they would now have Frangelico's fleet in pursuit. It would be nearly impossible for them to escape by sea.

Daria was stubborn and stronger than ever before. Just what means would Abramo have to employ to break her? Vincenzo clenched his hands again, remembering her insubordination, her failure to tell him the truth. She had deliberately misled him, made choices that could have brought harm to the guild. She had refused to heal his Tatiana when she clearly had the gift to do so. Rage flooded through him, splaying his fingers wide, then back into fists.

Abramo strode to one of the women Vincenzo had eyed upon entering the room, took a handful of hair in his hand, and forced her head up. "Come, my friend. Ease your passions here. Or here," he said, grabbing the sister. "These women are committed to our cause. They know the power of the dark, have sworn to serve it and us. Come, learn what we have to offer in a whole new way. Fully explore the power of passion and rage and the combination thereof. Know the dark. Tame it. Make it yours."

Stirred again, Vincenzo moved across the room.

CHAPTER SEVEN

"THERE are two in the outer reaches of the laguna," Basilio said. "According to another mosaic artist, he has laid eyes on them himself. Four peacocks, two on the bottom, two on the opposite side, with a round disk at the center of the square. Santa Maria e San Donato de Murano and Santa Maria Assunta de Torcello are the farthest away."

"San Giorgio was a simple conquest," Rune put in. "Waiting for us. The others will not be the same."

"And there are four among the inner islands of the Rialto," Basilio said, eyeing the group with warning. "Sant' Elena, San Zaccaria, Santa Giustina della Vigna, and as Giuseppe the mosaic artist told us . . . San Marco."

Vito blew out his cheeks and released a long breath. "That's fine. I feared you'd name a really difficult sanctuary to infiltrate."

Basilio rolled his eyes at the man's sarcasm and sighed heavily.

"How on earth are we to get into the doge's church itself?" Daria asked in a whisper. "Let alone all those others? If we're caught ransacking a church—it is as if we are signing our own death warrant. They shall hang us all."

"God will make a way," Gianni said with confidence none of the rest of them felt.

"Mayhap he already has," Vito said. "Our man Giuseppe is working as we speak in San Marco on their massive mosaic project. He does it for the money. But he is irritated that the priests are covering wall frescoes that his great-great-grandfather painted. We could use the conflict he feels and his need for funds to help us."

"God will prepare him. We will begin there," Piero said. "At San Marco. If we begin with others and word gets out, the richer churches will be more closely guarded, nearly impossible to infiltrate. If word reaches the lesser churches, it will be more difficult but not impossible. Yes, we begin with the most prominent of them all. If we're right, we will find the next glass segment there."

"And then we must find the others as quickly as possible, mayhap even split up and obtain two or three at once," Daria said.

"Nay," Piero said. "We are stronger together. We shall not split up."

"Captain," Ugo said, ignoring the priest. "The lady is right. Our only chance may be to get at least two at once, mayhap three. Strike before they suspect anything."

"Win the priest and you win me," Gianni said. "But if the priest says we stay together, we stay together."

Piero looked about, noting the expression of Ugo's frustration on several others. "Come, friends. Let us plan it out. We will devise several plans and then pray that God will show us which one to follow. We shall meet with this mosaic artist, away from here. He must never connect us to this house, understood?"

They all nodded. Piero's eyes halted on Tessa, again at the open window, deathly pale and still. "Tessa?"

Daria rose and went to the girl, sliding an arm around her small shoulders and looking out with her, obviously intending to comfort her. Instead she sucked in her breath and leapt to the side of the window, pulling the girl away with her.

Gianni rose and unsheathed his sword. His men did the same. Hunched over, they rushed to several windows and peered out. Daria and the girl were panting. In the silent room, all the men could hear them.

Gianni didn't see them at first, among the skiffs and barges. And then he spotted what had made Tessa pause, Daria jump.

Lord Abramo Amidei, in a long black cape, standing at the helm of a skiff. Two men stood behind him, poling along the canal. He was staring forward, away from their house, then suddenly turned his head and stared in their direction.

Gianni could see in his peripheral vision that Ugo and Rune leapt back to their hiding spots. But he held his position. Even if Abramo saw him, he'd draw more attention in movement. Abramo looked to the top of the mansion, where Vito was guarding. Would either man recognize the other?

He held his breath as Abramo stared upward, then turned in the other direction, tossing a command back to the men behind him. He had not noted their presence, or had not recognized Vito, or was cleverly disguising his discovery if he had.

Daria's wide eyes stared in Gianni's direction, and at her chest the child clung to her, staring at him too.

Tessa panted, tears welling in her eyes. "It is him," she gasped. "The Sorcerer . . . here!"

"It is all right," he said soothingly. "He leaves, Tessa, he is moving away. It is all right! There is nothing to fear."

But a big tear crested Tessa's eye and rolled down her cheek. "Sir Gianni, he knows we are here," she whispered. "He knows."

"Nay, child," Piero said, edging around the corner to peek outward. "He knows we're in the city, but he is not yet aware of where we are. Take comfort in the size of this city, our anonymity. Only God is omniscient. Never the dark. They know only what God allows. We still have time. We will move quickly and then make our escape. It will be all right."

But his expression did not meet the confidence that his words intended.

⚙ ⚙ ⚙

THEY spent several days preparing to infiltrate the great basilica, attending public mass, locating the peacocks and the green disk between them in the west nave. Vito and Ugo discovered the staircase that wound up to the upper level of the great church, and with a little assistance from Giuseppe, posed as workmen carrying buckets of mortar and cut mosaic tiles up to the masons and artists who worked on the high scaffolding among the upper arches even as the floor beneath them was completed.

The basilica was awe-inspiring, worthy of her fame and the doge's bid to make it the city's own church. It was here that Santo Marco's bones had been brought in the ninth century, stolen from a poorer church in Alexandria and smuggled out. "The way the story goes," Piero had told them, "the smugglers put the blessed saint under a layer of pork. When the Muslim guards inspected their cargo, they turned away in dismay without more than a glance and a sniff." Apparently, the green urns, etched with the sign of the peacock and containing Apollos's glass map, had accompanied the saint and his smugglers. They had arrived in Venezia, hailed as heroes, and Venezia had celebrated for days. The doge moved Santo Todaro aside and made Marco their patron saint. It was said that Marco appeared on several occasions and saved the city from foreign conquerors and sea storms alike.

It was Vito who noticed, from above, the peacocks' location. Around them labored more than fifty mosaic artisans, tiling the great arches and ceilings and domes of the basilica, covering frescoes hundreds of years old. From this location, they could walk the narrow, suspended wooden walkways and view the entire floor of the basilica. But it was the peacocks that drew his attention.

Vito and Ugo paused directly to one side of the dome that depicted the eve of Pentecost, when the Holy Spirit descended and entered each of the disciples with tongues of fire. Knowing that the church's principal structures continued through the floor to a shallow crypt and foundational layer below, the brothers had a good idea of where the underside of the peacocks would lie. Vito pulled his overcoat a little more snugly, feeling the comforting lump of sword strapped across his chest, and picked up his bucket again. Ugo pulled his chin up and met his gaze, silently telling him he would be guarding his back. Vito moved to another stairwell, heading down to the main floor of the sanctuary.

He was stopped as a cardinal swept by, a bishop and six other churchmen in tow, processing up the main hall of the basilica, obviously to pay their respects and pray beside the altar that sat upon Santo Marco's tomb. Vito took a step back and bowed politely, then stared from the corner of his eye at the man clad in red, struck by the fact he had seen the holy man somewhere else . . . but the cardinal was already past, no distinguishing marks visible. He *had* seen him before. Where?

Shaking his head, he turned the corner, walked down a short hallway, and then entered the staircase that led below the basilica. He passed two priests with a nod and proceeded down the long, dark hallway, illuminated only by occasional torches. He passed by what he assumed was the treasury of Santo Marco, where reportedly a good portion of the bounty of Constantinople lay. Two fearsome guards stood before the door, watching his every step. Giuseppe had instructed him to go on, three rooms past that point. He did as he was told and just as Giuseppe had told him, a lone guard stood just inside the entrance to Santo Marco's tomb. "You! Name yourself!" the guard barked at him.

Vito smiled and waved at him in a calming gesture. "I wish you and Santo Marco no harm, good knight. I am solely here to inspect the columns, as the doge wishes to know what funds it would take to tile these as well as those of the great naves above us. It is rather plain, is it not?"

"It is a crypt."

"But it is the crypt of the blessed saint himself!" Vito said. He waved his hands about. "These columns, this entire room should be bathed in gold." He glanced to the left and saw the narrow passageway Giuseppe had mentioned. He immediately moved to the other side of the room, pausing at each column and looking it over from bottom to top.

"I received no notice that the doge had asked for such an inspection."

"It is more an estimate on cost than any formal inspection. That shall come later. I hail all the way from Napoli. Is Venezia your birthplace?"

He moved off, ignoring the knight's response. His attention was on the columns. As he suspected, when he showed no interest in the saint's crypt, the guard relaxed. Vito counted the columns from the back and moved to the left. It was obvious that during the seasonal *acque alte,* or even at high tide, this room could flood. He could see the water marks halfway, even three-quarters up the wall. "Must you stand guard even when the room floods with water?" he asked the man across the room.

"Many a day, in the season ahead, I am waist deep in water," the guard responded. "We trade positions, once an hour, at high tides." He made a bawdy remark over the effect of seawater to his nether regions.

Vito laughed. He moved forward, inspecting the floor, and then saw it again, a passageway that led directly under the western nave. It was extremely narrow, barely wide enough for a man to enter, just as Giuseppe had described. He peered inward, but could see nothing. Why was it there? He edged toward a torch, intending to bring it closer, but the guard's voice halted his progress.

"I failed to ask your name," called the knight. "It wasn't but a day or two ago that another was in here, inspecting the infrastructure."

Vito raised his eyebrows. He heard the note of doubt in the knight's voice. "Indeed," he returned. "Apparently the doge is considering additional improvements. Mayhap they can make this crypt watertight. Would that not be an improvement? It would certainly aid me in keeping my tiles upon these columns. To say nothing of your comfort."

"To which guild do you belong?" the knight asked, suddenly right behind Vito.

"The Arte Mosaica, of course."

"Of course. It is odd, though. The doge's man. He never fails to tell me what to expect here. In ten years at this post, he has never failed to tell me." He studied Vito's face, saw the moment when Vito was searching for a response. Without further hesitation, he unsheathed his sword.

Vito raised his free hand and slowly set down his bucket of tile, freeing his overcoat belt at the same time, allowing him access to his sword. He raised both hands as if intending to surrender, but then, with a quick move, unsheathed his own sword. The two moved in a slow circle.

"You are a common grave robber. I will slice you to ribbons and be hailed the hero for saving Santo Marco."

"I hope not," Vito said. "Bloody ribbons," he said, pretending to shiver. "Much too messy."

He dodged the knight's first blow, not wishing for their skirmish to alert other guards that stood at the doorway of the treasury. The next narrowly missed his head and crashed into a column.

Vito pretended to lecture the knight. "Now the doge will be most unhappy with you. If that column was not weak before, it certainly is now. Please, take more care!"

It was then that Vito saw his brother, near a far column. Fortunately, the guard's attention was solely on him, his eyes ablaze with thoughts of glory and riches given in honor for killing the interloper before him. The poor sap had probably dreamed of such a day for the past decade, with each hour he stood in frigid, rising tidewaters.

The guard shouted and sliced left and right with his sword in a furious charge forward, nicking Vito's shoulder on the third strike. Vito ducked left at the side of the room and turned to face the guard, sword extended for the first time. The guard came to a halt, smiling in pleasure at the thought of real swordplay, and that was when Ugo struck, taking him down with one blow to the head.

"You couldn't have done that before he cut me?" Vito asked, fingering the slice at his shoulder.

"Just be glad I didn't let him get to your neck," Ugo returned. "Now, quickly. I bound one treasury guard and knocked out the other, but it won't be long before they come to or are freed."

"Over there," Vito said, gesturing with his chin to the far wall. "There's a cavern, extending directly beneath the peacock nave. If we can get past the door and squeeze inside, we may be able to obtain the prize without any further ado."

"Should I go and fetch the captain?"

"We only have moments before this knight or the others will be relieved and there is some cardinal above in the basilica. Guards will soon be upon us. Given that we've already been forced into the open, we must move quickly, see what we can discover on our own and then be away."

"Go," Ugo said. "You're more slight than I—see if you can get in there. I'll stand guard."

Vito grabbed a torch, hurried over to the last column, then counted three paces, making certain this was the right location. He unlatched the narrow door and opened it. *So this was what they wished to hide . . .*

ॐ ॐ ॐ

VINCENZO and Abramo rode on horses through the narrow winding streets and over wooden bridges that crossed the canals that webbed across Venezia. People, hungry for every inch of ground they could claim, continued to eat into the city streets, making some impossible to transverse via horseback.

They left their mares tied at a corner lot, paying a man to water them from a cistern, and hailed a skiff. Vincenzo knew not where Abramo was taking him, only that he had been asked to attend an important meeting. In minutes, they turned a corner in a canal and pulled up alongside a moderately sized dwelling that appeared overguarded. There were eight men within sight. Why the small army?

"Tell Lord Ricci that Baron del Buco and Lord Amidei are here to call," Abramo said regally to a guard at the water's edge.

"Yes, m'lord," said the guard with a stiff nod. He departed immediately.

The nearest guard turned to them. "You may take your ease here, in the shade, gentlemen, until Lord Ricci returns," he said, gesturing to the inner warehouse. Both men moved forward as indicated. Two other knights moved forward on either side.

They were pulling their riding gloves from their hands and the hats from their heads when Lord Ricci rushed into the room, hastily shaking their hands, chastising his guards for holding them up at all. "Come in, come in," he said.

They followed him up the stairs to the upper *piano,* settling into three low-slung chairs by a fireplace that glowed with afternoon embers. Lord Ricci summoned the chef to bring some refreshments. "Pardon my humble dwelling," he said, gesturing about.

"Gian, it is sufficient for one with such grand holdings across northern Italia," Abramo said. "Not every house can be a palazzo."

"Indeed," Lord Ricci said, leaning forward and waggling his eyebrows. "At least at first. I intend for that to change."

"Still making war upon thy neighbors, Gian?" Abramo asked.

"Only when I feel it is necessary," Lord Ricci said with a small smile, leaning back again and tenting his fingers together.

"You mean when you find they have something you want," Abramo said quietly.

"We have that in common," Lord Ricci returned. "So, Abramo, my old friend, tell me what brings you to my door. It's been two, three months? What has kept you away?"

"Siena, a lovely and fascinating city, has stolen my heart, I'm afraid. But Baron del Buco and I have returned to see through a new arrangement with Frangelico. He has agreed to a major import and export deal with the Sienese woolen guild."

Lord Ricci's eyebrows raised in appreciation, and for the first time he glanced at Vincenzo, clearly sizing him up. "It is your good fortune," he said. "I myself have sought a business arrangement with Frangelico for some time."

"Hmm," Abramo murmured. Vincenzo could hear no surprise in his response. He knew this all along. "How many of Frangelico's ships are you in need of?"

Lord Ricci's eyes darkened. He clearly knew he was being played. But it was to his benefit to consider anything Amidei brought his way. "Two, mayhap three."

"For?"

"My spice trade, but then you knew that." He leaned forward and poured each of them a cup of wine.

Abramo accepted the cup and leaned back into his chair. "Indeed. Consider that I may be able to persuade Frangelico to acquire a few more ships in order to run your trade. What would you be willing to trade me?"

Lord Ricci licked his lips and considered the question. "What is it you seek?"

"Five percent of gross sales. My *secretario* must have access to your books, of course."

"Done." He grinned, showing missing and rotting teeth.

"There is something else."

"Anything. Name it."

"Within the last few years you employed two knights."

"I employ many."

"There are two that I have a particular interest in."

"Who?"

"Sir Basilio Montinelli and Sir Rune of Germany. You remember them?"

Lord Ricci's grin faded into a frown. "I do. They insulted me and my house before they took their leave." Vincenzo glanced at the master; could he find out anything in any city? How had he tracked the knights back to this man?

"As I recall, they also stole your silver," Abramo led.

Gian started to shake his head, but then catching his eye, he smiled. So this was what Abramo wanted. "Yes. My silver. Every plate, fork, and knife."

"Tragic," Abramo said, slowly sliding a bag of silver across the table. "There was one knife left, yes? With the family crest upon it?"

"One knife," Gian said with a slow nod. He gestured for a servant and whispered in his ear. "The entire set was new, just arrived from

France, and worth a year's wages at least." He coughed, covering a con-spiratorial grin. "Are you saying you can find these thieves for me?"

"I think it only prudent to alert the local authorities that they are again in Venezia. Who knows who else they may rob? It is our civic duty to protect the people!"

Abramo stood and Lord Ricci awkwardly followed suit. They shook hands. The servant arrived and handed his master the knife, which Ricci then handed to Abramo. "I will see that the doge's men are informed," Abramo said. "We will have them in custody within a week's time, I'm certain of it. And when they are captured," Abramo said, pulling him close, "we will hold a celebration on the isle in your honor."

Gian grinned. Obviously, he had attended Abramo's banquets before.

"May I ask, m'lord, why you seek these men?" Gian ventured at the door.

"Nay," Abramo said with a smile. "But you might answer one more question for me. Where did the two knights go after they left your employ?"

"I believe they were employed by Bicoli for a time. Ilario told me they were disagreeable employees for him, as well, and departed for the south. Are you certain they are even here?"

"Oh yes," Abramo said. "Ilario Bicoli," he said with a breathy laugh. "That is most perfect. Come, Vincenzo. We must arrange for you to meet yet another old friend."

ॐ ॐ ॐ

It was an ancient Etruscan grotto. The countryside was littered with them. There were fewer in the far northern reaches and often, as it was here, other churches had been built atop the last. Marking superstition, or mayhap to show dominance, Christian architects constructed their buildings above the old, sometimes skirting, sometimes filling, but never leveling the grottos that had stood for ages. That was what had hap-pened here. Two boulders squeezed in from either side, but had not com-pletely covered the entry. Frequent flooding had played havoc with the marble walls that lined most of the tomb's far reaches, and evidently there was some reconstruction to be done here.

Vito sucked in his breath and pushed between the two boulders and into the tiny room beyond. It was simple in structure, a gentle curve in limestone, carved from some of the lone bedrock in all the lagoon. It was here that the Venetians had elected to construct the famous basilica, upon thousands upon thousands of pilings and this spare sector of rock.

But Vito's eyes were not on the ancient pagan grotto. His eyes were drawn to the ceiling, just five inches above his head. He ducked and moved farther to the left, pulling fist-sized rocks from a pile before him, one after the other. A green marble cylinder descended before him. It was what they sought. The question was, could he remove it without leaving a gaping hole in the cathedral floor?

He climbed up on an old block of limestone to get closer and peered at the cylinder, just within reach of his hand, recalling the priest and his care with the first.

"Vito," Ugo called out, wordlessly telling him to hurry.

Vito pulled a small knife from the back of his belt and began to pick at the wax directly beneath the disk. The trouble was that he could only reach it with his head cocked painfully to one side, and only with his left. He was right-handed. But a rock wall kept him from maneuvering to use his right hand. He flailed about, picking at the wax only once out of five tries.

"*Vito,*" Ugo called again.

"I'm working at it!" Vito called back in a hushed shout. "It's here!"

He lifted his torch and peered into the hollow that surrounded the cylinder. There was no way he had the time to pick at it in this fashion. If they were to escape, they had to move now.

Sighing, he pulled his sword again from the chest strap. Wrapping a cloth around a portion of the blade, he turned it over and stuck it in the hole, handle first, and then paused. He grimaced. The priest would keel over and die if he knew what Vito was about to do. But there was nothing for it. Taking a deep breath, he plunged the sword forward, the impact sending a tremor that reached his neck.

He picked up the torch and peered inward again. Did it hang at a slight angle now?

He exchanged torch for sword and hit it again, nudging it a bit to see if it gave way, then again, and again. On the sixth strike, it gave way at last, landing with a sickening *clunk* on the rocks directly below it.

Vito peered in again, relieved to see that no daylight showed through; the disk remained in place in the basilica floor above. With luck, the glass piece inside would be as well wrapped and as padded as the last. He grabbed the cylinder, pulled it out toward him, pulled the glass piece from its core, wrapped in cloth like the first, set the cylinder back among the rocks as if it had merely fallen down, and hurried out to his brother.

CHAPTER EIGHT

THE next day, the city was alive with rumors of men who had tried to steal the holy relics. "The way they tell it," Vito griped, "that lousy knight we knocked out turned away the devil himself. We were foreign invaders, bent on taking Marco's remains back to Alexandria."

"Let them continue to talk of it," Piero said with a barely concealed smile. "The more attention they grant the blessed saint's relics, the less they'll be aware of our real purpose in the crypt." He returned to the table and placed the second piece of glass next to the other. They did not fit together, but they obviously belonged together—both had the same coloration of tan and turquoise, as well as the delicate gold line. The second piece had small metal prongs as well.

"I do not suppose they all have underground crypts like San Marco's where we can pluck our urns like apples from the branch," Gianni said hopefully.

"Nay. Most crypts are shallow tombs, only directly beneath the altar for the relics. Few are as vast as Marco's resting place, spreading to form a foundation for the basilica itself. And the altar—it is some distance from the peacocks in these other churches. Anything is possible, but I am doubtful."

"I have thought of another idea," Daria said from a corner chair.

All eyes turned to her.

"What if Hasani and I approach the priests in these far churches—Torcello and Murano—and offer a handsome sum of money in order to bury my father's remains underneath the peacocks, our own family crest."

"Come out in the open with the peacock crest?" Gianni said. "I think not. Our enemies are about, Daria. We have seen them."

"Wait, Gianni," Piero said. He turned to her. "How would you persuade them to move quickly?"

"Gold florins speak volumes, especially to poorer parish priests," she said. "Murano, Torcello, they have seen their glorious days pass by. We could arrive with our own stone mason and Giuseppe, as well as a stated desire to be through with the funeral mass within the day."

"It may work," he allowed.

"Nay, it is too dangerous," Gianni said.

Daria turned to Gianni. "Our enemies shall not look for us there. They will assume we are trying to move in secrecy here, hidden in the city, rather than out in the open, in the outer reaches."

"Hiding in daylight. You really believe it may work to your advantage?"

"Nay," she said with a tight grin. "But we have precious few days before we are identified anyway. The Sorcerer is obviously determined to find us, tracking us all this way. And word of the healings . . ." She glanced at Tessa, who still stood watch at the window. "He knows we're here, Gianni. Should we not give way to using our identity rather than wasting precious days trying to preserve it?"

Gianni paced before a window. "How long? How long would you need?"

"We would travel to Murano, take a meeting with the bishop there in the morning, Torcello late in the day. They must each believe we intend to inter my father's remains in their church."

"Giuseppe has agreed to go with her," Basilio said. "And he has two companions he says can be trusted."

"You've brought them here?"

"Indeed. They were all here yesterday. They seem like honest men."

"Other than the fact they're willing to lie to earn a few extra florins. How is it, Father," he said, turning to the priest, "that we can spend an hour in mass and prayer each morning together and yet you can justify this conspiracy?"

Piero smiled. "To beat the serpent, one must be more wily than he." He turned to face the large knight. "The bishops will gain. What matter is it that no bones truly lie under a marble slab? They will have money to carry on with their charitable desires—feed the orphan, shelter the widow, tend to the ill."

Gianni understood now. This was Father Piero's plan, not Daria's. He turned on him in fury. "You would put m'lady in danger? You would force her to lie?"

Piero made a dismissive gesture with his hands. "You dare to lecture me? We are speaking of sin of omission, not an outward lie. But we will revise the story. She will simply say that her father's body is not available to her, that she wishes to remember him in this way, in this lovely sanctuary, beneath the peacock—her own family crest."

"Is a lie not always a lie, no matter how one phrases it? Let us think upon it, pray upon it. In a day's time, the Holy One will give us an answer."

"There is no time to waste!" Piero thundered.

They all stopped, staring at the small man. Seldom did he raise his voice.

Piero sat down, hard, on the edge of a chair. Gianni could suddenly see the weariness in the man's face and shoulders, the same exhaustion that plagued them all.

"I will tell them all that it is my quest," Daria said. "It is my quest to memorialize my father by placing a plaque beneath every symbol of a peacock I can find—in churches that allow it. And it will be the truth. It will honor my father. I pledge now to forever seek other locations where I can do the same. I will ask the priests and bishops to use my gift for the sick, honoring my mother as well."

Gianni recognized the resolution and determination in her eyes. There was no arguing with her when she got that spark. "So be it," he said. "With this plan, there is no need to move in such haste. We will consider it and pray over it for a day before we take action. Agreed, Father?"

"Agreed," the priest said.

"Hasani," the knight said, turning to the guard at the door. "You have seen no visions in regard to this, no warnings we must heed?"

Hasani shook his head, but his eyes slid to Basilio and Rune.

They noticed it too, and shared a glance of curiosity.

"Hasani," Piero said, rising and moving to the tall man. "Are the men in danger?"

He looked up at the ceiling, his face suddenly full of anguish. Daria strode over to him, laying a tender hand upon his arm. He looked at her and crossed his hands as if bound, then met the now stern gaze of Basilio and Rune. He communicated with Daria in low grunts and nods and hand gestures.

"He believes you will be taken prisoner," Daria said, confirming what they all feared he had seen.

"When?" Gianni said.

Hasani shook his head, misery in his eyes.

"You know not? Only that they will be imprisoned?" Gianni asked, running a hand through his hair in anxiety. "By whom?"

Again, the tall man shook his head.

Keeping his eyes on Hasani, Gianni spoke to Piero. "Father, can we do anything that would keep these visions from coming to fruition?"

Piero was beside him now. He looked up. "Hasani? Have any of your visions been unfulfilled?"

Hasani tucked his head to one side, sorrow in his eyes.

"Unfulfilled, yet," Piero supplied, "he thinks they will all come to fruition at some point." He looked to the ground and then up at Hasani again. "Have you ever noticed that your visions come to life, but different than you imagined? Can we alter the outcome?"

Hasani shook his head slowly, then eyed Basilio and Rune.

"We've spent more than one night in a dungeon," Basilio said. "For unrighteous reasons, of course."

"Come," Piero said, motioning them in.

Vito and Ugo moved in from the left, Basilio and Rune from the right. Tessa moved to Daria's side, wrapping her arms around her waist. They formed a tight circle with Hasani. "This is where it truly begins," Piero said.

"What?" Basilio asked sharply.

"Our testing." He took turns looking each in the eye. "This is when we will be proven worthy, or we will utterly fail. The danger will move from outside forces to those within us. The letter says we will encounter suffering, strife. That we must remain faithful, stand together. My brothers and sisters, this is when we will learn what we must do to fulfill the prophecy."

"Which prophecy is that, Father?" Basilio asked with a grunt. "We do not even have the other portion of the letter."

"Nay, but we have enough to know that we've been brought together for a purpose." He left the group to stride over to a cedar box on a marble table in the far corner and bring back the two glass pieces. "Our coming has been foretold for ages. We are here for a mighty purpose. And no matter what befalls us, imprisonment, even death," he said, willing belief into Basilio and Rune, "we must remain faithful."

"So that is it?" Gianni asked. "We cannot do anything to alter Hasani's vision of what is to come?"

"We can pray," Piero said. "We can pray that their imprisonment is brief, that we're able to free them, that we will all learn something from the hardship."

"Easy for you to say," Vito said. "You're not the man going to the dungeon."

Hasani's eyes had again turned to misery as he looked about the group. Gianni understood, then. They were *all* about to suffer hardship. Every one of them. Even little Tessa.

And there was not a thing he could do about it.

Chapter Nine

It was the middle of the night when Cardinal Boeri sat straight up in bed, a divine thought upon him.

He would find Daria d'Angelo and persuade her to be public with her gift of healing. He would bless her gift and petition that lousy pretender of a pope to grant her blessing. Given access to the public at large, she could do mighty works. She would gain attention throughout Italia and beyond. And she would need his protection and direction. He would become the healer's private spiritual counselor. She was surely outgrowing the capacity of the poor abbot-cum-chaplain. A woman of her stature, of her gifting, belonged in the company of princes and cardinals.

Slowly, they would introduce the others—her compatriots among the Gifted. They would mete out the revelations, the miracles, the petitions for sainthood. Make the people hungry for faith, bring them to respect the holy again. This is what the end of the letter referred to! An explosion of faith throughout the world. A faith led by the people. And Cardinal Boeri would be seen as the people's leader, embracing their own, campaigning for sainthood on their behalf.

Yes, yes, he said aloud, sinking back to the smooth linens of the doge's palazzo guest room, granted to him as long as he cared to stay. This was not a war that could be won in the refined wealth of the palazzos. It had to be won in the countryside and in the marketplaces across

Italia and France. They would love him for finding the Duchess, and later, the Gifted, their rightful place in society.

First he would win the Gifted, then Avignon.

They would beatify him. And with those things in place, he would be able to return to Roma, the cone-shaped crown of the pope firmly atop his own head.

ᛊᛊ ᛊᛊ ᛊᛊ

In an effort to keep Vito and Ugo out of danger for as long as possible, Gianni assigned them to guard duty within the mansion. They had all seen the armed patrols sent out from the doge's palazzo, searching the streets and canals as if seeking out common criminals. Gianni paid several men to find out if the guards truly sought Vito and Ugo, as they feared, or if they sought others.

It took only a day to find out that it was worse than they feared. "They seek two men on charges of thievery in San Marco's crypt," said the man, eyeing all the knights with greed. "And they seek two others, on accusations of thievery from one Lord Ricci, punishable in the Republic for up to five years' imprisonment. There is a bounty upon their heads. I must say that four of your number bear an uncanny resemblance to the descriptions."

"An unfortunate coincidence. We will pay the bounty for each month you remain quiet," Gianni said. "We have our own reasons for wishing to remain out of the doge's courts."

"And if you take my captain's money and then betray us," Ugo said, facing off with the man, "my brother and I will hunt you down. You don't wish us after you. You will not leave our encounter alive."

Fear edged into the skinny man's face. "Indeed. I would take a triple profit as a blessing from above and commit my time to prayer rather than speaking of it," he said, eyeing the priest now with a contrite expression.

"Well said, my son," Piero intoned, moving forward to wedge between Ugo and the spy.

"I do not trust him, Father," Ugo said.

"She thinks we can trust him," Piero said, nodding toward Tessa.

Following his gaze, Ugo took a step back, accepting the judgment if seconded by the girl.

The spy looked at all of them, curiosity alive in his wide eyes.

"Take this and go," Gianni said, tossing him a bag of coins. "Speak not of our meeting or this intrigue. If we have need of you again, we will call for you, and pay you handsomely for your assistance. You do not want to burn bridges with us."

"As you wish, m'lord," the man said with a nod, then turned on his heel and departed.

As soon as they arrived back at the mansion, Gianni whirled toward Rune and Basilio. "Tell me you did not steal from Lord Ricci."

The men did not flinch. "We did not," Basilio said lowly.

"You were given your horses, your mules? Your weaponry?"

"They were none but ours to give," Rune replied. "None of it belonged to Lord Ricci."

Gianni paced. "So what is this charge?" He rolled out the paper that the spy had brought them, issued from the doge himself. "Silver worth a year's wages? Every piece from the lord's home?"

"If it was stolen, it was not we who took it," Basilio said, irritation now plaguing his tone.

"It is a trumped-up charge," said Piero from the corner, striding toward them. "We have all seen how Amidei works. It is clear that he is behind this. He is attempting to smoke us out, take us down, any way he can."

"Oh? And what are we to do about that?" Gianni railed.

"Gianni, Gianni," Piero said in a calming fashion. "You have encountered this enemy before. We must take him on only when necessary. He is counting on pulling us apart with fear and fury. Do not let him get to you. Come. We must go to chapel and pray."

Gianni paced. "I confess, I do not feel like praying at the moment."

"Nay," Father Piero said with a gentle smile. "You look like a caged lion. Put wings on you, and you might be seen as Santo Marco himself. Come, come, Sir Gianni. Let us pray for you. Let us pray for protection over Basilio and Rune, Vito and Ugo. For us all."

Reluctantly, they all followed the small priest down the stairs, to the makeshift chapel they had erected in the corner of the water-level warehouse. There they communed together. "Take this bread, the body of Christ, within you and remember that he lives within each of us. No matter what happens to us, brothers and sisters, only God allows. We must trust him with our very lives to accomplish his good purposes." He turned and picked up a goblet of wine, an element of communion not used since the early centuries of Christian faith. They all shared a long look before Piero spoke. "Take this wine as the blood of Christ, washing each of us clean. Only in remaining upright, in answering his call and following his lead, will we be able to hold on to hope when all seems dark."

Quietly, each took a sip from the chalice and then turned to the next, whispering the words, "Blood of Christ, shed for you."

"Now you all listen to me," Piero said forcefully. "We are the Gifted. God has brought us together for his good purposes. This cause shall not die with us unless we allow it. You saw how God and his warriors defeated our foes in Il Campo de Siena. You have seen us discover his path in divine fashion. He is with us. He is with us! And if God is for us . . ." he led, reaching out his hand.

"Then who could be against us," the others returned, each laying their hands upon his.

"Come now," Piero said. "We shall pray over each one of us. Together, we are strong. And even apart, always remember that Christ is with us, inside us, leading us onward. We are on a holy mission. Let us not fail our Lord."

⚓ ⚓ ⚓

FOUL weather kept Daria from embarking for the outer islands on her mission to retrieve the glass pieces they now all assumed lay beneath the church floors all about them. Piero, Ugo, and Vito were attempting to find ways to infiltrate Sant' Elena, San Giacometto, and San Zaccaria, there in the city.

Rune and Basilio were restless, unaccustomed to long days indoors. So when Daria received the call to come and attend a man who needed healing, a man she only knew was near the arsenal, they were eager to accompany her. Having witnessed their frantic daily pacing, and with the other men on another mission, Gianni reluctantly agreed that they could come along as guards. The armed patrols out of the doge's palazzo had waned, apparently defeated or distracted in their pursuit of thieves within the city.

After verifying with Hasani that he had seen no vision that warned them of danger here, and knowing that Daria was likely to go with or without guard, Gianni made plans to accompany his lady to Castello, just beyond San Marco, across the canal.

They set out after supper, when the canals were still and empty, only pockmarked by the constant, drenching autumn rain. Hasani remained behind with Tessa, keeping watch as the girl slumbered, unaware that her mistress had departed.

Gianni studied Daria, standing in the bow of the skiff, face to the rain as if she could smell where she was to go. They all had a fierce devotion to her now, but what was stirring within his own heart was something he had not felt for some time. It brought him up short and he frowned in consternation. There was no time for such foolish imaginings. He had to stay alert, remain intent on keeping Daria safe and secure in the wild, uncharted waters ahead. Romantic entanglements would only weaken him, weaken them all. If Piero was right, they would again face multiple charges from the enemy. And if Rune and Basilio were imprisoned as Hasani's vision foretold, as the doge's hunt seemed to intimate was on the horizon . . . if he lost Vito and Ugo as well . . . no weakness could be allowed. He sighed heavily, and Daria looked back at him with wide, concerned eyes.

"You are weary, Sir Gianni?" she whispered, conscious that sound carried over the water. Many nights they had all heard conversations across the canal as if the speakers were in their very rooms.

"Heavy with thought," he returned in a whisper. Light from a nearby mansion reflected off the water and onto her face, illuminating every delightful curve, the length of her long, aristocratic nose, her wide eyes and lush lips, her slender neck . . .

She turned away, as if flustered by his obvious admiration.

"We must keep our heads on the task at hand," Piero said softly.

Was it so obvious to them all, his regard for his lady? Gianni swallowed the bitter taste suddenly alive in his mouth. He was a fool. The priest was right. He had to keep his head on the task at hand—keeping Daria safe. Keeping them all safe. Nothing else mattered.

They made their way, taking the long way around, choosing narrow, seldom-used canals to keep them from the waterways favored by the doge's patrols. In spite of their efforts, they came across a patrol, which hailed them to stop.

Basilio and Rune did not waver or cower. They stood guard as they had before they were spotted, pulling the skiff to a halt beside a dock as instructed.

"What are you doing out at such an hour? And in such foul weather?" a guard barked.

"I have business," Gianni returned, "and it is none of yours." It was imperative to keep Daria's identity hidden. She and Hasani were the most recognizable of their group.

The doge's knights drew nearer, holding up torches to each of their faces. They were nearing Basilio and Rune when another skiff came up the canal, from the opposite direction. "Hail!" cried the giant man aboard. "Hail there, men!"

Gianni looked more closely. The voice was familiar, one they hadn't heard in weeks, since the isle of lepers. He raised his chin, and noticed Piero glance his way, recognizing the fisherman too.

The fisherman pulled alongside them, and the doge's knights turned toward him.

"You must let these people go on their way," the fisherman said quietly.

"It is none of your affair. Leave now, man," said the leader of the patrol.

"You must let these people go," the fisherman said again. He stared into the man's eyes for a long moment. "You have no cause to hold them."

The man turned away. "Let them go on their way. We have no cause to hold them." He seemed not to recognize that he was parroting the fisherman's very words. But his order was immediately obeyed. All six guards boarded their two skiffs and headed out, disappearing into the wall of constant, gray rain.

"Sir," Piero said, reaching out to the fisherman as he poled away from them, in the opposite direction. "You are one of us."

"Mayhap," the man said, disappearing into the rain as the doge's men had before him. "In time, good priest. In good time, all will be clear to all of us."

Daria rose and stepped toward them. "Who is he, Father?" she whispered. "Why does he not join us, if he is one of us?"

"Apparently, because it is not time," Piero said, staring out to the dark canal as if he could still see the man.

"And his gift?" Gianni asked.

"Is it not obvious?" Piero returned. "We wondered over it on the isle of lepers. Tonight, I'd say it was confirmed."

"Saints above," Basilio said in dumbstruck wonder.

Miraculous powers, Gianni thought, glad the fisherman had moved on. The group was already hard enough to keep safe without drawing additional attention. Is that why the man seemed to steer clear of them? Or was such a one just the man they needed?

☙ ☙ ☙

FOR the sixth night in a row, Ciro watched the wretched man as assigned, wishing he could block the man's frantic cries as he beat his breast, clawing at his skin until his arms dripped with blood in the rain. A beggar by day, he spent every night like this, a torment of the soul. And listening to him, watching him, was slowly eating at Ciro. He had to escape, send the authorities to haul the man away to the madhouse. Or mayhap he would slice the man's throat, end his misery. It would be an act of service, really. The Duchess was never coming here to heal him. His master had been wrong . . .

He slid the dagger from his belt and was taking his first step toward the beggar, intent on ending the misery for both of them, when the skiff edged out of a cloud of rain. A patrol? Nay. Ciro edged back to his hiding place against the far building's wall and waited.

Five disembarked. In the constant rain and darkness, they were hard to make out. His heart raced. His master would want every detail. Five, yes. Three knights and . . . he smiled. It was the priest. And better yet, the Duchess. He was sure of it. Even in a hooded cape, he recognized her slim, lithe form, and the guarded actions of the captain of her knights.

Ciro knew that across the city, other spies stood guard over likely objects of the Gifted's attention. And yet he was the favored one, the one who would be allowed to tell the Master of her location. He licked his lips, thinking of the reward, the reward in flesh and coin and feastings. He must not foul up this task. He must not fail the Master again.

He leaned back, knowing his dark cape blended perfectly with the wall behind him. It was so very dark out, only a knight with a torch three feet away would be able to discern his presence.

☙ ☙ ☙

THE group neared the crying man. With each step, he cried out with greater pain and anguish, as if their very presence were a torture. "Away! Away from me, beloved of the Christ!"

Daria faltered, looking about to the windows above. It was much like that night in Siena, when the beggar had screamed and screamed, sending men running after them . . . Basilio and Rune paused too, looking with consternation to Gianni. They all shared the same frightening memories.

Only Piero strode forward, undeterred by the man's keening wail.

"Away! Away! We want nothing from you! Leave us!"

"Silence!" Piero said in a low, authoritarian tone. "In the name of the Lord Jesus Christ, you will be silent."

The scrawny man cowered, sobbing uncontrollably.

Piero waved them over with a pull of his head, kneeling beside the man. "This is the one?" he asked of Daria.

"Yes," she said, frowning. "But I know not how to minister to this one. What is his ailment?"

"He is diseased within, just as surely as one with a lung ailment or rheumatism. We must treat him as any other that you have been sent to heal. We will pray for healing. The Lord will take care of the rest."

"Nay!" the beggar screamed, as if breaking free of a gag.

"Silence!" Piero intoned again. "In the name of Jesus, remain silent. You shall not speak unless we give you permission. We are here to help you." The priest looked about the group. They had the beggar cornered; he could not escape. "Bring the torch closer." They all watched in silence as the flame, shielded from the rain by a metal roof, illuminated the man. He was pathetic, shivering in fear. From cold? Bloody, bruised, and as thin as the lepers. "Daria will need all of us to join her in this prayer. I will lead."

Piero held out his hands toward the man, praying in Latin and then in the common tongue.

"Father in heaven," Daria continued, "have mercy on us. Have mercy on this poor soul, beset by demons. Free him, Lord. Heal him now. We beg you for your mercy and your healing power, here, right at this moment."

"Hear us, Jesus," Gianni said.

"Hear us, Holy Spirit," Basilio and Rune said together.

"Heal him, Lord. Drive out these demons who cower before you. Send them away, into the waters and out to sea," Piero said.

"Nay," the beggar said through gritted teeth, as if holding on to the illness that rotted him from within. *"Nay!"*

"Yes, my son," Piero said sternly. "It is time. Allow the beast to depart and you shall find healing, wholeness. Embrace Christ's light within you. Let these words enter your mouth and heart. Speak the words. *Forgive me. Forgive me. Forgive me, Lord Jesus.* And you shall find healing."

"*Nay!*"

"Yes," Daria said, now sure of Piero's lead. This was the way. "Forgive me, forgive me, forgive me," she whispered. "Let them wash through you just once, and you are free. You will find healing. No matter where you've been. No matter what you've done. Just say the words in your mind and healing is yours."

"*Et dimitte nobis debita nostra sicut et nos dimisimus debitoribus nostris . . .*"

"Forgive me, Father, for I have sinned," Basilio said, sinking to his knees.

Daria glanced at him quickly. Never had she heard such a tone of intimacy from him.

Rune stared and then, looking up into the rain, sank to his knees as well, amid a puddle. "Forgive me, Father," he said, stretching out his arms, "for I have sinned."

Piero smiled in satisfaction at the men and followed suit. "Forgive me, Abba," he said, blinking upward into the rain.

The men formed a crescent around the beggar, who stared at each of them in horror. Gianni grimaced and sank to his knees as well, repeating his friends' words, thinking only of his own failures, his own fallen heart.

Daria looked to the beggar. Their honest, private pleas were like crumbling walls in his fortress.

"Nay. Please, nay," he whispered.

"It may feel painful, beloved," she whispered back. "But you will soon know peace. It is yours this night. I promise you. Simply believe. Trust. Reach for him. The Father, the Son, the Spirit . . . all are near." With that, she sank into the muck herself, barely feeling the cool seepage at her skirts. She stretched out her hands, completing the arc around the beggar, her fingertips touching Gianni's. But her mind and heart were solely upon her Savior. "Father God, I am but a sinful woman," she whispered. "Wash me clean, Jesus. Wash me clean. Use us. Heal this man, here. Now. In your holy name we pray, Christ Jesus. Amen."

As soon as she uttered her last amen, a jolt cascaded through them all, sending them sprawling, away from the beggar.

Rising on elbows and knees, they peered before them.

And they saw a brother rise.

ჶ ჶ ჶ

CIRO regained his feet, gasping for air, peering through the rain. The Gifted's torch had smoldered and died, forgotten behind the man they called Rune. It was difficult to make out. But it was clear that they all rose from the cobblestones, wrapped a blanket around the beggar—still mute—and made their way to the skiff.

Mouth agape, feet as heavy as stones, Ciro could not find the will or conviction to follow, as if a heavy hand kept him in place. Desperately, he wanted to follow orders, give chase, but could not. This was beyond what he had witnessed with the Master. With him, he had known power, earthly pleasure.

But here, beside the Gifted, he had witnessed God coming down.

This is why the Master sought them. He wanted their power to become his.

God within his hands.

And then no one could stop him.

CHAPTER TEN

"LET me be sure I understand you," Abramo seethed. "You watched the Gifted arrive, heal your designated target, then depart. You did not attempt to follow or give chase."

"It was magic," Ciro protested. "I was not myself. I was entranced."

"Nay, you fool," Abramo said, coming very close to the tall man. "You succumbed to the enemy. You are weak. Of no use to me. Get out and never come back."

"Nay, my lord," Ciro said, kneeling, hands locked in supplication. "Do not send me away. Forgive me for failing you again. Tell me thy bidding and I shall do it." Desperation shadowed his face.

Abramo looked down at him in disgust, shaking his head. "There is but one way into my good graces again. One way," he said, holding up his index finger. "Bring me the slave, the man who accompanies the Duchess." He stared at Ciro. "Only when you bring him to me in chains will I welcome you again within my fold."

Ciro swallowed hard and rose. "It shall be done, Master."

"Forgive me if I do not take you at your word," Abramo said sarcastically. "At this point, your actions will speak louder."

Ciro nodded wildly, desperate. He turned to go.

"Ciro," Abramo said from across the room. "Alert the Gifted by your actions, and I will behead you myself. You must work with utmost care."

"Yes, m'lord," Ciro said. "I understand. The slave and no other." He nodded once more and then departed.

Abramo joined Vincenzo at the window and smiled. "Excellent. I shall soon have two of the knights and the Duchess's most intimate guard. Then we can move on to the captain, the priest, and the other knights."

"What about the girl?" Vincenzo asked. "She recognizes you as soon as you draw near."

"Yes," he said with distaste. "She is a most unfortunate addition to their group. A liability. And I have no idea yet how to take her."

"I have an idea," Vincenzo said, almost involuntarily. "The perfect way to entice her to us . . ."

ॐ ॐ ॐ

"You have attracted their attention," Tessa said, walking to the window. She cast a sorrowful glance back at the group behind her, wrapped in dry, clean blankets. Hasani joined her at the window, looking outward into the dark night of rain, and then they shared a glance.

Their look made Daria shiver. "Let them pay attention," Daria said, feeling none of the bravado of her words.

"We have work to do before they discover us," Piero said, eyeing the beggar, now asleep in the far corner. The others drew nearer. "How did you fare at Sant' Elena and San Giacometto?" he asked Vito and Ugo.

"San Giacometto will be easy to infiltrate," Ugo said. "She has barely three priests to watch over her. We could take the priest on watch, bind him—without harm," he said, raising his hands in a gesture of intended innocence, "and dig up the disk right there and then. Giuseppe could come in and fix it behind us, so there is ostensibly no damage done. The priest might bear witness to foul play and noise, but not be able to discern what really transpired."

"I am certain our Lord will give us a way that is less intrusive for my brothers watching over the Lord's churches. Let us think on it." Piero gazed at Vito. "And Sant' Elena?"

"A more difficult conquest, to be sure," Vito said. "With the relics of the saint within, she has many more walking through her doors. But she is out of the way, separated. With a few of us, we could create a diversion, and we should be able to carry out the same plan as Ugo's. Or your alternative, Father."

"Time is of the essence," Piero said. "With Lady Daria unable to begin her plan on the outer islands, we must meet our goals here. Then, if we must, we can infiltrate Murano and Torcello, and escape."

"To where?" Vito asked.

Piero's mouth clamped shut. After a moment, he said, "I know not. Our Lord will show us where we are to go next, mayhap through these glass tiles. All I know is that we are to follow the clues already given us and those within Hasani's drawings."

His gaze went to Hasani.

But Hasani was gone.

ॐ ॐ ॐ

HASANI went to his quarters, a vision alive in his mind. Sweating already, his hand shaking, he bent to light a candle by his desk, dipped the pen clumsily in a well of ink, and set to sketching the image in his mind.

It was Daria.

Clothed in but an undergown, hands bound, tied so her arms spread in a Y formation. She faced the crossed bars of what? A cell? Large stones were behind her, almost as big as those that were laid in a castle's foundation. A dungeon? She was drenched, shivering.

He panted in fury, even as he sketched. Where? When? How would this transpire?

Hasani sat back, staring at the parchment. In the shadows, beyond Daria. He could see him.

Ciro. The knight excused from the estate outside Siena by Daria. A man with a grudge. A man bent on retribution.

Quickly, he sat forward and sketched the hulking man.

Then Hasani sat back. There was another, hovering in the shadows. To the left of Daria and Ciro. He couldn't quite make him out . . .

After a moment, he could see him, as if his eyes had adjusted to the dark.

Waiting. Watching.

The Sorcerer.

ॐ ॐ ॐ

DARIA awakened and left her room, determined to check on the beggar that God had healed the night before. She nearly stumbled over Hasani, asleep in front of her bedroom door. In all her life, she had seen him do this but three times. His hand was on his curved sword, but his mouth was slack with sleep.

She knelt and shook his shoulder.

He leapt to his feet, blinking rapidly, trying to focus as he faced an imaginary enemy. Only after a moment did he turn to glance her way.

She walked around him to view him in the face. "What is it? Whom do you fear, my friend?"

He only shook his head, pretending it was nothing, as if he always spent the night on guard at her door. He was walking away, but she raced after him, circling to face him again. She laid a hand on his chest.

"Hasani. Tell me. What did you see?"

In anguish, he rubbed his face and furrowed his brow in sorrow and confusion. He obviously wished not to tell her.

"Was it Basilio again? Rune?"

He shook his head, eyeing her from the side. His gaze went to the window, to the first sun they had seen in days. Fear cascaded into his face, and he looked back to Daria.

"It was you he saw," Tessa said, suddenly at her side. She sighed heavily, with more weight in her breath than a normal seven-year-old carried. The child took Daria's hand. "Do not be afraid, m'lady. God is with you."

"And ever shall be," Daria said with a grim smile. "Out with it, Hasani. You saw me in a vision that frightened you."

Hasani grimaced at her choice of words, pounded his chest in defiance.

"All right, all right. You were not frightened. You were alarmed," she said. "Simply tell me. Out with it. What else did you see?"

Hasani's wide eyes, bloodshot with the lack of a night's sleep, went from her to the girl and back again.

"You will be taken," Tessa said, instantly understanding the fear in his eyes.

"Taken by whom?"

Hasani told them with his eyes and Tessa whispered it, hand on her throat. " 'Tis the Sorcerer."

Hasani sighed then and turned away, rubbing his hand over his short-cropped hair.

"There is more," Daria said, raising her chin.

He turned and nodded once. He held up two fingers.

"There are two men in your vision," she said.

He nodded, raising his chin when Gianni strode into the room. "Two men?" Gianni asked.

Daria's eyes remained on Hasani, and his on her. "I will be taken. By Ciro. And the Sorcerer."

She saw the miserable truth of it confirmed in her old friend's eyes. And when she looked to Gianni, he was flushed and determined. "Nay, m'lady. They shall have to kill me before they reach you."

Hasani grunted and pounded his chest. *And me,* he was saying.

Daria looked back and forth between both men, on either side of her. She shook her head in sorrow and in gratitude, laying a hand on each of their chests. "Nay. Nay, you cannot sacrifice your lives on my behalf. If I am to be taken, I am to be taken. What good are you to me, to the Gifted, dead?"

ርጉ ርጉ ርጉ

"THERE is word of a madman healed," the doge said, sitting back, chewing his bread. He reached out to the dogessa and took her hand. "Tell him of it, my dear."

The dogessa, clothed in the finest of linens and bearing rouge on cheek and lip, looked the cardinal's way. "A madman, certainly. Almost dead with hunger, refusing any food for weeks. Screaming at all who came near. Possessed, certainly, of demons worthy of the Lord's own pigs," she said, referring to the story of the pigs into which Christ sent the demons—the same pigs that then plunged to their deaths over a cliff.

"And?" Cardinal Boeri said, trying to keep any edge of undue interest out of his voice.

"Today, healed, appearing in the Piazza de San Marco. Becalmed. Asking for food. Praising God for his healing."

The cardinal could not help himself. He set down his knife and leaned forward so that he might see the dogessa better past the vast candelabra and elaborate glass urn of their table. They dined alone, but they sat at a table that could accommodate twenty-four. "Did he credit anyone for his healing?"

The dogessa smiled and arched a brow. "A woman. Three men with her, and a priest. Yours, are they not?"

"It is likely."

"Your Gifted become more bold," said the doge, leaning forward himself. "Entering my city. Performing their miracles within my streets."

"Is there a law against miracles here, Doge?" Cardinal Boeri asked with a smile.

"Nay, nay. But I prefer to know when and where they will occur," the doge responded.

Cardinal Boeri raised his glass wine goblet in silent toast to the heavenlies. "Sadly, that is only the reign of the holy."

"Sadly," the doge allowed. "Tell me, how do you propose we bring these Gifted closer? Get to know them? Form an alliance as we have spoken?"

"We must rout them out. They are hidden. But they are close. Between your patrols and my own, we will find them." He swirled the wine in his goblet. "I know one other thing that might roust them."

"What is that?" the doge asked.

"The dark. Gianni de Capezzana, my knight who left to guard this healer, is dedicated. When he left the employ of the Vaticana, he was on the hunt of a man we called the Sorcerer."

"The Sorcerer?" the dogessa exclaimed. "How delicious!"

The cardinal ignored her ill-placed remark. "The man was foul. He performed unspeakable acts in dark caves, even catacombs of the dead. Sexual exploits, child sacrifice. Horror upon horrors." He looked up then, aware that the dogessa had not gasped when appropriate, and discovered the doge and dogessa sharing a furtive glance.

"He is here," the cardinal said in a low tone. "The Sorcerer is here."

"Not here," the doge said, meeting his gaze. "Nearby. But you may in no way disturb him. He is far too dangerous."

"You know who he is? His name?" the cardinal said, slowly rising to his feet. "You allow him to abide here? Do you not know what transpires in his ceremonies?"

"Sit down, Cardinal Boeri. Sit down!"

Slowly, the cardinal did as his host bid. "Your Sorcerer is but a man. A fearfully dangerous and powerful man. And he brings the Republic much wealth. We might find a way to use him to draw your Gifted out, but we must tread with utmost care. In fact, he may already be on the hunt for your Gifted. He came to me three days past, with the complaint of a friend, Lord Ricci. Lord Ricci claims that two knights of his former employ robbed him of the house silver as they departed. Based on Lord Ricci's word, and favors I owe this man, I immediately set my private guard on the hunt for these knights, reportedly seen in our city again."

"Two of Lady Daria d'Angelo's knights, I presume."

The doge took a sip of his wine and nodded slightly, recognizing that the noblemen were using him, powerless to stop it.

"His name?" the cardinal repeated. "I shall have his name!"

"Your Sorcerer is Lord Abramo Amidei."

CHAPTER ELEVEN

IT was a beautiful autumn day, the air crisp and clean. As the group headed for the outer islands, rounding Venezia in their boat, the canvas full of a brisk northern wind, they could see all the way across the wide-mouthed bay to the white-capped mountains that marked Italia's border. Tessa gazed in their direction.

"Mesmerizing, are they not?" Daria asked, laying a hand on the girl's shoulder. The child was gaining some weight, flourishing in a home and under care.

Tessa remained silent.

"Contessa?"

"Never thee mind, m'lady."

"Contessa." Daria turned the girl to face her.

"Why must I always be the bearer of bad news?" Tessa burst out.

Daria smiled ruefully. "I daresay that Hasani would say the same thing, if he could. We are surrounded by danger. We must watch every footfall. Or turn of the sail," she said with a gesture upward. "Tell me, child. Secrets are less of a burden when shared."

"I tire of secrets, shared or no," Tessa said. Seeing the determined look on Daria's face, she nodded to the mountains. "The dark grows in strength behind us, m'lady. He grows stronger, more bold. We have little time."

Daria let out a breath. "Well. Good, then. We shall count our blessings that we sail away from Venezia and toward her quiet outer islands. Let them seek us out! We are not there!"

Tessa tried to smile back at her.

Daria leaned close, looking out to the sea about them. "Contessa, the enemy is always present. Until we reach heaven, it will be the way of things. But we must keep our eyes on the Lord, our Savior. He is always present as well. Remember your words to me? God is with us. Always. And we must take faith in the fact that he is bringing us together for his good purposes. All we are to do is seek to serve him in that, and all will turn out well. It might be that we face the most difficult days of our lives ahead," she said, her eyes glazing over as she again stared toward the mountains. "But it will be well. Take heart, child. We are far from finished."

With a peck on the cheek, she left the girl then, striding back to Basilio, Rune, and Hasani, who accompanied them on this mission. Vito and Ugo remained hidden away from the prying eyes of the doge and his guards, who had doubled their efforts to find the "invaders of the crypt." Meanwhile, in Venezia, Gianni was scouting Sant' Elena and San Giacometto to see if he concurred with the brothers' plan to infiltrate both sanctuaries.

Daria's eyes scanned the others on the boat. Hasani, Basilio, and Rune, looking ill at ease, again at sea. They were clearly men used to soil beneath their feet. Giuseppe and two other mosaic artists, disguised as sailors, accompanied them. They scurried about, clumsily following the captain's orders at the helm, but were clearly better suited to laying tiny mosaic pieces into mortar than hauling on ropes and lifting sail. Still, their work was sufficient, bound to draw the attention of only the most detailed onlooker. And to most who gazed their way, they were but one boat in a hundred, hoisting sail.

The captain was a Venetian who was likely born at sea. Daria knew he could have run the waves blind, by the feel of the wind on his face, the rise and fall beneath his feet, the mist upon his lips. But this man was not without sight; he knew the stars above them like the freckles on his wife's back. The Venetians were famous mariners, like the Phoenicians before them. Born of the sea, raised with the sound of lapping waves in their ears, buried in her waters, never had Daria encountered people so closely aligned to water. Soil, earth, yes. But this connection was new to her.

She glanced at him again, and noticed his gaze was on the horizon, on another square-sailed ship that echoed their course.

He saw that she watched him and looked away.

Was he trustworthy? Protecting her from concern? Or did he fear discovery?

"What is it, m'lady?" Tessa asked, taking her hand again.

"Nothing," Daria said with a smile she did not feel. She doubted she fooled the girl, gifted as she was with discernment. But Tessa pretended she had, mayhap as anxious as she for things to be calm, even if for but a moment.

Daria glanced at the plaque with the d'Angelo family crest, nestled between Basilio and Father Piero, suddenly homesick. How she wished she were again in her own home, surrounded by those long loved! In her mind, she pictured dear Beata, faithful Aldo, each of the Sciorias. Even the hulking Lucan, the lone knight left to watch over her home. And then Ambrogio, dearest of friends! A smile edged her lips as she thought of him. Little Roberto, the boy so in need of healing upon his leg, and Bormeo, her beloved white falcon. She wished for him here, circling high overhead, watching over her.

ᖪ ᖪ ᖪ

Ilario, my friend," Abramo said, sliding into the Venetian merchant's third-floor *piano* with the grace of a king. He turned to Vincenzo, following behind him. "May I introduce my newest brother from Siena, Baron Vincenzo del Buco."

Ilario gave Vincenzo a barely cordial nod in response. "Your latest protégé, Abramo?"

"Hardly," Abramo deferred. "Vincenzo has already taught me much."

"Hmph," Ilario said, moving back to his desk. "So you have come to drink more of my wine, partake of my women again?"

"Nay," Abramo said, taking a seat that Ilario did not offer him, barely hiding his fury. Never had Vincenzo seen someone react so cavalierly in Amidei's presence. He sat down to watch such a curiosity unfold.

"You made it abundantly clear that I had crossed a line," Abramo continued. "For which I asked your forgiveness, attempted to make amends."

Ilario shot a cold, blinkless look across the table. "You impregnated my daughter with your child and left them here to rot."

Abramo met his gaze with equal force. "I have left ample coin in this house to pay for the girl and the child's needs, to say nothing of the business I have sent your way."

"You cannot buy back a woman's virginity. No one will marry her now."

"Is that what you wish? I can find a man who would gladly take a woman of such uncommon beauty and make her his own. I know ten men, right now, who would make her a suitable spouse. Men who are one with us, men destined for glory."

Vincenzo sat back. He had seen Abramo, in the shadows of their nightly frenzy, taking young women on a high altar. It was seen as an honor within their mass, a rite of passage, to sacrifice one's virginity to the dark lord. But never had he been witness to the repercussions.

A child. And an enraged father, seduced as much in the moment as was his daughter. Vincenzo knew the pull, the undeniable claim . . .

Abramo had a child. How many more were there?

Ilario stood suddenly and paced away, his face growing red with fury. He shook a fist at Abramo. "She pines for you. She will consider no other."

Abramo looked to the tiles beneath his feet, then back to Ilario. "Let me speak with her. I will persuade her to wed another. Name the man and I will arrange it within a fortnight. And I will continue with my support for her and this house." When Ilario lost the flush at his neck and lowered his fist, Abramo rose and went to him, laying a hand upon his shoulder. "I am well aware of how this house and her inhabitants have served me and our cause. Trust me, Ilario. Sacrifices will not go unnoted. You will see gain out of this."

He reached into a pocket of his jacket and withdrew a leather scroll.

With a silent question in his eyes, Ilario took it and went to the desk to unroll it, pulling the candle closer to read. His mouth dropped open. "You obtained it."

"Yes. The land you sought. And more you could not take by force. This will unite your lands. You will become one of the greatest nobles in all of northern Italia. Form your own kingdom, republic, whatever you wish."

Ilario shook his head, a slight grin edging at his lips. He dropped clumsily to one knee and ducked his head. "M'lord, forgive me. You come to my house to give me the deed I've sought for a decade, and all I've done is berate you. I pledge to you my sole allegiance. Never more will a word against you leave my tongue, nor will any be tolerated in this house. We are here to serve you."

"Good, good, my friend. Please, rise. I have something I must ask of you."

"Anything, m'lord."

"I am so glad you have come back to see that you are one of my own, Ilario. I do so hate discord among my people." He glanced at Vincenzo, who marveled at the turn in their host. Abramo was truly the Master.

"Ilario, it has come to my attention that you once hired two mercenaries, knights by the name of Rune of Germany, and a certain Basilio Montinelli."

Concern drew into Ilario's eyes. "Indeed. They left my employ some time ago."

"And what were the circumstances, if I may ask?"

"Uh, the men disagreed with how I was going about acquiring new territory. They took issue with plundering. They preferred to lounge about, eating another man's bread, without lifting sword or shield."

"I see. And so they left?"

"With nary a word to me. I was furious." He held back the question that Vincenzo and Abramo could see in his eyes. *Why?*

Abramo rose. "Ilario, I am worried about you and yours. I have been apprised of how these two men stole something sacred from your daughter."

"Stole? Nay, I do not—"

"Come now! There is no shame in admitting this, my friend. It is horrible when a lord gives his knights food and shelter and coin in their pockets, and they repay him by manhandling his prize, his daughter."

"M-manhandling?" he sputtered, a flush rising at his jowls again.

"Oh, Ilario . . . that they would dare to rape your daughter." He shook his head as if commiserating in memory. "Leaving her with an unwanted child."

Ilario kept his mouth clamped shut, staring at Abramo as he continued.

Abramo had walked over to the desk, running his hand over the land deed as if making it lie flat. "We'll see that these men are strung up between the columns of Marco and Todaro outside the doge's palazzo. Our patron saints will see that justice is served."

Ilario swallowed hard, understanding at last. "Justice," he whispered. He opened his mouth as if to let loose a torrent of rage and then, glancing at the deed, abruptly shut it.

"Yes," Abramo said, a grin spreading across his handsome face. "You are not the only one who was robbed. They stole from our friend Ricci as well—but only his house silver service, not a daughter. We are already hunting for them, on Ricci's charges. Add your own and there will be a citywide manhunt. We will catch them and bring them to account." He returned to the table and reached for his gloves, pulling them on slowly, methodically, his eyes never leaving Ilario.

"The authorities . . . the doge himself will be a part of this. They shall ask my daughter for her witness."

"And she shall give it to them. Bring her to me tonight. We are meeting on my isle at midnight. By the time the night is over, she will remember nothing other than what I tell her. And . . . our talk of her has awakened fond memories. I have need of her. The house of Bicoli shall serve me in this way?"

Beaten, hovering over the long-coveted deed, Ilario swallowed audibly again and nodded.

"Good. I see that I have chosen well in you, Ilario. We will take our leave and allow you to fully contemplate your new wealth. And I must rest before tonight's ceremony."

They departed without another word. Vincenzo glanced back to study Lord Bicoli, suddenly appearing as a shell of a man. He turned forward again and met Abramo's triumphant gaze. Abramo placed a hand on his shoulder as they walked down the mansion's hall and out into the bright of day. "Every man can be turned, Vincenzo. Regardless of their grievance, every man has a price. You've just borne witness to my power. The dark arts, wealth, and intelligence—they will make me, us, unconquerable."

They headed down a narrow street bordering a canal and turned several corners until they reached the lagoon that spread before San Marco and the doge's palazzo. The turquoise waters were alive in a light chop and the wind was crisp and cold.

"Are you going to tell me?" Vincenzo asked.

"About?"

"About Daria's men. What is your plan?"

"Know thy enemy, Vincenzo. The Gifted think they are strong. That with God on their side, they can push us aside. No one pushes me aside. No one. They are about to find out the full force of my wrath. They will be tested on every front. Their hearts, their minds, their very souls will encounter the dark at every corner. We must break them, turn them now. They are our greatest threat. Men are simpletons, easy to manipulate. The Gifted . . . they must be turned."

Vincenzo nodded, suddenly understanding his lord's direction, and looked to sea.

"We will have two of Daria's knights arrested. They will be accused of the atrocities just discussed with Lord Bicoli and then there will also be cause for Daria to doubt them herself. Baron, I need you to return to our fair Siena and destroy everything of the house of d'Angelo. Forever cut her off from the woolen guild, drive her people out, bring her house down. You must do this within a fortnight and return here, to me."

"A fortnight? That is quite a bit to accomplish. It will take more than two days to journey home—"

"A fortnight. That is all. The Gifted, they are moving quickly. I am disturbed by what I've heard . . . we must equal their pace. The letter is clear. When they become public, their powers will be unparalleled. God will shine and the day of enlightenment will begin. We must curtail their progress, cut them off now. You've heard yourself how Daria healed not only the lepers she touched but also those who touched those healed. That is a new level in her power of healing." He shook his head. "We cannot tarry. We must give them cause to break their stride, possibly lose their way altogether. We must know of what they seek here and take it before they get to it."

"What about the others? Ciro will pursue Hasani, but what of the knight, Gianni? The child, the other knights? The priest?"

Abramo's face broke into a full-fledged grin and he waggled his eyebrows as if he were about to let Vincenzo into the greatest secret of all. "Oh, I have plans for each of them. We will take them down, one by one. Moving from the outer edges in toward Gianni, Daria, and the priest. It is with them that it all began. They are whom we must take down last." He began walking again and Vincenzo fell into matching his stride. "It's like peeling an onion. We've already worked our way through the papery skin and the outer edges. We're making headway toward the heart."

Vincenzo shook his head. "Forgive me my disbelief, m'lord. But Daria is a very headstrong woman. If she believes that she is one of the Gifted, that her cause is holy and prophesied, I do not believe you can dissuade her."

Abramo nodded, hiding another smile. "That is how you will draw her to you, to us. At just the right moment, you will tell her that you have come across a portion of the lost letter, that there are drawings that clearly depict Daria and her troop. You will tell her that you have been incredibly wrong, beg forgiveness. Draw her in."

Vincenzo shook his head. "She saw me, Abramo. She saw me with you in Il Campo, when we attempted to capture them."

Abramo paused and faced Vincenzo, laying a hand on each of his shoulders. "My friend, do not fear. I will give you the tools you need to carry out this assignment. It is vital to our cause, to our future. Concentrate on this first assignment—return to Siena and obliterate that foolish artist. Begin dismantling the house of d'Angelo and all that Daria holds dear."

Vincenzo sighed, his heart heavy.

"Nay, nay," Abramo said, waiting until Vincenzo looked him in the eye. "Do not sorrow over this. This is for Daria's own good. We shall turn her, make her a princess in our fold. Her wealth shall be returned. Her prophesied day of enlightenment shall still come—she will merely see our way as her new path. It will be beyond our imaginings." He leaned closer and whispered, "She shall become ours. Ours for the asking."

"Ours?"

"Ours. I shall take my time with her, bring her around, seal her as our very own. Her strength will enhance what we do, making us mightier than ever before. And then she shall be returned to your side, Vincenzo. You have my word upon it. As beloved niece or as your lover. I shall leave it to your discretion."

"You will have to kill both the knight and the freed man to get to her."

"Mayhap. But it would bring me more pleasure to see them broken than dead."

Vincenzo stared into his dark eyes.

"Our cause is as holy as theirs, Vincenzo. But they wish to bow down to a God who is unseen. They are foolish to waste their talents on a God who cannot fully rule. We shall be gods on earth. Power. Wealth. Prestige. We shall become invincible. But these Gifted must be eradicated. Turned or utterly destroyed. My plan will succeed. Are you with me, Baron?" He paused for a breath. "Are you with me, brother?"

Vincenzo paused a moment, and then nodded slightly. "Yes, Master. I am with you."

Chapter Twelve

The captain rounded the island of Murano, beat upwind past the island's public docks, and then entered a large canal that roved through her middle. The city's glassmakers had been moved to the island fifty years before, Giuseppe told Daria, because the doge was deathly afraid of fire taking his mighty city. With kilns aflame from morning until night, the glassmakers took care to guard their fires, knowing that one wrong spark could bring them all down. Santa Maria e San Donato, the island's cathedral, was at her center.

The captain's eyes slid back to sea, and Daria knew he was searching for the other boat under the square sail. She glanced at Tessa, who observed them both carefully.

The child nodded to her mistress, telling her silently that she sensed no danger from the other boat. Daria relaxed and stared with vivid interest at the storefronts of glassmaker and village merchant alike. Soon the church came into view, positioned so as to display its most beautiful feature, the apse, to those arriving by sea.

"Ho!" called the captain suddenly to a man on a nearby dock. He immediately dropped the last remaining sail and they slid to a neat pause before the wooden pilings. Clumsily, Basilio threw a rope to the man the captain had hailed, and he caught it easily and looped it around a huge piling, bringing them to a full stop.

Daria still stared at the church, one of the oldest in the whole of the lagoon. It was a remarkable structure, predominantly of red brick. The magnificent apse line of blind arches met up with the first level, with a second line of arches and Istrian stone parapets in the gallery above. Between them were a line of triangles, decorated with crosses, animals, and flowers. The numerous arches gave an aerial grace to the structure, Daria thought, perhaps employing the intentional architectural tactic of design to cast a person's thoughts heavenward.

"Thank you, Captain," Daria said, tearing her eyes away, her heart pounding. Hasani took her by the waist and lifted her to the dock, three feet above the sailboat's deck. Tessa and the men all clambered out after her and they moved off toward the church.

"M'lady?" the captain asked, concern sheltered between his brows. He gestured toward the plaque bearing her father's name and family crest, Daria's stated cause in coming to the island.

"Oh!" Daria cried, her hand coming to her mouth. How could she have been so thickheaded? "Basilio, will you, please?"

"Yes, m'lady," he said, clambering down to the deck and reaching for the marble rectangle.

She looked to the captain. "You will remain here, waiting for us? I expect to be gone no more than half a day."

"I shall be here, m'lady. God be with you."

"And with you." They departed then, Daria chafing a bit at the subterfuge. But they had no other means to get to the clues they so desperately needed.

"God himself is watching over you," Piero said, suddenly at her side. God in his wisdom apparently allowed the priest to read her thoughts, giving her just the counsel she needed when weak.

"Will God not punish even his own Gifted if they lay waste his holy sanctuaries?"

"Pshaw," the priest said in dismissal. "We shall leave his sanctuaries even more beautiful than how we found them. And richer. We have Giuseppe and our stonemasons to make certain of it. We will simply unearth what we seek and depart."

"And you are certain that the priests will not stop us?"

"You have the coins in your purse, do you not?"

"I do."

"Nay, they shall not get in our way." They walked around to the entrance in silence. Then, "Daria, we are on a holy mission. There is a bit of deception here, but it is our only way."

"Why not try to bring them in on it? Tell them of our holy cause?"

Piero sighed. "They are not ready. Nor are we. We've been through this already. It is imperative that our identity remain as secret as possible until we have no choice but to risk exposure. Until we have the entire letter in hand, or God makes his way clear to us. We can only pray that they keep news of this occurrence to themselves until we are far from here."

It was Daria's turn to sigh. "Yes, yes. We have been through it before. It simply seems that things are going well, that God is making the way easy. We have yet to encounter the Sorcerer again, other than our glimpse of him. Our men have even been able to take our prize from San Marco itself. Surely that is God's workmanship."

"But the enemy is always on the hunt, Daria. Do not be dissuaded by these relative days of peace and quiet. He lurks. We must remain vigilant. And keep to our path."

The group rounded the church and entered a small, quiet piazza, then strode confidently to the church's front doors. Basilio, Rune, and Hasani all turned their capes to display the house of d'Angelo's coat of arms, a scarlet peacock on a bed of white. Daria smiled at the proud sight of them, mighty men at arms, wearing the d'Angelo crest. It had been too long. They turned and headed inward.

Daria sighed at the simple beauty of the church. Built on the lines of a basilica, with three naves separated by two rows of five columns in Greek marble. San Donato's remains, brought to the church a hundred years prior, rested by the high altar. In the curve of the front apse, a praying Madonna in blue, surrounded by golden tiles, drew her attention again and again.

Between the mosaic work and the marble pavement, the church bore more than a passing resemblance to San Marco, clearly influenced by the doge's improvements and echoing the work here. The flooring, as in San Marco, appeared more as an Oriental carpet than marble pavement. Bands of marble, finely knotted and woven into geometric shapes, covered much of it, but there were also complex pictures of animals—two roosters carrying a dead fox, symbolic of Christian vigilance over paganism and luxury; a pair of crickets; and what they had sought—the peacocks, drinking from a golden chalice.

Her eyes slid around the sanctuary and then back to the floor as they passed, just as Giuseppe had described, over to the right side. It was good, very good, this placement. Nobles frequently wished to be interred as close to the altar as possible. Chances were good that no nobleman had already purchased this as his burial spot.

A priest, sweeping the center aisle, looked up as they drew near. "May I be of service?"

"Indeed. We must speak to your bishop at once," Daria said.

"I shall go and fetch him." The young priest's eyes slid to the plaque in Basilio's arms, and then to the coin purse hanging at Daria's side, laden with coin. With one look, he revealed to them what they needed to know. The church appeared well off, but Venezia's wealth obviously remained closer to San Marco. Santa Maria e San Donato needed them as much as they needed her. Daria and Piero shared a small smile of gratification. This might prove easier than expected.

The bishop returned quickly, brushing crumbs from his robe as he entered, as if they had disturbed an early noon meal. He was flanked by the custodial priest they had met upon their entry and another at his right. "M'lady," he said with a nod, then turned his attention to Piero.

"Bishop, I greet you in the name of our Lord Jesus Christ. I am Father Piero, of late from Siena and Lady Daria d'Angelo's personal chaplain. May I compliment your lovely sanctuary? It is an honor to our God."

"Thank you," the bishop said, bowing ever so slightly. "Father, m'lady, how may I be of service to you?" His eyes went to the plaque in Basilio's arms.

"Bishop, my father passed from this earth several years past. He was a great man, possessed of great faith, as his father was before him. It is my desire to leave something of him in a great sanctuary. Given our family crest, Santa Maria e San Donato's fame, and the peacocks upon your floor, I had hoped that we might . . . come to an arrangement."

Talking about her father had brought surprising tears to Daria's eyes. The bishop reached out and kindly patted her shoulder. "Be at ease, daughter. Here your father's memory will find a welcome." He cleared his throat and stood upright again. "I assume your priest has told you that it is customary for a church to collect a gift in exchange for such an honor."

"Indeed." She reached to her belt and pulled a handful of gold florins out and dropped them lightly into the bishop's hands. "I have even brought masons and a mosaic artist from San Marco to ease the process. Give us but two hours and we will have the floor back in place, as if never disturbed."

"Excellent. And then we shall have the ceremony."

"Ah, my most worthy bishop," Piero interjected. "It is unfortunate that we must not tarry. It is of utmost importance that we continue on our way, as the lady has pressing business. Rest assured, I will see to the rites myself."

The bishop frowned. "I cannot allow—"

"I am happy to gift the church several more florins in exchange for this favor and courtesy," Daria interjected. She reached into her bag and drew out several more gold coins. The bishop reluctantly raised his hand to receive them. Before she dropped the last in his hand, she said, "My priest is well thought of in Roma and beyond. He will make sure all is well. But you and your priests must not be present. I wish to have a completely private ceremony."

"M'lady, what you ask is out of the ordinary," he said, nervous now that it would all fall apart. He looked down at Tessa, who held Daria's hand. "It is simply not done in such a way."

"I understand that I have placed you in an awkward position," she said. "If I were not a person who needed privacy, or if I did not need to hold to a most pressing schedule, I would not ask it of you."

The door ground open with a heave, and a large man entered. Against the harsh daylight, it was difficult to see his face. But Daria had seen him before . . .

"I give you my word, Bishop," Piero said. "Lady Daria is the finest of Christian women."

"I give you mine as well, m'lord," the man said, striding forward.

Daria held her breath. It was the fisherman. The one who had made a way for them to escape the isle of lepers and the street after she had healed the beggar.

The bishop greeted him warmly, reaching out to take his large hand in both of his. "You can vouch for the house of d'Angelo, Gaspare?"

"Indeed."

Daria could almost feel Tessa's smile. Her small hand was taut in Daria's, trembling with pleasure. So, here he was. Their comrade among the Gifted, whether he knew of it yet or not. She glanced to Piero, but the small priest remained face forward, a gentle smile of confidence upon his face, as if this were entirely expected.

"All right, m'lady," the bishop said. "Since this man has stepped up for you, I will honor your request. You may begin directly." He raised a finger. "But you shall promise me that every tile will be back in place before Sext. It gives you little more than two hours, but with your men, that should not be difficult, no?"

"They shall be done sooner than that, Your Grace," she said with a nod.

"I thank you for your generous donation to the church. May the Lord God grant you peace." He raised his hand and made the sign of the cross in the air before them.

"Amen," they all said together.

"Come," Daria said to Piero, and indirectly to the rest, "let us get some fresh air and catch up with our friend. We shall return to say terce with you, Bishop, and remain until all are cleared of the sanctuary."

"I shall look for you, daughter," he said.

The group turned and left the building. The fisherman's pleasant smile turned to a frown. "Send them away," he growled, nodding at the masons and Giuseppe. "They are not a part of a conversation it is time we have."

Basilio and Rune moved in to flank Daria, concerned by the change in the fisherman's demeanor. But she stood her ground, unwavering before his hulking mass.

"Gentlemen," Piero said over his shoulder to the masons, not letting his gaze leave the fisherman's. "Go and fetch some bread and wine. We shall look for you in the sanctuary after mass."

The fisherman's eyes flicked over their shoulders, waiting for the men to be a good distance away before he spoke.

"I would expect this is difficult," Piero said, breaking the silence and tension. "The Lord God has granted you a unique gift. I take it that you have not quite come to terms with it."

"You might say that," the fisherman grumbled. "Who are you people?"

"We are the Gifted, and we are seeking God's own path for us."

"The Gifted? What does that mean?"

Basilio and Rune took a step away, reading the fear in him, trying to bring him ease.

"It is much to take in. Come," Piero invited. "Let us go to that tree over there so that we might have more privacy and appear as if we are nothing more than a group of friends, sharing some conversation."

"I shouldn't be here," he said, pausing as if they were all drawing him along in a riptide.

It was Tessa who stepped forward. "Yes, you must." She reached for his hulking hand and took it. She pulled at him to take a step. "You are one of us."

With a great sigh, the giant fisherman stepped forward and followed them to the shelter of the tree. "Your arrival has set things on edge. There is a tension about Venezia that I have not sensed in some time."

Piero nodded. "I must tell you of our story quickly, for we have not time to tarry. Our gathering has been prophesied since the days of old. We possess a letter, possibly penned by Saint Paul himself, and in its margin are illuminations hundreds of years old."

"That is not so unusual."

"Nay. But the anomaly is in the illuminations. It is the most important aspect. The words are powerful, but it is the illuminations—they depict Lady Daria and me. Other depictions of our group show a knight in our company, Sir Gianni de Capezzana and Hasani, here."

The fisherman paused and studied the priest. "Illuminations, hundreds of years old, are of you?"

"Indeed. In one brief section of the letter, the author speaks of a gathering of the Gifted, people drawn together to bring light to the people, hope against the dark, and change in the holy Church. I was entrusted with the keeping of the letter many years ago, as a young priest. It was passed down to me from a long line of protectors."

"It is uncanonized?"

"Yes."

The fisherman sighed heavily. "Go on."

"Lady Daria came to a convent for which I was abbot outside of Roma. I recognized her immediately. And her gift was quickly evident."

"Healing."

"Indeed. Sir Gianni's gift is faith, and my own is wisdom. Young Tessa has the gift of discernment—she knows light from dark almost immediately—and Hasani has the gift of visions."

The fisherman eyed the tall man. "Your slave?"

"Freed man," Daria said.

He studied her with his light blue eyes; he flicked his gaze to the knights in their capes of white and red and then back to the priest. "A most unlikely crew you've gathered, Father."

"Agreed," Piero said with a wry grin. "Is it not perfect? Our Savior was not as his people expected. Neither are we. It was also foretold that we would be joined by one gifted in miraculous powers and another with the gift of prophecy. From what we've seen already, we're fairly certain that you are our man, gifted with powers that can come only from God."

The man studied him, saying nothing.

"You have been brought to us, now three times, at God's own urging. You've intervened three times for us, allowing us to make our way. You belong with us, Gaspare."

The fisherman heaved a sigh and put his giant hands to his graying temples, squeezing and looking upward. When he looked back to them, they were all surprised to see bright tears in his blue eyes. "I am but a simple fisherman," he tried.

"You have not been a simple fisherman for some time," Piero said fiercely. "Accept it. We know it's difficult. But accept it as the truth you know it to be. You were brought here, to us. To be with us. For God's own good purposes."

"There's more," Daria said, breaking in. "Evidence that God is in this, every step of the way."

"Evidence?" he asked, sliding a glance to her.

"More than the letter itself. Prophetic signs of our coming that we have discovered in everything from an altar tapestry to a fresco amongst the ruins of a Byzantine church to . . . other things we have discovered here, in Venezia. We are surprised by this, but God is not."

"And why are you here, at Santa Maria?"

Daria glanced toward Piero, silently asking him to answer. "Beneath her tiles, we will discover something more that we were sent to Venezia to gather."

"And that is?"

"Will you believe that this is God's path for you if we tell you before we unearth it?"

"Mayhap."

"Beneath that mosaic peacock is an urn with a peacock etched onto it. Lady Daria's own family crest."

"What cause have you to unearth such a thing? The lady can certainly afford to purchase her own urns."

"Within is a piece of glass, a portion of a glass map. We believe the pieces, once brought together, will show us where we are to go."

"If this is true . . . they would have been buried as each church was erected. This one we stand in has been about for more than five centuries."

Piero met his gaze steadily. "Our mosaic artist tells us that this falls in line with an old legend, one of Apollos, follower of Saint Paul. He created a vast glass map of Christendom. When the body of Santo Marco was brought to the doge, seven urns accompanied it from Alexandria. The instruction was to place one beneath the floor of each of Venezia's principal churches."

The fisherman studied him, chin in hand. "You've found one already?"

"Two. In the ruins of San Giorgio and beneath San Marco herself."

His eyes widened. "You ventured into San Marco? Brazen, you are."

"When it is called for," the priest returned. "We do not lay waste to God's holy sanctuaries. We are simply unearthing what God has left for us to discover."

The fisherman sat back and studied the small priest. "You are not like any kind of priest I have ever met."

Piero and Daria shared a smile, remembering similar shared words. "Nay," he said. "I am not. I am a priest who believes in Saint Paul's words—that we are all in the priesthood of believers, that we all share in Christ's holy mission, that we are all gifted. No one shall dissuade me."

Several long moments passed. "I am but a fisherman."

"Nay," Tessa said, taking his hand again in her own. "Inside, you shall know it as well as we. You are a mighty warrior."

CHAPTER THIRTEEN

A knock sounded on the massive wooden door, and Cardinal Boeri rose from his writing desk, setting his quill beside the well of ink. Bishop di Mino and a steward both rose to answer the door, but Cardinal Boeri waved them back to their seats. Few had come to their door. He would see who it was himself.

A steward bowed curtly. "The doge wishes for you to accompany him in the great hall. He said to tell you that a Lord Amidei is to be heard."

Cardinal Boeri tucked his chin and looked down the length of his nose at the steward. "Lord Abramo Amidei?"

"Indeed."

"Thank you," the cardinal said, shutting the door. He waved to his steward. "My finest robes and cap, at once." He looked to Bishop di Mino. "You must change as well. We must go, immediately." In minutes they were ready, and traveled down the long hallway to the massive public room, where the doge and the Twelve spent the bulk of their days, hearing complaints, resolving disputes, meting out punishments, governing.

They eased into the edge of the crowd, observing the day's meetings. Cardinal Boeri made his way forward, admiring the elaborate oil paintings that covered each wall of the room, until he was but ten paces away from the doge.

The last piece of business complete, a steward announced the next. "Lord Ilario Bicoli and his daughter, accompanied by Lord Abramo Amidei."

"On what charges does Lord Bicoli approach the court?" said another steward, furiously writing on a long parchment.

"Rape."

A murmur went through the crowd. The doors opened and the two stewards strode in, followed by three distinguished nobles. A pretty young woman clung to the older man's arm.

The doge sat back and studied the three. "Lord Bicoli? What is this loathsome charge? Who is the victim? And why are you here, Lord Amidei?"

Abramo stepped forward from behind the Bicolis. He was more handsome than the cardinal had remembered, charismatic in both stature and posture. All eyes were upon him, including the girl's. "It is I who convinced Lord Bicoli and his daughter that they must come forward," Abramo said.

"I see," the doge returned. "Go on."

"The entire city has heard of the thieves your court is tracking, those who stole from the house of Ricci."

"Indeed."

"Unfortunately, these two knights did not stop there. They went on to the employ of Lord Bicoli and stole something far more valuable from his house—the virginity of young Signorina Bicoli here." He lifted his hand and took the girl's hand from the older man's, pulling her forward. He wrapped a protective, fatherly arm about her shoulders, and she nestled in, looking shamed and afraid.

The doge studied them for a long moment. "These same knights. If the charges are true, Basilio Montinelli and Sir Rune of Germany are becoming quite the enemies of the Republic. Lord Ilario, I am unaccustomed to you remaining silent."

A quiet chuckle reverberated through the crowd. Ilario Bicoli was famously loud, in fact, the cardinal learned from two whispering behind him.

The short, stocky man coughed and stepped forward, beside Lord Amidei and his daughter. "You know my family well, Doge. But even you may not know that my daughter bore a child out of wedlock some months past. She wished it to remain her private shame, and I honored her request. But now . . . with the charges from Ricci, we knew we could not remain silent. Mayhap these men are guilty of still other sins, yet to be discovered."

"Mayhap," the doge allowed, still studying the men, and in particular Lord Amidei. He glanced toward the cardinal, and Lord Amidei's eyes followed the direction of his gaze, settling on Cardinal Boeri. Boeri returned his look without flinching, hating even being in the room with him. This was undoubtedly treachery. This man was the Sorcerer! One who sacrificed children upon his dark altar!

Lord Amidei gave him a slight nod and then returned his attention to the doge.

The doge rose and walked down several steps. He offered both his hands to the young woman of uncommon beauty, and she stepped forward, placing her hands in his. She curtseyed deeply, and when she rose, her cheeks had two glistening streams of tears running down. She bit her lip.

"Daughter of the Republic," the doge said gently.

He waited until she met his gaze. After a long moment, she did.

"I must hear it from you. You were raped by men in your father's employ?" he asked softly. "Left to bear a child alone?"

She nodded, looking to the floor again.

"And it was the men mentioned who did this to you?"

She nodded quickly.

"Daughter, these charges are most grave. Charges of larceny from Ricci would send these men to prison. If your charges are true as well, the Republic must call for these men to hang."

Her eyes slid to the left, to Lord Amidei. He nodded toward her, his eyebrows lowering as if in concern for her welfare. "Tell the doge what you must, *signorina*," Amidei said.

The young woman sighed and then lifted her head. "It is true," she said in a rush. "It is all true. Sir Rune of Germany and Basilio Montinelli mistreated me. I beg you, Doge, to see justice done."

The doge studied her a moment longer, then nodded once. "We are a city famed for her justice. These criminals will hang if they cannot come up with an adequate defense. Lord Amidei, who else is this with you?"

"Pardon my manner, Doge," Abramo said, stepping back and allowing the tall man to step forward. "This is Baron del Buco de Siena. He accompanies us because he has information that may prove helpful."

"Baron," led the doge, sitting down again in his ornate chair.

"Doge," the baron said, bowing. He rose. "This summer past, a woman, once my former co-consul of the woolen guild of Siena, hired her own retinue of guards. I believe the two you seek are in her employ."

The doge sat forward. "So the men we are hunting are actually in Siena."

"Nay. I have reason to believe they have traveled here."

"To Venezia."

"Indeed."

"What is this woman's name?"

"Lady Daria d'Angelo," he said.

The doge again looked to the cardinal and then back to the baron. "Are there others with her?"

"At least six. Three more knights, a freed man, a young girl, a priest."

"You know where they are residing?"

"Nay," the baron said, a flush rising at his neck. "The last I heard from her she had not yet obtained a suitable house. I fear her address is in a letter reaching my estate just now, and I accompanied Lord Amidei here unexpectedly. Doge, I fear for her. If these men in her employ have treated Lord Ricci and Lord Bicoli in such a foul manner, how much more will a wealthy merchantess de Siena be a target for them?"

"I understand your concern, Baron. Rest assured the lady will not come to harm in this city." He eyed the captain of his guard. "Double your patrols. Surely such a group will be found readily. That is all. You are all dismissed. I will summon your return when I have need of you."

A hundred people flowed from the room, and in minutes the room was clear but for the doge and the cardinal. "He is using you to track them," the cardinal said.

"Obviously," the doge returned. He threw out a hand, palm up. "But what choice did I have but to do as they wished?" He rose, came down the stairs, and walked alongside the cardinal. "Ilario Bicoli is a warlord. He has taken much land by force over the years, some by most despicable means. In the last years, he has continually campaigned for the Republic to go to war, lay siege, and expand our territory." He stopped at the doorway and stared at the cardinal. "Three days past I signed a deed from Lord Amidei, granting Lord Ilario a prime piece of land that will complete his conquests. He now has enough land to create his own kingdom."

"The two struck a deal. The girl's story was Amidei's price."

The doge tucked his head in a single nod of agreement. "But, my dear cardinal, they seek those that we seek, do they not? This gives us cause to find the Gifted and bring them into our fold. We cannot keep them safe from men such as Bicoli or Amidei. Our only hope is to bring them all to rest here, in my palazzo. From here, they can perfect their powers, and we shall consider how to best . . . aid them."

ぬ ぬ ぬ

AMIDEI looked across the darkening waters of dusk, from the isle off the Rialto's coast, studying the towering form of the basilica domes and how they glinted in the meager autumn sunset light. His eyes shifted to the two-story palazzo beside her belonging to the doge.

Cardinal Boeri. Cardinal Boeri de Vaticana de Roma. He knew him now, could place him in various wealthy salons and festivals during his time in Roma. The man was famous for his zealous faith, his intention to rout out heresy and evil from his city, his fervent desire to bring the papacy home to Roma. Why was he here, in Venezia? What alliance had he formed with the doge? It was obvious that the men were working together. Were they tracking the Gifted as well? Or were they planning some treachery against him, Lord Abramo Amidei? He smiled at the thought. No adversary made him fearful. He only wished to be prepared.

He remembered well the catacombs that bordered Roma. Within those dark, cool caverns, he had brought many to kneel at his feet. They were deliciously receptive in Roma. He had enjoyed forbidden pleasures beyond any he had ever experienced before. His powers had grown tenfold. And still they came, more and more, all simpletons seeking a new Roman emperor, a ruler of the dark. He would have remained there for months longer if it hadn't been for the knight de Vaticana, Gianni de Capezzana. The former captain of the cardinal's guard.

Yes, Cardinal Boeri knew all about him. The fabled Sorcerer. But Gianni had abandoned his post to serve Daria. Did the cardinal know of the Gifted?

ॐ ॐ ॐ

It was Ugo who spotted the doge's men, trolling by the mansion on a more regular basis than usual. "They are watching us," he said to Gianni, who joined him on the roof as the next patrol passed by. By outward appearances, he appeared unfettered, bored even at the sight of them. But a slight tremble in his throat gave away his fear. "Do you think they know of San Marco?"

"Nay. We would have heard word of it by now. The guards in the crypt know that the sanctuary was infiltrated, but they have no idea why. You left nothing disturbed. And they have not looked within the ancient grotto for centuries."

"Then why do they watch us?" Vito said from the deepening shadows of the wall.

"I do not know. We must proceed as if our enemies are alerted to our cause. Remain on guard, men." He left them there and strode down the stairs to the water's edge. Where was Daria? What was happening?

He berated himself for not going with her to Murano and Torcello. But then his presence would have endangered them. He had traveled with Cardinal Boeri more than once to visit the bishops of the outer islands of Venezia. The bishops would have recognized him as a knight of the Church, asked him questions he could not answer, drawn more attention to the Gifted than any of them wanted at this juncture. So he had stayed behind, forced to his knees repeatedly in prayer. There, before the tiny altar Father Piero had erected in haste for their temporary quarters, he had drawn some peace. But it was short-lived, always short-lived.

The devil was afoot. And he was bound and determined to meet him fully armed when he came to their door. But where was Daria? Was she safe? Had they found what they sought?

ॐ ॐ ॐ

The two ships pulled up to Torcello's docks as dusk was edging into autumn darkness. It was frigid upon the water at this hour, and Daria shivered beneath her cloak. Tessa clung to her, as if hoping to absorb some of her body heat.

As they walked a curving path toward the center of the island, Piero briefed her on Torcello's long slide from civilization. The island had been a Roman fortress, the first island that people fleeing mainland invaders had reached, and thus she was where Venezia had truly begun. Yet shifting tides had altered the rivers that crisscrossed her banks, silting them over and leaving them prone to the scourge of malaria. Within a few decades, her people had largely fled, leaving the island desolate and her church in perilous condition.

They passed dilapidated houses and collapsing barns, pushing toward the inner reaches, where they could see the peaking flames of a bonfire and smoke rising from several chimneys. They entered warm city streets, alive with villagers after a day of work. It was a tiny enclave, a mere remnant of what once was, casting a ghostly pall over their revelry. But Daria attempted to smile, engage the villagers who stood aside, mouths agape at the visitors.

They paused to purchase a salted ham and fresh bread, even two oranges, from several merchants and pushed forward toward the oldest church in all the region. "She has been here for more than three hundred years," Piero whispered to Daria in hushed reverence. "Built upon Roman ruins." He gestured toward an old white marble chair in the courtyard before the church. "The Roman governor's. This was a seat of power."

Daria's scalp tingled with anticipation. She could not wait to explore the sanctuary, gather their treasure, and return to Venezia and her mansion. To Gianni.

The thought caught her off guard. Even in the presence of the hulking fisherman and Basilio and Rune, it was Gianni who made her feel safe. She gained from his steadfast faith. Several times, in their conversation with the fisherman, she had longed for his interjection, his deepthroated vote of confidence. He never turned from their path. He could win men to his way of thinking with but a look alone. From the time she had brought him back from the edge of death in the woods, he had remained certain that they were on the one and true path. And he remained vigilant in his care and watch over her through it all.

What stirred in her heart for Gianni? Something deeper, beyond the sisterly love she felt for the friend of her youth, Hasani. She stared at her friend guiltily, knowing he thought of himself as her personal guard, and here she was wishing another man present. A hand unconsciously slid to her throat as she wondered at the feelings within her, feelings not explored since she had left Marco's side.

"Lady Daria?" Tessa asked in some concern.

She smiled down at the child. So intuitive, nothing missed her attention. She caressed the girl's cheek. "It will be well, Contessa. I was simply thinking—"

"Daria," Piero said, suddenly turning toward her. "The hour is later than I anticipated. They are in the middle of Vespers. Let us seek a bed for the night and approach the bishop in the morning. Gianni said the bishop is not one to favor those who interrupt his routine."

Daria held her breath. The last thing she desired was to tarry away from her temporary home in Venezia. But she recognized the wisdom behind Piero's words. "I shall abide by your direction, Father."

Hasani turned toward them, his dark eyes studying the villagers about them. He was on alert.

Rune and Basilio stepped forward.

"Tessa?" Piero whispered. "Do you sense anything?"

Tessa furrowed her narrow brow and concentrated. "Mayhap something . . ."

Hasani grunted and gasped for air, doubling, as if in pain.

"Hasani!" Tessa cried.

"Quickly," Piero hissed, well aware that the villagers studied their every move. "We must get him away."

The men gathered around, bustling them toward a quiet corner of the church, well beyond the village's main thoroughfare. Hasani collapsed there, crunching into a ball and weeping as he cradled his head.

"What is happening to him?" the fisherman asked, aghast at such a display.

" 'Tis a vision," Piero said grimly. "It shall be over in a minute. Basilio, make certain that no one travels this way. Take the masons and Giuseppe with you."

Tessa was beside Hasani, cradling his head in her lap, crooning to him and stroking his tightly cropped hair. She wept with him, as if seeing what he saw, sensing the darkness draw near through his wide, frightened eyes.

"Can we do nothing for him, Father?" Daria said, stricken in watching her friend's angst.

"Nay," Father Piero said grimly.

Daria gasped for air and turned away, wanting to weep at the exposure, the depth of feeling that emanated from Hasani in silent waves. Is this what happened every time? How could he have hidden such agony from her?

The fisherman stood his ground, staring steadily at the black man as if he could figure it all out in this moment. Basilio returned to them in a trot. "Bishop, on his way after mass. The villagers told him we were here."

This bishop strode with more regal stature than the bishop of Murano. He was a tall man, handsome, if a bit aged. What had he done to deserve such a remote post? This was a man who had known power and had been stripped of it. Rune, Piero, and Basilio turned to meet the bishop, blocking his view of Hasani and the tiny girl who comforted him. "Daria," Piero hissed. "You must act the part."

Daria turned at the last moment toward the four priests and the bishop who came their way, stepping up behind Piero, beside the fisherman.

"Bishop," Piero greeted him. "We hail from the house of d'Angelo de Siena. My lady has business with you in the morning, but I am afraid her man has taken ill. We seek lodging and permission to seek a proper audience with you in the morning—after you have broken your fast, of course."

The bishop, clearly pleased at the priest's deference, smiled slightly and nodded in Daria's direction. "Lady d'Angelo. I am Bishop Carpaccio."

"Bishop," she returned. "Might you have lodging for us? I must see to this man's welfare."

Bishop Carpaccio looked askance at Hasani. "We need not some illness upon us. Malaria has already robbed the island of her grandeur. We rather appreciate our lives. If I may ask, from what does your man ail?"

"It is merely a bout of stomach trouble," Daria said lightly. "We were on Murano this day, and I fear that he ate of some spoiled fish."

"Ahh. I see. Typical of Murano. If that is all that troubles you, then yes, we may grant you shelter. But your man, I must insist he sleep in the stable. And your other men too. I'm afraid we only have room for you and your priest."

"As you wish," Daria said after a second's hesitation. She ignored the furious, penetrating glances of Basilio and Rune.

"I do hope you might spend the day with us on the morrow, m'lady," the bishop said. "Our visitors are frightfully few and far between. I would value the company and conversation of a true noblewoman."

Daria shifted uncomfortably beneath his gaze. She did not like what she saw in his hazel eyes.

Piero took a half step forward. "We are on a pilgrimage of sorts, my lord. We seek a humble resting place for Lady Daria to bury a memory plaque, commemorating her father's life. As you have undoubtedly noted, the d'Angelo crest is the ancient symbol of the peacock. We've been told that your sanctuary has many symbols that relate. Thus, we were led to you."

"Very good, very good," the man said, his hungry eyes never leaving Daria. "This priest will show you to your quarters. This other will show you the way to the stables. But I must insist that I show the lady to her quarters."

Daria sensed Basilio and Rune directly behind her, edging closer. She practically leapt forward to take the bishop's arm. "You are so very kind, my lord. The Lord has granted us much favor in turning us over to your care."

"Very good," the bishop said, patting her hand with a bit too much familiarity. "Very good." He strode forward, leading Daria onward.

"Come and find me, Tessa," she called over her shoulder. "You may room with me." And in her call she found shame in turning to but a child for protection from a lecherous bishop.

ᛘ ᛘ ᛘ

GIANNI paced as but another patrol passed by the mansion, staring inward as if they could peer through the darkness.

"Whom do they seek?" Vito asked.

"I know not. Something is afoot. The doge has sent them to watch over us. Are they waiting for Daria? Piero? Mayhap we should set sail and be gone from this place."

"It is impossible, Captain," Ugo said. "We have yet to unearth our three pieces of the map. If our people have been successful in Torcello and Murano, we can move to those last three sanctuaries and then be safely away."

Gianni shook his head. "I do not like it. Mayhap Daria and Piero and the rest have been captured. We should never have separated." He resumed his pacing.

"You said yourself that God has sent us here. We must remain strong, vigilant," Ugo said. "They could have been waylaid. Father Piero said not to expect them back this night. To remain steadfast in our faith."

"A sharp-tipped blade is of use too," Vito said. He drew his sword suddenly, letting its smooth surface capture the light of the mansion torches—torches the doge's patrol had passed moments ago. "The sword of truth and shield of faith are our armor, Captain," Vito said. "But we remain at your side as your men-at-arms. We shall only leave you fighting."

"God himself will protect us," Ugo said. "He has not brought us this far to abandon us."

Gianni smiled and shook his head. "It is I who was foretold to be a man of great faith." He reached out and put a hand on each of the brothers' shoulders. "But it is you two who remind me of the basis of that faith in this dark hour."

"That's why you'll owe us a small fortune when all is said and done," Vito said.

Gianni laughed then. It led to another and then another, great belly laughs that washed over all three of them like salve on an open wound. When their laughter abated, Gianni lit a candle. "Come. We must pray for the rest of the Gifted. Father Piero has taught me to pray rather than fret. In our prayers, we must trust that God will hear us, that the Savior will protect our own until he sees fit to bring us into his holy presence."

"Amen," Ugo said.

As they walked toward Piero's small makeshift altar, Vito said, "If this vocation as a knight doesn't come to fruition, Captain, you really ought to think about becoming a priest."

⚓ ⚓ ⚓

DARIA unloaded her small trunk and set the plaque that Basilio had intentionally dropped off for her, checking in on her, against the door. She shivered as she thought of the bishop's eyes upon her. There was no lock upon the door. But if he tried to enter, he would have to force his way past the heavy marble plaque, giving her time to defend herself. She reached behind and felt for the long dagger lodged in her belt.

She hoped it would not come to that. She needed the bishop's favor, and was willing to cajole him, play the role of the oblivious lady. He might have taken advantage of others in her stead, but it would not come to pass here, this night. Mayhap his wandering eye was the reason he had been sent here. She would remain awake all night, if that was what it took.

Daria glanced to Tessa on the narrow cot they were to share, eyes wide with fear. "What is it, Tess?" she asked gently.

"I do not like it here. There is darkness here. The bishop is untrustworthy."

"I know it. Do not fear. Morning will greet us soon and before we know it, we will be away from this place."

"I hope you are right, m'lady."

"I am right, Tessa."

A knock on their shutters made them both jump. Daria drew out her dagger and edged toward the wood, unlatching them and pulling one aside while leaping away at the same time. Gradually, they could make out Hasani's dark face and white teeth, illuminated by the candlelight. He waved outward, ivory fingernails flashing in the night.

Daria gathered her skirts and clambered out as Hasani lifted her down to the ground. He reached back toward Tessa, who breathed a sigh of relief to be outside, away from what she obviously feared.

A thousand stars glittered across a dark sky, the sea's wind cold upon their cheeks. "You've made a fine recovery," Daria quipped to Hasani.

He grunted in return and tapped on Piero's shutter, then helped him outside. Basilio and Rune joined them, confirming that the masons and Giuseppe were sound asleep in the stables. The gentle hymns of Compline floated out to them in soft waves. It was haunting and beautiful, but one priest was horribly off-key. And loud. Very loud.

Daria peeked inward. Bishop Carpaccio presided, and all twelve priests in residence were in attendance. That was good. They had a bit of time before the service concluded, before Bishop Carpaccio might seek an audience of his own.

Hasani led the way to the back of the church and grunted. They were where he had collapsed on the ground, where the bishop had discovered them. He grunted again and struck a flint to a torch, which caught flame in a smoky, dim fashion, as if upon wet rags. Daria understood quickly—it was exactly what Hasani wanted, nothing that would attract undue attention. In this dim light, others who happened to be out would not be able to make out who they were. She cast a glance back to the village. All seemed deep in sleep.

Hasani made a sound that meant *there*. She looked to where he was pointing with his torch. A peacock, etched into the base of one of the rounded columns at the back of the sanctuary.

He moved forward, showing them one after another. At each corner was the symbol of the house of d'Angelo. They reached the back door, and the priests' voices were suddenly louder. Hasani gestured inward but they all hesitated.

"If Lady Daria or Hasani is discovered, there will be no explanation," Piero said. "If Basilio or Rune is discovered, there may be repercussions. I will go. I can claim a desire to be a part of the service."

"Then why not just enter? They are your brethren, are they not?" Daria asked.

"It is weak, but I will be sure it holds," Piero said.

"Nay," the fisherman said, suddenly beside them. "I will go. What is it you seek?"

They all studied him.

"You think you'll blend in?" Basilio asked mildly.

"They will not see me. Tell me what you seek."

They remained in silence.

"Tarry no longer. They are soon through."

Hasani began gesturing, making pictures with his hands, obviously wishing for parchment, pen, and a deep well of ink.

"I think he is saying that you might see frescoes, mayhap more. It is what he saw in his vision. Clues for us, here, in the sacristy."

Hasani nodded frantically, mumbling his assent. But then he paused and looked to the campanile across a small bridge, a bell tower they could only barely make out as a black silhouette against a tapestry of stars.

"There is more here for us, isn't there, Hasani?" Daria said.

He looked to her but seemed unsure.

"We must prepare ourselves for needing to spend more than this night in the bishop's presence," Piero said. "We must mine all the treasures of this place while we are here. Then we will make our escape."

"Father," Basilio said, "I do not know if you noted—"

"Yes," Piero said. "Lady Daria has caught Bishop Carpaccio's attention. It is a travesty. But we shall use the enemy's weakness for God's own good purposes. When we return, I will switch rooms with Daria and Tessa. If the bishop enters, I will feign surprise and confusion and make much ado about it, insisting I check on m'lady. He will be confused himself, embarrassed and without excuse. It will scare him off for a night. Meanwhile, Hasani, you shall sleep beneath Daria's window, able to come to her aid in a moment. If we're lucky, it will happen now, after the service, providing diversion and cover for you three, who will search out what is hidden in the church's recesses."

They all stood, mute as Hasani for a moment at the priest's audacious plan.

"Well, let us be off, then," Daria said. "Do not risk coming to my window this night," she said to the fisherman. "We will discuss your findings on the morrow."

Piero paused suddenly, listening to the cantor and his words. "We have but a few minutes before they are done."

"What of the campanile?" Daria asked.

"On the morrow. We must explore it on the morrow. We will have done well to have plumbed the sanctuary's hidden regions this night."

"Good." Daria reached forward with her hand, and the others covered it with their own. "If God is for us . . ."

". . . who can be against us?" the others returned in a whisper.

DRAGON FIRE

CHAPTER FOURTEEN

THE sun spread through the cracks of Abramo's shutters, pulling him reluctantly from the close embrace of the night's festivities. He sat up, pulling off the arm of a young woman to one side of him, while glancing down at the curvaceous form of another. The Venetians knew how to partake of his particular form of ceremony. His way was always made easy here, making it a stronghold for his plans. The doge himself was upon his throne partially because of Abramo's work. He owed him, and therefore forced the Church to look the other way, away from Abramo's dark island monastery. But the presence of Cardinal Boeri in the doge's own palazzo deeply troubled Abramo. He well knew that it was Boeri that had set Sir Gianni de Capezzana on his path and ended his time in Roma. And when he and his archers had trapped the company of knights, striking them all down, Gianni's vendetta against him grew a hundredfold. His cardinal could not be far behind.

Abramo rubbed his face and left the feather bed, one he had had imported from the north. He strode to the window, naked, opened the shutters to let in the bright, thin autumnal sunlight, and leaned against the sill as if forcing back his adversary. He loved the laguna. It was fitting that here, everything he had worked so hard to attain would come together, in spite of Boeri.

Somewhere, his enemies lurked. How did they conspire?

Vincenzo would be off this morn as arranged, due in Siena in two days' time. He would return within ten days, and Abramo's plans would be fully in play.

It was Frangelico who had been alerted to a merchantess of Toscana, here in the city, and discovered Daria d'Angelo's house, a mansion on a canal on the outskirts of the city. It was he who had tipped off Abramo. There was no way the doge's men could miss the Duchess's temporary home. Her knights would be arrested this day or the next, no later. Even in a city of more than a hundred thousand people, Daria d'Angelo was difficult to disguise.

It was just as well that Vincenzo was away. He needed more time to give the man strength, reason to remain in his stead as Abramo's second-in-command. Abramo was grooming him, training him in the dark arts, but such training took time. They both had taken a blow in Il Campo de Siena that fateful night three months past. Abramo recovered quickly. Vincenzo took more time. The lady and her Gifted were strong; he granted them that.

He glanced over his shoulder at one of the lithe women in his bed, Ilario's daughter. After a second night in his bed, her loyalty was assured. She had pledged her devotion and fealty to him.

Abramo smiled.

And so it would begin. Ahh, yes, and it would only be the beginning of the first great challenge he had felt since Siena. He could hardly wait. He would see the Gifted to their end here, in Venezia. Here, he would vanquish them one by one.

In the end, it would only be Daria.

Daria . . . the lovely, elusive, captivating Duchess de Toscana.

ぉ ぉ ぉ

BISHOP Carpaccio surprised them all by not coming to her room that night. Piero blinked awake as early morning light peeked through the boards of his shutters. Mayhap they had misjudged the fellow. But then he thought of Tessa and her squeamish reaction to the man. Nay, he was not trustworthy. He must be watched. Mayhap there could be a bit of ministry here for Piero, to help get the bishop back on the path.

He donned his robe and tied the rope around his waist, leaving the room to attend Lauds with his brothers, as expected. He padded down the earthen hallway and stepped up onto a stone path that led the way to the sanctuary. Once there, he paused outside the doors, waiting for a brother to come along and invite him in, as was customary. A moment later, a priest turned the corner and waved him inward with him.

The church was magnificent, climbing two stories in height, with wide windows on the western flank that allowed the pink light of impending daybreak to softly illumine the sanctuary. At the front, above the altar, was a mosaic of Mary, crafted much like the one in Murano. But here, the mosaics were more elaborate. On the back wall was a complex mosaic done predominantly in blue, depicting the Last Judgment, Christ and his disciples, heaven and hell. His eyes searched the sanctuary floor until he spied the peacocks, making him almost trip when he noted there were four of them, covering a much larger square than the space in Murano. It would take more effort to dig up this panel. He began breathing again when he noted there was still a large green disk at the center. They would begin there.

He got to his knees and recited the Lord's Prayer silently in Italian. When they left this place, when they no longer needed to hide and were on the move, then they might be able to resume their ministry to the people. Here in Venezia, their task was clear. To find the clues their God had left for them to find, avoid capture, and move on.

Piero confessed his trepidation over the bishop, confessed his need for forgiveness, and begged for understanding, the wisdom to lead the Gifted in the direction his God wanted to take them. His Lord felt strangely distant here, as if blocked. But Piero knew that no one but himself could block the Almighty. It was something within him.

He stayed on his knees for an hour, even after the service of praise ended. With a sigh, he said his amen, crossed himself, and then rose. Unexpectedly, he was alone in the sanctuary. All had gone to break their fast and left Piero to the privacy of his prayers.

Free to wander, Piero took in everything. The church was in the form of a Greek cross. Signs of the peacock were everywhere. On the iconostasis that formed the presbytery were marble panels carved with lions and peacocks in heraldic pose. A Roman sarcophagus, holding the relics of Saint Eliodorus, rested at the foot of the altar. Above the altar, in the apse, was a mosaic of Mary. On it were icons of the disciples, hundreds of years old. Above the icons hovered a wooden, painted crucifix, probably completed in the same era. Below them was a row of marble carved panels. On the panels at the center, peacocks sipped from a basin.

The peacock had once been a pagan symbol, Greek in origin, but it had long been adopted by the Christians because of the legend that a peacock's dead body never decomposed. With the surprising flash of the male's tail feathers, the peacock became a lovely symbol of the Christ and his followers.

Piero wondered why and when Daria's forefathers had chosen the symbol as their family crest. He mused again over the time his Lord was willing to take to do his good work, planting images and clues for the Gifted, hundreds of years before they were born. Piero chided himself at his own wonder. Had not the Root of Jesse been prophesied a thousand years before his Jesus came to be born? Even so, it was hard for even him to believe at times that all of this was happening to them, Christ's lowly, humble followers.

The expression on Gaspare's face came back to him then, when they had told him of who they were, who he was. He was frightened, clearly not wanting this mantle. But he would come back around eventually. They need only wait for their God to woo him to a place of acceptance.

"In your time, Lord Jesus," Piero whispered. "Bring him to us in your time. And keep us all in your care. Amen."

The church was deadly still, and Piero held his breath for a moment. Mayhap there was time for him to steal into the sacristy and view the frescoes that the fisherman may have discovered. In the light of day, he might be able to see more anyway . . . Piero had to know what it was.

The custodial priest entered just then, nodding to Piero. Piero forced a small smile and moved out into the light of day as if that had been his plan all along. He spied Daria and Tessa right away, eyes ringed with lack of sleep. Between fear of the bishop and the news of the frescoes that lined the back of this church, there had been entirely too much going on to sleep.

Piero joined them in the quiet covered walkway and then ushered them to the stables to speak of their plans. Basilio and Rune shared day-old bread to break their fast as they walked a short distance from the masons in order to speak without inhibition. The fisherman was gone again, with no further word to them.

"He has fled?" Daria asked the men.

"It appears so. He exited the sacristy, spooked. He gave us none but the bare bones of what he saw, then rushed off. We were going to steal inside, but then we heard someone coming, so we left for the stables."

"Will he return?" Daria asked the priest.

"He has come to us three times already. Our God is at work on his heart. This one simply does not wish to take this holy path. He understands the potential cost. He is not at ease with his gift. And so he fights it. He was probably surprised to see something of the Gifted in the frescoes, the very day we unearthed a portion of Apollos's glass map. It is all much to absorb."

"You are confident he will not betray us?"

"We must leave our lives in the Lord's care. But no, I think not."

"All right, today's task is to obtain permission to unearth the peacock in the church and find the next glass piece. Daria will see that we have entry. Mayhap you can also talk the bishop into giving you a tour of the bell tower, Daria, so we can see what might be hidden there. You must engage him in lengthy conversation so that he does not return to the church to see us at work. Tessa and Basilio will find a way to accompany you so that you are not endangered."

He turned to the men. "Rune, I need you to keep watch outside. I will be inside the sanctuary supervising the work. Hasani, if there is an opportunity to enter the sacristy and see what the fisherman saw, I would like to take it. I need to know that it was what you saw in your vision. That we're not missing something else we are to see."

"He seemed certain it was Daria, and you, depicted in the fresco," Rune said. "Is it worth the risk to see if there is more?"

"Yes. He was frightened by something he did not share with you. We must know what it was."

"I can use my work in importing supplies for the Church's artists to engage the bishop in conversation," Daria said. "I shall ask about the church's artwork, old and new. He will love to boast of it. Mayhap show them to me, in case you do not have the opportunity to steal inside."

"Do so," Piero said. He looked around their group, meeting each man, woman, and child's gaze. "Keep an eye on one another, friends. The stakes continue to rise and we must take care. Come, Daria. Let us seek our audience with the bishop."

ა ა ა

So you seek a place to inter your father's remains," the bishop said, staring at Daria.

"A plaque in his memory, my lord. It seems perfect, your sanctuary. There are symbols of the peacock everywhere, from the presbytery to the marble paving. My father would have been honored to know I had memorialized him in this place. Such history! Such grand artwork!" She did her best to become positively effervescent in her compliments.

Daria turned and grabbed the coin bag at her waist and slid it across the table to the bishop. "I understand that a proper donation must be made in exchange for such an honor," she said. "I am confident that you will find more in there than you've ever been given before."

The bishop's eyes widened as he studied the bag. She could tell his fingers itched to open it but decorum kept him from doing so. "I have only two requests of you," she said quietly. This was the difficult part. Would he agree?

"Name them, daughter. With such a donation, you shall always be a friend to Santa Maria Assunta."

"You are more than kind, Your Grace. You see, it was my grandfather who began to import dyes and other materials for the Church's artists. It is my particular passion to study the finest of art and even more, the oldest in our churches. So much has been destroyed or covered up. As an example, I assume Santa Maria once had frescoes in that front apse, did she not?"

The bishop's pupils swelled with interest. He clearly saw this as an opportunity to make a *patrona* out of Daria, just as she had hoped. He coughed and then said, "It was before my time here that the mosaic went up. But yes, there once were frescoes. Of various saints, I believe."

Daria's face fell with disappointment. "Oh, I had so hoped that a church with as grand a tradition and history would still have some frescoes on display. Not that your mosaics are anything less than perfection, that is. I simply have a certain passion for the artists of old."

"You are uncommon, daughter. Such an interest is rare among nobles. Most only take interest in the new."

She cocked one brow and glanced at Piero with a wry grin. "That is what our dear Father Piero tells me too."

Bishop Carpaccio leaned forward over his arms. "Do not let the priest dissuade you from your passions, m'lady," he said.

She smiled back at him, hinting at demure flirtation.

"There is something that may be of interest to you in the back of the church, in the sacristy. Something that few have seen."

"Oh, Bishop. Are you saying—"

"Yes, yes, m'lady, I shall show you. I believe you are worthy of unusual access to our sanctuary."

Daria noticed he had dropped calling her "daughter" and had moved to "m'lady." He was playing right into their hands.

"You are far too generous to us, Your Grace," Daria purred. "I would love to know your grounds from campanile to narthex to baptistery. When I return to Siena, I want to picture my father here, in this beautiful place. He would have appreciated it."

"Well then, I shall see it done."

Daria leaned back in her chair, placing a hand upon her heart. She glanced over to Piero. "You were right, Father. This is the perfect place for us."

Across from them, she could feel the swell of pride and hope within the bishop.

"One more thing would make it perfect, Your Grace."

"Name it, m'lady. Name it."

"My father . . . he was an intensely private man. In honoring his memory, I would like to have a private ceremony as we inter his memory plaque."

The bishop moved as if in protest.

"Again, I will gladly honor the church with more gifts from my coffers in exchange for such an honor. I am aware my request is unusual."

"I will see that it is done in a respectful and holy manner," Piero put in. He reached to his belt and pulled a smaller bag of coins from the rope, handing it to Daria. She slid it across the table toward the bishop.

After a long moment, he looked to them both and said, "I will take you, m'lady, to show you the frescoes, and then on to the bell tower. Meanwhile, your priest can oversee his masons in doing their work in preparing the ground for your father's plaque."

Daria clasped her hands together and pulled them to her breast. "You are like a gift from God, Your Grace." He was, truly, with his willingness to do all they asked.

"Not at all, not at all," he said. "I hope that this is but the beginning of a long and glorious affiliation."

"You are too kind," Daria said.

"Too kind," Piero echoed.

He led them into the sanctuary and made sure that the masons and Daria's people were to be left alone after two of the peacocks and the central obelisk were removed with utmost care. Satisfied that that would be enough to unearth what they sought, Daria thanked him profusely and he gestured toward the sacristy, a room hidden behind the altar. "Come, m'lady," he said. "This way."

"Oh, wonderful!" she said, not missing a beat. "Basilio, Tessa, come, join us," Daria called lightly as she followed the bishop. She ignored his expression of displeasure. "I fear they have caught my passion like some strange malady. They have traveled a great distance with me in order to see such treasures."

"I see," the bishop said stiffly. With little choice, he led them forward and through a small door to the left of the altar. They went down several steps and walked around the convex curve of the apse, directly behind the high altar and Episcopal throne flanked by the choir. Like many church sacristies, it was filled with old, discarded artwork, threadbare stoles and robes. Old crucifix and Marian figures, processional crosses broken or misshapen. It was stuffed to their left, leaving only a narrow pathway to the right. In only one or two steps, Daria's breath caught. The frescoes. Beautifully preserved, here in the half light of the narrow window to their left. She paused. The hues were bright, brighter than she had ever seen in remnants of frescoes that typically remained in contemporary sanctuaries. On the far right was a life-sized ancient knight, standing, as if on guard, bordering the fresco. But to his left, the scene had been done in great detail, the figures tiny, some only an inch in height. It was a map of Venezia and her surrounding islands, of sorts, but certainly not to scale. There was the Lido, flanking Venezia. The curve of the Giudecca. Le Vignole. Sant' Erasmo. Murano, Burano, and Torcello.

Tessa squeezed her hand as they neared the great fish-shape of Venezia. The artist had depicted a massive storm, setting the waves to such heights that they threatened the few sailboats cresting her waves. "It is beautiful, extraordinary," Daria mused, suddenly aware that they had been too silent, pausing too clearly before the storm.

It was then that she saw the large ship heading out of the lagoon. Square sails, not like the sails of old, atop three masts, more like those of their modern day. She moved past it, as if not intrigued, pretending she was looking at the next scene. But her eyes slid back to the square-sailed vessel. A giant fisherman was at the wheel of the first, and a woman with long, curling hair blowing in the gale, a knight on either side, and a priest between them, laid out as if ill.

In small boats behind the ship, all with swords and shields, as well as archers, obviously giving chase.

"M'lady," Tessa said with urgency, suddenly spying the two ships as well.

Daria tugged her along. "Yes, Contessa, I know. It is marvelous, isn't it? The finest frescoes we've seen in some time. Basilio, isn't it wonderful?"

"Wonderful," he grunted, now staring at the ship himself as they all moved to the left.

"Your Grace, something must be done to preserve this artwork. I would like to set up a fund to be certain it is never destroyed. Others should have access to this. It is a part of Venezia's proud history!"

The bishop thawed a little at her words. "I can certainly see that done, m'lady. I have long thought that this would be of interest to the doge."

"When did you say this work was completed?"

"There is written reference to it as far back as two centuries or more."

"I see, I see." She noted the far less populated city of Venezia and old, plain single-story buildings that had been replaced with more dramatic mansions and palazzos by now. The map extended onward, ending in another bordering life-sized figure, this one of a bishop.

"I believe that may well be the bishop of Altino, who brought the blessed saint's relics with him and founded Torcello. There is a sketch of him in the written record of this holy place."

"Very good, very good," Daria said. "You have done a most wonderful job in preserving this. You are to be commended, Bishop. It is a miracle, a true miracle."

He smiled down at her. "I have been here but a decade, m'lady. It is largely due to my predecessors."

She waved off his dismissal. "I know well how such things transpire in our holy dwellings. I commend you for safeguarding this treasure during your sojourn here. Now please, we would dearly love to see the view from the campanile. I have heard it is magnificent."

They emerged from the far side of the sacristy, out a narrow door that exited through a small tunnel to the back of the sanctuary, where Daria and the men had conferred the night before. The bishop waved at the small etching in each curved wall of the back of the church, small peacocks. "Are you certain that your ancestors did not spend time here? Mayhap it was in this place that they adopted the peacock as their family crest."

"It is possible," Daria mused. "My people are said to have abided in Italia since before her kingdoms were born."

"Then they may have been among the first to flee to these islands, running from the invaders, much like the bishop of Altino and his people."

"Possibly," Daria said. She realized then that she had no verified history beyond her great-great-grandparents. Her great-great-grandparents had settled in Siena just as the city had come into her own. She knew not from where they hailed. Only that the house of d'Angelo had been theirs. Her great-grandparents had then purchased the country estate as their wealth grew.

The bishop offered her his arm as they crossed a small bridge over a canal, still and murky green with moss. She could feel the tension in his forearm, his slight hesitation, as if he looked for a reason to cut away from Basilio and Tessa.

"Tessa, you will simply love the bells in this fine old tower. Might she ring them for you, Bishop, when it is time to call your people to mass?"

"Nay, nay, we could not allow that. The girl might fall, injure herself. The tower is more than two hundred years old. I must say, I believe a campanile is a poor place for a child. Mayhap we should leave her here, safely aground."

Daria laughed lightly and ducked to enter a short door into the tower. "Why, Bishop, what a novel idea! In almost every city, is it not an altar boy who assists the priests in ringing the bells? I would think that your priests would welcome the respite from walking such a long lot of steps. Come, Tessa, you will love this! Basilio, you too!"

Daria and Tessa moved forward, ignoring the pause before the men followed them.

"M'lady?" the bishop called, bringing her to a halt, midway up the second set of steps that wound around the square tower.

"Bishop?" Daria asked.

"There is hardly room for two up at the top. In the interest of your safety, I beg you to allow me to see you to the top myself. When we return, your knight and the child can take their turn."

"Nonsense," Daria said lightly. "I have traveled a great distance and am well used to going where I wish. If there is but room for two, you take your ease, Bishop. I know it is quite a climb. Basilio can see to my welfare."

Basilio moved to the staircase and paused behind Tessa. All three of them looked to the bishop.

"Ah, that is a generous idea, m'lady. I can see that is your nature, always generous in spirit. Fine then. Be about your way. Simply take care at the top to watch the girl, and yourself, m'lady. There has been more than one priest who has fallen to his death on these treacherous stairs."

"I do so appreciate your concern, Bishop. We will simply take in the view for a time and then return. Mayhap we can share a pot of tea and discuss how we might preserve Santa Maria's treasures."

Bishop Carpaccio brightened. "Very good. Have a priest show you to my social quarters when you are sated with the view."

"Good enough. Thank you, Bishop. You continue to capture me with your kindness."

"As you do me," he said, a smile spreading across his cheeks.

CHAPTER FIFTEEN

"I must leave this house." Gianni said, pacing as the noon bells rang across the city and then settled into silence. "Waiting is useless. I will take to the streets. I'll attempt to discover why the doge's men now keep us under such close watch. Possibly locate Lord Abramo Amidei's lair."

"You should not go alone on such a mission," Vito said. "Let me come along. Without Ugo, I doubt I will be recognized. He can remain here."

"Very well," he said. "Ugo, you are all right? Keeping watch with no other?"

"How hard can it be, brother?" Vito interjected for him in response. He waved toward the canal. "You have your own palazzo guard!"

Ugo hid a small smile at his brother's gallows humor. All three men recognized the threat. And what did it mean, that Daria and the others had not yet returned? They had anticipated that their return would have been an hour past, at the longest. Had they run into trouble?

"Pray, rather than fret," Vito reminded him, clapping him on the shoulder. "They'll be along shortly. Let us distract your mind with other thoughts while we wait."

They moved out into the Sestiere di San Marco, pausing to ask along the *riva* if anyone had heard of Lord Amidei or did business with him. It took an hour to come across a man unloading crates of sardines. "Aye, I've heard of Lord Amidei."

"Excellent," Gianni said. "Might you be able to point me in the direction of his home or place of business?"

The fisherman straightened and studied them. "What business do you have with him?"

"I am an associate of his from Siena."

"He will welcome you, then?"

"As a man who greets his cousin."

The fisherman paused, assessing them through narrowed eyes. "He abides in two places. An isle off our coast and in the San Marco district, not more than a few blocks north from the piazza."

Gianni glanced across the Canal Grande. So close was his nemesis! No wonder they had caught sight of him that day! "My thanks to you, friend," he mused, already turning away, Vito right on his heels.

⚓ ⚓ ⚓

THE bell tower proved to be a phenomenal viewpoint, but it bore no further evidence for the Gifted. There were no other peacocks, no other adornment of any kind in the tall tower. They had even inspected the massive bells, inside and out, seeing nothing but the mark of the foundry from which they came.

"M'lady," Basilio said, his voice taut with concern. Daria joined him at the eastern wall. A group of nobles approached the church, bearing a lady on a blanket. Even at this height, they could see the woman was great with child, and writhing in pain.

"Come," Daria said to Tessa and Basilio. "I must go to her."

They raced down the stairs and toward the living quarters of the priests and their bishop. Daria doubted that nobles often came this way. What had made the woman travel in such an advanced state of pregnancy?

They rushed down one hall and then another, following the woman's cries. She passed by an open door.

"Wait!" called a frail voice. Daria turned in confusion from the group of men huddled in front of the bishop's door, in deep conversation. The noblewoman was reaching out to her, her white-faced maid standing aside. "There you are. I knew you would be here. I knew you could save my babies."

"M'lady?" Daria asked in wonder. She had never seen this woman. "Have we met before?"

"Nay. But the Lord told me to come here. He told me you would save us . . ." She pulled her legs toward her chest in agony as another contraction wracked her body.

"Gracia?" a man's voice queried from the hallway.

"This is the woman who will see our children to safety," Gracia said tiredly. "I told you she would be here."

"How did you know?" the lord asked, kneeling by his wife's side. He glanced up to Daria and offered his hand. She placed her hand in his and he kissed it, tears running down his face, filled with wonder. "I am Conte Martino Morassi de Venezia. Last night, my wife went into labor. She refused to have anyone in attendance. The midwives have all told her that our children will likely die before they are born. She says the Lord himself told her to come here, to you. I thought it was nothing but a dream, but since no one could be of help to us in the city, and she seemed so certain . . . we set off to find you."

"Did you say children?" Daria asked, moving toward the lady.

"Children," the lady said, misery in her eyes. Few twins were born that lived. They either died before birth, killed their mother in their attempt to exit, or died afterward. Once in a while, one would live, usually the larger of the twins. Obviously, these nobles had been told all of this as well. There was defeat in their faces, but in the mother's eyes was a spark of hope, faith.

Daria took Gracia's hand. "Listen to me, m'lady. I am Daria d'Angelo. I tell you the truth. If God himself sent you to me, he intends for you to be safe, for your children to be safe. Do you believe your God when he speaks to you?"

Gracia panted through another contraction, gritting her teeth, but her eyes remained on Daria. "Save us, sister. Save us all."

"Not I. God. God will save you and see you to a happy family union." She tore her eyes away from the frantic woman, back to Basilio and Tessa. "Go and fetch my basket of herbs. Fetch Father Piero. Clean blankets. Water. Many buckets of hot water."

❧ ❧ ❧

GIANNI and Vito headed out of the famous Piazza de San Marco. The streets were busy this day. Winter was quickly closing in and the city hurried to complete its gathering of provisions and end of business, before the seas became too rough to be trusted. Gianni too felt the urge to complete their business and be free of this place. There was something on the wind he did not care for, a quiet queasiness to his stomach. His belly tightened as they drew closer to the mansion described, across a wide canal just around the corner.

Suddenly it was in view and they stepped to the side, behind columns to hide their presence. Vito took out a knife and worked on his fingernails as people passed them by, as if waiting. Gianni took a piece of parchment from his vest and read from it, as if trying to follow a map.

Carefully, they studied the limestone mansion, larger than their own by half. In front of it, many barges moved in and out, dumping their loads and taking others out. As he did everywhere, Lord Amidei was doing a prosperous business in trade. Gianni's eyes flicked to the roofline, guarded by three men. Two more were visible in the third *piano,* two more on the canal.

A deep voice surprised them from behind. "Gentlemen, gentlemen. Please, come in. You'll get a much better view of my home from inside."

They whirled, resisting the urge to draw their swords when they saw he was unarmed.

Abramo Amidei.

ॐ ॐ ॐ

GRACIA screamed in agony. Daria dismissed the men and lifted Gracia's skirts to expose her belly, like a giant basket atop her narrow hips.

"Contessa Gracia, meet my Contessa," she said with a smile, introducing the girl to the noblewoman. "We call her Tessa."

Gracia gave the child some semblance of a miserable smile and then turned back to Daria. "You are a midwife?" Gracia panted, sweat rolling down her temples. Tessa moved to sit by her head, mopping at her brow with a rough brown cloth. Had this lady ever even felt a cloth that was not the finest of silk, cotton, or wool?

"Nay," Daria said, looking her full in the face. "I have delivered only thirteen or fourteen children in my lifetime." She took the woman's hand. She was lovely, even in such a dire state. "However, I tell you that if God sent you to me, he will see you and your children through this."

"Do not be afraid, m'lady," Tessa said, wiping Gracia's forehead with the cloth. "If Lady Daria is your attendant, all will be well."

Gracia seemed to take strength from the child's solemn words and stared at Daria. "Who are you, friend?"

"I tell you the truth. I am a healer."

The contessa seemed to absorb the news as if she had expected it all along. Daria turned her attention to the noblewoman's belly, feeling across the skin, drawn perilously taut. "Have you felt both children move, Gracia?"

"As late as yesterday. There is one at the bottom, sideways. The last midwife we had told me that the child would be the death of us all. She tried to turn him, but could not. It was then that I knew our only chance was to set sail and find you."

"Wretched. I am sorry you had to hear such things," Daria said, feeling along the woman's lower belly. Sure enough, she could make out a child's leg and shoulder. She returned to take Gracia's hand and look her in the eye. She waited while another contraction wracked the woman's body. "These are the first of your children?"

"Yes," Gracia said, panting. "I miscarried, a year past."

"Listen to me, Gracia."

The woman turned still eyes upon Daria.

"The midwife was right about one thing. Your child is breech. We will pray and God shall turn him. I watched my mother do such a thing when I was about Tessa's age. It will be a painful process, for I must push and pull at the child. And we must trust that the Lord will see him to his proper place and that you will be delivered of your children, whole and healthy."

"Proceed! Do what you must."

"What I must do is have my priest come in. He can stand on the other side of that screen, to give you privacy. But we need his prayers. Agreed?"

Gracia gasped through another contraction.

"Agreed?" Daria asked urgently. Time was short for the twins and their mother. She could feel the cool of death's edge steal into the room, making her pant for breath, for life. It was a feeling she had not felt since the isle of lepers, and before that, Il Campo de Siena before the Sorcerer . . . She shook her head. She must keep her mind upon the holy, the light.

"Agreed," Gracia said.

"Go and fetch Father Piero and the anointing oils," Daria commanded of Tessa.

The girl fled the room.

⚭ ⚭ ⚭

I prefer to know where the wolf lives," Gianni said, circling Abramo, "rather than enter the wolf's lair."

Abramo smiled. "And I like to know where the lamb lives. One never knows when one will have a hunger."

Gianni's lips turned into a snarl. "Do not threaten me or mine."

"Ah, the Duchess is yours now? Is she aware of that?"

"It is none of your business."

"On the contrary. It is my most essential business." He paused and they ceased their circling. "You think you defeated me in Siena? You merely escaped me."

"We are people of the light. You are of the dark. Light always pierces the darkness, Lord Amidei."

Abramo smiled again. "At times, indeed, at times. But when all goes well, the dark prevails. The dark snuffs out the light, like a candle in the wind." His eyes flicked over to Vito, and he smirked. "Young knight, you must come to one of my ceremonies. I hear you have fellow knights in your company with a wild taste that I could see assuaged. Mayhap you all share such wild tastes. Come, come with me. We shall end these unfortunate spats and become one."

Vito spat on the ground. "You do not know me or my comrades."

"Nay, I know all of you. Each of you. Shall I tell you of what I know? There is the priest, an ugly little man who has a bit of wisdom in his odd-shaped head. Gianni de Capezzana here, once a knight of the Church who pursued me," he said, lifting his brow as if in humor at Gianni's hopeless cause. "There are two who once lived in this city, a certain Basilio. A tall German, Rune by name." He paused to smile and pulled off his glove to inspect an errant fingernail, as if harboring a secret, goading them. Then he was at once all deadly intent. "You and your brother hail from the duchess's country manor district." He circled Vito this time. "You play instruments and provide the Gifted with levity from time to time. I enjoy men in my company who can make others laugh. Come, come and see what me and mine have to offer one such as you."

"Never."

"So you say," Abramo said, disbelief rife in his tone. "Who else? Yes, the tall slave."

"Freed man," Gianni said.

"Yes, of course. *Freed.* He, I'm afraid, must go. He will do nothing but get in our way."

"We are not on your side," Gianni growled.

"Not yet," Abramo said tonelessly. "But you shall be." He faced off with both of them. "Then there is the lovely, enticing, thrilling Duchess. I envy you your close proximity. But do not become accustomed to it. Soon, that will end and she will be where she belongs."

Gianni scoffed at his audacity. "What? With you? Do you not know that she reviles the very sight of you? You turn her stomach!"

Abramo cocked one handsome brow. "Is that what she told you? A pity. It will simply take me a bit longer to turn her. But make no mistake; I shall turn her."

Gianni drew his sword then. "Enough. You shall speak no further of my lady."

"No more?" Abramo asked tauntingly. "Very well. But hear me, now. The dark shall win this round. You may fall into step with me, or you will fall hard, beaten and dismantled. I shall not allow you to remain together. I shall destroy every one of you. Just as I cut down your men in that grove . . ."

Gianni growled and rushed toward the tall man, until the point of his sword hovered before his Adam's apple. Ladies cried out. Men shouted. Abramo's eyes remained on Gianni. "Good, very good. Men of passion are always the grandest to turn. Your fall will be one of my greatest triumphs. Right after Lady Daria, of course."

"Draw . . . your . . . sword . . ." Gianni whispered, pulling away to give him ample opportunity.

"Nay. It is not the time, knight," he said, straightening his overcoat. "We shall do battle on a different day. My day." With one more long look, he ducked past the tip of Gianni's sword and strolled toward his mansion.

Gianni panted and paced in fury, raging within. As Abramo turned the corner, Gianni gritted his teeth and gave out a guttural cry, knocking his head to the wall with such force that he came away bleeding.

Vito joined him and sheathed his sword. "Well, I guess we now know where Amidei stands," he said dryly.

Gianni put a hand to his brow and wearily sheathed his sword. "I must find Daria. If he knows all he says, he knows exactly where she is. He knows where we all are."

ෙ ෙ ෙ

PIERO blessed the oils he poured into Daria's hands and prayed constantly, some in Latin, other words in Italian. He spoke to the contessa about how Jesus had illustrated his impending death and temporary separation as a mirror image to a woman in labor. "Our Lord said, 'A woman giving birth to a child has pain because her time has come; but when her baby is born, she forgets the anguish because of her joy that a child is born into the world.' So with you: Now is your time of grief, but I will see you again and you will rejoice, and no one will take away your joy."

He leaned closer to the contessa. "I want you to believe, Gracia, believe that your children will be born and rest in the assurance of the truth of it, just as you rest in the assurance that you will one day see your risen Savior. He also said, *Siguid petieritis Patrem in nomine meo dabit vobis.*"

" 'Ask anything in my name,' " Gracia whispered, translating the Latin herself.

" 'Ask and you shall receive, and your joy will be complete,' " Daria went on.

Their words seemed to calm Gracia. Her breathing and contractions settled into a more quiet rhythm. "I . . . I have not heard the Word in our own tongue," she panted. "Have not dared to translate. It is beautiful."

"Concentrate on those words, Gracia," Daria counseled. "Know that Father Piero and Tessa and I are praying them over you every second. God has brought you here; he is present. The Holy One is present. Do you believe?"

"I do," Gracia said through eyes slit in pain again.

"Very well. We must move quickly." She turned her attention to her Lord, feeling him envelop her with his holy presence. He had brought Gracia to her. She was to heal her. And healing, she suddenly saw, meant giving her her children, and her life. "Father in heaven, holy God, mighty Lord, be present with us," she whispered, covering Gracia's tight, rounded abdomen with oil. "You have brought this woman to me, Holy One. Move through my hands, my Lord. Move through these hands and move these children into their proper places."

She took the breech child at his rump with her right hand, and his sibling above him by the head. No, that was not right. She felt the pause within her gut. All at once, she could feel her arms surge with strength, the proper pathway on Gracia's stomach as if an arrow had been drawn for her. She moved to the other side of the cot in order to put her right hand on the breech baby's head, and her left on the sibling's. Yes, this was the right way. "He's showing me, Gracia," she whispered. "I see where the children should be. Hold on. Concentrate on the Christ, here with you. Concentrate on his promises. His hands are upon mine. Ask it of him. Ask it in his name. He will deliver you!"

All at once, she shoved, pushing the breech baby to the left, into proper position, head down, and his sibling to the side in order to make room.

Gracia screamed in agony.

But the babes moved into place.

Chapter Sixteen

The Conte and Contessa Morassi each held a child in their arms and beamed at Daria the next day. "There is no way to repay you, m'lady," the baron said through a broken voice, as if he were choking back sobs. "No way."

"You have given us the greatest of gifts," Gracia said.

Daria smiled. "Not I. Your Lord."

"Our Lord," Gracia said, bending to nuzzle her son.

"We have named them," her husband said.

"Excellent," Daria said, rubbing the fuzzy featherlike hair of the nearest twin.

"The boy is Angelo. The girl is Daria. Both in your honor, m'lady."

Daria's hand flew to her throat. "Oh, m'lord. It is too much."

"Nay." He bent to one knee again. "I begged you to help us and you did. You allowed God to use you in a mighty way, and because of it, we will never be the same. We are forever in your debt."

"The Lord's debt."

"Yes, yes. The Lord's. But I pledge to you, Lady Daria, that if you are ever in need of anything, anything at all, if it is in my power, I shall grant it to you. Be it land or house or men or protection. Name it."

Daria stared down at the man, his tiny baby nestled in the curve of his arm. "All I ask is that you teach these precious babes that they were claimed by Christ from the start. That he longs to know them, that he watches over them. Can you do this?"

"Every day. But what may we do for you?"

Daria squirmed. "I shall remember your pledge, Conte Morassi. Mayhap I shall have need of your assistance one day," she said, reassuring him with a pat on the shoulder. Finally, he rose.

"May we see you and yours home to Venezia?" he asked.

Piero nodded slightly. All was in order.

"That would be lovely. We are a bit cramped in one ship. It will make our return a bit easier."

"Consider it done. It is safe to move Gracia now?"

"Indeed. Treat her as any convalescing mother, but one that is fully healthy. The Lord is watching over you." She turned to go.

"Lady Daria?" Gracia called.

Daria turned.

"We have one more favor of you to ask."

"Yes, of course."

Gracia glanced to her husband. "We wish you to be little Angelo's and tiny Daria's godmother. Will you honor us in this way?"

Daria put a hand to her heart. "Of course!" She grinned. "It is an even greater honor than their names!" She smiled at the parents and then left to gather her things.

Piero fell into step beside her. "You realize what you just pledged?"

"To be the children's godmother. Isn't it magnificent? Mayhap these two are our next generation. Surely it is the Lord's own work—"

"Daria, this is the *Conte and Contessa Morassi*. Does their name mean nothing to you? Do you remember the massive palazzo along the Canal Grande? They now have twins, born healthy, despite all odds. What kind of baptismal ceremony do you anticipate? The entire city will go wild."

She could feel the blood drain from her face. "Forgive me. I was not thinking. But I . . . I cannot go back on my pledge now."

"Nay. But somehow, you must persuade them to hold a private baptism ceremony. We must not yet be so exposed."

Daria sighed. Why must every step be so difficult?

Siena

BEATA pulled the dead flowers from the vase and added a fresh arrangement of multicolored fall leaves from the hills outside Siena. The boy Roberto had ridden there alongside her grandnephew, Nico. As she had hoped, without the competition over the girl, Tessa, the boys had become fast friends. Each day they took Bormeo, Daria's prized white falcon, to the hills to hunt rabbits and flex his wings.

Agata entered the kitchen. "Pretty," she mused, fingering the edge of a wide, golden maple. Against the deep green of a pine bough, it practically lit up the room.

"Those two boys are as fast friends as Lady Daria, Lord Marco, and Ambrogio once were. Remember how they would steal away each eve? They believed themselves so stealthy."

"Never knowing that Daria's father had Aldo trail them." Agata eyed her. "Those were days of great joy in this household."

"Great joy," her sister agreed. "Do you believe our mistress and the others might return home in time for Michaelmas?"

"Aldo says that it isn't likely," Agata said, referring to her brother, Daria's steward. It was Aldo who oversaw everything for her from guild business to running the country estate and this massive city manor. For generations, the Scioria family had served in the household of the d'Angelos. Loyalty and devotion had long run deep between them.

"Ahh, well," said Beata, a smile pushing her round, rosy cheeks even as she pushed her spectacles—a costly gift from Daria a year past—up the bridge of her nose. "We shall then pray for Eastertide. An Eastertide reunion will be lovely." She turned to the fire, crackling inside the blackened hearth. "That smells divine, sister. I hope you are cooking an extra portion."

"What? To feed that hulking knight?" Agata blustered.

But Beata simply turned away, a smile hidden on her face. Despite her stern words, Agata loved having another man in the house. Just as Beata loved another child in the house. Agata felt protected with the knight around, even though few came to their door without Daria at home. Mayhap it was his big appetite, and the amount of Agata's good cooking the kind giant put away each day. Beata headed up to the solarium with her arrangement, intent on settling it on the long table and then finding the boys to set them to chores.

Life would be wonderful when Lady Daria returned home. But now, here and now, Beata believed that life was still good.

ঙ ঙ ঙ

VINCENZO mounted his horse and, with six of his men, rode toward the d'Angelo abode.

He had strict instructions. Cut Daria off from her stream of guild income, dismantle the house of d'Angelo, kill a portion of her beloved staff, bring the others to Venezia in chains. It was difficult, this task, but she had brought it upon herself. At times the mightiest of men had to fall hard in order to learn. Daria was no different. It had taken losing his third wife and his child to see the way of it. The path he should take. And he wanted Daria on that same path—even if he had to destroy her in order to build her up again.

"Tell your lord that Baron del Buco is here to see him," Vincenzo said to Jacobi's men. He glanced to Daria's home and anger surged through his veins. Stupid, foolish girl! Why did she push him, press him to this? He had once chased the despicable man from his claim on the land beneath the d'Angelo south tower. He would have remained Daria's protector had she not so betrayed him.

The fat lord soon greeted him, wiping his mouth as if he had just interrupted a greasy meal. "Baron—"

"Here," Vincenzo said, tossing a document to the dirt at his horse's hooves. He did not wait to watch Jacobi open it. He turned to go and made his way up to the d'Angelo mansion, gritting his teeth against the glee he could sense behind him in Jacobi. It was an official document allowing Jacobi claim on the south tower of Daria's house. She would be defenseless. But Vincenzo would make certain that she could not retreat this time—he would destroy her fortresses behind her. He had already dispatched men to burn her country manor.

"You have engaged me in battle, Daria," he whispered. "That is never wise."

He dismounted and his men did the same. He knocked on the door. A small window slid open. "Baron del Buco!" cried the Scioria boy.

"Go and fetch your mistress, child," Vincenzo said tonelessly.

"Lady Daria? She is not here."

"No. Of course not. I speak of your grandmother. And I have need of discussing business with Rossellino."

"One moment, m'lord." The window slid back into its place. A lone knight peered over the precipice of the house.

Ambrogio himself appeared at the window. "Baron?"

"Open the gate, Ambrogio. We cannot discuss business in such a manner."

The younger man hesitated for a moment and then slid open the giant metal rod that secured the improved front gates. It would prove to be the last time it was to bar Vincenzo. He signaled to his men and they drew their swords, rushing inward.

The Sciorias shouted, as did Ambrogio, surprised at this attack. They had expected trouble from Lord Amidei, but never Baron del Buco. Simpletons!

Vincenzo held Ambrogio at bay by pointing his sword against the man's throat.

The artist stood there, helplessly watching as Vincenzo's men gathered the Sciorias together from the kitchen and great room.

ॐ ॐ ॐ

ROBERTO was heading down from the third floor, belatedly following his playmate to respond to Beata's call, when Lucan passed him in a rush. "Hide yourself," the great knight hissed over his shoulder. "Hide well." The kind, hulking knight pulled his sword and moved quietly down the stairs, out of sight.

Roberto, a child of the streets, did not ignore a warning. As if in a dream, he turned and entered the knights' hall, empty now except for Lucan's solitary cot, and in the corner, his own. He paused, hearing the clang of swords and then the guttural cry of his friend, wishing he could go to his aid, knowing it would be foolhardy. Slowly, he went to the narrow passageway through which they hauled water for baths.

He could hear boots upon stone, rushing toward him.

Roberto scurried over the ledge and took to the rope, sliding out of sight and then stopping his descent, listening, praying that the rope would cease swinging and that he might remain safe.

꧁ ꧁ ꧁

THE lone knight above gave the intruders a good fight on the second floor, but was no match for so many against him. The sound of swords striking soon abated.

"Stop!" Ambrogio shouted, shoving away Vincenzo's sword tip, knowing that the sudden silence meant Lucan was either dead or captured. He whipped his head toward Vincenzo. "You have already had me removed as co-consul. Why this attack? Why?"

"Where is the boy? The cripple?" Vincenzo growled, ignoring his questions.

"He is away," Beata said with a tremulous voice.

He studied her. She was a poor liar. "Join the others and find him," Vincenzo shouted. One of his men hustled away, passing other del Buco knights on the stairs. Another joined him to search the rest of the house for the child. The two that remained casually wiped their swords of bright blood on Daria's finest tapestries before sheathing them.

Beata whimpered in terror.

"Baron, we are defenseless," Ambrogio said as the knights continued their descent down the stairs. "What is it you want? Ask it and it shall be yours."

Vincenzo thought that this would be difficult, but he was having trouble feeling anything at all, only the goading push to get this gruesome work done. "I want you to also forfeit Daria's seat on the guild's council."

"The co-consul seat is yours. But I promised Daria I'd hold her place on council—"

Vincenzo lifted a hand to his right and a knight thrust a dagger into Beata's belly. Her face twisted in surprise, and then she gasped and fell to her knees, then to her face. Her glasses shattered and skittered over the floor.

"Nay!" cried her sister, Agata.

"Baron!" shouted Aldo, Daria's trusted steward.

Ambrogio's face was devoid of any customary humor. "You are the foulest of the foul," he said, staring at a man they trusted in their youth. "What has happened to you? You have just killed one of the finest women of Siena! An innocent! A woman who has fed you, served you, for decades!"

Vincenzo lifted his arm again and another knight put an end to the old man's life.

"Nay! Nay!" Nico shrieked, crying hysterically. His grandmother, Agata, caught his shoulder, and weeping, pulled him backward, to a wall, clinging to him, hoping against hope to protect him. Aldo sank to the ground, lifting his hand to see his own blood upon his fingers.

"I am sorry that the Duchess left you to your demise," Vincenzo said over his shoulder, still looking at Ambrogio, who stared in mute horror at the old steward, struggling for a breath. "She has betrayed me. Dared to make light of our partnership by placing this impostor in her stead. She will know the full force of betrayal in her own heart as well."

"I hope they kill you," Ambrogio said. "Better yet, I hope her men make you suffer before you die."

Vincenzo let a colorless smile spread his lips in a sneer. "Ah, Ambrogio. Always the romantic. I appear to be past the point of feeling. Suffering. All I care for now is power. Glory. And you and yours are in my way." He pointed with his chin, and two of his men took Ambrogio and hauled him across the room to a table, forcing him to his knees before it. A third knight menaced Agata and the boy with his blade. Agata sobbed.

"You there," Vincenzo called to a fourth knight. "Go to the roof and retrieve the white falcon. Then go to the solarium. You will find there a box on a table that Daria holds dear. Bring it to me. But before you return, douse the entire floor with oil."

Agata whimpered anew.

He bent to retrieve Beata's shattered glasses and pocketed them. Foolish Daria, spending a fortune on a servant. She had always been tenderhearted to the point of idiocy. It would prove to be her undoing.

He pulled his sword from his belt and strode over to Ambrogio. "Tell me what you know of Daria. She must have written to you, told you where she is."

"She has not. We have not heard from her these past months."

Vincenzo lifted his chin again and the men each spread one of Ambrogio's hands upon the table.

"Nay, Baron. Not my hands! 'Tis my livelihood!"

"Oh? I thought you fancied yourself a guildsman now." He brought the hilt of his sword down heavily upon the man's left hand and Ambrogio screamed in pain. He allowed his head to collapse to the table, gasping, choking on the pain. Only Vincenzo's men kept him from crumpling to the floor. Vincenzo took a fistful of hair and hauled the artist's head backward. "You still have your right hand," Vincenzo said. "Tell me where she is."

Ambrogio grimaced and then spit in his face.

Vincenzo cried out in fury, lifting the hilt of his sword and taking aim at the man's right hand.

"Nay!" Nico cried, wrenching away from his grandmother. Tears streamed down his face.

His grandmother screamed at him to be silent.

But the boy's eyes, bloodshot, remained on Vincenzo. "Do not do it, Baron. Ambrogio does not know where she is. But I do. I do. My granduncle," he paused on a sob, "he read me her last letter."

Vincenzo smiled and straightened, sheathing his sword. "Very good," he said to the boy. He already knew where the Gifted were. What he needed was this . . . one of Daria's own to betray her. And to use them against her. It would tear her down, take her to the brink of demise. And then he and Abramo would remake her. Remake her as their own. Without Daria, her connections, her funding, the rest of the Gifted would easily play into their hands. Abramo had convinced him. And he believed it.

The knight returned from above and handed Vincenzo the bird and the box.

Vincenzo turned to the two who had been upstairs. "Did you find the boy? The cripple?"

"Nay, m'lord. There is no one else in the mansion."

"Very well. Bind them and bring them to my home," he instructed, waving at Ambrogio, the old woman, and the child. "Leave from the back gate so no one sees you. And as you depart," he said, looking around the great hall for the last time, "burn it. Burn it all to the ground."

CHAPTER SEVENTEEN

GIANNI and Vito returned to the manor in a trot. "Ugo!" Gianni cried. *"Ugo!"*

"Yes, Captain," the man said, running down the manor steps.

"Any sign of them yet?"

"Nay."

"We must go after them. They have been absent for far too long."

"Captain, wait," Vito said.

Gianni pulled up short and cast a furious look in Vito's direction.

"Think it through. The Sorcerer may be counting on you doing just that. Leading him to our lady. If we allow them to return home, we can at least face the enemy together. If he knew where she was right now, do you not think he would've already descended upon her?"

Gianni paced back and forth, running an anxious hand through his hair. "I am listening."

"Lady Daria has about as much protection as we could afford her. Hasani, Basilio, Rune. They are all very capable, Captain, worthy and strong fighting men. Even Father Piero is decent with a sword."

Gianni sat down hard, head in hands. "All right, all right. But what could be keeping them?"

ෆ ෆ ෆ

ROBERTO narrowly escaped the burning mansion, sliding down the rope and out through the kitchen and courtyard, to the streets beyond, long after the building was heavily ablaze. He had seen the old man, Aldo, and the kind old woman, Beata, slain on the ground, but could not near them, so heavy was the fire.

There was no sign of the others. Vincenzo had killed people dear to him in the household—sweet Beata, kind Aldo, playful Lucan. He had kidnapped the others. For what cause? To where did they take them?

Roberto's eyes narrowed in conviction. He had to take to the streets again, follow them. The Duchess would expect it of him. Nico, his friend, his brother, would expect it. He would not disappoint them.

Hot tears ran down his face as he went to the stables and released the horses from their burning prison. The last was a mare he had ridden for months, wild in the eye in fear at the flames, but still accepting of bit and rein. Roberto clumsily climbed a rail and threw his crippled leg across her middle. "Go, girl, go," he whispered, and they jumped over a burning timber and out the back gate of the house of d'Angelo. "Never to return," Roberto whispered in sorrow.

He cast another look back at the grand mansion, flames now spreading from her roof to the next mansion. Would this fire bring down the entire city? What madness was this?

⚓ ⚓ ⚓

IN the end, it was Piero who convinced Daria to attend the baptism. The Morassis had cajoled and begged, pressing Daria when she evaded answering them directly. They were plainly powerful people used to having all they desired. And they fervently desired to honor her. "We shall introduce you to the most powerful in Venezia. Whatever you seek, we and our friends can help you obtain it."

"God has made a way," Piero told her. They all knew that news of Daria's memorial gifts to both churches in Murano and Torcello would spread quickly, as would her miraculous midwifery of the contessa. Piero recognized the thirst for power in the bishop's eyes. Torcello was a dying island, her grandeur long faded. His only hope of escape and glory was to be noticed and moved to a more prominent location. He would talk.

"Our time grows short. We must race against those who may expose us, get to those last three churches, and then escape the city," Piero said lowly to Daria and Hasani. "The Morassis will be able to win us entry faster than we can talk our way in." It took some cogent reasoning, but in time, they gave in to his plan.

"Come. Let us be away," Daria said. "Gianni must be going mad with worry."

"Who is that?" the conte said, drawing near. "A suitor, mayhap?"

"The captain of my guard," Daria said. But she felt another odd stirring at the baron's words.

"Ahh. And we have kept you here longer than expected."

"Indeed."

"Then let us be away at once."

He ordered his men to collect Daria's meager belongings, as well as his wife's, and the two ships set sail across the bay to Venezia. The conte unfurled celebratory flags on his larger skiff, and Piero, used to their long months of secrecy, fought back a wince. This new papa deserved to celebrate—there was no possible reason the priest could give him not to do so. Still, he met Daria's worried gaze with one of his own. "God help us," he whispered, leading her to the front of the ship.

He gestured to Hasani, Basilio, and Rune, and they gathered. The masons and Giuseppe were together in the back, sharing their own good fortune with a bottle of wine and musing over the knowledge of this odd group they had served. Piero figured it would only be days before one of them shared their story, despite all their solemn promises. It simply was too intriguing to escape the desire to share in gossip.

"We will have to move very quickly once home," Daria said. "The Morassis will have the twins baptized in two days' time. My entire household will be invited, as will every noble acquainted with them, including the doge. Conte Morassi has promised to introduce me to patron families of San Zaccaria, Sant' Elena, and San Giacometto, if Gianni has not yet found a way to infiltrate them. The following day, we will gain entry to each church, lay claim to what we seek, and then flee this city, mayhap even under the cover of darkness."

"To where?" Rune asked.

"I am hoping that once we have the rest of the glass map, that will be made clear to us," Piero said.

"And if it is not made clear?"

"Then we will pray that God will make a way."

"You fear the Sorcerer?" Basilio asked.

"I fear that he will waylay us, keep us from our holy task. At some point, he must be won over to the light or destroyed. But for now we must stick to the path that God has shown us and let not evil dissuade us."

They hugged the coast of Venezia, making their way to the other side. In another hour, their neighborhood came into view, and they waved good-bye to the Morassis.

ᚕ ᚕ ᚕ

DARIA stood, laying eyes on the mansion for the first time in days. A shout was heard from her rooftop and the captain brought their rented skiff to an expert halt right beside their dock. Then Gianni was immediately outside, lifting her out, pulling her inside, shielding her from view. "Enter, all of you, at once!"

Once safely inside, she stood her ground, pulling Gianni to a stop. "What is it?"

"Where have you been?"

"In Torcello," she said, crossing her arms. "You *knew* where we were. What is this about?"

"But you planned to return yesterday."

"We were delayed. Something transpired—"

"Yes, well, something *transpired* here too."

Daria shut her mouth abruptly and stared up into his handsome face, rife with agitation. Something significant had happened, all right. A threat of some purport to push him toward such rude and gruff behavior. She turned to Hasani. "Pay the captain, Giuseppe, and the masons and send them on their way. Remind them of their pledge of silence."

Hasani grinned and fingered his long, curved blade, departing at once with another sack of coins.

"Come, knight. Let us sit as civilized people in a circle and share what we know with one another."

Gianni reluctantly followed her, gesturing to Vito and Ugo to keep watch from the windows so they could hear, but still protect the Gifted.

Piero clapped him on the shoulder as they walked. "I see it is indeed time for us to immerse ourselves in the Word and in prayer. The devil is about, I take it."

"Just across from our own neighborhood," he said, as they all sat down on the benches that surrounded their long dining table.

Daria's breath caught. "So he remains here, in the city."

"A stone's throw away. All Vito and I had to do was spend a little time asking about him, and we found directions to the door. And it is not like Siena. Abramo Amidei already has deep ties in this city, having lived a portion of his years here. We will find no friends that he has not already touched."

Daria and Piero shared a long look. Were the conte and contessa God's form of protection for them in a friendless city? Or were they already attached to Lord Amidei in one way or another?

"So you went to spy upon his house . . ." led Piero.

"And he came out to us from behind. Either he circled around or happened to be out when we arrived."

Daria sucked in her breath. "What did he say?"

"He greeted us as old friends, invited us in, then made veiled threats about every one of us." Gianni rose and paced. "Make no mistake. He is planning his attack, and his friends here are many. We must be away. Immediately."

Piero stood.

"He will attack any way he can. I cannot protect all—"

"Sir de Capezzana!"

Gianni paused abruptly and stared at the small priest.

"What has happened to you? You are our man of faith. Great faith. Is this where your faith leads you? You think it all boils down to you? One man? Where is your God?"

"This is where my head leads me," Gianni said fiercely, pounding the table. "We are called to be faithful, but are we also not called to wisdom, priest?"

"Of course! We are all to be using our gifts. But you seem to have forgotten that we are all in this together. It is not all up to you."

"Which is all very well and good. But Amidei is a physical menace as well as a spiritual one."

"One that our God has fully prepared us to engage in battle, should it come to that. But we are weak. We must return to the Word, prayer.

Take it in like a fine cut of meat as sustenance. If Lord Amidei was here, he would be thrilled to see us, forgetting from whence we've come, what God has shown us, taught us. Arguing." Father Piero paced around the group. "He wants nothing more than to divide us. One by one, he has a better chance to conquer us. That is why the Lord has brought us together." Briefly, he told the men who had remained behind what had transpired on Torcello.

He studied the group around him. "We are the Gifted. But we are forgetting our giftedness—our faith, our trust, our service to our Lord. Instead we have become absorbed by sin or weakness. It is time we remember our place in this world. Come." He shoved away from the table.

"Where are we going?" Basilio asked.

"To chapel. We will do nothing but fast and pray this night. The Lord will show us what we seek, if we seek him first." He reached out a hand to Gianni. "The dark is not to be feared if we are awash in light. Are you with us, knight?"

Gianni paused and then took his smaller arm in his own powerful grip, staring him in the eye. "I am with you, priest. Forgive me. I succumbed to my fears. It will not happen again."

"May it be as you say," Piero said lightly. "All of you, gather candles. Daria, bring your family Bible. Gianni, we need us all together, even our guards at the roof. We will pray that God will protect us as we commune, and believe that he will."

Gianni paused for a long moment, then turned and walked away to fetch the men.

Daria leaned toward Piero. "Are you testing him?"

"I am reminding him. He is off the path. As are the rest of us. We must quickly find it again before we encounter the dark."

⚭ ⚭ ⚭

ABRAMO floated on a skiff outside the manor, alone but for the boatman who had brought him, shivering at the back but saying nothing. There was little light from the night sky, but high above him a soft, flickering light pressed outward from the second piano. He could hear the prayers of the Gifted. Their voices cascaded outward and over him like sleet in the cold. But still he remained.

They were gaining strength, not falling apart as he had hoped. He had to move quickly. Very quickly.

It would all begin as soon as Vincenzo returned to the city. Then all would be in place.

And the Gifted would turn to him.

Or they would fall.

Chapter Eighteen

Cardinal Boeri entered the doge's private quarters and was shown to a large, comfortable chair. Candles about the room flickered in a slight draft, and the cardinal shivered, pulling his overcoat a bit tighter. Venezia would be a cold city come winter, surrounded by water as she was. The chill seemed to seep upward from the very stones beneath his feet.

A steward arrived with a steaming mug of mulled wine and left. The cardinal could hear voices speaking in hushed undertones in the next room. In a moment, the doge entered, with Bishop Carpaccio behind him.

"Cardinal Boeri, I assume you know Bishop Carpaccio de Torcello," the doge said, glancing back at the tall man.

"Indeed," returned the cardinal, nodding toward the bishop.

"The bishop has just arrived this eve from Torcello. He has an interesting tale to tell." He gestured toward the bishop, and the man quickly told of Lady Daria d'Angelo's arrival, her interest in the peacocks of the old church, and the miracle of Contessa Morassi's birth of two healthy children.

"The contessa had been told that she and her children would die in birth, given that one of her twins was breech."

The cardinal glanced toward the doge, and the man raised a brow and gave him a look that told him it was true, not folklore. "Why did she come to Torcello?"

"She knew that Lady d'Angelo would be there. She had been given a dream," the bishop said, "a dream from our Lord that told her to come to the island. That Lady d'Angelo would save her and her children. And she did!" He was clearly enjoying the uncommon drama of his tale. The cardinal was certain that prior to this, the doge had given the bishop little notice.

A steward entered the room and refilled their mugs of steaming wine. "What of her interest in the peacock?" asked the doge.

"It is her family herald. She wished to bury a memory plaque beneath our peacocks."

"Beneath the peacocks?" the doge repeated. "Beneath the mosaic tiles?"

The bishop paused. "Why, yes."

"And you allowed it?"

The bishop paled a bit. "I did. She gave the church a handsome sum. It is quite common—"

"Did you oversee the process yourself?" The doge rose and paced before the fireplace, the embers of a dying fire glowing within the hearth. The steward hurried to add two split logs to the embers. "Did you watch as they buried the plaque?"

The bishop paused again. "Nay, m'lord. The lady specifically asked for privacy. The priest, he promised that all would be done in holy fashion and nothing would be disturbed. May I ask, what is your concern?"

"You know not of the legend of Apollos and the peacock urns?"

"N-nay. As you may remember, I have only resided in Venezia over the last decade of my life. The lady seemed to have a considerable interest in old frescoes, not mosaics."

The doge threw up his hands. "My dear bishop. The lady may have left a plaque beneath your church floor. But I'd wager she took with her something far more priceless, as she did from the churches of Murano and my own San Marco."

"What are you saying, m'lord?" the bishop asked, rising on shaky legs. "She robbed us?"

The doge eyed the cardinal. "*Robbed* is a strong word. I believe she simply took something that she believed was hers all along."

♉ ♉ ♉

PAID well as a spy in the doge's palazzo, the steward made his way out into the dark streets of Venezia, heading a few short blocks away to the city mansion where Abramo Amidei resided. He knocked upon the massive side door, away from prying eyes, and a guard gave him quick entrance to the kitchen, then farther into the dark house.

Amidei emerged from his bedroom in a robe and listened to the tale of Bishop Carpaccio and the doge's response. He nodded with pleasure, a slow grin spreading across his handsome face. He laid a hand on the steward's shoulder. "Great shall be your reward." He turned and then handed the man a box, heavy with silver. "This is but the beginning. I have long waited for such a breakthrough as you have provided this night."

"I am pleased to be of service, Master," said the steward.

"Before you go," said Lord Amidei. "Do you know the other churches where the peacocks can be found?"

"The doge mentioned the seven principal churches of Venezia, those that have been around for at least several hundred years. There are few that meet those criteria. Sant' Elena and San Zaccaria are two of them, for certain. I can find out the others on the morrow. The city sleeps at this hour."

"Many sleep," said the Master. "But not us. We must move, and quickly. We will go to those churches and wake their priests. We shall see for ourselves this night, before the sun rises, if the legend of Apollos is true."

⚓ ⚓ ⚓

FATHER Piero, Daria, Hasani, and Gianni set off in a hired skiff for Sant' Elena as the morning sun struggled to break free of a dense fog. Daria pulled her overcoat closer, tucking her chin down and into the neckline. She looked up in surprise as Gianni neared, a blanket in his hands. "You appear as chilled as you do weary," he said.

She smiled up at him and took it, wrapping herself in the thick, raw wool. "I wish there were time to rest, catch our breath," she said to Gianni as he took a seat beside her.

"I understand." His hazel eyes searched hers. "The healing . . . what you did for Contessa Morassi. Did it sap your strength?"

Daria smiled. "That or remaining awake the whole night. I do not know which was harder." She rubbed the edge of the wool blanket. The feel of it made her miss the luxurious fabrics of home—as co-consul of the Sienese woolen guild, the house of d'Angelo had long since become accustomed to the finest of linens. Her thoughts went to the Sciorias— Agata, Beata, Aldo, Nico—and little Roberto and her friend, Ambrogio. How were they all faring? Might she get home to them sometime soon in the new year? She had been gone too long already; home felt distant, unattainable.

The small skiff soon rounded the point of Castello and tied up at the docks and the four disembarked. Gianni asked the man to remain with the skiff and await their return, and he tossed him a silver coin. They set off along the canal, Gianni in the lead, Hasani behind Piero and Daria, and began to turn a corner when they glimpsed a monastery and church. Gianni turned back suddenly, grabbing Daria's arm, then Piero's, leading them back the way they came. Out of sight around a monastery wall, they huddled their heads together.

"There are three priests outside the church door, speaking animatedly to six men in a patrol of the doge's guards. Quickly, Father Piero, might you near them and try to discover what is happening?"

Piero nodded once and set off down the *calle* that led to the church. In minutes he had returned with a grim expression, leading them forward, back to the docks. "The church floor was dug up in the dark of night," he whispered, looking back over his shoulder.

Daria let out a breath of sorrow. "The peacocks?"

"It is gone."

"Who? Somebody is after the same map?" Gianni asked.

Piero stared at him. "We have been discovered, Sir Gianni. We must move quickly to try to obtain the other piece before him, then decide if we need the two he has."

"Two?"

"San Zaccaria suffered the same fate as Sant' Elena."

"They will assume it is us," Daria said, her voice rising as Gianni moved her along the *calle*. "It will only be a short time before the bishops of Murano and Torcello link our interest in their peacocks to the travesty that occurred last night. We were in the city last night. They shall link it to us!"

"Take your ease, m'lady," Gianni said firmly. "It appears grim, I grant you that, but nothing escapes our Lord and God's attention. He sees the thieves in the night and he sees his servants by day. We do not walk alone."

Daria took a deep breath and then accepted his arm, walking to the docks. "We must head immediately to San Giacometto," she said, using the affectionate name for the tiny church more formally known as San Giacomo di Rialto.

"Nay," Piero said. "We must return to the manor and pray. The entire city's churches will be on guard now, every move questioned and observed. Not even our enemy will be able to slip in unnoticed and rob another sanctuary. We must find another way, another way."

The man who poled their skiff eyed them nervously as they neared the manor. Hasani rose silently, regally, hand on the hilt of his sword, and then looked back to Gianni with fear in his dark eyes. Three large skiffs bearing eighteen men in total had disembarked and surrounded the mansion. There was not even room for the rented skiff to pull up alongside. Gianni bent and spoke to the man and they paused a short distance away. Gianni and Hasani hesitantly took their seats again.

A young captain unfurled a scroll and began to read in a loud voice. "By decree of Doge Bartolomeo Gradenigo de Venezia, we hereby arrest Basilio Montinelli and his cohort, Rune of Germany, on charges of rape and robbery."

"What nonsense is this?" Ugo asked, coming outside to meet them.

"You are harboring two men who have raped one of our noblemen's daughters, and stolen a bounty in household silver from another."

"Which noblemen have made such a claim?" Rune asked, joining Ugo.

"Sir Ilario Bicoli and Sir Gian Ricci."

"They are lies, blatant lies," blustered Basilio, now on Ugo's other side.

"You shall have your opportunity to plead your case before the doge himself in less than a fortnight," said the captain unwaveringly. "Until then, you will be imprisoned in the doge's prison."

Daria's hand flew to her throat. Less than a fortnight! And imprisonment! How would the Gifted resolve their business here and move on if two of their own were waylaid? She made as if to rise, but Gianni laid a gentle hand on her shoulder, wanting her to remain inconspicuous.

"Surely we can make some assurances to your doge that we will keep these two under close watch," Ugo said. "We shall bring them to the court on the day of their hearing."

"We cannot allow that. You are not even a citizen of this city. You would flee as soon as we turned our backs."

"I give you my solemn word. We shall not flee," Vito said, joining the group below.

So brave, her knights, Daria thought. Facing the very patrols who had hunted them these last weeks, in order to stand up for their brothers.

Hasani rose, fear again rife in his eyes. "Bring us closer," Piero said suddenly. "I must get to them. Something is going to go wrong," he said, rushing to the end of the skiff as if he intended to jump in, looking back to the terror on Hasani's face. "Quickly!"

Hearing his raised voice, the young captain of the doge's knights eyed the priest across the water with a frown and then turned back to the men. "We cannot allow it." He lifted his chin and his men surrounded Ugo and the others. All reached for their swords and unsheathed them.

"Wait!" Piero shouted, leaping to the nearest patrol skiff and skipping across a seat and to the dock. "Hold! *Hold!* It will do no one good to die this day." He waded into the sea of armor and swords, pushing aside one and then the other until he stood before Basilio and Rune. "Please, friends. Go with these soldiers and trust that God will free you."

Basilio eyed him over his elbows, drawn back as if to strike the nearest soldier with his broadsword. "Father, this is treachery. Rune and I are innocent."

"I know it as fact," Piero returned. "But you must live if we are to free you. If God is to free you. Basilio, Rune, do you trust in the God we serve?"

"Indeed," Rune said.

Basilio gave him a short nod.

"Then go with God. He will not abandon nor forsake you, or us. This is but an attack. We are in a war. We give up this battle in order to win a larger one."

Daria could see the unanswered questions that plagued Basilio and Rune, but reluctantly they tossed away their swords and raised their hands in surrender. The knights grabbed them roughly and hauled them toward the skiffs.

"Gently, men, gently," Piero urged, following them. "These men are your brothers, falsely accused, regardless of what you've been told. Please treat them as you would wish to be treated in their place."

⚜ ⚜ ⚜

CARDINAL Boeri paced outside the doge's public quarters, awaiting a private audience. Bishop di Mino had heard of the d'Angelo knights' capture, and had come to Cardinal Boeri with the news.

It took the doge hours to complete his business and then allow the cardinal entry. Cardinal Boeri simmered and continued his pacing. At long last, the doors were opened to him and the cardinal strode into the wide, empty hall. The doge sat at a desk a step above, at the end, attended by two stewards. "You had them arrested," the cardinal said lowly.

"That should come as no surprise, given the conversation you witnessed," the doge said, dipping a quill in ink and signing his name to the bottom of a document. He handed it to a steward, who fanned the ink with his free hand, encouraging it to dry. The doge waved away the second steward and both exited the cavernous hall.

"But what shall you do now? You said yourself you would have no choice but to put them to trial, and that in all likelihood they would hang."

The doge sat back and studied Cardinal Boeri above steepled fingers. "Do you believe your God would allow his beloved Gifted to die?"

"Nay . . ."

"Nor do I."

"So this is some sort of test?" the cardinal asked, pacing before the doge. "It is never wise to test our Lord and our God."

"It is not him that I intend to test. It is your Gifted. If they truly have miraculous powers, then they shall find a way to free their brethren." He stared back into Cardinal Boeri's eyes. "Be at peace, Cardinal. This brings them closer. Strife always has that potential. You can question the men, find out whatever you need." He rose, walking down the step to stand beside the cardinal. "Were it my prerogative, I would bring them all into my prisons. They would be safer there than on the streets, hunted by Amidei. This is just the first attack, Cardinal. I've seen how this man works. He will do all in his power to destroy them. His reach is too great; his hold on my city too secure. I myself owe him, in large part, for bringing me to power. None can stop him, it seems. He weaves his tentacles deep and tight before a city even realizes that he is stealing her very breath."

Cardinal Boeri remained still. "So what of our conversation? What of the Church, and how she might aid you in power?"

The doge waved his hand dismissively, as he had done a moment ago with his servants. "Frankly, Cardinal, winning over the Church is a future, potential hope. I have a driving, immediate need. I am compelled to seek out the Gifted to assist me here and now."

"You wish to make a way for the Gifted to destroy Amidei?"

"If possible," the doge said, a slight smile lifting the corners of his mouth. "He owns an island off our coast where dark things occur. I continue to get reports that . . . disturb my court. They coincide with your stories of the Sorcerer of Roma, giving me no choice other than to believe we have a common devil in our midst. And since his return from Toscana, the stories grow. If it continues, then Lord Amidei becomes not only a spiritual threat to the good Christians of Venezia, but a threat to this seat of power." He gestured up and about, toward the magnificent halls and the rest of the palazzo.

"Then do as we discussed," the cardinal urged. "I shall go to them, convince them of their proper path. We will return with the Church won, and together as a force destroy Amidei."

"Nay. There is this matter of these first two men, falsely accused. My people will see justice done or there will be an outcry. The men shall stand trial and be freed as innocents or be sent to the hangman's noose."

"You would kill two of God's own chosen ones?" the cardinal blustered.

The doge smiled. "Come now, Cardinal. Do not be so theatrical. I am no Pontius Pilate. I said they would be sent to the hangman's noose. I never said I would allow it about their necks." He took his arm and they walked down the hall. "I know you wish to be away with your precious Gifted, so intent are you to win over your Church. But don't you see? Facing an evil one in their midst will merely add to their strength, prepare them. Amidei is mighty, but he is but one man. They must be prepared to face many if you are to take them to Avignon." He paused outside his door and released the cardinal's arm. "It happens here. Now. If God is in this, he will bring your Gifted victory."

"And if he is not?" the cardinal asked in a whisper.

The doge shrugged and opened his door. "Then I will find another way to face my devil, and you will do the same with yours."

cb cb cb

GIANNI paced on the ground floor as the others gathered, back inside. "This is Amidei's doing."

"Certainly," Piero said. "Do not give in to fear, Sir Gianni. It will all turn out as God has foreseen it. He has need of us. He has given us his good work to do. He prepared us for this, gave us Hasani's vision. No one will get in the way of his way, ultimately."

"Hasani saw Lady Daria imprisoned as well, by the Sorcerer himself. Do we simply wait for that to occur?"

Piero eyed Daria mournfully. "It is bound to occur. We will find a way to free both our men and our lady. It will serve a purpose, their imprisonment."

"And what of Rune and Basilio? How can we coexist in this city for a fortnight with Amidei hovering near?"

"We shall not. We will move on without them and return in two weeks' time."

"You . . . you plan to leave them behind?"

"Only to follow where our God is leading us."

"Nay," Gianni said, slicing a hand through the air sideways. "Nay! We shall not abandon our people!" His eyes cut to Daria. "Any of our people!"

Piero waited for a long moment for Gianni to bring himself under control. "Gianni, we are on a holy mission. We will do our best to protect and preserve our people, but there may need to be sacrifices . . ."

"Sacrifices?" Daria said. She strode to Gianni's side and faced the priest. "This is unacceptable. We must go to their aid, immediately."

"We must pursue our plans as we have outlined them," Piero said calmly. "Attend the baptism this day, obtain the next glass piece from San Giacometto, see if we must retrieve the stolen two, discover where God wishes us to go next. This is our charter, as the Gifted. To follow as God leads. No matter the cost. He will show us the way."

"Even if that means abandoning our friends?" Gianni thundered.

"Even if it means abandoning our friends *temporarily*," Piero returned. "You must dress at once. We shall be late if we tarry any longer."

Gianni and Daria stared at him for another long moment.

"Come, my friends. We cannot think about what lies behind us— only what lies ahead. We will pray that God shows us a way to free Rune and Basilio. But even if we cannot, we must trust that God will protect and keep them."

The group turned to trudge up the stairs, Tessa trailing behind. The girl followed Daria into her apartment and assisted her with dressing and with her hair. Daria chose a soft cream underdress and a burnished bronze overdress, a modest ensemble appropriate for a baptism. She had discovered that Tessa was gifted with hair, often asking her to try to bring her wild curls into some semblance of order.

Tessa chose a crown of three strands of freshwater pearls and wove the rest of Daria's long hair into a twist that she pinned up in the back. As she was putting the final pin in Daria's hair, leaving a sweet wreath of soft tendrils around her neck, Tessa clutched her stomach and moaned softly.

"Tessa?" Daria said, turning on her stool to look at the child.

"I am fine, m'lady. I must have eaten something foul this morning. It shall pass."

Daria frowned at her, then turned to the dim looking glass to place the last pin herself.

A pitiful cry made her whip back around. Tessa was on the ground, clutching her stomach.

"Tessa!" Daria cried, going to her at once. "Ugo!" she cried, knowing he was on guard outside her door.

He entered and hurried over to them. "What ails her?"

"I know not," Daria said grimly. "Place her upon my bed. I will fetch some tea and my herbs."

Piero watched her as she descended the stairs. "We must go at once. Mass will begin shortly and you cannot be late."

"Tessa is ill. She thinks she ate something ill advised. She needs me," Daria said, brushing past him and to her basket.

"Daria, she will be fine," Gianni said, moving away from the window. "Her stomach probably is upset after the trauma of this morning.

We really must be on our way. If we do not follow through with our plans, then giving up Basilio and Rune makes no sense."

"I cannot leave her alone."

"Vito and Ugo shall be with her. They cannot risk being recognized. We were fortunate that they were not recognized by the doge's men this morning. Come. Let us go."

The others had gathered around her, urgency etched in each of their faces. "Very well," Daria said, passing a handful of dried herbs into Vito's hands. "See that you steep those for several minutes into a dark tea and make certain Tessa drinks every drop."

"I shall be as good with the kettle as I am with the sword, m'lady," Vito quipped.

Daria sighed and followed the others out to the lone skiff and set out for the Canalazzo and the church in which the twins would be baptized. She glanced around the group as she got settled but stopped breathing when she spied Hasani, staring resolutely back at the mansion with angst in his eyes.

"Hasani?" Daria asked.

Her question shook him out of his reverie and he tried to smile at her. "Is all well?"

He nodded.

But Daria did not believe him.

CHAPTER NINETEEN

VINCENZO brought his captives into Abramo's home—Agata, Nico, and Ambrogio, huddled over his mangled hand. They had all been bound and gagged, tossed into the hold of the ship and then over the backs of donkeys to bring them here.

"Excellent, excellent," Abramo said, clapping his hands together in pleasure at the sight of Vincenzo and his bounty.

Vincenzo expected to feel warmed, gratified by his master's praise, but again he was struck by the void he felt in his heart. The gratification would come; he was certain it would come.

Abramo spoke to his guards, who led the prisoners to the back of the first-level warehouse, into a bricked-off room that would deaden any cry they dared utter. They would move them to the isle this night or the next.

"It may take more than these people to persuade Daria to enter your lair," he said, pulling off his gloves and sitting in a chair.

Abramo poured a goblet full of wine and handed it to him. "Of course." He filled another and then sat across from Vincenzo.

"So what will you do?"

"Let us consider for a moment. I trust that your return means that you have cut Daria off from her guild and her bankers."

"And her home is in smoldering ruins."

Abramo grinned. "You are a wonder, Vincenzo. That is perfect. What of the others in her house?"

"Dead."

"Any evidence of that?"

Vincenzo dipped a hand into a deep pocket of his jacket and tossed out Beata's glasses.

"What of Marco Adimari?"

"He arrived in a separate vessel. Seeing me with the remnants of Daria's household may have . . . confused him. I elected to keep them apart."

Abramo lifted his glass in silent toast, then rose and went to a tapestry along the wall, pulled it aside, and exposed a cabinet beneath. He pulled a key from his belt and unlocked it, reaching around several objects within to pull out a scroll.

"The letter?" Vincenzo asked.

"Indeed. We will use the letter, Marco, the servant's glasses—whatever means necessary—to draw the Gifted out on our terms."

"You intend to give up the letter?"

"A copy. You will make your way to Daria, tell her you've seen the error of your ways and desire to find restoration to her side. The healer in her, her love for you, will be unable to deny you. And this letter, coveted and sought by the Gifted, will be your key to entry. If not the letter, then these." He turned back to the cabinet and withdrew two objects, swaddled in yellowing, rough cloth.

Vincenzo sat forward and picked up one glass piece, and then the other. "What are they?"

"They are the reason the Gifted still linger here. They are seeking the glass map of Apollos."

Vincenzo sat back to listen to the legend, of how Abramo had beaten them to two of the churches and stolen the peacock urns and their enclosed treasures, just ahead of them.

Vincenzo let out a humorless laugh of wonder. "So how will we bring them to us?"

"We will find a way. Hauled along as our prisoners, or lured along by our treasure."

"But what of the girl, Tessa? She screams any time you or I draw near."

"We shall find our way around her."

"And the others?"

"Trust me, Baron, trust me. I received the most appealing invitation; to a baptism, of all things. You must don fresh clothing. The tide is turning, my friend. The Gifted will soon be ours. And it all begins this night."

ↄ ↄ ↄ

THE baptism was like a thousand others before it, holy words spoken in Latin, anointing with chrism oil, holy water sprinkled from the cardinal's fingertips, a holy cross traced on their foreheads. Piero closed his eyes and prayed that the Holy Spirit would take hold within these children's lives, that they would be forever claimed by the blood of Jesus. He prayed they would know their God in a vital and vibrant way, that people who knew the Christ as a living God would come beside them and mentor them.

The mass ended, and it seemed that the entire cathedral poured outward and traveled en masse to the Morassis' palazzo on the Canal Grande. When the Gifted arrived, there was no room for their skiff. They were all on edge, disquieted by the morning's arrest, Tessa's illness, and the potential of encountering people they would rather not. Gianni shouted at a deckhand, insisting that room be made for them. But after a moment, it mattered little. Another group of nobles arrived, tying their skiffs to Daria's, creating a makeshift dock. So many people did the same that the Canalazzo was soon almost shut off, narrowed to a point that only one vessel at a time could pass.

People trudged across them all, all flowing into the magnificent Morassi palazzo that peered over the Canalazzo like a queen. She was one of the ten finest homes along the canal—once three separate mansions that had been combined into one, with a new façade to tie them all together—and the Venetian people claimed that someday all would equal her in presence.

"Brace yourself, friends," Piero said softly to the Gifted. "I would not doubt that we will face off with the enemy in some fashion here. But we must carry on, carry through it. Keep your eyes on our joint goal, our ultimate call. Understood?"

He looked about and all gave him a nod.

Two men appeared before the palazzo and waved them forward.

"M'lady," said one. "The conte and contessa would like you and yours to join them at the head table. Come. Follow me."

As they were entering, three guards grabbed Hasani and shoved him to a wall. He grunted quietly and Daria cried out.

"No slaves inside," barked a knight toward her.

"He is no slave," she said, coming around him, side by side with Hasani. "He is a freed man."

"Show your papers, then," said the knight to Hasani.

Hasani reached for the small satchel he had worn forever at his waist. Inside were documents that Daria's father had signed long ago. He opened them and handed them to a guard.

"That is not necessary," said a voice behind them.

Daria whirled.

Vincenzo del Buco. And Marco.

Daria took a step backward, confused in a twin desire to both run from them and run to them. Vincenzo! Marco! The desire for home surged through her. Gianni's hand came to her elbow, and she suddenly was aware of his presence behind her. It gave her strength.

Vincenzo spoke to the knight holding Hasani, but his eyes were only on Daria. "I can vouch for the man. He is a freed man, all right. No need to check his papers. Impede the lady's progress no longer. The contessa has asked for her."

Daria studied him carefully. He appeared reserved, but she could see none of the hollow darkness she had seen in Il Campo. He looked rather well, far better than earlier in the year, in fact. Had he changed? How did he know the Morassis? And what of Marco? She dared to let her eyes meet his. He seemed agitated, but more reserved.

"I, too, can vouch for the man. Return his papers and leave him at once," Marco said to the guards.

"Yes, m'lord," the knight said, reaching for Hasani's satchel and stuffing his papers back in. He stared into the tall black man's face, but Hasani's eyes remained on Vincenzo. "You may proceed inward, but your kind is not welcome above the first *piano*. Understood?"

Hasani nodded once, used to such gruff treatment. Interrogation, doubt, displeasure. He seemed to let it roll past him. But his eyes looked where the rest of his friends looked—upon a man they had not seen for months, a potential enemy.

"Daria, we must speak to you in private as soon as possible," Vincenzo said. Up closer, Daria could see that his eyes were wreathed in sorrow, pain, and Daria longed to embrace him.

"Nay, I cannot allow that," Gianni said, stepping between them.

"We have urgent news of Siena and the guild," Vincenzo said. "And more. Please. Let us find a moment this night. It cannot wait. You may have Gianni and the others with you. I have made grave errors. I long only to make amends. And to tell you what we must."

Daria paused. She had prayed for a way to bridge the gap with Vincenzo, Marco. To find healing . . . and what of the guild? Urgent news? She had to allow them a moment. She glanced at Piero. His eyes were wary, but he did not shake his head at her unspoken question. "I will consider your request, Baron. Forgive me my guard. Considering our last exchange—"

"Of course, of course," Vincenzo said, waving her words away. "I understand. I deserve nothing. But I ask it of you anyway."

"Very well," she said. "We will try to find the opportune moment to speak." She moved away, to the grand staircase, conscientiously avoiding looking at Marco again. Her people closed in around her, Gianni offering her his arm. She took it, gratefully, suddenly feeling as if she could not breathe well among the crush of people.

"I do not trust him, Daria," Gianni said.

"Nor do I," Piero said from her other side. "But everyone deserves a chance at redemption. Let us not be quick with judgment, Gianni. Even the lowest of us can find forgiveness from heaven. Mayhap the baron and Adimari have seen the error of their ways. Mayhap they have been sent to help us battle the Sorcerer."

"Mayhap it's all a ruse," Gianni said. The muscles in his cheek tensed and relaxed repeatedly. His green eyes scanned the people before them.

Daria began breathing so rapidly that she paused, suddenly feeling as if she were drowning in the folds of her dress.

"Daria?" Gianni said anxiously, scanning her face. He pulled her out of the crush of the crowd and to a narrow room, then inward.

The room was spinning around Daria and she could feel her knees give way. Gianni picked her up in his arms and carried her to a bench in the corner, laying her gently upon it. "Daria? Take deep breaths, m'lady."

Piero came around and took her hand. "It is much to bear; I know, daughter. But God has given you the strength to see this through. Find that within you. Find it. 'For who is God besides the Lord? And who is the Rock except our God? It is God who arms me with strength and makes my way perfect.' "

Daria focused on his words, repeating them, letting them seep into her bones. *It is God who arms me with strength, God arms me with strength, God arms me with strength* . . . And as she did so, her breathing became more measured, calm. She opened her eyes to study Gianni, so close, so caring, then brought a hand to her forehead, embarrassed. "Forgive my foolishness. It was . . . Vincenzo and . . . I, uh . . . and Basilio. Rune. I—" She shook her head and rose to a sitting position. "I am once more the fool."

"Nay, m'lady. You are never foolish in my eyes," Gianni said. "Are you ready? I will be beside you every step. I shall not leave you. Do you trust me?"

She studied his fervent, devoted expression. "Come. Let us get on with it."

He took her hand and assisted her to her feet, staring intently into her eyes.

She glanced quickly toward Piero, but he had already moved to open the door. They rejoined the crowd who were climbing the stairs, then moved out to an open back porch, planted heavily in the style of an English garden. Containers were kept free of weeds and watered liberally from several cisterns that served only this palazzo. A giant willow was at its center, a lovely imported gem that was showing the impact of its transplant by the drying leaves on her limbs. Daria knew that in a wealthy household like this, it could be replaced the following week with a new import from the mainland.

Huge tables had been draped in the finest of silk cloth, a delicate pearl. Never had she seen such fabric used for a table! Daria ran her hand across it, remembering different times, happy times when she could do the same in their guild warehouses. The guild seemed far away, forever and an age past since her fingers had touched such finery . . . she looked up to scan the crowd for Vincenzo and saw that he stared in her direction. He gave her a tender smile, as if recognizing her thoughts, and she involuntarily returned it. What was that, right behind his eyes? Sorrow?

She turned away, frightened by what she was feeling, doubting herself. She well remembered that last dark night in Siena. When she closed her eyes, she could still feel the cold wave of fear and a sheer drop wash over her. A sheer drop, that was what it had been. Normally, she felt the push back of humanity within others. But that night, that night when she had stared into the eyes of Amidei and Vincenzo, she had known nothing but emptiness, a wasting away that took her very breath. Death. *Leave the dead to tend the dead,* her Father had said to her. Had Vincenzo escaped? Was he free? Had Marco come to his aid? Deep within, she knew she would need to hear them out. They had all shared too much to not give them that.

Gianni again offered his arm and led her to the table, beside the Conte and Contessa Morassi. Gracia Morassi smiled at her and kissed her on both cheeks. She promptly turned to a nursemaid, took the tiny Angelo from her arms, and placed the child in Daria's. He was tightly bundled and sound asleep, a precious, beautiful babe. Daria smiled and stroked his soft cheek with a finger.

A chill, like a cold breath upon her neck, brought her head upright. She scanned the crowd. She had not felt such a thing since, since . . . there.

Abramo Amidei. A young woman hung on his arm. But his eyes were only on Daria.

Daria fought for breath, to appear unfettered. Her eyes went back to the baby and she attempted to smile down at the child as if she feared nothing. "Gianni . . ." she said, still staring at Angelo as if speaking to the baby, not her captain.

"I see him. Pay him no heed. He will not try anything here, Daria. The doge is making his way up the stairs as we speak. Do not let him spook you. Simply carry on. Pretend as if this were a celebration that your own parents host, and you were surrounded by loved ones. Can you cling to such a vision?"

"Mayhap. Is Vincenzo anywhere near him?"

"Nay. He is on the opposite side of the gardens. Speaking to another noble, along with Adimari. He appears . . . troubled by Amidei's arrival."

"Mayhap they had a falling out. Mayhap Vincenzo truly is seeking forgiveness."

"Mayhap it is a ruse." He stared at her until she met his gaze. "Promise me you shall keep up your guard."

"I shall," she promised.

The doge and his minions arrived then. They paraded into the garden—four priests, two bishops, two cardinals, the doge and dogessa—his third wife—then six guards, straight to the table set on an elevated plain, as if they had done so before. Mayhap they had.

Daria studied the curious older man, edging into his eighth decade to be sure, and his fine robes and pointed, bejeweled hat. The duke of Venezia. A power who dared to taunt kings and pope alike. The jailer of her comrades. What did God intend for her here? Would she have the chance to speak to him? Could she do anything? Or was it best to hope he would not notice her at all?

She noticed Gianni's rigid posture and followed his gaze to one of the cardinals. She had seen him somewhere before . . . "Gianni?"

The cardinal looked over to them and smiled softly.

"He is my cardinal," Gianni whispered lowly to her. "Cardinal Boeri. Cardinal Boeri de Vaticana de Roma."

"De Vaticana?" Daria whispered. She could ask no more. The doge neared and she turned to pass the baby back to the nursemaid.

"Doge," Conte Morassi said, bowing regally to the doge. "You honor us with your presence."

The doge sniffed and held out his hand for the conte to kiss. "I had to see for myself the miracle of your twin children. Did the midwives not all tell you that they would die and take your wife with them?"

Daria stirred in anger at the callous, thoughtless words of the old man. He even sounded disappointed that all had not turned out as they thought it would. Conte Morassi swallowed hard, then nodded soberly. "It was as you say. But God sent us a miracle."

"So I have heard," the doge said, his eyes flitting toward Daria. "The fabled Duchess d'Angelo." Escaping notice was apparently impossible. Somehow, he already knew of her. "May I ask what brought you so far from your home, m'lady?"

The entire group had grown silent, all eyes upon Daria and the doge.

"Ah yes, your reputation precedes you," the doge said smugly, stepping toward her. "There is little in my fair city that I do not know. And when a noble secures one of our finest mansions, then proves to be the employer of men brought to my prisons, and the savior of two of my youngest citizens," he paused to smile over the infants in the Morassis' arms, "I set out to know more."

"Venezia is the finest city I have ever seen. Is that not reason enough to bring me to your domain? And as to the events of the morn," Daria said, "I believe you will soon know Sir Rune of Germany and Basilio Montinelli as the innocent and honest men that they are."

He paused and smiled. "You are obviously as courageous as you are beautiful. We shall see if your words bear truth. But in the meantime, accept my gratitude for aiding our lovely Contessa Morassi and the birth of these fine children."

She curtseyed deeply, took his hand, and kissed it. "You are more than kind, Doge Gradenigo. And I believe my men shall find freedom in due time, in this city, famed for her justice."

"Intriguing," he said, his cold, old eyes still looking her over. "We have much of which to speak," he said. "You shall stay for the entire evening?"

"Nay, I am afraid—"

He leaned close, so only she could hear him. His voice was as crisp and clear as his eyes. "My dear girl, you *shall* stay for the entire evening. I will know more about the intriguing Duchess d'Angelo, healer of lepers and savior of twins and employer of scoundrels. Now raise your head and say, 'I shall be honored, Doge.' "

Daria raised her head at once, but kept her eyes to the ground. "I shall be honored, Doge."

CHAPTER TWENTY

As the feast began, Daria took the opportunity to sink into her seat at the Morassis' table. She tried to lift a goblet for a sip, but she was shaking so badly, the wine threatened to slosh over the side. A massive hand covered her own, beneath the folds of pearl silk. Gianni. It was highly inappropriate, but she welcomed the warmth, the strength of his fingers, and could not find it within her to pull her hand from his. It steadied her. He meant it as a bond of friendship, solidarity. Did he not?

Wave after wave of servants came to the gardens then, serving them first delicious fruits, then sumptuous soup, and finally five giant, roasted hogs, their jaws clamping down on a baked apple, each beast carried by four men. They were placed between the many tables, and carvers set to work to distribute the precious meat. Others carried fresh breads, hot from the ovens.

"Fresh pork is always the meat of choice for Venetian feasts," said the conte, waving a chunk in her direction upon his knife. "Due to the fact that it was a layer of pork that shielded the precious shipment of Santo Marco."

Daria sat back after only a few bites of the meat. The thought of spoiled pork in a ship's hold threatened to turn her stomach. Her mind immediately went to Tessa, wondering if she was all right, what she had eaten . . . and then to the glass pieces of Apollos's map that had been smuggled from Alexandria along with the body of Santo Marco.

Angelo began wailing then, and immediately his sister joined in.

"Time for the wet nurse," the contessa said, raising a brow. "Come. It appears you have had your fill as well. Will you join me, Lady d'Angelo, in taking the twins to the nursery?"

"Of course," Daria said, rising. All the men at their table rose as well. Gianni took a step as if to go with them.

"Nay, nay," the contessa said. "You must eat far more, Sir Gianni. I will look after your lady. You enjoy the feast."

Gianni cast anxious eyes from their host to Daria.

"It is all right, Sir Gianni. We can look after the babies. You stay here and make certain all remain as you do, eating until you can eat no more." Her tone was light but her words carefully chosen.

"You demand much of me, m'lady," Gianni quipped, pretending to be delighted at the thought of more food, and the contessa laughed.

Gracia led her into the palazzo. The back hallways were narrow and serpentine, turning and climbing in ways that made Daria's head spin.

"The owners of these mansions before us," Gracia said, "kept adding to them, building them bigger and bigger. Thus the floors are not all level and the necessity of the stairs. I would have sent the babies with one of our nursemaids, but I must confess, I love holding them, caring for them." She paused and turned in the dim hallway. "You have given us such a gift, Daria. I shall never be able to repay you."

"You are overly generous, Gracia. You owe me nothing. It was an honor to be a part of God's holy work."

"What did the doge say to you?"

"He wishes to speak with me further, later in the evening."

Gracia turned and took her hand. "I heard of the men arrested from your home this morn. Hiring good knights with sterling reputations is more difficult than most would imagine."

"My men are innocent," Daria said, lowering her chin.

"Of course they are. But see that you take care with the doge, friend. He appears old, but he is ruthless. You do not wish to cross him. It was good you agreed to stay for the festivities this night as he required." They passed a narrow, high window, and Daria realized that the feast had gone on for hours, the afternoon soon over. Winter was edging near and the days had become very short.

"I . . . I had not planned on staying, Gracia. I have nothing but this dress to wear, and it is hardly suitable for dancing."

Her hostess turned to study her in the dim light. The baby squirmed in her arms, whimpering and preparing for a full wail of hungry complaint. "You are about my size, just a bit taller. We will return to my apartments and you shall try a few of my dresses."

"I could not."

"Nonsense. You have been through so much this day, and still here you remain, honoring us all with your presence." With that, she disappeared into the nursery. Daria sighed, and as the tiny girl in her arms began to wail too, she entered the dark room. Did everyone she met feel they could order her about?

༒ ༒ ༒

"Come," Gracia said. "Let us go and see if any of my gowns will fit you. If not, you shall need to send that handsome knight to your home to fetch one for you."

Daria smiled. "I doubt that he would appreciate such an errand."

"I believe that man would do anything for you."

"What do you mean?"

"Why, he is desperately in love with you, Daria. Can you not see it?"

"Nay," Daria said, hand on her throat. She was glad for the encroaching darkness in the cramped back hallways of the palazzo, for surely the contessa would have laughed to see the blush climbing her neck.

Gracia leaned in. "Open your eyes, m'lady. He is a fine catch. He simply needs encouragement from you."

"Nay," she whispered, wondering at the thundering within her heart.

"Yea," the contessa returned with a flash of teeth. "He cannot have come from nothing. Surely he has enough to be a suitable suitor. Let me guess . . . younger son of landed gentry?"

"I believe so, but—"

"And he became a knight. It's lovely, really. There is nothing more winning to a woman than a man who can defend her. Wouldn't you agree?"

"Well, yes, but—"

"I will see that you two are side by side in the dances tonight. If he can manage as well on the dance floor as he certainly does in battle, I see not—"

"*Gracia.* Please. This is hardly suitable conversation. I do not wish to have a suitor."

Her new friend stepped back and tried to study her in the dim light. "You may say that now, Daria. But if you can fit into the gown of which I'm thinking, you'll have more than one tonight."

She turned and walked away, obviously assuming that Daria was following her. Again, Daria had no choice. She did not like the dark walkways, and wished she had found an excuse for Gianni to follow them. Hasani was downstairs, relegated to the first-floor hallway, even as a freed slave. Piero had been squired away by the other priests, longing for word of Roma and Toscana. Again, it had hardly been suitable for him to cling to his lady. Remaining together had proven much more difficult than expected.

The hallways widened as they neared the contessa's apartments. Try as she might, Daria had no sense of where she was in the palazzo. She tried to think of a question that would lead Gracia into telling her where she was, but nothing sounded right in her own ears. So she remained silent.

Suddenly, the contessa paused and leaned hard against the wall outside her apartment.

"Contessa?" Daria said, walking around her. "Are you well?"

"Just a bit weak, I'm afraid," she returned, bringing a slight hand to her brow.

"This is a great deal for a new mother to manage, so soon after the birth," Daria said. "Are you bleeding?"

"Very little. I am fine. Simply weary."

"Well, you must rest upon your bed while I try on the gowns."

"I believe I shall."

The contessa called for a maid, but all appeared to be out in the gardens.

"It is all right," Daria soothed. "Please, be at ease, Gracia. Direct me to the trunk where I will find the dresses and I shall get right to our task." She helped the shorter woman to the bed, admiring the golden gown the contessa was to don for the dances, already spread across the bed.

"Over there, in the far trunk. There are two that have not been altered yet for me and may be a good fit for you. One is an ivory silk, the other is deep blue."

Daria strode over to the corner and opened the heavy lid. Dresses of every color were neatly folded within. She searched for the ivory and blue and pulled them from the piles and flung them outward. Each had a small train and was made of some of the finest fabric she had ever seen, probably imported from England, possibly France. Rarely had anything like this come through even the guild's warehouses . . . and when they had, they were sold for only the highest prices.

She carried them over to a dressing screen and stretched them over the wooden frame, admiring the cut of each skirt, the fine craftsmanship. It made her long for her dresses at home, in Siena, left behind in their flight. Even if she had sent Gianni back to the mansion for another gown, he would have been able to choose from only three others, none of them suitable for a formal dance. She glanced back at the contessa.

Her hostess already dozed, snoring softly from her bed. Daria smiled at the incongruous sound from such a lady and circled around the dressing screen to disrobe. When she was down to her undergarments, a sound in the room gave her pause.

"M'lady?" she called.

But she was greeted only with a soft answering snore.

Daria ducked her head around the screen, peering in the dim light to see if she could spy anything amiss. She chastised herself. It had taken only a brief meeting with Vincenzo and Marco and a glimpse of Abramo to set her teeth on edge.

She returned to the dresses, attempting to save Tessa's work upon her hair, trying the dark-blue gown on first. There was no underdress to these, only one long piece that was far more fitted than she was used to. This was the higher-necked one, touching the hollow at the base of her throat but reaching off the shoulder. A bit tight, she thought.

She managed to unbutton the back and slip out of it. Daria listened for the contessa's soft breathing, then turned to the ivory gown and slipped it over her shoulders and down across her narrow hips. It plunged daringly low at the neck and even came in a bit at the waist. Daria frowned. Never had she worn such a thing. Surely this was not the fashion rage among her neighbors to the north! She would have to send Hasani or Gianni to the mansion for one of her gowns after all, if this was as scandalous as she thought . . .

Daria ventured from behind the screen and went to three candles on the nightstand, bending to light the second and third from the first. There. Much more light now. She gazed over at the contessa and smiled. The poor lady was incredibly weary, desperate for all the rest she could get! Such foolishness was this, a feast and festivities so soon after being delivered of two children!

She sighed and went to the long looking glass, held by a frame of wood and angled so that one could see oneself from head to toe. Never had Daria seen one of such height or clarity. The mirror was speckled with black, but boasted large areas of clear silver. She edged in front of it and gasped a bit at her image. The gown was entirely too fitted, clinging to her shoulders and arms, exposing the long length of her narrow neck, the peeking edge of rounded breast and shadowed valley of cleavage, even the ebb and flow of hip. It plunged to the floor, reminding Daria of a fish's tail as it scooped outward behind her.

But the design was effective. As a guildswoman of cloth, she was a bit spellbound at the daring craftsmanship. She turned left and right, willing herself to take it off, determined to find something more suitable.

"Goddess," whispered a low, gravelly voice.

Daria whirled. Cold air washed over her neck and down to her breast.

She turned again and again, trying to plumb the shadows as if she could see in the dark. From where had he spoken? Who was it?

The three candles were not enough for the cavernous room.

"You are beautiful," said a voice clearly.

Daria turned toward it. A hulking man leaned against the wall, but his voice becalmed her. "Gianni?"

She whipped back around to face the mirror, embarrassed to have Gianni see her in such a gown as this. This was not the dress of a modest noblewoman!

But then his arms moved around her, pulling her gently against his hard chest. She tensed at first and then relaxed, liking the feel of his strong arms wrapped about her waist. A man's arms about her . . . not since Marco . . . He kissed her then. Softly, so softly and tenderly upon her head. Then, slowly, reverently upon her shoulder. Then again, a bit farther up toward her neck, making his way steadily toward her ear. She kept her eyes closed, feeling the rush that danced across her skin as he kissed her again and again. "Gianni, we should not . . . the contessa . . ."

"She shall not wake." He kissed her harder then, and his hands began cascading across her body, across the flat of her belly, across the swell of her hips, down her thighs, up to her breasts. "You smell of orange blossoms. It is just as I imagined . . ."

Daria shook her head. "Wait. Wait. This is not proper. We must not . . ." She took his hands, keeping them from roving any longer, and stared into the looking glass.

But the man who stared back at her was not Gianni de Capezzana.

It was Abramo Amidei.

ҩ ҩ ҩ

DARIA screamed and kept screaming until several servants came running from the far reaches of the palazzo, until the contessa shook her and she clamped her mouth shut.

"Daria, Daria, you are safe. No one is here but us."

The contessa stood before her. Daria had backed into a corner. "There was a man in the room. He was . . . there was a man in this room."

"You are safe, friend. You are safe! It is only us." She attempted a shallow laugh. "You must have dozed off as quickly as I and had a nightmare."

"But I did not sleep. I was trying on your gowns . . ."

"And I see you found a lovely one. Come, my maids will help me into my gown and we shall join the festivities. Can you hear the music? We've undoubtedly been missed by now. Most inappropriate to tarry so long. The doge himself will be looking for you!"

Gianni appeared then in the doorway, panting from exertion. "M'lady, there you are. I have searched this entire palazzo for you."

She raised her eyebrows, staring at him in confusion. It had been he, had it not? His voice, his touch? He and Abramo were of similar height, but Amidei was a bit taller as Gianni was a bit broader. What black magic was this?

"I am glad you found me," she said.

He immediately took a step inward, disliking the weak tone of her voice.

"Nay, Sir!" cried the contessa playfully. "I know your lady looks like a queen, but you must wait to see us down to the dance. Out, out. We shall accompany you in a moment."

Gianni reluctantly bowed and left the room. "I shall be right outside your door, m'lady," he said, staring into Daria's eyes.

She nodded. "See that you remain right there." Did his arrival mean that Amidei or Vincenzo had departed the gardens? Had it truly been Amidei here, in this room, or had it only been a nightmare? And why had she accepted the kisses, the embrace, when she believed it to be Gianni? She lifted a hand to her head.

In minutes the contessa was changed and ready for the dance floor. "Come," she said, taking Daria's arm. Daria snapped out of her trance. "I cannot. I cannot go out in such a dress."

"Of course you can! This is all that anyone is wearing in among the Frankish or English. You shall begin a new trend here in Venezia and garner all the attention you deserve. Come, Daria. I have yet to introduce you to the patron families of San Giacometto, as you have asked. We cannot tarry any longer."

She walked behind the contessa, feeling the hot, confused stare of Gianni as he looked at her with open compliment in his eyes, then looked away, appearing embarrassed. It was an unsuitable dress, but there was nothing for it. They turned one corner and then another, drawing near to the revelry. Shouts were heard, along with lively music—strings and a delicate drum.

They entered the wide expanse of the third *piano,* and Daria paused. The walls were ringed with dripping candles, casting warm light across the entire room. The windows were wide open to let in the cool winter evening air to counterbalance the heat of the dancers. Rings of people cascaded by, smiling and glistening with their exertion.

Daria was thankful that they were all preoccupied. It kept their attention from her. She needed to speak as briefly as possible to the doge, meet the patron families, seek out Vincenzo, and then make her escape. The doge was seated on the far side of the room, with a cardinal at one elbow, the much younger dogessa on the other, watching the festivities. Daria noticed many of the women had donned more exotic gowns, some as daring as her own, although the men remained in their morning church attire.

She searched the room for Abramo, Vincenzo, and Marco—spied only the last two—glanced over her shoulder repeatedly to make certain that Gianni was with her, and slowly made her way through the crowd.

There were certainly more than two hundred guests, and it appeared all were dancing, in celebratory, raucous rings. Repeatedly, they were asked to join in. The contessa had already joined a circle.

One song ended and another began. As it did, there was no choice but for Daria and Gianni to join in. Here, she could feel the wandering, curious looks of the men, and the resulting blush from her neck upward. In time with the music, their small circle joined another and another, until there was a large ring that drew together and apart. In the next stanza, a group of four parted and faced one another. Gianni moved away, barely keeping step with the dance.

Daria focused her attentions on her own, aware she might fall if she did not pay more attention. They moved left, right, then inward.

And Daria came face to face with her love of long ago, a man whose face would forever remind her of Siena, of home.

Marco Adimari.

CHAPTER TWENTY-ONE

SHE knew he was there, of course, thought herself prepared for such a meeting. His presence no longer made her heart leap with grief; it merely left her feeling melancholy. Seeing him, across from her, in a dance . . . a hundred memories from their childhood and their young adulthood and their handfasting cascaded through her mind, capturing her with sudden, surprising homesickness and longing. Daria dropped her arms abruptly and made brief apologies as she departed in a rush. Marco came right after her, out into the hallway.

"Daria, we must speak to you in private."

Lightning flashed, making the revelers scream and laugh. Servants passed them with trays full of wine goblets. Gianni was there, then, beside her. Vincenzo came to them then too.

"Speak now, if you must."

Marco glanced from Daria to her knight. "It must be in private. I assure you, our business is most urgent."

She glanced at Gianni and then led them both toward the far hall. They turned a corner and entered an empty room, lit only by a corner candle. Another flash of lightning lit up the room, followed by a crack of thunder.

"Speak freely," she said to Marco and Vincenzo. "Gianni must hear anything you have to tell me."

The men glanced at the knight again and then Marco began pacing before them. "Daria, I am afraid we bear bad news."

"Out with it."

"We must speak of your seat on the guild council. But there is something more dire you must know. Daria, your home has suffered a fire."

Daria was not that surprised by his first statement. But the second threatened to send her to her knees. Her home? Burned? Her eyes went to Vincenzo, saw the truth of Marco's words within them. Gianni edged closer, as if willing his strength into her without touching her.

"The Sciorias? Our knight? The children? Did all escape unharmed?"

Lightning flashed again and thunder shook the palazzo walls. In the flash of light, Daria had seen the grim look upon both Marco's and Vincenzo's faces.

"Nay, nay," she moaned. "All of them? All of the Sciorias? What of Ambrogio?"

Gianni's strong arm went around her lower back and held her firmly at the hip.

"None remain," Marco said steadily. "Oh, Daria—" He reached for her, but Gianni stopped his hand.

Marco ignored the knight, staring at her. The tears now flowed as she thought of Beata, Agata, Aldo, Nico, Roberto . . . She fought to focus on his words, hoping this was but another nightmare. "Nay. 'Tisn't possible. Nay . . ."

"Listen, Daria. I would protect you if I could. But there is no way for me to do so. My wife is not even aware that I traveled here to see you— she thinks I am here on business; I must return immediately. Please. Only Vincenzo can help you. Jacobi has laid claim to your land again. If he is successful in holding it, there will be no way to rebuild. He is threatening suit against your estate for damage done during the fire, as are your other neighbors. More than twenty mansions were burned to the ground."

"Jacobi?"

"Only fate kept the wind from sending the fire in his direction."

Daria thought of the Bergamos and the Fiadonis, fine families who had lost their homes! And still, Jacobi's stood! More tears came then, bitter tears. And the Sciorias . . .

"Listen, you are liable to lose everything. Everything your father and grandfather worked to attain. Everything that you rely upon."

"It is nothing, nothing, naught but wood and brick and memories . . ." Daria said, weak from the impact of his dark words. She stared up at the ceiling and tears streamed across her cheeks and into her ears. "Were they given proper burial?"

Marco met her gaze. "I will see to it myself. You were formally removed as the guild's co-consul the morn of the fire. Vincenzo fought for you. He fights for you still, to hold your council seat. He came to me and asked that I travel here to tell you. He feared—"

"I feared you would not believe me," Vincenzo said, speaking for the first time.

Marco shook off Gianni's arm and glared at the knight, but Gianni remained where he was. "Daria, listen to Vincenzo. You can trust him. He will guide you on what to do about the guild, the estate."

"Why listen to either of you? You have both betrayed m'lady."

Marco nodded slightly but frowned toward Vincenzo in confusion. "My betrayal is something for which I will never forgive myself. But I never lied to you, Daria. Did I?"

Daria was slow to answer. Then, softly, "Nay, Marco. You were always honest with me." Her eyes again went to Vincenzo, hovering in the shadows. "He took no part in removing me from my position?"

"From what I know, he fought for you to the end. Please . . . I cannot remain here with you. But listen to him. Listen to him. He is your only hope."

Daria raised her chin and stared out as the storm raged, sending sheets of rain into the room.

"I have with me several documents," Vincenzo said. "They are legal documents that will help you begin your fight to keep your seat on the guild's council, for your estate and for access to your bank accounts."

Daria's eyes went wide. "My bank accounts? Why would I not have access to them?"

"My dear, the fires, they ravaged many. Marco can tell you that the Nine are busy, hearing all those families lay claim to your fortune to cover their own losses. It will take some time, but I believe I can help you salvage a portion."

"And as co-consul? What of that position?"

"Daria, you know as well as I that you can no longer maintain a seat. You abandoned your responsibilities on this mad quest you are on . . .

you left Ambrogio, of all people, in your stead. Surely you did not think he could fill such a post."

"Nay," Daria said, lifting a hand to her head. "I did not truly realize how long I would be away. And now . . . it matters not. None of it matters. The Sciorias . . . Ambrogio . . . all is lost."

"Not all," Gianni said.

"Daria, there is something else." Vincenzo paused, with his hand half under his jacket, and glanced to the door.

"I must return to the dance to pay my respects to the doge and the conte, and then depart. My task here is done," Marco said graciously, turning and walking to the door. "I pray that you shall listen to Vincenzo, Daria, and that he will assist you in righting the wrongs against you and yours. I will see to your beloved servants, Daria. They were dear to me too."

"Thank you, Marco."

"Farewell," he said, breaking their intense gaze.

"Farewell, Marco."

Daria turned back to the table where Vincenzo now stood, unfurling documents. He pulled a quill from his pocket, as well as a tiny corked silver well of ink.

"I hope you do not believe that I shall sign these now, without a thorough review."

"Nay?" He raised his eyebrows. "Very well. Take them. Sign them when you wish. But be advised that every day you tarry is a day that goes by in which Marco could fight for your cause in Siena. He leaves at daybreak. Are you certain you do not wish for him to carry these with him?"

Daria paused. "Mayhap. But I must read them, at the very least. I shall need a moment."

"Take it," Vincenzo said. He strode to the windows and closed the shutters as she read, Gianni close at hand and reading them as well. Daria knew Vincenzo was moving slowly, methodically, waiting for her to be done with her task, giving her the space she needed to focus. She had read through the first document and was halfway through the second when he spoke.

"Someday you will be done with your odd task and will wish to return home, Daria. I look forward to that day. In that light, I have taken something from Abramo Amidei to assist you. Something you and yours would very much like to see."

He slipped his hand under his jacket again and pulled out an ancient lambskin scroll, tied with a leather riband, so similar to . . .

Daria's breath caught and she could feel Gianni straighten behind her.

"I hope this will convince you that I am not your foe, Daria," he said, drawing near. He tossed the scroll to the small table.

The storm was raging now, lightning cracking overhead again and again, thunder rocking the walls around them. She felt it resonate deep within her, not remembering such a storm in all of her days.

With trembling hands, she reached for the scroll and then pulled away, glancing at Gianni. He moved around her and reached for it, untied it, unrolled it, and slipped the sheets from its folds. "Daria," he said with a heavy breath. He spread the three sheets across the table. They were part of their letter.

Illuminations screamed to them from the margins. A fisherman upon the sea, surrounded in waves, casting his nets. A sea monster menacing a knight, priest, and lady on the shore . . .

Gianni moved aside the sheet to expose the last. Vincenzo was across from him, leaning down as if to study the letter himself. But Gianni and Daria were staring at the man in black, a dragon on his chest as if it were a coat of arms. They both knew him. Their enemy, once Vincenzo's friend. Abramo Amidei.

"That you would allow us to see these, Vincenzo . . ." Daria said. "You have parted ways with Amidei? Seen him for who he really is?"

"I well know Abramo Amidei for who he is," Vincenzo said grimly.

Daria's heart softened. "I have prayed so fervently for you . . . that you might know the truth . . ." She reached out a hand to him, and he took it. She returned her attention to the table and Gianni, the letter. She picked up the first page and began to translate the words in her mind.

Gianni looked at his fingers and lifted them into her line of vision, showing her how a fine white dust coated them. It seemed to coat all three pages. He rubbed his fingertips together, feeling the fine grit of it. And then he looked up at Vincenzo. "You have brought this for us? You are giving it to us?"

"I wish to assist Daria. If this is what she seeks, it is hers. Abramo seemed intent on keeping it from you. I assumed it would be of some assistance to your cause. He will do all he can to bring you down. I knew I must come to your aid."

Daria's heart leapt. Mayhap this was the Lord's way of making things right for her. Restoring Vincenzo to her. Helping the Gifted along their way.

"Daria, I beg you. Sign these papers. Be on your way, with Abramo's letter, wherever you must go. But let me return to Siena and fight for what is yours. So you have something to return to when your task is complete."

Daria looked up at him and saw love and compassion in his eyes, her old uncle, the man she had once known. In this most sorrowful of days, he had brought her hope. He still fought for her! He had found his way. The agony over the loss of her home, the Sciorias, warred with her triumphant joy that Vincenzo again was entering her life.

Her decision made, she reached for the silver inkwell and uncapped it, dipping the quill.

"Daria . . ." Gianni said.

"I must," she hissed, irritated that he might question her. This was right . . . her hope. Her future.

She signed the first document and then the next and then the next.

She had expected Gianni to speak out again, particularly on the last one, which she hadn't even cursorily read. Daria glanced up at him.

He was sniffing his fingers, staring at them with wide eyes, fighting for clarity, understanding. He appeared as if someone had struck him across the crown.

"Gianni . . ."

The knight fell to his knees then, leaning so hard against the table it began to tip.

"Gianni!" She looked to Vincenzo for help. But he was not looking in their direction. He slipped a second glove onto his right hand and gingerly picked up the documents Daria had signed.

"Vincenzo," Daria said, dread cascading through her in nauseating waves. "No," she said, tears of renewed grief again stinging her eyes.

But now he had moved on to stacking the precious sheets of the letter.

Gianni appeared frozen, hands clinging to the table's edge, eyes wide and unseeing. "Poison," he whispered. "Poison."

Daria looked from him to Vincenzo as her once-beloved uncle completed his stacking and lifted the papers in her direction as if to hand them to her.

"Daria?" he said, lifting them up to her chin. They cupped in a half funnel. She was reaching for them, as if in a dream, when she saw him turn aside, take a deep breath. When he faced her again, he blew, sending a cloud of the fine white dust toward her.

She gasped, and in that second, smelled the bitter odor as it entered her nostril, felt the burn of it upon her tongue.

☙ ☙ ☙

ABRAMO Amidei was joined by several others, and he began his incantations, circling the palazzo, laying his hand on section after section. He lifted his face to the sky, feeling the cold rain upon his face like the baptism of his dark lord. He grinned as lightning cracked so close that he felt the hairs on his neck raise and could feel the rumble of thunder in his bones.

Never before had this palazzo held so many. It was burdened. Her piers and supports were weary. He whispered dark words, envisioning the walls come down before him. Over and over, the lightning cracked, hovering above them. His peers went to their knees and echoed every word he uttered. By now, he was shouting to be heard. He entered the garden and continued to cast his spell, arcing hands toward the palazzo. Inside were his enemies. Inside were the remnants of the Gifted. Tonight they would be brought to their knees . . . tonight they would begin to fall.

A lightning bolt cracked behind him, hitting the old willow and sending a surge through Abramo like he had never known before. Using every ounce of strength within him, he cast an arm out toward the palazzo roof. Another bolt of lightning struck the willow again. And as the lightning arced to the palazzo roof, even in the midst of the rain, a smoldering fire began.

☙ ☙ ☙

SHE stumbled away, her mind fogging, fighting for clarity. She fumbled her way backward until the wall met her back, held her there.

He reached out to her, offering his hand. "Dear Daria. My darling Daria. Come."

She leaned against the wall, cold, so cold. And weak. What was happening here? Why did she feel that all the hard, good work she had done alongside the Gifted was slowly unraveling? Was it all over? Or was she ill? She needed help.

Help . . .

Vincenzo walked toward her, and suddenly there were two of him, striding toward her at an impossible angle.

"Uncle!" she cried in fear.

He was there then, taking her in his long, lanky arms. He held her close, shushing her with his whispers.

"Uncle, the Sciorias . . . something terrible has happened."

"I know, Daria. Shh. Shh. It will be all right. It will be all right."

ლ ლ ლ

"Something is amiss," Piero said, joining Hasani. "We must be away immediately."

Hasani rose from his place at the wall, hand immediately on his curved sword.

"I went to join Daria and Gianni and they are absent, not to be found in the gardens nor with the others who still dance above. I cannot find them anywhere. Worse, Amidei, Vincenzo, and Marco are gone as well."

Hasani turned and ran with Piero back up the stairs, past the guards who had detained him earlier. They shouted in outrage and gave chase.

Hasani and Piero continued upward, racing up the stairs. "This way!" Piero said quietly. They ran down a dark hallway and ducked into a small room, hoping the guards would pass them by. The two men rumbled past.

It was then that Piero first smelled the smoke.

He glanced toward Hasani. "You return to the gardens. I will go back to the dance room. Look in every room as you pass. If you find them, escape at once. We shall meet again outside."

ლ ლ ლ

"Fire!" someone screamed outside their door. "Fire!"

"Get out! The palazzo is afire!" screamed another.

A group of people lumbered past. A woman fell right before the door. Others trampled over her, clambered over her, wouldn't let her up. She fought for a moment, got halfway up, and then was pushed down again. It was a mass of people all trying to get through an impossibly small hallway. To freedom. To the water. Away from the flames.

Vincenzo led Daria to the window and looked back and forth. "There is room. We're only a floor up from the canal!" He reached out his hand. "Daria. Do you trust me?"

Daria looked to Gianni, who appeared to be asleep on the floor, even as rain from a shuttered window that had burst open now covered his face in drops and drips. Dimly, she wondered if she should go to him, but she knew she could not make it . . .

"Daria," her uncle said soothingly.

She was wavering on her feet, fighting to stay upright. Daria glanced back to the hallway. Another had fallen, right before their doorway, making it a slight wall. People were screaming and shoving, a constant, moving mass.

Choking smoke billowed down the hallway. In seconds, a brown haze filled the room.

"Daria! We must jump!" Vincenzo cried.

Daria stepped toward Vincenzo, feeling as if she were watching herself in a dream. She looked to him, then to the still waters of the canal, just ten feet below.

"Gianni . . ."

"First I see to your welfare," Vincenzo said firmly. "Then him."

Daria looked outward, barely keeping herself from tumbling out the window. A narrow spot was right below them, where a skiff had been tied earlier. Crimson and pumpkin flames reflected in the water in an eerie dance. She could hear screams behind her, but it was as if she were already under water, unable to hear them in anything but a muffled pulse in her ears.

She leaned heavily toward Vincenzo, no longer able to keep her feet. "Uncle . . . Gia . . . Gianni. He said . . . said poison. What if . . ."

But she could not complete her question.

Vincenzo picked her up, leaned through the open shutters over the water, and released her.

CHAPTER TWENTY-TWO

IT was a nightmare. The crush of people, faces covered in soot and fear. So many people, and not yet Daria or Gianni. Where were they? Had they already escaped? Piero searched hallway after hallway, again lost in their maze in the dark and the smoke.

He came face to face with Cardinal Boeri, a man he had known in his days in Roma, but who had seldom given him the time of day. Piero had never been ambitious or political enough.

"Father Piero!" the cardinal intoned, taking him by the shoulders. "Where is Sir Gianni? The Duchess?"

"I know not! I seek them as well!"

"I will go this way and you go the other."

Piero frowned. Why would the cardinal go to such lengths for a knight who had abandoned his post? But it mattered not. The house was immense. If the cardinal would help him search for Daria and Gianni, he was glad for the assistance.

He turned a corner and climbed a flight of stairs, where he found the nursemaid, slumped to the ground, wailing in fear. "The babies!" she cried. "I could not get them out!"

"Where are they?"

"They are dead! There is no way they could still live! We will all die here!"

Piero took the girl by the shoulders and shook her. "Where are they?"

"Down there!" she sobbed. "Down *there!*"

Piero turned to where she had pointed. The hallway was a mass of flames, licking up the walls, climbing across the ceiling. The door to the nursery had smoke pouring from beneath it.

"Nay!" he cried. "God did not save you to die here!" He barreled down the hallway and struck the door, rolling inside. The room was full of smoke, but was relatively cool. No fire here. Yet. He turned, looking to a second small room where the babies might have been laid down to rest. Nothing.

He rushed to the next door, seeing it made sense as placement for a nursery. He tentatively tested the wood for heat, then gruffly pushed it open. The room was fairly free of smoke, but it billowed toward them from the hall. The babies coughed lightly in their sleep, barely aware that death lurked so near their tiny beating hearts.

"Thank you, Father. Thank you, Jesus. Help me. Help me get these children to safety."

He took a corner basin and filled it with water, then soaked a blanket for tiny Daria and another for tiny Angelo. "God is here," he cooed, as he wrapped one sleeping, squirming infant and then another. "God has sent me. He is covering us all. He will get us out." Tucking both swaddled infants in his arms, beneath his jacket, he opened the door and stepped back. Fire had made the hallway a tunnel from hell. As he watched, a portion of the floor fell away.

"Hold tight, little ones," Piero said to the babies, now beginning to cry in sleepy complaint. And with that, he ran forward, leaping across the chasm.

ꝏ ꝏ ꝏ

DARIA swam for the surface, gasping for air, gasping at the cold, gasping at the shock.

"Over here!" urged a man.

In the dark, she could barely make out his hand, a silhouette against a backdrop of a palazzo aflame. She reached for the hand and a powerful arm brought her up, up out of the water and before him.

Abramo.

He pulled her close and brought a hand to her throat, pinching her airway shut, whispering into her ear. He smelled of smoke and heat. But his hand was icy upon her wet skin. "Give in, Daria. I shall not kill you here. I have plans for you. Simply give in to the dark. Give in to sleep. You are in my care, Daria."

She struggled weakly against him. But he was too powerful, his arms like iron about her waist. The poison had done too much damage. Her vision spun in swirling fashion, gaining speed. She could not get enough air. The palazzo spun and a wall of black climbed. She had been so foolish . . .

"Very good," Abramo said soothingly, lifting her.

And then the darkness took her.

ණ ණ ණ

Gianni came to, the rain lashing at his face with pounding drops. Moaning with an ache that threatened to split his head, he gained his feet. "Daria?"

Even as his voice cascaded around the empty room, he knew she was gone. There were no more voices within, only fire eating away at the palazzo's skin, moving its way to her very marrow. He took a step, cried out at the pain within his head, and then forced himself to take another. They had been outsmarted, the enemy using the very letter that had brought them all together in order to bring them down.

Gianni entered the hallway and stumbled forward, despite the stinging heat that threatened to melt his cheek and brow. He could smell his hair burning.

Down, down he went, skirting holes of fire in the flooring, leaping and rolling a few times, hard-pressed to rise again and continue.

He very narrowly escaped the palazzo before the roof collapsed to the third *piano*, the third *piano* to the second, the second to the first, the first to the warehouse floor. Within an hour it was a pile of white-hot embers and smoking linens. Ladies covered in soot wandered about, almost unrecognizable, crying, calling out for loved ones. Time after time he stopped a woman, thinking it was Daria, only to be disappointed. He looked about wildly. Had she made it out? Had Piero? Hasani?

ණ ණ ණ

THE twins wailed with the pitiful mewling cry of newborns. They were wet and possibly hungry. Piero widened his focus. He needed to find the conte or contessa, let them know their children were safe.

There. Past twenty people, Piero could see a woman on her knees, crying, hands clutched to her head, facing the building as if wanting to dig through the burning embers. A man clung to her, desperately trying to will comfort into his wife. The conte and contessa.

Piero made his way across the makeshift dock of skiffs, passing many others. The burned palazzo cast off so much heat, no one could remain too near. Finally, the babies' cries drew the contessa's attention. On shaking legs, she rose and looked about madly, trying to determine where they were. Her husband held her by the shoulders, joining in the search.

Piero reached the last group of people that separated them, and went around. When the contessa saw him, she uttered a small moan and ran to him. "Oh, my babies, my babies!" She threw her arms around Piero. "Oh, you have saved them! You have saved them!"

Piero smiled, and when she withdrew he gently passed one twin to her mother, the other to his father.

"Father Piero," the conte said. "Now we owe you and Daria for our children's lives twice over."

"You owe our Lord for sparing them," Piero said, gently clasping him on the shoulder. Streams of tears cleared the soot from the conte's face where the rain had not done its work. "I was merely where my Father placed me."

"Thank you, Father in heaven," the conte whispered, looking up into the silver rain that emerged from a bank of darkness.

"Piero!" shouted a man. The priest turned and spied Gianni, making his way through the crowd to them. He had been struck by something, leaving a huge cut above his right eye. Blood streamed down from it.

"Are you all right?"

"I . . . I am fine."

Piero could easily see he lied. His face was rife with pain.

"Do you know where Hasani or Daria are?"

"Nay. I was hoping they would be with you."

Piero turned toward the Morassis, willing his lips to form the words that must be spoken. "Conte, do you know if everyone made it to safety? Was there anyone trapped inside?"

The man looked up from his tiny son to the knight. "Nay. You and I were some of the last out. I think all were clear before the palazzo fell."

Gianni squinted and looked about. The entire canal reflected the glow of the dying palazzo fire. They stared at every man, every woman. "Do you see them?" he asked Piero, who stood beside him doing the same. *"Do you see them?"*

♋ ♋ ♋

"You have killed her," Vincenzo said, cradling Daria's head in his lap as the oarsmen took them out to sea.

"Nay. She is merely sleeping. When the drug wears off, she will be safely inside our fortress."

"You found it necessary to take her near death?"

"It will only be the first time of many, Vincenzo. You must steel yourself for what is ahead. Daria will not be easy to break. She will hold out against us. But she must be broken. When she does, it will weaken the knight. And without Daria and the knight, the priest will play easily into our hands."

Vincenzo sighed heavily. "What of Hasani?"

Abramo laughed. "I do not believe that Ciro will fail us again."

♋ ♋ ♋

Hasani jumped off the skiff and ran across the island, intent upon finding another vessel on the other side of the island and giving chase to Abramo, Vincenzo, and Daria. He made better time on his long legs than upon the water and ran with everything in him, pausing only to turn one corner and then another. At one point, he thought he had lost his way, and then he spied a tiny neighborhood church that gave him his bearings.

Sputtering candles above icons in alcoves here and there were his only light. The night was even darker than usual with the constant, pounding rain. He ran with his hands out, one before him, one beside him to trace the edge of one building and then another.

He turned a corner and collided with two men, stumbling backward to the cobblestones. He rose up on one elbow and peered, cockeyed, into the rain.

He heard the dreaded sound before he saw them. The metallic clank of iron manacles.

Another man raised a torch. "Runaway?"

"Appears to be a runaway to me," said another.

Hasani went for his sword, but the third man kicked him to his back.

"Nay, nay," Hasani shouted, the best he could.

"What was that?" asked the man with the manacles.

Hasani groaned and reached for his papers. He must get the facts straight. Right here and now. Abramo and Vincenzo would get away with Daria! For the first time in some years, he tried to speak. "Fee. Fee," he tried. *Free. Free.*

"What was that?" repeated the man. "You want me to pay a fee to enslave you? Nay. I've already been paid. And I'll get paid again when I deliver you." He smiled. Hasani could see the flash of ivory teeth even in the dark. Why was he familiar? He was a giant of a man, as broad in the shoulder as . . .

Ciro.

Hope within Hasani came crashing down like the palazzo behind him. It could not have been chance that put this man, this man who had dared to insult Daria, who had tried to infiltrate their enclave in Siena, here.

Ciro leaned down and held out his hands. "You were reaching for your papers, were you not? Go ahead," he said, laughter in his voice. "Give the man room. Lift that torch, there. You all will want to see his face when he gets a look at his *papers.*"

Hasani's mouth went dry even as rain pelted his face. He reached into his pocket and pulled the old leather packet out. He rose to a seated position, shielding the precious papers that bore the mark of master Giulio d'Angelo, that testified that he was a free man, that would keep him from men such as these, as they had done a hundred times before. He pulled them out a bit, looking for the familiar writing, the red wax imprint with the house of d'Angelo's mark of the peacock. . . .

He moved them closer to the torchlight, turned them over.

Blank. They were completely blank.

Ciro began laughing. "Just as I thought!" he crowed. "A runaway! My newest acquisition! This one will fetch a nice price. Take him."

CHAPTER TWENTY-THREE

DARIA awakened and moved a bit, dimly aware of the cool, stone grit beneath her cheek, a dull pain in her shoulder. She moved again, feeling sluggish, as if she had been consuming wine all night. Her head pounded. It was difficult to open her eyes. Where was she?

Vaguely, she realized her hands were bound before her, as were her feet. She groaned and rolled to her back, trying to find a care within her that she was lying on a stone floor in utter darkness. But she could not. Her body cried out for slumber. She was tired . . . so tired. And every time she opened her eyes, she began to spin, spin . . . To say nothing of the horrendous thoughts, memories that loomed over her.

It was better to sleep. Sleep. Sleep.

಄ ಄ ಄

"ARE you mad?" Gianni shouted at the priest.

They had returned to the mansion, hoping against hope that Daria and Hasani had found their way there and then spent the remains of the night in heated debate. Vito and Ugo and tiny Tessa hovered near, staring at them.

"Nay. I am simply asserting that we stay with our plan. We cannot resume our journey without the remainder of the map."

"And even if I agreed to ignore that m'lady and three of our men are gone, we could not even obtain your precious glass piece without Daria," Gianni spat out, pacing. "We have gone over this and over this. She is the only one who could gain us entry to San Giacometto."

"Nonsense. After last night, the Morassis feel that they owe as much to me as they do to Daria. They will assist us."

"Under what guise?"

"I have not made it through all the steps—"

"When you do, send me word. I am going to find them." Gianni strode to the door.

"Excellent. Will you stop and pick up Basilio and Rune on your way?" Vito called. He smiled contritely when the knight whirled on him in fury. "Beggin' your pardon, Captain, but the priest speaks words of wisdom."

"When your comrades fall in battle," Ugo put in, "you have no choice but to continue forward with your attack and then circle back to pick them up."

"Nay," Gianni said. " 'Tis not the same."

"Yes. It is," Ugo said. "We've spoken of this as a battle. We've simply been divided and addressed by the enemy."

Gianni ran anguished hands through his hair and turned to stare at the pink of daybreak streaming through the windows.

Piero joined him there. "We must be fervent in our prayers," he said. "Right now. We must turn to our Savior to show us how we are to move forward."

"It came so fast in Siena," Ugo said, pacing now, behind them. "Sign after sign. Our path was so clear there. Why is God remaining silent here?'

"I know not," Piero said. "I only know that in times of trial, we are told to go to our God and await his direction. Think of Jesus himself in the garden of Gethsemane. For all intents and purposes, he was alone in his darkest hour. And yet he chose to walk the path of utmost faith. We must follow him." He looked solemnly from one face to the other. "Our gathering was foretold. Our end was not. How far are we willing to go in trusting our God?"

None looked him in the eye nor answered his question.

"Come, brothers. Little sister," he said tenderly, holding out a hand to Tessa. "We begin with prayer. And we will go to our God like the persistent widow, begging our Lord to save them, free them, lead us to them."

ර්ර ර්ර ර්ර

WHEN Daria next awakened—a day later? more?—she found herself in a cavernous room on a luxurious bed, draped with rough cloth. Her hands were unbound, and a cold winter breeze flowed over her from a gap in the shutters of the nearby window, making the tip of her nose cold.

She sat up slowly, dropping her feet to the wood plank floor. She was still in the contessa's white dress, although it was very dirty and ripped in several places now. Her feet were bare. Her head throbbed with ache and she put her hands to it. Had she dreamed up her time on a stone floor, bound? Where was she?

Daria searched her mind, trying to remember. But try as she might, she could not. A confusing mash of memories flooded her brain at once—Gianni, Marco, Vincenzo, the doge, the Conte and Contessa Morassi, the lovely twins . . . Abramo Amidei.

She rose on unsteady legs and went to the door, pulling it by the handle. But it refused to budge, apparently barred from the opposite side. Daria did not bang on it, hoping to avoid her captors until she had a better understanding of where she was and why she had been taken. She went to the window, unlatched the shutters and eased them open. Cold ocean air swept freely into the room now, giving her mind a bit of clarity. She squinted into the harsh winter light, staring across a choppy gray sea. To Venezia.

She was on a tiny isle away from the city, with nothing but open sea and treacherous tides between them.

Her eyes went to the grounds beneath her. A small fortress wall bordered the small island. Impeccable gardens, tilled and winter dormant, stretched out in even boxes. A priest in brown robes moved out along the path. Had she been brought here to recuperate? Had she been injured?

"Father!" Daria cried, trying not to be any more noisy than necessary. "Father, up here!"

The priest turned and, shielding his eyes, looked up the gray stones to the third floor where she waved. Spying her, he stared for a moment, then turned and walked away without a word.

And that was when Daria saw the sword hanging at his side.

The door opened behind her and Daria whirled.

Abramo Amidei smiled and spread his arms wide. "Welcome to my abbey, Duchess." He bowed lowly.

"Men . . . men such as you do not find lodging in holy abbeys."

"I beg to differ. This has long been a stronghold for me." He nonchalantly strode toward her and she backed into the corner between bed and window. He kept his hands behind his back and paused at the window. He pointed outward with his chin. "It is here that they come, my dark flock, to be trained and sent out."

Daria's eyes widened. An abbey. A sanctuary for the dark arts, masquerading as something holy.

Abramo smiled and cocked his head. "Ah, yes. You understand. It is here that you will come to my side, serve me at the high altar. You are my finest conquest. I shall not be denied."

"Never," Daria mumbled, casting a gaze she hoped reflected only defiance. But her head throbbed with pain and she was feeling sick, so sick. . . .

"I am a patient man, m'lady," he said, stepping toward her. He placed one hand against the wall to her right, the other to her left. She stared at the ground, willing herself the courage to meet his gaze. But she could not. *She could not.* She was shaking with fear. Shame washed through her. Where was her strength? Her courage? Why could she not summon the strength of the Spirit within her?

He was massive, twice her size. There would be no fighting him off.

Abramo leaned in, close to her bare neck, and inhaled deeply.

Daria squeezed her eyes shut, bracing, but he conspicuously kept from touching her, in the barest of fashions. Memories of the contessa's looking glass came flooding back, of his touch, his hands . . . she had thought it was Gianni! Gianni! But it had been him, this evil one she had allowed near. And now she could not escape him.

"I dream of your scent, m'lady." He inhaled again, and again. "And you shall find that I am good at finding weaknesses within people. Tell me," he said, leaning so close that his whispering lips traced over the curve of her neck as he spoke, "what is your weakness?" He hovered there, his breath hot on her skin, waiting for her response.

"You quiver, m'lady. You seem to have a weakness for men. For Marco Adimari. For Gianni de Capezzana. Even your uncle, Vincenzo. Might I form in you a weakness for . . . me?"

Daria's head spun. She fought off the mad pull of him. She would not fall, never fall before this man. He could not entrance her. She merely needed an ounce of the strength her heavenly Father had afforded her in Il Campo. Daria cast about in her mind for Scripture, for words that would bind this enemy . . .

Not a phrase came to her rescue.

Abramo raised his head and stared down at her, sensing her fight, tasting her weakness.

Daria looked him in the eye. Words entered her mouth and spilled outward. "Our Father, who art in heaven, hallowed be thy name—"

Abramo struck her so suddenly and with such force it cast her sideways, to the bed. "Blasphemy," he chided. "You are in my dark house now, dear Daria. I will not tolerate your foul prayers here."

Daria swallowed hard, reaching up to wipe the blood that seeped from her torn lip. She tried to rise, but the force of Abramo's slap had sent her head into a serious spin. "Thy kingdom come, thy will be done—"

Abramo reached for her with a roar, pulling her to her feet, and threw her across the room. Daria hit the floor and rolled, feeling the scrape of stone on her cheek. But despite his abuse, she could feel the strength of Jesus' prayer washing through her. She could not stop now, must not stop. "On earth as it is in heaven." She raised one arm to her Lord and stared at Abramo. "Give us this day our daily bread and forgive us our trespasses as we forgive those who trespass against—"

Abramo ran to her and pulled her up by the hair, rushing her to the far wall and slamming her against it. "You shall cease," he ground out.

She remained silent, letting him think he had won. But she had rediscovered her source of strength. She would do this battle, to the death if that was what her God called her to do. This demon had to be contained, driven out, destroyed.

Appeased, he released his handful of her hair and let her turn. She sprang away from him and wiped her lip with the back of her hand. She lifted her chin and cast him a small smile. "Lead us not into temptation."

Abramo lunged and missed her.

"And deliver us *from evil.*"

"*Daria!*" He came after her again, narrowly missing her as she turned and ducked. Her head was completely clear, the ache gone as if it had never come. She remembered Il Campo and how Abramo had been turned back by angels, by Scripture. She raised her arms to the ceiling. "For thine is the kingdom and the power—"

He caught her this time. With one hand he clamped down upon her slender throat, lifting her to her toes, strangling her, pushing her to the bed. Dark spots began to cloud her vision and she writhed, pulling at the hand that clamped down upon her airway. "I am the only power here, Daria. The sooner you understand that, the sooner this will end." With a growl, he released her and strode out of the room, slamming the door behind him.

A heavy latch locked into place, but Daria was focused on her prayer, on taking in even one breath. "And . . . the . . . glory," she finished. She closed her eyes, reaching for her God. "Amen . . . and amen." With each word, her breathing eased, her vision clearing. "Amen and amen and amen and amen."

But even she was aware that she curled into a ball, bleeding upon the bed.

⚓ ⚓ ⚓

GIANNI fought to focus on the priest's words, fought to concentrate on his prayers. But all he could think of was Daria, and what dire consequences she might be facing. It was one thing for Rune and Basilio and Hasani to face harsh treatment, imprisonment. They were warriors, fighting men. It was another thing for the lady, the Duchess d'Angelo, to face the same.

Fury raced through his veins. Why had she insisted on speaking to Marco, to Vincenzo? He had tried to warn her, tried to protect her . . .

She had not been thinking clearly. She was confused, entranced. From the moment she had spied Abramo Amidei in the garden crowd, she had become unhinged. She seemed to draw strength from Gianni when he had held her hand, but then after she had left with the twins and the contessa, something had changed. He frowned. What dark magic had happened within that room? What had Abramo done to her?

"Gianni!" the priest said sharply, bringing him out of his reverie.

The knight opened his eyes in surprise. The priest was in the act of communion, but Gianni had not heard a word he had said.

Piero clamped down lips of anger and set his chalice and bread aside.

Gianni could feel the heat of Ugo and Vito's sidelong stares from either side of him. Piero took the knight's big head in his small hands and stared into his eyes. "Our only hope, *our only hope,* is to rely not on our own wits, our own strength, our own vision, but upon God's."

Never had Gianni seen the priest so fierce. He was twice the size of the man, but in that moment, kneeling before him, his hands clasped to his head, Gianni felt like a boy being punished by his grandfather. The old man stared down at him.

"We must find our path again, Gianni. God is allowing this because he wants our attention. He desires to shake us up, bring us around, head us in his direction again. But we are stubborn, thinking our own thoughts, even in the act of communion."

Gianni felt the heat of embarrassment climb his neck. "You are right, Father. I have sinned in more ways than one." He dropped his eyes to the priest's robes. "I confess I have been thinking of revenge, of hate, of fear, of pride. I am blaming Lady Daria in my thoughts because it is easier than blaming myself. I cannot stop thinking about it, how I failed her. How I failed you all. I confess my desire to find our way out of this myself rather than wait upon the Lord."

Piero paused, waiting for him to finish. "It is good to confess to us, your brothers and little sister. Even better to confess to him," he said, gesturing to the crucifix on the wall of their makeshift chapel. He tore a chunk of bread and handed it to Gianni. "You must remember, it is only by *this* body and blood we are saved. No matter what we do or do not. In this world and the next. You may choose to sacrifice your life in the battle. But only by our Savior's body and blood shall we win the war."

CHAPTER TWENTY-FOUR

HE left her alone for hours, offering her neither food nor water. Daria thought she might go mad with the misery and fear that collided in her mind and heart. She had been over every inch of the room, looking for a weakness, a way out, but it was a stone fortress. Every brick was set perfectly atop the next, the mortar still fairly new and binding. Every tile of the floor was firmly in place, cracking nowhere. She had no instrument to pry it up, even if there were.

Daria went to the window again and stared out to sea, across the waves to Venezia. How she wished she were there, safe beside Gianni and her other knights! She looked down the face of the tower, again wondering if she could survive the jump, idly wondering if God might allow her to heal herself if she broke either back or legs or both. There was no climbing down it, not without a rope.

She glanced at the bed. Her captors had thought even this out, leaving her but one blanket upon the feather bed. It was the bed of a princess with the rough, woolen blanket of a pauper. A blanket that would be impossible to rip into strips to form a rope . . .

Daria continued her pacing, trying to get her mind off her empty stomach and aching throat. Part of her torture, no doubt.

Fury was preferable to grief. When she stopped thinking of Abramo and Vincenzo, her mind went to sweet Beata, strong Agata, stalwart

Aldo. Of Ambrogio, her dear friend, whom she had left behind in her stead. The sweet, giant knight, Lucan. Of precious Nico and Roberto. Had they tried to run away from their murderers?

Rage and sorrow cascaded through her heart and she sank to the floor in the corner of the room, hands covering her face. She had thought her tears were gone, her body too dehydrated to relinquish any more liquid, but still they came. She covered her face as her body shook with the weeping.

Who was she fooling? She was weak. She could not fight this monster. Not on her own. Not on her own . . .

♺ ♺ ♺

ROBERTO leaned against the wooden crates, wincing at the deep ache in his leg and hip. Never had he ridden so far in his life. When he reached the sea, he left the mare with a farmer, promising he would be back for her and pay the farmer for keeping her.

He edged around the corner of the stack of crates, eyeing the sailors, loading the ship, speaking of wintering with lovers and spring journeys to warmer climes. He struggled to hear mention of Venezia, wanting to make certain that they traveled to Venezia on the morning tide.

Roberto knew not what he would do when he got to the city, how he would find the Gifted. All he knew was that he had to go, warn the lady of her friend's treachery, his betrayal, the murder of her loved ones, the destruction of her house. He leaned back behind the boxes, thinking of Tessa, his friend of Il Campo. Together, they had survived much. If he did not get to the lady, warn her, would Tessa be killed as the Sciorias had been killed?

He squeezed his eyes shut, wishing he could remove the memory of old Aldo's body, barely visible among the flames and dancing heat waves. Had they killed them all? Even Nico? For all his trials as a beggar on Il Campo, none compared to the travesty of that day, just five days past. He had not always gotten along with Nico these last months, but in the last few weeks, things had eased and their friendship had grown stronger by the day. Was he gone? And what of Ambrogio? Ambrogio, more of a big brother . . . Killed alongside Nico?

His hands curled at his sides. He would not let Vincenzo near Tessa. Not if he could do anything about it. Roberto's heart raced.

What if he was already too late?

஧ ஧ ஧

"I⊤ is only because the Morassi family has asked this of me that I allow this," the priest grumbled to Father Piero as they entered the sanctuary of San Giacomo di Rialto. "You have undoubtedly heard that the churches of Sant' Elena and San Zaccaria were robbed, not a week past."

The priest stopped and turned to Piero, glancing over the three knights, the girl, and the stonemason, questions looming large in his mind. The fragment of the Gifted had agreed to never part again. Every step forward was to be together as one. They would complete their mission, find their missing, and move forward to where God showed them they should go next.

The priest's eyes hovered on Daria's coat of arms upon the knights' chests. The peacock. In an all-out war, one wore his colors bravely, the knights had told Piero, and he had concurred. Their time of hiding was over. It was time to stand or attack.

"Are you those responsible for the peacock mosaics dug up and destroyed?"

"We are not. I give you my word."

"Then I ask you again, brother, what business brings you to my church?"

Piero paused. "We are on a holy mission. Of that, I can tell you no more. Only that your church undoubtedly will take her place in history if you aid us."

"By doing . . ."

"Please, my brother," Piero said. "It is imperative that we move quickly. By my word, by that of the Morassis, might you give us but an hour alone within?"

"The Morassis and their friends are important to this church . . ." the priest said.

"May every Christian church find her *patronas* as you have," Piero said with a soothing nod.

"Yes, well," the priest sniffed. "See to your business and leave my sanctuary in better form than you found her, or I shall scream for the doge's guards. Please know that this is a favor I do not wish to honor twice."

"It will not be asked of you," Piero said, with another slight bow.

ප්ප ප්ප ප්ප

"You are weakening," he said, circling her.

"When I am weak, my Lord is strong," she said.

He ignored her bait, continued circling her. "You need some water? Wine mayhap? A bit of bread? Or some broth? It's been two days since the baptism feast. Ask me for it, and it is yours, Daria."

Daria tried to swallow, but there was nothing in her mouth.

Abramo continued walking around her. "I brought you a gift."

She refused to look at him.

He came before her and held it in his large hand, a small wooden box with a riband about it. "Go on. Open it. Open it and I shall order a pitcher of water and a loaf of bread immediately sent to your room."

"Nay. I shall not accept any gift from you."

"It is your choice, Duchess. I leave it here, for you." He set it down on the corner of her bed. "You are in need of a bath. Fresh linens. Food. Simply accept my offer."

She folded her arms and turned away from him. He circled her again.

"No? Then consider another offer. One meal. Once a day. For a week. We shall engage in a bit of civilized conversation and I shall get to explore your sharp feminine mind."

Daria scoffed. "And what will I get from such wasted time?"

Abramo laughed and threw out his hands. "Sustenance. Where will you be if you do not accept that? Dead? Is that what your Lord wishes for you?"

She stared back at him, unwavering. "I would rather follow him unto death than follow you unto eternal damnation."

Abramo stared back at her. "You're looking a fright, Duchess. You are in need of a hot bath, a fire in your hearth. You're weary. Alone. Dehydrated. Famished. You cannot keep this up much longer."

"I am not afraid," she said, lifting her chin.

"Oh . . ." he said, as if her words were tragic. "You will be. Someday soon, you will be." He strode to the door, tapped twice, and then stood there as the guard opened it.

Abramo gestured to the gift upon her bed. "Open it. And when you have, I shall take it as acceptance to my invitation. You shall be bathed, don a new gown, and we shall dine together."

ർ ർ ർ

DARIA sat in the corner and stared at the package for hours. What if it contained sweetmeats? Tender, flaky rolls? He was right; she was weakening. The fall winds rattled the shutters and made their way into her stone room. The hearth remained void of wood, cold now for days. She huddled under her rough blanket, wishing to be free of her tight gown and again in the welcome folds of her soft Sienese dresses. She longed for Beata's call to supper, for Aldo's droning reports on the fields, the imports, the exports. She wished that Ambrogio would appear and make her smile. She remembered roaring, crackling fires in the hearth that chased away the damp of winter.

No such comforts were available to her.

She stared at the gift.

Mayhap this was the Father's way out for her. What good was this, anyway? Starving, dying of thirst? She should be gaining her strength, looking for a way to escape. She was playing into Abramo Amidei's hands, letting herself go like this. She would take a meal with him, once a day. She could do that.

She threw the blanket aside and stepped across the cold wooden floors. With a shaking hand, she reached for the box and untied the riband. It fell to the floor. Taking a deep breath, she opened the lid. It came off with a squeak of protest.

In the shadows of dusk, it was difficult to see.

Daria went closer to the table aside the bed, and the candle, almost melted away. She frowned and then reached in, fingers touching wire. Shaking her head back and forth, she pulled it out anyway, holding it up to the sputtering candle flame.

And then she dropped it to the floor with a cry, scrambling backward to her corner, tears coming again.

Beata. Beata's glasses. Beata, Beata, Beata . . .

She closed her eyes and could almost hear Abramo's cruel laughter, his smile of victory. And now she had done it. She had accepted his challenge of a week of dining with him.

Daria balled her hands into fists and struck the floor. He thought he had her. This was only one of many ways that he would try to beat her into submission. Hunger, thirst, fear, sorrow, doubt—pain if necessary.

He would use any weapon he had to divide her heart from her Savior's, from the Gifted, and meld it to his.

She sat up suddenly, clinging to the surge of anger. Anger drove away her grief.

She would rob him of some of his power. She would eat and drink and gain physical strength. She would dine with him, mayhap even stroll the grounds with him so she could plan her escape. She would not go too easily. It would be necessary to convince him that he had truly beaten her, not that she was playing a game. He was frightfully keen. But he could not know her inmost thoughts. Only her Creator knew such things.

Daria shook her head and sighed, wiping her face of the tears. "Lord God, lead me on. One footfall at a time. Lead, Jesus. And I shall follow, even in the valley of the shadow of death."

ᚼ ᚼ ᚼ

"You are our man, gifted with profound faith. Do you have faith enough for this task?" Piero said from the shadows.

Gianni stared out to the pounding rain and gray seas. "Where could they have taken her?"

"The Lord shall show us the way, Gianni, when the time is right."

Gianni let out a dismissive snort. "I care not for how the Lord is managing things at the moment."

The silence grew between them. In the quiet, they could hear Tessa's sobs from the room above. The girl had been crying for days, ceasing only when they were out, looking for her mistress or about the Gifted's business.

Each cry seemed to weigh upon Gianni like a stone between his shoulders. He ran his hands through his hair. "How is this to turn out? How could this possibly turn out well?"

Father Piero sat down heavily upon a chair. "Sometimes it must be our darkest hour before we can find our way to the light."

"Oh, that is grand!" Gianni said sarcastically. "So our Lord allows us to wallow in the darkness?"

"If he must. We are to learn something key here, Gianni. Your faith fails you. I am unable to see the wisest path. What are we to learn?"

"I know not. I know not! Do not harangue me with puzzling questions of the faith."

"But we are his chosen ones. It is exactly we who must puzzle this out. We must go to our God and ask, ask that he show us what he wishes us to see."

Gianni gave out a roar, picked up a chair, and threw it across the room. "I tire of being a pawn upon my Lord's chess field!" He took one chair after another and sent them sailing across the room, six in all.

Father Piero groaned and put his head in his hands, elbows on knees. He shook his head. "Ah, Gianni, Gianni. How far we've strayed."

Vito and Ugo, hearing the commotion, came running.

"I know not of what you speak," Gianni ground out.

Tessa appeared then too, eyes bloodshot and puffy from her tears.

"After all that we've seen, all that's been shown to us, how can we doubt that the Lord will not show us what to do next? How can we fear that our comrades will be left to rot in prison or worse, as the captives of our greatest enemy? Do you not see? Do you not see what is happening?"

"Nay. I do not see. Tell me, and quickly," Gianni said, sinking down onto the floor across from the priest.

It was Father Piero's turn to rise and pace. "Our enemy has found a way to weaken us. He seeks to divide us, rob us, threaten us, make us fear him. He is the father of lies. And we are beginning to believe him."

"What lies?" Vito asked warily.

"That we are weak. That we are dividable, gullible, dupable, conquerable. We are, of course. On our own. We falter, fallible, prone to sin. But we are *not* prone to such failures when we are living in the Christ who lives within *us*." He faced each one, looking them in the eye. He pounded his chest with one fist. "He cannot beat our Savior. Not the Christ who lives within us! Not him who lived and died and rose again! Not him! Not him!" he shouted in righteous glory. "Not him! *Not him!*"

His words fell upon them like gentle rain, even though they were shouted.

"You are right, of course," Gianni said. "I am casting about, rather than donning my shield of faith."

Piero cast a tender eye in his direction. "As are we all. My friends, our enemy is wily. He will use every device available to him in order to bring us down. Stand strong, come what may, and remain on this path. Believe in our God that saves. Remember he has a call upon our very lives. For that cause, must we be ready to live and die. But in him, we cannot fail, no matter what we suffer or endure. In him, we cannot fail."

⚓ ⚓ ⚓

THE next morning, the fisherman pulled in his nets as the rain continued to fall and the cloud-covered silver orb of a sun struggled to rise off the horizon. His hands were on the knotty ropes, his movements practiced and easy as he pulled in a handsome catch of red mullet. But his eyes were on a small fortress of an island, once inhabited by a northern prince, but long the domain of the dark ones.

A female swallow rose and dipped and took a sudden curve past the bow of his boat, her white breast a mere flash against the gray sea. His eyes went again to the stones of the island wall, where here and there, bushy green Crysthe Marine clung to chinks in the masonry. On the far side of the island two scrubby, stubborn sea pines struggled to live on the edge of the water, outside the wall, one even reaching to the top.

He was not sure why his Lord had called him here, to this island. But he was certain it had to do with the Gifted. Two days ago he had been fishing off the island's shore and seen a woman look out the tower window. And the lady looked strikingly similar to Lady Daria d'Angelo.

He had returned to this same shore each day, searching for a glimpse of the woman, but the shutters on the high tower remained shut. No doubt it was cold in the small fortress. His eyes watched as a man dressed in a monk's robes traded with another in the tower. He was not fooled. They were men dressed to appear as monks—to make the entire isle appear as a monastery. For the ships that passed in and out of the laguna, it provided adequate cover. But the men who fished these waters knew the truth and were either drawn to it, or repelled by it. Foul things were happening inside the island's walls, deeply disturbing. He knew it, within.

This was the devil's lair.

So why was the lady there? Had she been won over? Or was she held captive? Or had he been mistaken? Was it not her after all?

He finished hauling in his nets and cast one more glance toward the high walls that surrounded the island and the three guards in plain sight. He sighed heavily, wishing again that his God would allow him to rest, leave his gifting to others. He was getting to the age when he ought to be leaving the fishing to a son, cuddling grandchildren by the fire, but instead he was alone, always alone. The Lord had never allowed him a wife, as if keeping him married to this purpose alone.

The fisherman went to the mast and hauled his sail upward. He shook his head to free it of the drenching rain and then blinked up into the sky that continued to send down showers. "I did not ask for this," he said.

The old refrain was his answer. To obey, always obey.

And yet he still was not sure he was ready. "Why me?" he asked the gray, billowing clouds, heavy with rain. He would have shouted the words, but he did not wish to rouse the island guards' attention. He knew that someday soon, the guards would regard him with idle attention, comfortable that he was the same fisherman who had been fishing these same waters for weeks. And that would be the day his Lord would ask him to move.

CHAPTER TWENTY-FIVE

THREE women entered the room. Dangerously dehydrated and weak, Daria watched with dull eyes as they set a large washtub in the corner and poured two steaming buckets of water inside. The third set down a trunk and pulled a soft ivory underdress and a beautiful dress in gold silk from it, along with a dainty pair of slippers. She bent and pulled out undergarments and laid them atop the dress, glancing quickly in Daria's direction.

It was then that Daria knew her. Zola. Abramo's woman. Deceiver.

It was she who had allowed her master entry to Daria's home in Siena, when they had so narrowly escaped. She who had almost brought them all down. Poor Rune had practically given this woman his heart. And it was all a ruse. All a terrible ruse. She had fooled them all. "We welcomed you into my home, Zola," she said dully. "My men rescued you."

"I did what was necessary, m'lady," Zola said, busying herself across the room, not daring to look her in the eye.

"You must have had the gift of tongues at one time. How could you pervert such a holy gift into something that would ensnare God's own?"

"It was the only way." Zola dared meet her gaze then, eyes full of misery. "I freely give the Master everything I have. It is required."

"You are the ultimate traitor to our God. You have sold your soul,

Zola. The Holy One has gifted you with the blessing of his own, holy language, and you threw it in his face! Please! You must come away and beg our Father's forgiveness. He will have you back. All you need do is ask."

"I have chosen my path. You would be wise to do the same. The Master enjoys nothing more than bringing God's special ones to his side. He is relentless."

Daria shook her head in disbelief.

"It need not be painful, m'lady. But if you tarry, if you do not soon give in, it will be excruciating." She turned away from Daria then and wiped her face.

The first two women disappeared to retrieve more water, and Zola continued to pull items out of the trunk. A chunk of soap. A brush and a comb. A small mirror. A gown for sleeping. A second, more simple work gown. She paused and looked at Daria, patting the last item of clothing. "This is not for this evening, Duchess. The Master wishes you to wear the gold. We shall wash and repair your gown," she said, nodding toward the gown she had been wearing for days.

The other two women entered again, dumping three more buckets of water into the tub. In her other hand, the second had a basket, which she handed to Zola. She bent down, waiting for Daria to look in her direction. "You must take it slow, m'lady. There is a hard roll and a bit of water here," she said, opening the basket and pulling them out.

Daria grabbed the corked bottle from her hands, feeling half-mad in her haste and need. She drank from it greedily, like a crying infant finally offered her mother's breast, ignoring the slight chalky, limey taste.

"Easy, m'lady, easy," Zola soothed. "Take it too fast and it's bound to come up again." She reached to place a hand on Daria's shoulder, and Daria wrenched away. But Daria sighed and wiped her mouth with the back of her hand, willing herself to slow. She knew the woman was right.

"You are still angry with me," Zola said.

"There are hardly words," Daria said, staring in her direction. "Deep was your deception. You are merely a puppet of the Sorcerer, but you have gone against my Lord and my God. I do not understand! When one recognizes her gift, knows it fully, she knows God more fully. How could you turn away from him?"

Zola rose, as if brushing off her words. "There will be a full supper with the Master, of course," the woman said, "but you would be wise to take this first." She unwrapped the small hard roll and offered it to Daria.

Daria took it and ate it, as slowly as she could, watching the three women move in and out of the room, adding water to the tub, lighting a fire in the cold hearth. Zola left the room for more wood.

"I need to leave this place," Daria dared as soon as she had swallowed the last bite of roll.

The other two women paused for a moment, but then continued about their tasks as if she had not been heard.

Daria reached out and grabbed one of the women who was packing up the basket again. "Please. I need to leave. I'm here against my will."

The woman cast hard eyes in her direction. "And here you shall stay, Duchess, until the Master tells us otherwise."

Daria let her hand drop to her lap.

The second woman came to stand beside the first. "You have a place of honor here, Duchess. Do not fight the Master. Give in to him. The sooner you give in, the sooner you will resume your life of ease."

They reached for her and helped her stand. Daria felt light-headed and woozy, wondering if she had eaten and drunk too fast. Defeated, she allowed the women to unbutton her gown and slip it from her shoulders, then ease her into the blessed, steaming waters of her bath.

They dumped buckets full of water atop her head, lathering her long, dark hair with a soap that reminded Daria of Siena. Mayhap it had been purchased in Toscana. It smelled of milk and lavender and piñon pine berries. The aroma made her cry, longing for home, for her loved ones, now all gone.

"Shh, shh," Zola crooned. "It will be well. You shall see." The women scrubbed her back and feet and wounds and then left her to soak for a time. Daria sat back and fought the utter weariness, tears still streaming down her face. What was happening to her? She felt like a princess being readied for her prince on her wedding day.

The thought brought her suddenly upright. No, she whispered. No, no, no . . . The darkness called to her, pulled at her. And yet she felt as helpless as a swimmer working against the fierce current of a whirlpool. She could fight, and fight, and fight, or she could relinquish her fate to her God and let him fight it out with the devil himself. Surely if he meant her to live, he would find a way to save her.

The maidservants returned and assisted her out of the tub, toweled her off, and helped her into the clean clothes. They dabbed salve upon her scrapes and scratches, the cut at her lip, her chapped lips. They brushed out her hair and pulled it up into pearl bands so that some of it fell about her face and neck in wet coils. Dimly, Daria remembered that Marco had loved it that way.

The dizziness ceased and Daria sat upon the bed, watching the fire in the hearth gain life. One of the women went and added several logs to it, remarking that she would be nice and warm this night.

But Daria could not keep her eyes from the flames. It was as if all her senses were heightened. She could hear, smell, and see with greater clarity than ever before. She strained to hear what might be happening down the stairs, so that she might be prepared.

It was then she knew. She had been drugged again. She knew she should be outraged, she should fight it. But she felt stronger, invincible, more alive than ever before. Mayhap the drug would work for her, against them. She liked it. Liked this feeling . . .

Zola bent to speak lowly in her ear. "Give in, Duchess. Give in to it. It is so much easier than fighting. And there is much here for you to enjoy. Give in, give in," she whispered.

The other two took Daria's arms and led her down the stairs. "The Master will be so pleased," said one.

"So pleased," murmured the other.

He appeared at the base of the stairs, looking up at them with a broad smile. "Ladies, what a vision are you all!"

He spoke to all of them, lingering on Zola, but his eyes settled upon Daria. He offered his arm, but she kept her hands to her side, clinging to her own skirts like a desperate child.

"Very well," he said calmly, gesturing forward.

Daria stepped into an elegant room set with exotic foods, difficult for even royals to come by this time of year. Oranges and grapes and dates cascaded from a plate between the two trenchers set on either side of the table. A manservant entered the room with a golden-brown baked chicken upon his trencher. Daria took her place and Abramo went to his.

Candles were set about the room and a fire roared in the hearth, giving the room a warm glow. She glanced at Abramo and admitted to herself that he was handsome, suddenly having difficulty remembering why she hated him.

Abramo poured her a generous cup of wine, and the manservant set several slices of steaming chicken upon her plate. A brown crust, laden with seasonings and borne on curling tendrils of steam, sent heavenly smells to her nostrils.

She could feel her hold loosening and fought to care. "Wh-where is Vincenzo?" she tried, grasping at the first thing that came to mind. She stabbed a fork into the chicken and placed the succulent meat upon her tongue, closing her eyes with pleasure. Never had she tasted any food such as this! Never in her life!

Abramo smiled across at her. "Vincenzo is near," he said. "Do you wish to see him?"

"Nay," Daria heard herself say, feeling as if she had not a care in the world.

"Good, good," Abramo said. He ate from his own trencher, but his eyes were only on Daria. "It is satisfying to see you so relaxed, Daria."

Her name upon his lips sounded entrancing. She stared at his full mouth as he spoke, not hearing his words, imagining she could see words forming in his throat, coming at her in soft clouds of vapor.

"It is as if you have always been here," he was saying. He reached across the table to take her hand and she allowed it, watching as if she stood at the end of the table, out of her own body. "I want you to stay, Daria. Here, with me. I want to show you the mysteries of our cere-monies. I shall keep you this relaxed, this content. I shall teach you our ways. You are a woman of uncommon presence. Your gifting . . . it could be utilized for so much more. By my side you need not fear. No one can touch us. I own people in power from here to Napoli. We can travel the entire length of Italia and rule her as we ought." He leaned over the table. "Join me."

A shudder ran through Daria, breaking her reverie. She sat up straighter and frowned. What was happening to her? It was more than the drugs that cascaded through her system, she knew. It was some sort of spell . . .

"Daria," Abramo said, a note of frustration in his voice.

Daria stared at the fire. A prayer sprang to her lips as she watched the flames. "Father of light, be with me," she whispered. The flames immediately changed, at once appeared in less vivid colors; she no longer felt as if she could hear a mouse in the corner of the room. The drugs were fading, mayhap mitigated by the food in her belly. Or was it her prayer?

Two women entered the room, dressed in dark clothing, hair down about their shoulders in the manner of whores. They took the wine bottle from the table between Abramo and Daria and, laughing, poured wine into each other's mouths, giggling as they wiped it from each other's chin and cheek. One sat down upon Abramo's lap and the other moved behind him, staring idly in Daria's direction, then leaned down to kiss Abramo's neck in territorial fashion, still staring at Daria.

Daria shifted uncomfortably upon her seat, still trying to focus through the remnants of her stupor. Was this real? Or all illusion?

"They are pleasing, but they interest me not compared to you," Abramo said, bending his neck to accept another kiss. "Come, m'lady. Let us show you the wonders of the dark. You will discover more of life than you ever dreamed. It is more intoxicating than the drug in your belly or the wine we share," he said. He seemed not to be concerned that she knew, knew that he had drugged her. Probably knew the pull of it, the instant desire for more, more as it faded away . . .

"Nay," Daria whispered, leaning back as if still fighting a visceral force.

Abramo waved away the women and they huddled together as they left the room, laughing. "We shall await you, m'lord," called one suggestively.

Abramo leaned forward. "Come, Daria. What is the harm in seeing what we offer? Surely your God is not so jealous that he won't accept you looking. Once."

"One step is all it takes to fall off a cliff," she returned. "And my God is fiercely jealous. I . . . I do not want what you offer."

"Ah, you lie." He sat back with a grin and sipped at his wine. "You are curious. You feel the pull." He said each word slowly, hypnotically. "Pulling . . .pulling . . . pulling. You wish to know more. More . . . more . . . more . . ."

Daria gripped the table ledge, suddenly panting with the effort of resisting him.

Abramo rose, walked around the table, and came to stand behind her. He leaned down for a long moment, letting his breath wash over her again, before he spoke. "Come. Offer yourself to me. I shall not take you by force. You are curious about matters of the spirit, knowledge. You shall learn more than you ever anticipated in my care. If you still wish to depart on the morrow, I shall open the door and set you upon the boat myself. All I ask is that you do not leave ignorant. You are learned, Daria. Come and learn, Daria. Come. Come . . ."

"Nay . . . *nay*." She gripped the table as if he were lifting her. What was this madness? Why was she mulling over his words, considering them?

He moved to her other shoulder. "Do you fear your God is weak? Do you fear that he cannot protect you here?"

"Nay!" She turned to face him.

Abramo knelt and waited until she looked into his eyes. Try as she might, Daria could not tear her gaze away. Deep within, she knew he was using his powers upon her. What was she to do? She was a healer! She did not have the faith of Gianni, nor the wisdom of Piero! How was she to fight this man?

"If you trust in your God, why not confirm in your mind and heart that we offer nothing? Surely he would not allow one of his Gifted into my abode unless he wished you to be here. Certainly you, one of the Gifted, can see that you are only here because of God's plan. Are you questioning God's wisdom?"

Daria blinked rapidly, trying to focus. His words resounded as truth in her ears, but her gut clenched with fear.

Abramo took her hand and stroked it with his other.

Scripture began cascading through Daria's mind, filling her chest until it spewed out of her mouth. " 'They fly like a vulture swooping to devour; they come bent on violence. Their hordes advance like a desert wind and gather prisoners like sand.' "

Abramo dropped her hand and stood up abruptly.

Daria stood too, upon trembling legs. " 'They deride kings and scoff at rulers. They laugh at the fortified cities; they build earthen ramps and capture them.' "

Abramo took a step away and passed a hand through his hair. Daria stood, unable to keep herself from speaking. With each word, she gained strength, found herself, her God again. " 'They sweep past like the wind and go on—' "

"Cease," Abramo growled, rushing to her, pushing her back to the wall, kissing her then, hungrily, as if trying to pull her back to him.

Daria tried to pull away, panting, now with righteous fury rather than against his spellbinding power. " 'Guilty men,' " she continued, " 'whose strength is their god.' "

"Daria—" he warned, pushing her harder against the wall.

Daria stared upward. " 'O Lord, are you not from everlasting? My God, my Holy One, we will not die. Your eyes are too pure to look on evil . . .' " She stared at Abramo when she said these last words of Scripture, seeing again the hollow core of the man.

He threw her, then, across the room. She tumbled and rolled to her back, rose on one arm even as he advanced upon her again. " 'Why then do you tolerate the treacherous?' " she shouted to her God as she came to her feet and scurried out of Abramo's reach.

Abramo paused and wiped his mouth with the back of his hand. He smiled. "You are not the only one who knows Scripture. What follows those words, Daria?"

She frowned, hearing them in her mind.

He took a step toward her. "Let me assist. 'Why are you silent while the wicked swallow up those more righteous than themselves?' " he said to the ceiling with a sneer. " 'The wicked foe pulls all of the righteous up with hooks, he catches them in his net.' "

Daria backed away, confused. Her armor, the Word was flawed!

" 'He gathers them in his dragnet,' " Abramo continued, smiling in victory as he closed in upon her. " 'He sacrifices to his dragnet; and burns incense to his dragnet, for by his net he lives in luxury and enjoys the choicest food.' " He paused to gesture back toward his table and then it was Daria's turn to smile in victory. She dodged out of his way, putting the table between them.

" 'See, he is puffed up; his desires are not upright . . . indeed, wine betrays him; he is arrogant and never at rest.' " She shook her head, seeing the truth of the Word, living before her! " 'Because he is greedy as the grave and *like death is never satisfied,* he gathers to himself all the nations and takes captive all the peoples. Woe to him who piles up stolen goods and makes himself wealthy by extortion!' "

Abramo stood upright and folded his arms before him. "Are you quite finished?" People were rushing by their room, down the hallway, laughing and plainly drunk. Women shrieked and men laughed in gluttonous pleasure. They were all making their way to Abramo's dark ceremonial room.

" 'Woe to him who builds a city with bloodshed!' "

"Daria . . ."

She stood straighter and then advanced upon him, spitting out the words now, righteous in her anger. " 'Woe to him who gives drink to his neighbors, pouring it from the wineskin till they are drunk, so that he can gaze on their naked bodies.' "

He stared down at her, nostrils flared, eyes narrowed in fury.

Daria sensed the danger but could not stop herself. " 'You will be filled with shame instead of your glory. The cup from the Lord's right hand is coming around to you, and disgrace will cover your glory.' "

His hand came then, lightning fast, and grabbed a handful of hair, yanking back her head. He pulled her close with his other arm, locking her arms to her sides. He stared into her eyes, cheek muscles working in fury. "Enough. You *shall* come to me, Daria," he ground out. He paused a moment, his tone mellowing. "Take refuge in your invisible god if you must, your meaningless Scriptures. But at some moment, you shall come to your senses and bow to me as your new god. And then you shall make an offering of yourself. The longer you tarry, the more full shall be *your* woe."

He pulled her head back even further, hovering near her lips as if he meant to kiss her again, barely touching them with his own, closing his eyes.

Abruptly, he pulled his head back, still holding her in place. "Listen to me. I must attend the ceremony now, and you will be taken back to your room. On the morrow, we shall resume this interplay. Be advised, I always win. Always. There is a reason why Habakkuk lamented his fate and that of the world—because the dark rules. The dark will either win you over or beat you into submission, Daria. Either way, you shall be ruled. Would it not be better to pledge your loyalty rather than become enslaved?"

With that, he allowed her to stumble away from him. He straightened his overcoat and turned from her.

She shook her head, more clear on the truth than ever. "No. Never," she said, shaking her head. "The dark believes it rules at times, but it is the light that prevails."

But she spoke to an empty room.

Chapter Twenty-six

Hidden within the hold, cradling his sick stomach against the incessant swell and fall of the waves, Roberto heard the sailors speak of the isle for some time and the ceremonies to come, before he truly knew of what they spoke. But through the fog of his queasiness, he understood at last that the Master they mentioned might well be the same man who had drawn so many to the caves outside Siena, the Master who had almost claimed him.

The sailors leaned together and spoke so that he could not make out their words, but Roberto knew by their bawdy laughter of their subject matter. When grown men, sailors, withdrew to hushed undertones, they spoke of something truly shameful. And yet they reveled in it.

Roberto's pulse quickened. What favor was this that Providence had put him upon a ship bound for Venezia, with sailors who knew of the Sorcerer? Or rather what cursed luck was this? If he was discovered, they would surely throw him into the sea and not look back.

A sailor came lumbering down the narrow steps, searching for something among the supplies of ropes and pulleys. Roberto moved deeper into the shadows, leaning on a creaking board. He froze.

The sailor looked in his direction, squinted, and then looked away.

Roberto took a deep breath, thanking God for his preservation and asking for a day longer to serve the holy, to serve the Gifted in some way before he died.

"Please, Lord God, Your Holiness, Your Most Worshipful," he whispered, trying to think of any complimentary name he could, working to get within the Divine's good graces. He could not let Lady Daria, Tessa, down now. Not after all they and the Sciorias had done for him. He clenched his hands and lifted them up to a shaft of light. "Please, Jesus. Let me serve."

⚭ ⚭ ⚭

"**WHAT** purpose does this serve?" Cardinal Boeri asked Bishop di Mino, as he paced the floor of his quarters for the fourth day in a row. "The Duchess has been gone since the fire—and mark my words, she did not die within the palazzo."

"So you've said," intoned the bishop tiredly. "Mayhap we should press on, to Avignon. If the Gifted are to do battle with the dark ones, and the doge refuses to intercede, we can do little but pray our own find strength to overthrow the dark. The doge is correct—if they can beat the Sorcerer on his own turf, they will grow stronger, and our common enemy will be put down."

"Or it will merely enrage him further. He is strong, Bishop, stronger and with more pull in more cities than I ever imagined."

"But he is still merely man."

"Yes," Cardinal Boeri said, staring out the glass disk of a window pane to the sea. But inside, he wondered if that was true.

⚭ ⚭ ⚭

DARIA was more careful over the following days, smelling the water and wine before she partook, on guard for the citrusy odor of the drug that had almost been her undoing. She prayed for more of the Word to become her sword, and each eve when Abramo sought her out, the Lord gave her new Scriptures to use in their fight between light and dark.

Abramo seemed to enjoy the challenge, and no longer succumbed to anger or abuse. But Daria knew that he would soon move to other means of persuasion when he grew tired of their verbal swordplay.

"Release me. You will not persuade me to join you," she said. They were in the main parlor, and she went to the window and stared out at the gray seas through the wavy, smoky glass.

"Oh no?" He leaned against the stonework that framed the window, arms crossed, staring at her, bemusement in his voice.

"Nay," she said. "Because I have found the sword that you cannot strike down."

"Bah," he said. "You must know that I have more of an arsenal than a simple reliance on old, useless words."

"I do not fear you, Abramo," she said, tossing him a contemptuous look.

He grinned. "You are brave, m'lady, but a poor liar." Abramo stepped away from her, hands behind his back while he paced. "You believe yourself ready for the rest of my arsenal?"

"Bring forth what you wish," Daria said.

Abramo grinned and narrowed his eyes at her in curious delight. "Be you knight or be you lady?"

"The Lord God on high is my strength and my shield," she said, staring up at him. She tired of his games. "You could kill me and my Lord would still claim victory in my resurrection."

Abramo's eyes covered her and he smiled a thin smile. He glanced over at one of his men. "Bring them."

Daria folded her arms and turned, watching the guard depart out the doorway. Abramo bent toward the fire, raising his hands to the flame. Daria bit her tongue, refusing to ask what was ahead. Instead she turned back to the window and prayed furiously.

She heard the bird before she saw him. "Bormeo!" she cried, when the first guard entered with his cage in hand. She rushed across the room and smiled in spite of herself. She thought he had died in the fire! But here was her bird! The white falcon screeched, welcoming her, wanting out of his cage.

Abramo was directly behind her, hands on her shoulders, speaking softly in her ear. "Everyone has a price, m'lady. Might you agree to attend our next ceremony if I return your bird to you?"

Daria sighed, trying to brush off his hands. "Nay."

"Hmmm. Bring in the others."

Daria's eyes narrowed. She braced for what was ahead.

They came in then, one after another, manacled and led by guards dressed as holy men.

Daria's hand went to her mouth. Each entrance was like a blow to her belly.

She cried out, taking a step to rush forward, but Abramo held her shoulders, forcing her to stand where she was. Daria battled between euphoria in seeing her loved ones alive and horror at their condition.

First was Ambrogio, battered, his left hand an awkward clump in bloody bandages. They pulled him farther into the room and it looked as if he could barely keep his feet. He stared at her through one slit of an eye. "Daria?" he breathed, as if she were an apparition.

"Brogi," she whispered, tears slipping down her face.

Right behind him was Agata, wearing a threadbare gown and appearing as if she had aged fifteen years in the months since they had parted. She cried out at the sight of Daria, reaching an old hand out, but she was roughly pulled to the side. She let out a pitiful cry.

Daria shoved down a sob, the tension building in her chest.

That was when they arrived with Nico, just a boy, not yet a young man. They dragged him in and his head hung limp from his shoulders.

Daria cried out, then, unable to tolerate another moment. "Nay, nay!" she cried, wrenching free of Abramo's grip, rushing to the boy, weeping. "What have you done to them?" She whipped her head around and stared at Abramo. "You are evil itself. Entirely corrupt."

Abramo took in her words with a passive expression and no retort.

"Release him," she said to the guards holding Nico. "Release him! Release them all!"

She turned a furious gaze upon Abramo and he flicked out his chin, giving the guards his permission.

Ambrogio sank to the ground with a groan. Agata fell to her knees beside Daria and threw her arms around the younger woman. Daria shuddered at the foul smell of her, but pulled the old woman tight for a moment. "Oh Agata, I had mourned you. Are the others alive as well? What of Beata? Aldo?"

She pulled back to look into the old woman's face, but the woman only cried, her tears washing away clear, waving paths in the filth that covered her face. "Nay, they killed them, m'lady. Murdered them before us."

Daria pulled her close, shuddering at their combined grief. The boy coughed, choking, red bubbles at his lips. Daria turned to Nico, unconscious upon the floor.

"What did you do to him?" Daria spat out at Abramo. "He is but a child!"

"He refused him, m'lady," Agata whispered, weeping and casting fearful eyes upon Abramo. "He wanted the boy to come to their ceremony. But you would have been proud . . . he took blow after blow and still refused them, refused them until they left him for dead."

Abramo smiled and Daria felt rage build within her. He gave her a small shrug. "You refused me, m'lady. I went in search of another means to soothe my needs that night."

"You are a monster."

He waggled his eyebrows and smiled more broadly. "It is as you say. Some look upon me as monster, others as benevolent father. I ask you to consider which is a more pleasant viewpoint. It remains your choice."

Daria turned to Nico and ran her hands over his slender chest, feeling the odd dip of a broken rib in several places. She leaned down and listened to the boy's breathing. It was ragged, full of liquid. Did he bleed within? She dipped her fingers into his mouth and pulled them out. Pink. How long would he live?

"Will you heal the child, Duchess? I would like to see you work."

"I cannot."

He raised a brow. "You cannot?"

"Not with you in the room."

"You are saying that your God is not mighty enough to work if his enemy is present?"

"Nay," she said, shaking her head.

"Then why not go to it? Do you not feel him?" He smiled again, leaning toward her, eyebrows raised in glee. "The angel of death. It is as close to your God as I wish to get. It is where our dominions collide. And each time I feel the angel of death near me, it is a thrill. I think I shall take each of these loved ones of yours, Daria, to death's door, merely so I can feel him hover about." He closed his eyes and shivered. "Mm, delightful."

"Cease," muttered Ambrogio. "Do not listen to him, Daria."

"It is always unwise to ignore me for long."

Daria clamped her mouth shut against a retort—thinking of it as wasted strength—and went to Ambrogio. She bent over him and gently reached for his left hand. He cried out, but still she moved, unwinding the bandage. A huge knot formed in her throat as she saw the mangled fingers.

She drew a hand to her mouth, hoping to cover her gasp, failing. If it had been his right . . . The artist . . . pride of Siena . . . no longer able to paint. It reminded her of Giovanna Maria, the nun she had first healed in the abbey outside Roma. But she had been surrounded by holy ones there, others who prayed alongside her . . .

"Daria," Ambrogio whispered, touching her face with his right hand. "I failed you. Forgive me."

His words made her weep anew. "Oh, Ambrogio, my friend. You did not fail me. It is I who failed you. I should never have—"

Abramo's hands clamped down upon her arms then and lifted her up to her feet, away from Ambrogio's side. Agata wept.

She struggled to get away, but he held her easily against his chest, forcing her to stare at her injured loved ones. "Hmm," he said. "This must be the finest torture possible. People you care for, hurt, dying. And yet I will not let you near them any longer. The healer in you must be screaming. Your loved ones, here, so near, and you, unable to act."

"You must allow me to care for them," she said, struggling anew. "Please."

Abramo sighed in satisfaction. "Say that again," he whispered in ecstasy.

Daria winced, hating his revelry in her weakness, hating his power over her. She leaned away from him, but he held her easily by the elbows. Nico took a sudden, ragged breath, as if it might be his last, then choked. Agata leaned toward him, stroking his forehead, crying, wiping blood from the boy's lips.

"Please. I must tend to them." Tears ran down Daria's nose and dripped to the floor. She gave in to the sobs, unable to hold them back any longer. "P-please . . . please!"

"Daria, you only must agree to one thing, and then I shall agree to your every request."

Daria stopped struggling and just shook her head, caught, weeping in frustration.

"Do not do it," Ambrogio said. "Daria, do not give in to him. He cannot force you to do anything evil. But if you follow him willingly—"

His words faded into a scream of agony as a guard stepped on his mangled hand.

"Nay!" Daria cried. *"Nay!"*

"Take them away," Abramo said. The guards immediately bent and took the three out the door. Agata cast one last glance at Daria, her eyes mirroring Daria's pain and confusion. Even Bormeo screeched unceasingly as they carried him out and down the hall.

Daria gasped for air as she wept, frustration and fury rendering her helpless.

"Ah, the mighty Duchess," he said, pulling her upright and against his chest, forcing her head up, still staring down the hall, now empty. He felt like a stone wall behind her. "I told you, I will win this war, Daria. Give in, give in to me now. You are vanquished. Agree to serve me in our ceremony this night . . ."

"Nay," she said, shaking her head, her eyes blurred with tears. "I shall never serve you. I belong to the light. I belong to the light. I belong to the light . . ."

He let her go, then, and she turned to face him, sobs wracking her body.

He folded his arms. "You weaken, my love. Mayhap it will take the boy dying, then the artist. Finally the old woman. I will make them suffer every moment they live. I shall force you to watch. Or you can agree to my terms."

"Away from me, Satan. Away from me."

He smiled at her with a hollow look, sighed heavily, and then left.

Daria turned to the wall and bent her forehead to the cool stone, praying through her sobs. "Oh my God, my God. Come to us. Save us. Save us. Please, Lord Jesus. Please." She sank to her knees, still weeping. "I beg you. Please Lord. I cannot watch my loved ones suffer. I cannot. Come to us. We are fragmented and weak. Fight for us. Free us. We need you. *We need you.*"

CHAPTER TWENTY-SEVEN

"WE have five pieces," Gianni said, pacing. "He has the other two." Tessa stood at the window, staring out with a stricken look on her face as she had all afternoon. It unnerved him, her fear. *They gain strength,* she had said earlier. What kind of warrior awaited his enemy to become stronger before he attacked? Their delay was foolhardy!

"We have what we came for," he continued, "but we cannot leave without Daria, Hasani, the men. Do we not have faith enough to take on the leviathan?"

"We have faith enough, my son, but wisdom tells me to hold."

"For how long? How long must we wait? Our enemy only becomes stronger!"

Father Piero, Vito, and Ugo stared at him from their chairs.

"Captain, we do not yet know where he has taken her," Vito said. "How do you suggest we go and find Lady Daria? Hasani? We've combed the city, looking for them. To say nothing of Basilio and Rune in the doge's prison . . ."

Tessa stood up straighter and smiled. "Help is coming," she said, smiling at them as if she knew a secret. She turned back to the rainy night, so dreary and dark that the front oil lamps barely made a dent outward.

Gianni went to the girl and peered outward. "Who, Tessa? Who is coming?"

"Our fisherman," she said, smiling wide.

The others stood and joined them at the window.

Within minutes, a skiff appeared in the soft glow of the lamp. A powerful man stood at the back, poling his way to their landing.

Vito and Ugo rushed out, not pausing for their capes, and helped him pull the skiff to the dock. The trio hurried inside, out of the rain.

Gianni reached out an arm and the fisherman took it, pulling back his hood. His bearded face was wet with rain.

"I shall have your name this time," Gianni said, still holding the older man's arm.

The fisherman sighed, his eyes flicking to Tessa, who smiled up at him with a beatific smile. "Forgive me, Captain, for being late. It is as you have said. I am one of your own. It took me a bit to agree to the Lord's terms."

"His call is at times exasperating and yet relentless," Gianni said with a smile. "I take it you are here to join us at last?"

"At last."

"And your full name?"

"Gaspare. Gaspare Belluci." He turned to shake Vito and Ugo's hands and then the priest's. At last he turned to Tessa and tousled her hair.

"I knew you would come, Gaspare."

"Ah? I thought it was the black man who was gifted with visions."

"Nay," she said sweetly. "Hasani knew you would come one night, out of the rain. He showed me his picture of it. But I knew you belonged with us, from the start. I can see the light within you."

Gaspare smiled and, with a grunt, went down to one knee. "Forgive me, girl, for being so stubborn. I might have spared you and yours some pain had I come earlier."

"Nay, all is as it should be," Piero said. "All is coming to pass as the Lord has seen it. We must simply be upon his way."

ல ல ல

DARIA fell asleep in the early hours of the morning, exhausted by her tears. She had thought she had found a way to keep Abramo at bay, but never had she considered the alternative lengths he would be willing to take. Vincenzo . . . the depth of his betrayal clawed at her heart.

Not only had he taken her captive at the Morassi palazzo, he had captured or killed her beloved Sciorias and Ambrogio, set fire to her home. He had been in that mansion when Daria's mother had given birth, been there when her father had asked him to be Daria's godfather. Had been there when her mother died, and then her father, three days later.

He had held her, comforted her, counseled her, planned with her, all within those walls. And then he had killed people he had known as long as her, set fire to the walls, taking down the last of her physical defenses. He had even thought to bring Marco with him in order to draw her in.

This was why he had been so conspicuously absent since her arrival. Amidei had wanted her to feel the impact of this punch. The devastation of a friend so totally removed and placed against her. He wanted her to know the full reach of his power. Abramo Amidei owned Vincenzo. Owned him.

Deep within, Daria knew they would all suffer further at Abramo's hands. He meant to own all of them, as he did Vincenzo. The darkness within him reveled in bringing despair to the world, for in their despair, people at times turned from the light and embraced the dark in a desperate search for relief from the pain. Daria had seen it within Vincenzo. Seen his hope die with his beloved wife, his love turned to anger, anger to hatred, hatred to the foul, the foul to the desperate, the desperate to a pitiful grab at power.

Images from Siena cascaded through her mind. On some level, she could understand Vincenzo's fall. But what she could not get past was his utter betrayal. At what point had Daria become his enemy?

Was it when she refused to tell him of her gift? She paced back and forth, remembering his expression when she was unveiled in Piazza del Duomo, when he believed she had played him for the fool rather than simply protected her secret.

Daria considered another attempt at reaching out to him, asking for help. Might history ultimately prevail? Shared memories? Shared lives?

She shook her head. She would not speak to Vincenzo ever again. He had murdered her loved ones, abused and taken captive still others, removed her from the guild, and burned down her home. At some point he had come to see her as an enemy. But over and over, he had proven himself as an enemy himself, rivaling Abramo.

Her hatred for both men wearied her, and she sank to the bed and gave in to a light, fitful sleep.

ch ch ch

"I know where the lady is," Gaspare said, taking a swig of wine and staring into the fire.

"Daria? You know where Daria is?" Gianni cried, leaping to his feet. "Where is she?"

The grizzled fisherman stared up into his face. A blush grew at Gianni's neck and all were silent for a long moment. "Tell me. Where is she? We must be off at once."

"Nay," Gaspare said, shaking his head gently. "You are not thinking as captain, gifted in the faith of the ancients. Search your heart, man. Is this moment the right one to go and fetch your lady?"

Gianni's cheek muscles worked in frustration as he stared at the fisherman. He turned away suddenly, clamping down upon his temples with the third finger and thumb of his right hand. After another moment, he looked over his shoulder. "I take it you have another plan."

"I do."

They all waited expectantly.

"We will go and free Basilio and Rune first," Piero said, staring at the fisherman and suddenly recognizing the right course of action. "We will need every fighting man we have."

"They are to appear before the doge himself on the morrow," Vito said. "Are you suggesting we simply enter the palace and free them?"

"God shall make a way," Gaspare said, still staring into the fire.

"That's an extravagant feat, even for God," Vito said.

Gaspare's head whipped around and he stared at the knight dolefully. "Are you suggesting, after all you have witnessed, that you believe your God cannot do as he says he will?"

Vito frowned. "Nay. Um, I only meant . . ." He clamped his mouth shut.

"Go on," Ugo said to Gaspare, throwing out his chin.

"They are charged with rape and larceny, are they not?" Gaspare said.

"Indeed," Piero said, sitting down across from the man.

"And the charge will demand payment. Venezia is a city that prizes justice over all else."

"Even if justice is not served?" Gianni asked. "Even if innocent men are sent to the gallows?"

"Certainly," Gaspare said dryly. "The *idea* of justice holds sway over justice itself here. If it serves those in power and appears just, it is enough."

"We have not yet tried going to the conte and contessa," Ugo said.

Gaspare raised an eyebrow. "That idea may have merit."

"It is easier to have the conte free them than fight their way out on the piazzeta," Ugo said.

"The conte is powerful," Gaspare said, tucking his chin into his hand. "But the people are stronger yet."

Gianni narrowed his eyes. "What do you mean?"

Gaspare looked about the room. "You are the Gifted. We are the Gifted. This time and place has been foretold for the ages. God has shown me this. What he has set forth, no man can deny. Although the dark shall try every route possible to dissuade us, our God is stronger yet."

Piero rose, chin in hand, nodding. "It is within my own heart as well. For days now, I have felt the pull to the people. To reach out to them, speak to them."

Gaspare gave them all a stern glance from beneath bushy, graying eyebrows. "I propose that we allow your men to stand trial and take their sentence. When they are led to the gallows on the piazzetta, we will move."

"But we shall not move alone," Piero said.

"The people will rise and support us?" Vito asked.

"Yes," Piero said, his eyes wide with understanding.

"And if they do not?" Ugo asked.

"Then God shall," Gaspare said. "Be not afraid, Gifted. You are fragmented, but God on high has chosen this moment to bring you back together."

"He wished for us to remember," Piero said thoughtfully, staring into the fire.

"What, Father?" Tessa asked, taking the priest's hand. "What did he wish us to remember?"

"That he is our God, and we are but his children. Gifted or no," he said, looking beyond the girl to the men, "We are all but children in his eyes. When we take our eyes off him, we lose our way."

"But when lost," Gaspare said, "one must first recognize that one has left the path. Then one can go and find it again."

ॐ ॐ ॐ

THE maidservant set down her pitcher of water and the basin and paused, listening for Daria's breathing.

Daria breathed in and out slowly, as if in deep slumber, and after a moment, the woman departed.

Just as the door was about to close, Daria flew across the stone floor on tiptoes and grabbed it, right as it was about to latch shut again. She held her breath, listening to the maid flirt with the guard.

"Leave your post, man. Come to the ceremony. The lady sleeps. She is exhausted. And even if she escaped, where would she go? The Master would not be angry with you for wanting to partake of the feast this night."

Daria moved to see through the slit in the door. The maid and the knight embraced, kissing passionately. He moved her to the far wall of the hall, lifting her hand and pinning it there, ardently kissing her.

The maid succumbed to his advances and then cocked a brow, eyeing him brazenly. "You've hungered for me for weeks." She lifted up on tiptoes and bit him playfully on the chin. "Come with me."

"Vixen."

"Come," she repeated in invitation.

Daria allowed the door to slide shut, holding the latch from taking its place, locking her within. Her heart pounded as she imagined the guard turning to study the door, making sure it was shut. She prayed that he would not try the door, not look in upon her to make certain she was as sound asleep as the maid contended. Swallowing hard, she laid an ear to the door and heard the musings between man and woman. Then . . . footfalls fading away down the hall.

Whispering a prayer of thanks, she eased open the door a crack and peered out. Empty. She opened the door wider. She looked one way and then the other.

Nothing but a solitary, flickering torch, casting deep shadows.

Daria shivered. Did she have the courage to do this?

Moreover, how could she not?

Steeling herself, she moved down the passageway. She could hear the laughter and cries and shouts of the ceremony reaching its apex, down off the main dining hall. This was the fifth such ceremony since Abramo had brought her here as his captive. In spite of the rain, there were more people here than ever before; Abramo's power and hold grew in and around Venezia. She knew that the ceremony would last well into the night.

Could she free Ambrogio, Agata, and Nico and flee to one of the boats moored at the isle's edge? She thought of Nico's severe injuries, Ambrogio's wounded hand, and shook her head. It would take an act of God to free them. A bigger act to see them safely beyond the isle's shores and to safety.

All she knew was that she had to move now, in order to try to heal the boy. If she did not, he would be dead before morning.

Sighing, she moved down the passageway and peeked around the wall of the staircase. All appeared empty. Below, the frenzy was building. She wished she could block out the animalistic cries and moans, but they grew louder in her ears, pounding at her like hungry dogs at her heels. She would have to pass the doorway to make her way to the other wing, where she believed the prison was.

Daria edged around a corner and peered down a long, empty passageway. Three torches flickered and danced in the darkness. A drum began beating and the crazed sounds within the ceremonial room grew in tandem with it. Abramo was speaking, droning on in an incantation that Daria blocked out with whispered, concentrated Scripture. She prayed for safe passage, for them not to see her as she crossed the doorway. She prayed for blocked vision, for holy protection.

With that she rose from the edge of the passageway and squared her shoulders. The doorway was but a few feet ahead. If they saw her, what would happen?

Lord, protect me. Set your angels about me. Before me, beside me, behind me. Protect me, protect me, protect me. With that she began walking, concentrating on the end of the passageway, turning not left nor right. *Protect me, protect me, protect me.*

As she passed the doorway, the dark pulled at her like a cloying arm, sticking to her leg, her arm, her shoulder, her neck. She closed her eyes and whispered, *Jesus, Jesus, Jesus* . . . Her ears filled with the *whoosh* of her pulsing blood and she managed to put one foot in front of the other, in front of the other, in front of the other.

She stopped and opened her eyes, aware now that she was at the end of the passageway. She glanced back, expecting pursuit. But there was only emptiness. And a dreadful silence.

No more crazed sounds from the ceremonial room.

Nothing. Terror overcame her.

Daria turned and ran.

She turned one corner and then another, pausing to listen, hearing only the pounding of her own heart in a rush. She ran up one set of stairs and then another. She entered a cavernous room, full of pillars and terribly dark. She was lost, no closer to her loved ones than when she was in her room. Daria sank to her knees behind a long, stone wall that came to her waist, panting and listening.

"M'lady?"

Daria sucked in her breath and held it. It was Abramo, across the room.

"Daria?"

Her eyes widened. Vincenzo. Vincenzo was with him.

A man took in a deep, heavy sniff from across the room, the sound of it filling every crevice of the room. Abramo chuckled softly. "Ah yes. You are here. Do you not know that when you pray, you begin to smell of the Gifted? I would know you anywhere." He was moving, searching for her. "Shall I demonstrate?"

Daria closed her eyes, fighting to not give in to the fear.

"Vincenzo, take that flame out and leave it, then return here, to the doorway. I shall show you how to search out the Duchess in other ways."

Daria's eyes widened as the torch was taken from the room, leaving them in utter darkness.

Abramo laughed lowly. "Ah, yes. I shall find you, Duchess. And this night, you shall be mine. I am coming, Duchess. Do you hear me? I am coming to claim you. You belong with us. Come, come to the ceremonial hall and take your rightful place."

Daria struggled to not gasp. He was nearing her, frighteningly close.

He was silent for a long moment, listening. "I hear your heart, beloved. Fluttering. Like a sweet butterfly. You fear me. It is intoxicating. Give in to your fears, Daria. Face them. I shall teach you how to conquer them. I shall show you ultimate power."

Daria longed to stand and face him, to shout out words that would combat his own. But she could not, she was too afraid, could only pray for protection, a way out.

"*Pa-dump, pa-dump, pa-dump,*" Abramo said, just across the stone wall from her. "Your heart is pounding, frightfully fast. Hear it, Duchess? It fills the room. *Pa-dump, pa-dump, pa-dump, pa-dump, pa-dump.*"

Daria's brow furrowed in terror. Could he hear her heart? He was reaching out to her, guessing. Using her fear. He could not hear her heart! He could not!

But still, his words were timed uncannily close to the true beat of her pulse.

"I shall have your heart, one way or another," he said, stepping forward until he was beside Daria. But he was not reaching down, did not know she was there, right there.

"Duchess, come to me." He turned in a slow circle, his voice echoing off the opposite wall, then to her right. "You are here. I am upon your scent. Our charming game of cat and mouse is over." He inhaled deeply. "Piñon berries and milk and honey and cloves and oranges . . . It is you. There is no escape. Offer me your heart. Serve me this night. Pledge your devotion and I shall free your loved ones. Stand apart from me and watch them die. One way or another, I hold your very life in my hands. This shall be difficult or it shall be easy, so easy. *Pa-dump, pa-dump . . .*"

Daria held her breath, feeling the cool tendrils of the dark reach out to her, pull at her, like tongues of the dead.

I will not succumb, she prayed. *Lord Jesus, do not allow me to succumb. Deliver me, deliver me, deliver me, Father of light . . .*

"Master," Vincenzo said across the room. As he spoke, Daria turned and crawled around the wall, away from Abramo. "The others . . . they grow weary of the wait. You take them to a point of frenzy and then make them await your orders."

"Silence!" Abramo said.

Daria paused, several feet away from him now. She felt the Lord's urging, continued to crawl as silently as she could, pausing to pull the skirt from beneath her knees when it threatened to cripple her.

The grit of the stones dug into her knees, but she kept moving, feeling her way away from Abramo, down to the right. She paused, aware of Abramo behind her, but from this angle, she could see Vincenzo's tall form silhouetted in the doorway.

"She is departing," Abramo said. "Bring back the torch."

Vincenzo turned away and Daria immediately scurried to the next room, rising to her feet. The dance of flame lit the doorway behind her, but she was already moving away, turning a corner and then another. She gave up trying to remain silent and fled headlong down a staircase, almost losing her footing.

Daria paused at the base of the stairs. She heard the heavy footfall of another in pursuit and glanced over her shoulder to see the light of a torch nearing the top of the staircase. Why were they not rushing after her? Was she trapped?

She turned and collided heavily against metal bars.

She cried out, the impact stealing her very breath, knowing then that escape was futile. An attempt to flee was useless.

"Oh, Daria," said a heavy voice behind her.

So Abramo had sent him. Her betrayer.

Daria reached up to hold the bars, willing her Lord to send her the strength she needed. "Vincenzo," she said in barely more than a whisper. Still she did not turn. She could not face him.

Vincenzo lifted his torch and Daria looked into the cell, expecting Agata, or Ambrogio, or Nico.

But instead, she saw the naked form of her oldest friend, Hasani, his back flayed from repeated whippings. Beyond him were images upon the wall, images painted crudely, as if with fingertip and blood. It was blood. Blood, so much blood.

Daria sank to her knees. "Hasani," she whispered.

He did not move.

"Hasani?" she cried.

Vincenzo lifted her to her feet.

Abramo was there, then. "Speak not to my slave."

"Slave? He is no slave!" she cried, fury momentarily replacing fear.

A man came out from behind Abramo. Daria fought to place him. His face was in deep shadow, but he was frighteningly broad and muscular, his neck nearly as wide as her waist.

He had to speak but a few words before she knew him. The knight, the knight from her country estate, the one she had sent away . . . Ciro.

"Need me to take care of this woman while you see to your business, Master?" he asked, leering over Daria.

"She is my business," Abramo said lightly. "But mayhap I have been too lenient these past days with her. Chain her up as our slave has been. She still believes herself too strong. That she can escape me. We will show her what weakness truly is."

Abramo turned toward the tiny, barred window and paused.

"What is it, Master?" Vincenzo asked.

"The rain."

"What of it?"

"Do you sense the shift? It is ceasing."

Vincenzo shook his head quizzically.

"Seek within you, Vincenzo. There is a check there, such as when you feel an enemy afoot."

"Can it not simply be a change in the weather?"

Abramo stared at him then gave a quick shake of his head. "Nay. It is something more."

Ciro opened the cell next to Hasani's and pushed her inward, yanking her hand up and clamping shut the first of the manacles.

CHAPTER TWENTY-EIGHT

GASPARE raised his hands to the sky and bowed his head. After several minutes in prayer, he uttered but a few words. "In the name of Jesus, cease."

The group of citizens huddled in the small piazzetta beside the neighborhood church the conte and contessa claimed as their own gasped as one. They were sleepy and bewildered, called from their beds at such a late hour, and in the rain, at that. It was only in deference to their priest and the *patronas* of their church and an idle curiosity that brought them out at such a moment.

But when Gaspare called upon the skies to cease their relentless drizzle, and the skies heeded his call, they stood a bit straighter.

Gaspare nodded toward Piero.

"Good citizens," said the priest, speaking not in a shout, but a hushed whisper that was handed back through the waves of the crowd, from person to person. "I call upon you at this moment to search your hearts and determine for yourselves whether or not I speak God's holy truth."

He paced before them. "Venezia is a city of the just, priding herself for holding up the righteous. I beg you to understand that I have been called to this city, as have my compatriots." He waved in Vito, Ugo, Gianni, Tessa, and Gaspare's direction and the crowd visibly shifted a step in respect.

"We have been called to your city for God's holy purpose," Piero said. He looked to the conte meaningfully.

The conte stepped forward. "I can attest to that. It is because of these people, and those among them who are unable to be here this night, that my twin children live." He paced before the crowd, waiting for his words to be passed back to the outer reaches. "My children were said to be dead within my wife's womb," he said, reaching back to put an arm around the contessa. "And a healer among these people saved them all."

A murmur went through the crowd, people conferring on what they had heard and what they knew to be true.

"Not only that," the conte continued, "but if it were not for this priest," he said, laying his hands upon Piero's shoulders, "my children would have died when the palazzo burned to the ground. He emerged from the flames and smoke unhurt, my children with him."

Piero waited for the conte's words to be passed along. "We share this with you, friends, because we are in need of your help. We are in a fierce battle with those who wish us dead and gone. We are God's holy ones, and you are our protectors. We have been called here, and yet the evil ones wish our cause squelched. I beseech you, brothers and sisters, to rise to this call. We are in need of you."

He waited for his words to work their way to the back of the crowd. "I beseech you to search your hearts and determine for yourself if we speak the truth," he said. "God has called us here on his own holy mission. And yet we are wounded, unable to go on. Some of our own have been captured, taken by the evil ones. Others are held by the doge himself."

Piero paused again, waiting for the ripples to pass backward. "To be sure, we believe the doge does not understand what treachery has come to pass. But it is the truth of it. On the morrow, the doge will sentence two of our own to death, on charges of rape and larceny. But upon my life, they are innocent."

The priest paced back and forth, waiting, praying that there were no spies among them. But together, the remnant of the Gifted had prayed, and God had shown them this as the one and only way.

"I beg of you to see the idiocy of this claim, the obvious movements of the dark in this foul moment. They have been framed for crimes they did not commit, and will perish on the morrow upon the gallows if we do not have your help and intervention."

A long moment of silence followed his words. Then a man stepped from the crowd. "What would you have us do, Father?"

Piero paused and looked to the ground, then to the night sky. "This plan only works if you all remain true to it. If we remain together . ." He went on to detail the plan and then prayed over the group.

He looked up. "I thank you, friends. For considering coming to our aid. I leave it to our Lord and Savior to see it through."

A long second passed. "How do we know you are God's own?" shouted a man in the back of the crowd.

"A good question, that," Piero said, motioning to settle the agitated crowd. He glanced at Gaspare. "I pray that the Lord Jesus Christ, and his Holy Spirit, and the Father in heaven, will give you assurance thrice over. As you return to your homes, let the gentle rain upon your shoulders be your answer."

"What rain?" scoffed another from the right.

Gaspare was already down upon his knees, hands lifted up to the heavens.

As one, they looked skyward, and felt the rain fall upon their faces again.

They could have claimed trickery.

They could have fought the truth.

But with wonder and awe, Piero watched as the crowd turned and, with bent heads, made their way home in the rain.

Vito and Ugo turned to follow their captain home, Tessa between them. But Gaspare paused and looked back to him, and Gianni stopped and turned, staring at Piero expectantly.

Suddenly, staring across the empty piazzetta as the last of the men and women departed, Piero could see it, how it would all work out for God's own purposes.

He faltered, feeling the hard stone meet his bony knees. He bent low and then slowly rose, lifting his face to the rain. "And so it ends, Savior? Here?" he asked the sky.

His mind raced and his heart pounded. And yet deep within, he felt peace pervade his entire being. Utter confidence. Security. And a tinge of sorrow. But all at once he saw the wisdom of it, with a clarity that surpassed the ages.

He would die. Sacrifice himself for this cause.

But he would die well.

ക ക ക

BASILIO rose when keys jangled and the large metal door to their prison cell scraped upon the stones. He nudged Rune, asleep on the stones, and the man sleepily came to a sitting position, squinting against the sudden torchlight that filled their cell. The doge's jailer and a bishop came into view, and behind them a cardinal. Rune came to his feet.

The cardinal dismissed the jailer and waited as the man padded away, clearly displeased to not watch this interchange.

"Come to hear our prayers, priest?" Basilio spat out. They had spent more than a week in prison, and their trial had been a travesty, their former masters and Ilario's daughter telling no semblance of truth. But Ricci silver had reportedly been sold to a merchant who identified Rune. A housemaid claimed to have seen them stealing into the girl's bedroom. They had been in Venezia at the time; it was shortly thereafter that they had set off for Siena and a new land, a new captain, and run across Gianni de Capezzana.

"I can hear your prayers," the cardinal allowed, ignoring Basilio's slight in calling him a priest. "But it is not why I have come."

"No?" Rune asked.

"I am Cardinal Boeri de Vaticana de Roma," said the man, studying them both.

Basilio shifted. "Our captain's former employer."

"One and the same."

"What do you want of us?"

"I wish to aid you."

Basilio scoffed. "Mayhap you have not heard, Your Eminence. Tomorrow we are to die."

"I have heard," the cardinal allowed, eyeing the bishop beside him. "I have heard that you have been sentenced to die. But your sentence has not yet come to pass. I am here to tell you that your friends and your God have not forgotten you. Chances are high that on the morrow, you shall make your escape, and return to the Gifted."

Rune's eyes shot upward, meeting his.

"Oh yes, Sir Rune, I know all about you, as does the doge. But be at peace. I am here as friend, not foe."

❦ ❦ ❦

DARIA looked over to Hasani, motionless as he hung from the manacles that held his arms and legs out in a large X against the wall. Was he dead?

Ciro lifted her other hand and slapped the manacle shut. She had to stand on her tiptoes to keep the irons from digging into her hands, tearing the flesh. Daria carefully avoided looking at her captor, only at her friend. In fact, Ciro had chained her against Hasani's cell wall so she could do little else.

"He lives, yet," Ciro said. "The Master is not done with him. He will serve the Master. As shall you, Duchess."

He held her by the waist and she dared to eye him over her shoulder, his features hidden by shadow, the torch flickering behind him. Abramo and Vincenzo hovered behind him. When she saw the glint of the knife in Ciro's teeth she gasped, involuntarily leaning away, only succeeding in an inch's gain, before she swung back.

Ciro took the knife from his teeth.

"What are you doing?" Daria asked.

"The Master honors me, with this task." He grabbed the shoulder of her golden overdress and slid the knife beneath it. With a flick of the wrist, he cut it at the seam, then moved to the other side, studying her profile.

Daria knew dismay, and fear filled her eyes, but she could not help herself, could not hide the horror of this moment.

Ciro smiled and then yanked at the gown, looking down at her as it fell to the floor. He moved behind her and cut a slit into her undergown at the center, then with one savage pull ripped it open, leaving her back bare and exposed. *O God, O God, O God,* she chanted in her mind. This could not be happening. Not now. *Lord, Lord, where are you? Come to me! Come to me! Rescue me! Rescue us all!*

"I shall pay you a king's ransom. Please, free us."

None of them answered her.

Ciro brought the knife to the back of her neck so she could feel the long, cold shaft and slid it slowly down the length of her spine.

O God, O God, O God . . . What of young Nico? Agata? Ambrogio? Hasani? Were they all to die here on this miserable isle, tortured to death?

"The Master wishes me to break you. To teach you fear," Ciro said. He reached for a whip, coiled upon a peg, and slowly let it loose.

Her heart pounded, reminding her of Abramo, mimicking its beat. She grimaced. She was playing right into their hands. Again.

Paul's words flooded through her mind and out through her lips.

" 'Praise the Lord, O my soul." Her voice cracked. "I will sing praise to my God as long as I live.' "

Ciro's whip fell to the ground with a dull thump, like a massive coil of snake upon the stones.

"Uncle!" Daria cried, looking over her shoulder at Vincenzo.

He moved forward, to her side. "It does not have to be this way, Daria. Say the word, just say the word that you will join us, and this shall cease."

She shook her head, again surprised at how far Vincenzo was willing to go to follow Amidei. " 'Do not put your trust in princes, in mortal men, who cannot save,' " Daria continued in a rush, her voice gaining strength. Vincenzo resumed his position in the shadows behind her. " 'When their spirit departs, they return to the ground; on that very day their plans come to *nothing*.' " She spat out the last words in Abramo's direction.

Abramo lifted his chin and the whip came then, lightning fast, parting Daria's lips in silent agony. Abramo brought his hand to his chin and watched her intently.

" 'Blessed is she whose help is the God of Jacob,' " she whispered, tears sliding down her cheeks, " 'whose hope is the Lord her God, the Maker of heaven and ear—' "

She cried out as the whip again crossed her back, panting against the searing pain. She fought to concentrate on the Word and her faith, her only protection. She fought to block out the countless stripes across Hasani's back before her, and the vision of her own in similar tatters.

" 'The Lord remains faithful forever. He upholds the cause of the oppressed and gives food to the hungry,' " she said, staring toward Abramo. " 'The Lord sets prisoners free . . .' "

The whip came again, licking around her rib cage, slicing open a portion of her undergown. She glanced down; the blood climbed up the soft ivory cloth toward her right breast.

"Where is your God now, Daria? Why is he not setting you free?" Abramo said, suddenly beside her, hissing in her ear. "He has left you, abandoned you to us. Join us. We shall never abandon you."

Daria forced herself back to the Scriptures. " 'The Lord gives sight to the blind,' " she said, panting, " 'the Lord lifts up those who are bowed down.' " She looked again to Abramo even as the whip came across her back, making her arch this time. " 'The Lord loves the righteous and frustrates the ways of the wicked!' "

The fifth blow cut deep. Her vision swam and she sank to her feet, allowing the manacles to dig into her hands, hanging now. Tears flowed down her face.

She slowly lifted her face, her back a searing mass of agony, recognizing that Abramo was now on her other side.

"I told you, Duchess. You can come to me easily, or you can come vanquished. But you shall come."

Daria shook her head slightly. "It is you who does not yet understand. I belong to no one but the Lord God, who was and is and is to come. Who was and is and is to come. Who was . . . and *is . . . and is to come.*"

Abramo stepped backward, his mouth closing in distaste. He turned and glanced at Ciro. "Ten more lashes. A bucket of saltwater at the end. Leave her alive but sure of my words about her absent God." Then he departed, not looking back again even as the whip cracked and Daria at last gave way to screams.

Chapter Twenty-nine

THE knights of d'Angelo did not wear their colors the next day. The day had dawned with no more rain clouds in sight, crisp and cold. The sea was again a delicate green, rather than the gray they had become accustomed to. And with a plan in mind, a bright late-autumn sun in the sky, and knowledge of where Daria was held, Gianni felt the first stirrings of hope that he had felt in weeks.

He came down to the main floor, pulling on his gloves. Vito was beside Gaspare, saying, "Can you not simply create a diversion for us? Make it hail or the like?"

Gaspare rolled his eyes and stood. "I do only as the Lord bids. It is not my sense that he will allow it now."

Vito sighed and stood beside his brother. "I was afraid you'd say that. Why is it the Gifted cannot act when we wish it?"

Piero smiled and padded behind him, gathering his belongings. "Think on it, Vito. Does it not become clear that God acts at just the right moment? Always in his time, his way. Be it frustrating for us to wait upon him, it is always right."

Vito sighed again and turned to gather his sword and shield.

Gianni motioned them all forward, pulling Tessa into the center of their circle and onto his knee. "You shall remain by my side at all times, understood?"

She nodded, the very picture of serious intent that they all now shared.

"Everyone has what they need?" Gianni asked. The boats were packed and loaded, ready for them. "We have Hasani's things?"

"Here, Captain," said Ugo, raising a canvas satchel.

"The knights' weapons and clothing are stowed?"

Vito nodded.

"Our map pieces?" Gianni asked of Piero.

The priest gave a gesture of assent.

"And you are ready to leave your city? Leave everything behind?" Gianni asked of Gaspare.

"I am but a fisherman, used to nothing but the clothes on my back and the sea beneath my feet."

Gianni gave him a small smile. "How are you with a sword?"

"Regrettably, fairly poor," Gaspare said. He pounded a meaty fist into the palm of his other hand. "I am an old man, but I am yet strong."

Gianni reached out a hand and laid it upon his shoulder. "Strong of fist, mighty in faith. You are exactly who we need at this moment, Gaspare. Praise the Lord on high that you have answered this call."

Gaspare sighed and nodded, staring at the space of floor between their feet. Gianni knew he must be wondering what was to become of him—just last night, the fisherman had said he had never been away from the lagoon, having felt the rock of her waves since he was a babe, believing he would die here.

"We shall see that you return, if at all possible, my friend," Gianni said gently.

"It shall be as it shall," Gaspare said with a shrug.

᚛ ᚛ ᚛

HASANI gasped and lifted his head, staring at the wall that depicted Daria, Gianni, and the others in his own blood. He saw Father Piero in the vision, dying, sacrificing himself, just as he had seen Daria bound and captured. He bent his head and shook it, wishing his gift of visions would dissipate like the rain. He could hear it had ended, smelled the sun on the bricks outside the small window of their prison.

"Hasani," Daria said lowly.

Hasani brought up his head with a start, thinking he was hearing things. At his right, a golden sedge warbler flitted to the window for a moment and then departed, leaving him feeling more alone than ever.

He turned to the left and looked to the cell beside him, long empty. And then he moaned and let out a cry of despair.

Daria stood as she had in his vision, clothed only in a ripped under-dress, chained to the cell wall. Old blood climbed her undergown in odd splotches. But she stared at him, her eyes clear.

Hasani bent his head and wept, wishing it no more than a vision, not yet truth.

She allowed him several moments, and then spoke with clarity, in a tone she had not used since they were children. "You have been hurt, as have I." She paused, took a breath, difficult in her position. Hasani well knew the battle. The feeling in his hands, arms, and shoulders had long become numb. Even his chest had little feeling to it, the blood pooling in his legs. The only blessing was that it put a halt to the pain in his back; he prayed for the same blessing for Daria.

"We are not abandoned," Daria said sternly.

Hasani raised his head, stared at the images drawn in blood, and then glanced her direction. He made a sound, one he knew she could interpret.

"We are not abandoned," she repeated. "The others are yet alive. Our God has not forgotten us."

Hasani swallowed hard, wishing for a bit more saliva in his mouth. The stub of his tongue cascaded over dry cheeks. "Bai'o," he said with a slur. "Wue," he managed. It had been a long time since he had uttered a sound at all. But if these were their final moments, he did not wish pride to get in the way.

"God will see to Basilio and Rune, and the others," she said, nodding toward the drawings on his wall. From her angle, she probably could only see a portion.

She eyed him meaningfully. "Hasani, you must cling to hope. Hope in the Christ. He will save us. He brought us together. He shall save us."

Hasani bent his head. All he could think of was his papers, Abramo setting them afire from a candle and tossing them into the hearth. The only other copy had surely burned in the mansion in Siena. Abramo had delighted in telling him of the fire that had taken down the house of d'Angelo, collapsing over the corpses of Beata and Aldo . . .

"Papeh," he said, trying to get her to understand about his papers that had long held captors at bay, freedom in close proximity.

"Your papers?" she asked, wincing as she moved. "What of them? Did they take them?"

"Bank," he managed, wishing for a bit of water. "Bank, bank," he said in despair, shaking his head.

"Blank? They were blank?" She groaned and leaned her head back. Then she groaned again and shook her head. "When we entered the Morassi palazzo, the guards, they questioned you, looked at your papers . . ." She sighed. "I am sorry, my friend. You have my word that we shall get it straight when we reach safety."

A long moment passed, and then uncommon humor entered Hasani's mind. Safety? She would see to it? He allowed a small, manic laugh and it gave way to another and still another.

Daria frowned at first, but then giggled a little, making Hasani laugh louder. It had been years since Daria had heard the deep bass of Hasani's laughter. Daria threw her head back and laughed, letting it flow through her until tears of joy streamed down her cheeks.

"So it does not appear as if we might reach safety anytime soon," Daria said. "But Hasani, I gain strength simply by being near you again, friend. They have not beaten us yet."

Hasani glanced at her and, for the first time in days, drew as deep a breath as he could. She was right. Together, they could fight off the monsters.

God had seen them to this place.

God would lead them out.

Even if it was not in the way Daria imagined it.

Footfalls and voices at the top of the steps drew their attention forward, and Daria watched for their approach. Hasani looked from right to left, but chained with his belly to the wall, he could not see.

He grunted, drawing her attention.

"Ami'ei," he said, gesturing with the top of his head, he whispered madly, frustrated by the intelligible sounds. They were coming down the stairs, three maybe four of them.

"What?" Daria asked, confusion on her face. "The letter? Abramo's letter?"

Hasani nodded madly. "Ge' i," he said. "You. Ge' i."

"Get it? I've seen it. He poisoned me with it."

" 'aria."

She shushed and looked at him intently.

"Ge' i. I' way."

Daria frowned. "The letter? The way?" she whispered. "We must get it from Abramo?"

"Igh. Can'e."

"The light," she whispered, remembering the map that was illuminated when they had held the first three pages to the candle. If they could get the three that Abramo held, they might indeed see a map, just as they had seen the way in their first portion.

Hasani nodded, staring at her meaningfully as the men entered the room behind him.

Two paused at Hasani's cell and Ciro bent to unlock it. Daria watched the men, listened to them talk, and in seconds knew them as slavers.

Nay, nay, she thought. Nay! She cried out silently to her Lord. *Not this! Please!*

Hasani's eyes remained on hers, willing her to be silent, confident in the knowledge of the holy—the same knowledge she had used to speak hope into his heart earlier.

She could not tear her eyes away, even as she heard her own cell door open with a metallic groan, knew Abramo and Vincenzo were with her.

"You are certain this was necessary?"

"Less than called for," Abramo said lightly. "I told you to expect difficulty in this pursuit."

The men were looking over Hasani like a woman checking over a chicken in the marketplace.

"We'll give you fifty," tossed a slaver over his shoulder, patting a hand on Hasani's mighty deltoid. Turkish, Daria thought, remembering many encounters with other merchants of their homeland. Cutthroat and mercenary, by and large.

"Would've given you sixty had you left him with some of his black hide," said the other. "It will take a good bit to sew him back together."

The other moved to haul back a corner of Hasani's lip to examine his teeth.

"He is not for sale," Daria ground out. "He is a free man."

The slavers stood straight and looked in her direction for the first time. They came to the bars that divided the cell and stood there, gawking. "Who's the woman?" asked one. "She for sale too?"

The other laughed, letting his eyes slide slowly down her tattered, bloody dress and back again. He was missing many of his bottom teeth.

"I am Daria d'Angelo," she said, lifting her chin. "My father freed Hasani when he was a boy. He has not been a slave in twenty years."

The first man eyed her warily and squinted, as if recognizing her name. He looked to Abramo. "Does she speak the truth, Amidei?"

Daria could feel Abramo shrug. "I have not seen his papers," he said. "And I have no use for another servant. I think it best you take him and not ask any more questions."

Ciro moved into Hasani's cell and unlocked his manacles. Hasani slumped to the ground, his arms, shoulders, and back so numb that he could not stop his momentum. He cried out as his back curved, the whip's wounds breaking open.

Daria gasped.

Vincenzo leaned forward. "You can save him, Daria."

"Get away from me."

"Ah?" Abramo asked. "You would allow one of your oldest friends to be sold into slavery?"

Hasani was shaking his head, wordlessly telling her to remain quiet. The two slavers hauled him to his feet and he lifted his chin, ever strong. Her first knight. Hasani, Hasani . . .

"Say the word, Daria. One word, and I will keep him here," Abramo said from the other side of the bars.

She cast helpless eyes in Hasani's direction. Was there no way to save him?

He shook his head, telling her to let him go.

" 'May the praise of God be in their mouths,' " Daria murmured dully, as the slavers hauled Hasani out and up the stairs, feeling none of the fire of the Scriptures that usually accompanied them. " 'A double-edged sword in their hands, to inflict vengeance on the nations and punishment on the peoples, to bind their kings with fetters, their nobles with shackles of iron, to carry out the sentence written against them.' "

Abramo held his ground, watching her. "Is it not you, noblewoman, who finds herself in fetters? Do you realize how foolish and empty are your words?"

" 'This is the glory of all the saints,' " she returned tiredly. " 'Praise the Lord. Praise the Lord. Praise God in his sanctuary; praise him in his mighty heavens. Praise him for his acts of power . . .' "

Abramo growled and cast a fist to the right, as if plunging a knife into an unseen adversary to the right. Then he strode out of the cell and up the stairs, two at a time.

" 'Praise him for his surpassing greatness,' " she whispered hollowly, Hasani now out of sight, his departure tearing a deeper chasm in her heart.

She stopped speaking then, willing the power of the Word to give her strength for what was ahead. Vincenzo unlocked the manacles and she fell as Hasani had toward the floor.

With a grunt, Vincenzo lifted her and carried her to a dirty straw tick, live with vermin. They scattered as he lowered her down, setting her on her side. Tears dripped down her cheeks as her arms became intolerably afire, blood returning, even as blood seeped down her back. She could feel the cool damp of it anew.

Vincenzo sat down heavily on a stool across the cell, legs akimbo, elbows on knees. He cradled his face in his hands for a moment and then looked at her, fingers still covering his mouth.

"Leave me," Daria whispered, her eyes blurring in grief. The depth of what he had done to her and hers left her breathless.

Vincenzo looked to the side, appearing suddenly older than his years. "This can all lead to good, Daria."

She turned her face away from him slowly, as if he had slapped her. Then, pushing against the searing pain in her neck, shoulders, and back, she slowly rose to a seated position. "You have murdered and stolen what was mine," she said slowly, with as much agony now in her heart as was upon her body. "Burned my home. Killed my beloved servants. Sold a free man, an honest man, into slavery. Watched as I was whipped."

"You have always been too stubborn," he said. "This is what happens when a woman is allowed in a man's world. I tried to tell your father—"

"Do not speak of my father. You are not worthy to ever utter his name again."

Vincenzo sighed and leaned back from her. His eyes hardened. "If you are to survive, you must give in to your conqueror."

"I am not conquered," she said, shaking her head slightly. "You and yours might take my friends, my home, my livelihood. But you forget what gives me life and breath—my God."

Vincenzo scoffed. "Your God is not the ruler of this world."

"More than you have yet realized."

He sighed and ran a hand through his hair. "Daria, you must know I did not wish to kill them. It was our only way to bring you to submission. To teach you this was no game. You must cease your mad task and join us." He rose and paced, hands on hips. "We shall give you power, stature, wealth, wealth beyond your dreams."

Daria shook her head. "You speak only of the temporal, forgetting what lies ahead. 'God will give to each person according to what he had done,' " she said, quoting Romans. " 'To those who by persistence in doing good seek glory, honor, and immortality, he will give eternal life.' "

"This life has not been what I had imagined. I will take my glory here, now. Not wait on some fable of eternity."

"Fable of eternity? 'Tis no fable, Vincenzo. 'Tis truth! A promise." She leaned her head back against the wall, careful to keep her back from touching it. " 'But for those who are self-seeking and who reject the truth and follow evil, there will be wrath and anger.' "

She swallowed hard, suddenly, unaccountably feeling sorrow for her old friend again. It surprised her, and she pushed it away, preferring her righteous anger. But then she saw the wisdom, the simple, stark hope of it. "Vincenzo, he says it very clearly in the Holy Writ. 'There will be trouble and distress for every human being who does evil.' Turn, turn now while you still can. Help me, help us. Get me to safety, back to my people. Turn back to God and find healing, wholeness, forgiveness. This is the way. This is—"

"Save your strength," he said, holding up a hand. "My lot has been cast."

"Nay," she said. "There is still time. I will pray that God will allow me to forgive you in time. But I know that God is standing here, ready and waiting to forgive you, at this very moment."

"Halt your speech," he spat out. "Your God long ago turned his face from me. Do not speak of him being here, seeking my return. I do not want his forgiveness. It is he who must ask it of *me*."

Daria waited for a long moment to pass. "I know that you have suffered unspeakable hurt. Anger. Fear. Well do I know those feelings myself, now. And you wished to turn those things from your life. But Vincenzo, you are signing your name upon a document from hell, one that will keep you in *eternal* anger, fear, hurt. You have found but temporary escape; the consequences shall be long."

"Never mind me," he said, crouching down before her. "I am a man, grown. Think of yourself now, Daria. Abramo will send Ciro back here to whip you again this eve. Hasani bore such torture for five days. I might talk him out of it, convince him that you have become one of us. But there is one condition."

Daria scoffed, casting an incredulous look in his direction. Could he no longer hear? "One condition?" she asked idly.

"Swear allegiance to Abramo. Serve me."

"Serve you? I thought Abramo wished me to serve him upon your foul altar." She tossed it out in exasperation, feeling the disgrace of every word.

Vincenzo fell to his knees before her and took her hands. Daria winced as the movement tore at the skin of her back. "I will protect you," he tried.

She opened her eyes wide to stare at him, feeling the dull heaviness of his presence like a cloud surrounding the evil one. "Vincenzo, my oldest friend, my newest enemy. You were like a brother to my father, an uncle to me. But now you are my betrayer, in every sense of the word. *Protector*, I fear you shall never be again."

THE RECKONING

CHAPTER THIRTY

THEY spent the afternoon canvassing the grand piazza that spooled out before San Marco, and the smaller piazzetta beside the doge's palace that led to the lagoon, plotting their movements, scheduling the event to come as closely as possible. After several hours, Gianni stood looking out to the gray-green waters, past the ruins of San Giorgio, imagining he could see beyond the Giudecca, the island that blocked his view of the isle that was Daria's prison.

"I must free her," he said, as Piero came to stand beside him.

"As you shall," Piero said. He patted the tall knight on the shoulder. "First our men, Captain. Then we shall take on our enemies, stronger for it."

Gianni eyed the priest. "So we free the men, go to Daria and free her. What of Hasani? Where do we go next?"

Piero pursed his lips and rocked back and forth on his feet. "I know not. Only that God will show us, in his good time. He has brought us this far. He will see us through the next steps."

"You are certain."

"Never more so."

They stood there in companionable silence for a time, watching the boats and ships move about the lagoon. A crowd was already gathering behind them, a hanging always bringing hordes of people.

"Will it work out right?" Gianni asked, eyeing the rising tide. This time of year, the great square flooded each day.

"It will be perfect. Be at ease," soothed the priest. "Gianni . . ."

Gianni cast a curious glance at the short priest. But the holy man's eyes were far away, staring out to sea. "Father?"

Piero startled, as if surprised again by earthly language. Then his expression sobered. "If . . . That is . . ." He paused and searched Gianni's eyes. Gianni turned to face him, alarmed now. The priest reached out and took his arm in the gesture of solidarity among fighting men. "Gianni, should something happen to me, promise that you shall see the Gifted through to the completion of their mission."

Gianni frowned and studied the man. "You shall be with us every step of the way. We have need of you, Father. We know not where God is leading as of yet."

"Mayhap, mayhap," Piero soothed, but still he held on to Gianni's arm. "Swear it. Swear that you will trust the Lord to see you through."

"Father, I—"

"Give your word."

"I do not know why—"

Piero pulled him forward, making him rock on his toes, surprising him. "Give me your word," he said fiercely.

Gianni stared down at him. "Upon my word, upon my life, I shall serve the Lord's own goals among the Gifted. As it has been. And this day and evermore."

Piero inhaled deeply and visibly relaxed. "Good, good." He relinquished Gianni's arm.

"Father, is there something else you wish to say?"

Piero flashed him a grin. "Nay. All is as it should be." He left then, going to speak with Vito farther down the *fondamenta*. But Gianni failed to feel the comfort that his words intoned.

ↄᴆ ↄᴆ ↄᴆ

"I think it unwise," Vincenzo said, as Abramo reached for the white falcon.

"Nonsense," Abramo said, casting about for the bird's legs.

"No one but Daria or the boy has handled that bird for years."

"It is high time, the—" The bird struck the tender side of his unprotected left wrist with his sharp beak, drawing blood. Abramo whipped his hand out of the cage of reeds, cursing. He slammed Bormeo's keep to the ground.

The bird fell, then hopped to his feet. Spying the new hole, he took to the air.

At the last moment, Abramo reached up for the tether that trailed from behind the falcon, yanking him backward. With one swift move, he pulled the tiny leather hood over the bird's head, instantly becalming him.

Abramo smiled over at Vincenzo. "As difficult as his mistress, is he not?"

Vincenzo returned his smile and nodded his sorrowful assent.

Abramo now had the falcon perched on the leather glove that covered his right arm. He raised him, stroking the long, white feathers that made Bormeo so striking. "I take it you made no progress with her?" he asked, never taking his eyes from the bird.

"Nay," Vincenzo said, shaking his head. "I do not think we can turn her, Abramo. She is too deluded, pigheaded."

"Nonsense," Abramo soothed. "The Duchess has only encountered the first of our volleys. She will soon give in. She must give in." He raised a finger to Vincenzo. "It is a delicate dance, this. The lady has encountered terrible strife, trauma. But I do not wish her to be beaten. My bride must be strong, if we are to accomplish what I have envisioned. So we must break her spirit, but she must be able to still hold her head high."

Vincenzo studied him with irritation in his heart. She was his, not Amidei's! "Abramo, you ask the impossible. If watching Hasani hauled out by slavers will not break her, I do not know what shall."

"Patience, patience," Amidei soothed, still stroking Bormeo's long white feathers.

"Time is growing short," Vincenzo said, rising to walk to the wall that looked out from the tower, across the lagoon, to Venezia through a narrow passage between the Lido and the Giudecca. "Today, the knights will be hanged."

"And the Gifted will be far weaker than ever before," Abramo said with a grin. "Scattered. Beaten. In chains. I would say the tide has turned in our favor, my friend. The dragon shall sink his teeth into the peacock at last."

"So be it," Vincenzo murmured. But he felt none of the victory in his heart that his mentor's words intoned. "What weapon will you next use upon Daria?"

Abramo paused, still fingering the bird's feathers. "Hope," he said.

ᚸ ᚸ ᚸ

BENEATH the Piazza de San Marco was a network of support pilings, canals, and drainways, engineered to send rainwater toward the Canal Grande and attempt to control the rising tides, keeping the grand church and the neighboring doge's palazzo from tidal floods—at least on a routine basis. Every few years, an uncommon tide, the *acque alte,* rose, flooding the crypt of the sanctuary, even the first floor of both basilica and palazzo. And as the decades slid into centuries, some remained, some pilings rotted away, leaving a serpentine path beneath the city.

It was said that the church had been constructed upon thousands of white larch, and the palazzo atop thousands more. Each one had been driven into the *caranto,* solid clay beneath the surface. Not that Vito could tell if it was true, he thought, making his way, with a construction engineer the conte had sent to him, through a drain canal beneath the piazzetta. The pilings were certainly more spare here.

"You are certain this is the way?" Vito asked.

"Come ahead," the engineer said, hearing the fear in his voice. They lay upon short, flat rafts, no more than a few boards wide, barely watertight, dragging two others behind on ropes, destined for Rune and Basilio's use, if all went well.

Water seeped atop the makeshift boat, leaving Vito's belly cold. He shivered, glad not to be swimming through these miserable, encrusted pilings and dilapidated causeways in the frigid water. His eyes searched the pitch dark, the relative light of dusk upon the lagoon long lost among their passageway. Then he studied the engineer, so easily found among the city. It was too simple, his availability. Vito did not trust it. Would he be forced to slit the man's throat?

He cursed his luck in drawing the short straw on this duty. Ugo always received the more choice of positions. Always the younger brother, regardless of their youth long past! Surely they would be discovered, lost to soldiers who had long hunted them—Raiders of the Crypt de San Marco, as the heralds proclaimed. He rather liked the title, Vito thought smugly. It held some *braggadocio,* swagger to it . . .

"Over here," said the guide.

Vito veered left, hit another cursed piling, partially submerged, then moved on toward the flickering lantern. Dim light streamed from the iron cover's wide holes above them.

"Excellent," he said sourly, reaching out to flick the gray, encrusted piling with his knife, marking the water level. They could barely sit upright atop their boards, so near was the piazzetta's flooring above their heads. "You are certain this is the right one?" he whispered.

"Yes," the engineer said with a nod. He looked upward. "The doge's guard will bring the men right past here."

"And we will spring, grab my friends, and then make our escape."

"Indeed. It will be imperative that you get the prisoners settled upon their rafts and make your way out behind me. We must not tarry. They will give chase."

"Of course they will," Vito said dourly. "Would it not be best for us to make for the lagoon and take our chances?" he asked again, hoping the engineer would have changed his mind.

"Nay. If they see them escape, that is the first place they shall look. Be at peace. I know the way out."

"I am fervent in my hope," Vito said. He eyed the neighboring piling again, saw the finger-width climb above the knife mark. "I do hope they make haste," he whispered. "Please Lord of sky and sea, help them to hurry upon their way."

The crowd above them surged and shouted, and several men stepped atop the iron cover. It was beginning. The prisoners would soon be brought out! But people stood atop the grate above them!

Vito's eyes found the engineer's. "Well, that is not good. That is not good at all."

෴ ෴ ෴

ROBERTO slipped from the ship late in the afternoon, angry at himself for falling asleep. He had waited so long in the cramped bow of the ship, hiding while the sailors unloaded their freight. And after being up all night, sleep had overtaken him. Weakness! He would never be the knight that he and Nico had dreamed of becoming.

He moved up into the fading sun of the hatch and carefully up the stairs. The ship was empty, as were most of those around him. One man on a neighboring boat eyed him briefly and went about his work. Roberto had to get to the Duchess! Gianni! Tessa! As fast as he could possibly find them.

His eyes went wide as he took in the vast marina, the wall of buildings that met the sea. Moving carefully, he shifted his weight over the edge of the ship and dropped to the dock. He winced, favoring his good leg. His cramped position had left the bad leg stiff.

"Hey, boy," said a gruff voice from directly behind him. A heavy hand came down upon his shoulder. "What'd you do? Stow away?"

Roberto squirmed away from the hand and stumbled away, down the dock, to a pier, toward the city. He glanced back, glad the old sailor did not give chase. Two others stopped their work on their nets and idly watched him limp by.

Roberto felt some relief when he reached the stonework of the seaside *calle*. It was a strange city, the first of any outside Siena he had been to. But he knew how cities worked. He was a child of the streets. He could find his way.

This section of the city seemed largely abandoned. He heard word of a hanging and knew how people reacted to such occurrences. They had all probably turned out to see some poor saps hanged. Roberto instinctively knew he needed to stay as far from that as possible.

He reached out to stop a boy, about his own age, as he ran by.

"You are going to the hanging?" Roberto asked.

"*Si, si,*" said the boy, a grin crossing his face. "It is not every day you see a German strung up."

Roberto stilled. "German?"

"Yes, a tall one at that. And his friend too." He made a motion, as if he were being hanged, sticking his tongue out. "Do you wish to come? We have to hurry or we'll miss it!"

"Mayhap," Roberto allowed, as if truly interested, walking alongside him. "Tell me, is the man's friend also German?"

"Nay," said the boy. "Unless they name boys Basilio Montinelli in Germany too!"

ᚖ ᚖ ᚖ

DARIA rose to a seated position again, aware that she had dozed off, as someone opened a creaking, metal door and peered inward.

"Who is there?" Daria called. It was growing dark, the light in the small window now pink with dusk.

Daria was wary, for the noises came from her right, from another bank of dungeon cages.

Agata peeked out, her head reminding Daria of a frightened bird peering from her nest.

"*Sh, sh*, Agata, it is well. I am alone," she soothed.

Agata stared at her a moment and then turned, helping Ambrogio haul the boy in.

Daria forced herself to her feet, trying to hide the intense pain of every movement. There was no way that the child still lived . . . was there? Slowly, she made her way to her prison's front walls.

"M'lady, what have they done to you?"

"Pay me no heed," Daria said, sinking to her knees, her eyes upon Nico. The boy's skin was waxen and his breathing labored, barely visible. Pink blood still ringed his lips. "How did you gain your freedom?"

"Stupid guard," Agata scoffed. "Ambrogio slid a bit of wood in the lock, so it did not latch."

Daria's eyes flicked to the staircase. How long did they have? Her hands pulled toward the child as if God were moving them himself. *Make haste. Make haste!*

"Has he awakened?"

"Nay," said his grandmother sorrowfully. Angst knit her eyebrows together. "He is leaving us, m'lady."

Daria reached out and took the old woman's hand. "Take heart, friend. God will not see this one lost. Here. Move him as close as you can to me so I can assess his condition."

Ambrogio, wincing as he wrapped his bandaged hand around the boy, lifted him by hauling upward.

"Careful!" Daria cried, louder than she intended.

All eyes went to the staircase. But it remained silent and still.

She saw Ambrogio's eyes slide past Hasani's cell and then felt his attention lurch backward. He rose and went to the door of the cell, then entered, studying the wall, painted with the man's blood.

"Who was here? Who did this?" he whispered.

"Hasani," Daria said, her hands running the length of one rib within Nico and then another.

"Hasani! Where is he now?"

"They took him."

"Where? Who?"

"Amidei sold him to Turkish slavers."

Agata regarded her with doleful eyes, and Daria glanced up at Ambrogio. Once, she might have given in to a fit of hysterics. It all was so much . . .

"Bring that torch near, Ambrogio," she said.

Reluctantly, he pulled himself from the painting, took the torch with his good hand, pinning its root at his hip, and hovered near. "You never told me Hasani was an artist."

"You should see what he can do with proper instruments," she said morosely, her eyes still searching every inch of the boy's chest. She could better see the bruising that crisscrossed the boy's chest now, with the light near.

"Yes, well, you should see what I can do with broken, mangled fingers."

"Do not give in to despair, Brogi. God knows you were injured on our behalf. He means to heal you. And it is your left hand, not your right. You will paint again."

"It's been too long," Ambrogio said. "I am to live out my life as your court jester. My days as an artist have come to an end."

Daria smiled. "As delightful as that vision is, I have neither court nor means to keep you. We must return you to gainful employment again."

Ambrogio raised an eyebrow. "Back to my hovel, is it? I warned you, warned you that if you left me in your stead, I was liable to lose it all."

"You did. I put you in a most unfair position, Brogi. But I had no choice."

"I believe I now have the right to know, Daria. End your secrets. How could Vincenzo so thoroughly have turned against you? He is mad with rage, murdering dear Beata and Aldo! And what does Amidei hope to gain, with you and yours imprisoned?"

She eyed him carefully. "My brother, you have stumbled into another realm, one occupied by a lord of the underworld, who has imprisoned us, and the Gifted, me and mine who seek to do the Lord's bidding."

Ambrogio sat back on his heels and regarded her for a long moment. "Of what do you speak, Daria? The Gifted?"

"Our presence, our gifting, has been prophesied throughout the ages. Father Piero has the gift of wisdom; Sir Gianni, faith."

"And you, healing," he whispered.

Daria nodded. "There are others . . . Hasani has the gift of visions."

"Thus the paintings."

"And Tessa, the child, she knows things . . . deep within, she sees whether people be good or be they evil."

"Discernment." He paused, waiting. "Are there others?"

"Yes, I believe so. A fisherman, with unaccountable powers." She shook her head. "I have never seen nor heard of anything like it. And there is still one to come, one we must find. One with the gift of prophecy."

Ambrogio studied her. "How exactly do you do the Lord's bidding?"

"By following where he leads. By doing this," she said, bowing her head and reaching out through the bars, praying through the pain, concentrating on Nico and only Nico. "Pray with us, Brogi. Pray with us and believe my words are true. Believe our God can do all he says he can do."

She covered the boy with her hands, lightly running her fingertips over his chest, feeling the heat of the puncture within his lung, the swelling of blood within a sac meant for air. In contrast, the desperate cool of his forehead. She prayed, prayed for Jesus to be present in their prison cell, for the child to live and return to full health, for a miracle to pervade this den of darkness and squeeze light and hope into them all. "Please, Lord Jesus. Please, Great Physician. Move into his lungs. Drive out the blood. Heal his wounds. Straighten the bones. Bring him back to us, Father of life. Bring him back."

The Spirit moved among them, covering them with a warmth and a pulsing sound in their ears that brought them comfort. A heavy pounding built, slowly, slowly, then in a rush, pushed them backward, as if a wave had washed through the room.

As Daria, Ambrogio, and Agata regained their feet, Nico sat up, blinked, and then smiled.

And it was then that footsteps sounded upon the staircase.

CHAPTER THIRTY-ONE

VITO eyed the dark waters. It was getting more difficult to see. Even the holes of the iron cover above them held precious little daylight and his guide's lamp illuminated but a couple of feet around him. He reached down into the water and touched the mark he had made with his knife. Five inches. At this rate, they would be drowned, never seeing the stars of the lagoon again, let alone rescuing Basilio and Rune.

The doge's trumpeters made their announcement and the people cheered. More stepped atop the iron cover, making Vito mumble a curse. "Make haste," he whispered, staring upward. "Make haste! Where the devil could they be?"

"They shall arrive soon," said the engineer, hovering on his skiff, his face made ghoulish in the light of the lantern.

Vito sighed. "It is difficult to believe a man who looks like the grim reaper."

Ь Ь Ь

ALL was going as planned. The conte and contessa had hired performers to build the human pyramid that usually only accompanied feast days. They had also seen to it that a rope was strung from the roof of the doge's palace to the piazzetta floor, allowing for the "Bird of Venezia"—a man, sailing down the long expanse of it—to fly, again something rarely seen outside the annual festival. Other hired men wandered the crowd, pouring wine from casks, free of charge. People continued to move into the square, drawn by the rumors.

The doge surveyed the crowd, unaccountably large. "Good people of Venezia," he cried in greeting.

The crowd roared in response. The smaller side piazzetta was packed; the larger piazza of San Marco square was full, halfway back. A thousand people milled about, more arriving by the minute.

"I give to you two prisoners who have been tried and found guilty of both larceny and rape."

The crowd bellowed their complaint and outrage. Tomatoes flew toward Basilio and Rune, who dodged them easily, but frowned.

Gianni's eyes ran across the doge and his companions, fretful that the sailing spoiled fruit might mess up his plan. The timing for distraction . . . It was then that he saw Cardinal Boeri at the doge's side, among other churchmen. The cardinal arched a brow and gave him a small nod. Why did he not show any surprise in seeing Gianni here? His heart leapt. Could the cardinal do something, say something to end this nightmare? He appeared to have the doge's ear! But the crowd surged, almost taking Gianni from his feet.

It was up to the Gifted, and God, to get his men free. Gianni eyed the wooden gallows, hastily constructed between the columns of Marco and Todaro. Made of Egyptian red and gray granite, the columns stood as tall as seven men and dwarfed the gallows. But the sight of the ropes over the crossbeam, the men awaiting his knights to set the noose around each of their necks . . . it made him say a quick prayer of protection, deliverance.

Gianni pushed his way through the crowd to the iron cover, directly along the route the doge's men would take to move Basilio and Rune from palace to gallows.

A wine merchant with a cask upon his back followed behind him. Three villagers who had been present with them the night before walked alongside them. They pushed forward, prying the wine merchant loose of clogs of people who asked for a cupful as he passed. The doge droned on for a good bit; then his man listed the full extent of the knights' crimes and went on to extol the good and righteous decisions the doge had made.

"On with it!" cried a man in front.

"On with it!" echoed the crowd.

The doge clamped his lips in distaste and then nodded to his guards. The men, four in number rather than the anticipated eight to twelve, surrounded the prisoners and led them down the stairs and into the crowd. Gianni stood with mouth agape for a moment. What stroke of good fortune was this? Only four men? How could they be so thick-headed? There were only two possible conclusions: Either the people would tear the prisoners to pieces, or the prisoners would escape. He eyed the doge and the cardinal again. Cardinal Boeri stared straight at him, as if speaking without words. He had planned this! He had made a way for Gianni!

The crowd separated, creating a narrow avenue toward the gallows, as if anxious to see the condemned men to their end. Each prisoner was flanked by a guard, and there was a third at the front, a fourth at the back. But the meager guard could not keep the prisoners from being spit upon, harassed, slapped. Gianni saw several people from the night of Gaspare's rain push aside others who taunted the prisoners. Still, onward the group of six made their way forward.

One more moment, he said to himself. *Wait, wait, wait . . .*

The men were coming closer, close enough for Basilio to catch sight of his captain and raise his eyebrows in recognition. Gianni nodded to a villager next to him and the man sent his hat sailing into the air; seeing the signal, a man came flying down a rope, a cape spreading out behind him like the wings of a bird. The crowd gasped and lurched, closing off the avenue that had been opened for the doge's knights.

At that moment, a tenth man reached the top of the human pyramid and people shouted, and pointed, moving again en masse. A crush of people moved forward, all laughing and cheering, the prisoners forgotten.

Confused, the doge's knights did not even get the opportunity to un-sheathe their swords. Two were carried off, their weapons quickly stripped from their sides. The others were walled off from the rest of their group, blocked by what appeared to be drunk and disorderly citizens. They shouted and shoved people aside, but the townspeople were doing as Gianni and Piero had asked, simply blocking the way. Being disorderly in every way possible.

Gianni and Ugo moved in from opposite sides, each hauling a guard to the ground and out of view of the doge and the rest of his men. Townsmen moved in to cover them. In quick order, they were bound and secreted off among the people.

Basilio and Rune ducked, using the people as a barrier from anyone who now attempted to reach them. Gianni reached down and, with his sword, quickly broke the lock that held the iron grid in place. Ugo hauled it open. Even among the din of the crowd, the *creak* of it was still unaccountably loud. He motioned for Basilio and Rune. They hurried forward.

"Go, go! We shall meet you soon," Gianni said, motioning down to the water. His eyes narrowed as he spied the rising tide and Vito's proximity.

"Make haste," Vito hissed up at them. "If you do not, you shall have avoided the hangman's noose only to drown beneath the gallows."

Rune jumped down into the water and disappeared. Basilio hung back. "I am not a good swimmer."

"Now's the time to learn," Ugo said, pushing him in.

Gianni slammed down the grate, and the winemaker stood atop it at once. Another man set a new lock in place.

The doge stood at the rail of his platform, searching the crowd.

"Guards!" the doge screamed, hands now upon the railing. *"Guards!"*

But Gianni saw the small, victorious smile that passed between him and Cardinal Boeri as he glanced back. The Gifted were now clearly indebted to the doge—and Gianni's former employer.

♣ ♣ ♣

ROBERTO paused in confusion. He had run toward the square, fought his way through the crowd, trying to be heard, trying to put a stop to Rune and Basilio's execution, crying "Innocent! Innocent! Innocent!" until his throat was hoarse and gave out altogether. He had no idea of how Rune and Basilio had gotten into such dire straits, but he was certain it was through unfair means. There was simply no way any of the Gifted could be involved in such treachery! It had to be more of the Sorcerer's work . . . or Vincenzo's.

The thought of the man who had so savagely killed the Sciorias and set fire to Lady Daria's home sent a burst of energy through his body. He forced his way through a last knot of people and again tried to cry, "Innocent! They're innocent!"

He had just reached the doge's steps when he saw the small, old man rise, with his famed pointed hat atop his head. But it wasn't the hat that brought Roberto up short.

It was the swell of the crowd, the sudden shoving and swaying behind him. And the doge's red face as he screamed for his guards. Roberto turned, searching the piazzetta, trying to find the men. He saw the doge's knights, scuffling with the crowd, trying to make their way through. But he could see neither Rune, nor Basilio, nor Gianni, nor any of the other Gifted.

His heart sank. Were they not here after all? Had he misunderstood?

⚓ ⚓ ⚓

It was no use. They were coming too quickly, their boots clumping down the steps. Daria grabbed hold of the bars and let her head slump forward, praying. Ambrogio stood, as if he meant to guard the old woman and child outside her cell. Agata scrambled backward, hauling her grandson with her, back toward the door where they had been imprisoned, but she did not even make it three steps before the men arrived.

Abramo and Vincenzo stood there, studying the group. Abramo allowed a grim smile to cross his face as he looked them over. "Well, just as I had suspected. I could smell you all down here. Such a sudden draft of oranges and cloves!"

Ambrogio moved to try to block him, but Abramo simply took the smaller man by the neck and shoved him against the bars of Daria's cell. He studied the child in the old woman's arms. "Yes, yes, yes. I knew you could not keep from it. Not if he was brought to you like an offering."

Daria lifted her face slowly to look upon him, wishing she had the strength to rise. "It was God's bidding that brought the child to me; it was he who asked me to heal him. You had little to do with it."

Vincenzo and a guard moved in to hold Ambrogio where he stood. Ambrogio stared at Vincenzo with hatred in his eyes. "How could you? How can you now? Stand by and watch this happen to Daria? You loved her once! You loved her! She called you Uncle!"

"Cease," Vincenzo said, glaring at the younger man.

Abramo knelt down, studying Daria through the bars like a hunter inspecting curious prey. "It robs you of strength, this healing, does it not?"

She looked away, weary. Of what use was it? When would their God deliver them of this monster?

"My ceremonies feed us, my love. They do not sap us; they build us, making us stronger."

"And yet you destroy others in your ceremonies. You sacrifice children upon your altar, among other despicable, evil things."

"You are guessing. There is a reason for everything we do. A divine order to it all. It makes sense, once you are present. Come and experience it. Then you will know. Then you will understand."

"Get away from her," Ambrogio ground out, staring down at Abramo.

"Vincenzo told you to cease," Abramo said, never looking from Daria.

"I will see your throat slit one day," Ambrogio spat out, looking wildly from Vincenzo to Abramo. "Both of yours."

"Brogi!" Daria cried. "Please, do not give in. Do not play their games. It is just what they want."

"You are tired, and wounded," Abramo said, as if neither she nor Ambrogio had spoken. "Come, come let me tend to you. Care for you. Show you the true way to greatness, strength that never leaves you. This makes no sense. Your God would not wish this upon his creatures, not if he loved them."

She raised her eyes to meet his at last, words again cascading through her mind. " 'The foolishness of God is wiser than man's wisdom, and the weakness of God is stronger than man's strength.' "

"Daria," he warned, his eyes going from compassion to fury in half a breath.

She pushed back, so he could not reach her through the bars. " 'God chose the foolish things of the world to shame the wise—' "

"*Daria.*"

" 'God chose the weak things of the world to shame the strong.' "

"*Daria!*"

" 'He chose the lowly things of this world . . .' " She smiled as he stood and backed up from her cell, staring down at her in utter fury again.

"Let us go on our way," Ambrogio tried. "This is no use. You shall never turn Daria or us to your ways."

Abramo, frenzied, tore the younger man away from his captors and hauled him to Daria's left.

"Nay!" Daria cried, stumbling to her feet. She followed along from the inside of her cell, then over to the bars that divided hers from Hasani's old prison. Abramo rushed her friend in, opened manacles chained to the floor, and slammed Ambrogio's ankle into one, making him cry out in pain, and then went to the other. He pushed the man down to his back and Ambrogio's head slammed against the stones.

Ciro entered and held down Brogi's left arm and shoulder. "Bite down on this," the hulking knight said to the slender artist, jamming a piece of wood between his teeth.

Daria stood there, gasping for breath against the pain in her back, trying to keep her feet.

Abramo knelt on Ambrogio's right forearm and accepted a fearsome hammer from Vincenzo. He eyed the artist's right fingers. "The pride of Siena. The great Ambrogio Rossellino. Will he paint again?"

Daria shook her head in horror.

Ambrogio wrenched violently to one side, surprising the two men. Both pushed back. "Turn to me, Daria," Abramo said savagely, wiping his mouth with the back of his hand, eyeing her from the side.

"Nay," she whispered. "It is as Ambrogio said. We shall never be yours."

Abramo lifted his chin. "You shall be mine, Daria. Or you shall die."

"Then I shall die."

"You try my patience sorely. Never have I encountered such a stubborn one as this," he said to Vincenzo. He turned back to her. "But I do not believe you, Duchess. Your words are pretty and bold. But I know the ways of weakness. And I shall exploit every one of yours until you give in to my wishes. We have only yet begun. You shall give in."

"Nay," she said, feeling the weight of his warning.

"You make a grievous error in your choices, Daria," he said, his voice softening. He left Ambrogio to Ciro and neared her. She backed away as if he might come through the bars themselves, fighting to keep her feet. "All I ask is that you come to our ceremony on the morrow."

"To worship the dark one?"

"Among other things. You will discover—"

She laughed then, a hollow sound that echoed about the prison walls.

"I am to worship the Lord my God, and no other. I am *his* servant. Never will I be another's."

"Who is this God you serve?" Abramo snarled. Daria heard Agata crying then, hunched in a corner, her grandson in her arms.

"You know my God well, for he is your enemy."

"Oh?" he said, cocking a brow. "And so . . . does that make *you* my enemy, Daria?"

"In every sense of the word."

Abramo sighed heavily as if hurt by her retort. He glanced over at Ambrogio and then back at her. "You have become fond of quoting the Scriptures in my face. Do you know it is written that God will command his angels to guard you carefully?"

"Well I know it."

"Where are they now, Daria?" He moved over and lifted the hammer.

"Here," she whispered, eyes on the tool.

"What was that? I couldn't hear your retort."

"They are here."

"They are here? In this cell? With us?" He moved the hammer from one hand to the other and gestured at Daria with the handle of it. "Do they see me? Did they watch as you were whipped? Your back ripped to shreds?"

Daria nodded slightly.

Abramo turned without pause and slammed the hammer to the stones, destroying Ambrogio's smallest finger.

Daria closed her eyes as her friend screamed.

"They rescued you in Il Campo, in Siena, did they not?" He gave her a little smile. "They were with you then. But I ask you, where are they now?" He lifted his arm and destroyed the next of Ambrogio's fingers.

Daria closed her eyes and pushed backward to the corner of her cell, wishing she could block out the dull sound of the hammer, Ambrogio's shrieks. She collapsed into the corner, as far from Abramo as possible, hands over her ears, eyes shut tight, gasping with each blow. She sat down heavily, feeling every wound in her own back as one she deserved for bringing Ambrogio into this nightmare. If it hadn't been for her, for her, for her . . . No more paintings of the Christ, his disciples, his angels. No more blessed Mother. No more of Elijah or Moses or David . . . no more of Ambrogio's precious gift, no less holy than her own!

The sounds ceased at last, and the only sound was Abramo's panting and Ambrogio's sobs. Daria covered her face, unable to force herself to look. But Agata's cry forced her eyes open.

Abramo stood before her cell, holding the boy in front of him, who stared desperately in Daria's direction. "Speak to your Lord's angels, Duchess. Why are they not fighting us off? Guarding you? Call him down, m'lady. Ask him to come and save you. He was just here, was he not? Was it not he who saved this boy from death, through you? Where did he go? How could he be silent at this moment? Where is he, Duchess?"

She remained silent, taking each question like a punch to her belly.

He sneered and shook his head. "He cannot be trusted. You follow an absent and uncaring God."

"He is here," she insisted. "He is here."

"Where?" Abramo asked, eyes wide, looking about in parody. "All I see is a faltering noble, a broken artist, a weeping old woman, and a boy who will serve on the morrow in our ceremony. Tomorrow eve, it shall be our grandest yet. I have people coming from every sector of the laguna. Yes," he said, bending down to stroke Nico on the cheek, "I owe you, for saving this one."

Nico wrenched his head away from the man's hand and struggled to get away, but it was of little use.

"Please," Daria said, trying to rise, failing. She crawled toward him, weeping. "Please. Not the child." *Not the child, Lord, not the child, not the child, not the child . . .*

He ignored her and spoke to a guard. "Take the old woman back to her cell." He looked over his shoulder. "Think long and hard on this moment," he said. "Remember it well and consider this . . . mayhap it was not I who misled you. You have always known me for who I am. But who is your God? Is he trustworthy? He has saved you, yes. But why would he allow this?"

He turned to go.

"Wait!" Daria cried, sitting back on her knees. "Not the boy. Please, not the boy. Take me," she said, weeping again.

"Daria, do not!" Ambrogio said through his sobs.

Abramo lifted his chin and studied her. "You are offering yourself? You shall join us in the ceremony?"

"Yes, yes. Just leave the child," she begged. "Leave him."

He left Nico with the guard and came to her cell, knelt down outside it. "Shh, don't cry, my queen. It is an honor to join us. You shall know the truth of it once you've experienced it."

"This has nothing to do with truth," she said, scoffing at how he could so swiftly twist words. "This is ransom, me for the child."

He pulled back and then gave his head a slight shake. "You followers of the Way. Always so willing to sacrifice for another. It is touching, really." He sighed and rose. "It matters not to me, how you come. Only that you come on your own accord. The rest will follow." He looked to his guard. "Go and fetch bandages and salve for the lady's wounds. I will send the women to tend to her."

He turned to go and grabbed Nico's arm again.

"What are you doing?" Daria cried. "Leave the child here!"

"He'll be safe with me, Daria," Abramo said. "And I think it will be good for you to know he is up in the tower, as you once were, ripe for the picking. Just in case you change your mind."

CHAPTER THIRTY-TWO

RUNE emerged from the inky waters and immediately reached for Vito's raft. "Back, back behind me," Vito urged, now so close to the floor of the piazzetta above him that he could barely lift his head all the way. Basilio came down then, with a clumsy, heavy splash. Vito just caught a glimpse of Gianni before the captain slammed the grate shut. Vito could hear people stomping atop the iron cover, even in the midst of Basilio's sputtering emergence from the water.

"Basilio!" Vito hissed. "Calm yourself!"

But the short, broad man was panicked, casting about, taking in choking mouthfuls of water. In a moment, he was under water; in two, he did not emerge again.

"Vito!" Rune urged, from behind him. "He does not fare well in the water."

"Obviously," Vito said. With a grimace, he left his raft and slid into the water, casting about in the dark for his comrade. He was irritated at first, frustrated that they were wasting precious time as the tide rose. But as his breath gave out and he was forced to the surface, he became concerned.

His guide lifted his lantern toward him, barely above the surface of the water, but Vito went back down. He cast about, finding hope once, twice, only to discover he had touched a rotting pillar, not a man. *Please, gracious Father,* he begged, his second breath now waning. *Please let me find him.*

He thought of the miracles he had experienced in his time with the Gifted, the sweet deliverance of his own faith. *Please, Lord,* he repeated silently. *One more sweep here. One over there . . .* there.

There. He touched the flailing arm of Basilio, who had sunk like a stone, much deeper than he had anticipated. Vito kicked and took the man by neck and shoulder and swam for the surface. They came up so hard, he bumped his head upon a support of the piazzetta floor. Wincing, he pulled Basilio backward, toward the guide's lamp and his waiting raft.

The knight was coughing hard, taking deep draughts of air and coughing some more.

"He lives?" the guide asked dolefully.

"He's coughing. Can you not hear?" Vito groused. "Help me." Vito positioned himself on two pilings about three feet apart, struggling to gain a footing upon their slimy surface. But a way down there was another submerged, cracked piling that gave him a better toehold, and then, holding just so . . . he yanked and pushed Basilio upward toward the raft, nearly turning it over, as Rune and the guide tried to hold it steady.

In another moment the knight was upon the boards, panting and looking in Vito's direction. "I never took to the sea," he said.

"As I've observed," Vito returned with a grin. But his grin faded as he heard the crowd move as one above them, driven by something. The doge's guard? And Basilio barely could fit upon the raft and stay beneath the piazzetta supports. "We must move quickly," Vito said. "Take them. Lead them out. I will follow behind upon the last raft."

The guide, apparently as concerned as Vito now, immediately moved out, pulling Basilio's raft behind him, and Rune's behind his. Vito treaded water, feeling the rope slide between his fingers. And then his raft arrived.

With a grunt, he hauled himself atop it and began to pray that they would escape the dark labyrinth of drainways before the climbing tide claimed them all.

ෆ ෆ ෆ

GIANNI and Piero and the others hurried down the *calletta* that ran between the doge's palazzo and San Marco. Most ran away from the palace, disappearing down the alleys and *calles* and canals like liquid through a sieve. Gianni worried they would stand out, moving in the opposite direction.

"Do not fret," Piero said, nearing his elbow. The priest was a surprisingly good runner. "They will be more than occupied behind us. The conte will see to it."

"Had something planned, did he?"

"Several things," the priest returned with a wry smile. "The Lord is good. He made certain we made just the allies we needed in this city."

"Indeed," Gianni said, wondering again over the sudden appearance of Cardinal Boeri. They turned a corner and then another, finally arriving at the rendezvous point where the knights and their guide should emerge upon a small canal. Gaspare came down the narrow canal, poling his skiff toward them in a lackadaisical manner common among fishermen.

It would be barely large enough for them all, but it would do.

When Gaspare neared, they leapt aboard, eyes searching the dark waters for their friends. "Come, come," Gianni whispered.

Several long minutes passed, but still the men did not emerge.

"They should be here by now," Gianni whispered to the priest as an old woman and her daughter passed by, casting curious looks at the group of men and Tessa.

"Something is wrong," Piero said, eyebrows knitting in concern. "We must pray. Come," he directed Tessa, Gaspare, Ugo, and Gianni. "Come, circle together. Let us lift our brothers up to the Lord."

Reluctantly, Gaspare moved toward the priest, and Tessa stood between them. She smiled, and the light of it made them all smile back. She looked up at Gaspare with a sage expression. "We were good at praying, even before you joined us."

"I can well imagine, child," he said, closing his eyes and bowing his head.

⚓ ⚓ ⚓

THEY were constantly bumping into crossbeams and in another moment, all were in the water. Vito wrenched apart his makeshift raft, sliding one board in Basilio's direction. "Here," he said. "I don't care to save your heavy arse twice."

"*Grazie,*" Basilio said, not bothering a retort. He was worried about the rising tide, as were they all.

Vito swam toward the guide, who had taken the candle out of his lantern and left it atop a long board from his own raft. It was their sole light. "Where are we? Shouldn't we be there by now?"

"Yes," the guide said. "I fear we took a wrong turn."

Vito swallowed an angry word and took a deep breath. "Think, man. Where did we take the wrong turn? How far back?"

The guide frowned.

Please, Father, Vito prayed. *Show him. Show him our means of escape.*

He turned, recognizing their predicament. The drainways went in four different directions. Was it down to two options in the guide's mind? Or three? He willed himself to be patient, to wait upon the Lord to show them the way, as he had seen Gianni and Piero do many times before. *Show him, show us, show him,* he chanted silently, concentrating on treading water, hoping he could beat back the frigid chill of it.

"I think," the guide said at last. "I think it was back twenty yards. I should have turned right. I believe we turned left."

"Yes," Rune said. "We did."

"All right, back then," the guide said. "Twenty broad strokes, knight. Then we should be close."

Rune and Basilio led, Vito behind them, then the guide. By the time they got back to the point where they had made their error, there was barely enough room for them to take a breath. The candle hit a crossbeam and tumbled into the water, leaving them in darkness.

"There," Vito said, turning his face sideways to take a breath and speak. "Up ahead."

Without the candle, they could see the barest glint of light, fifty yards ahead.

"Swim, men," the guide said. "Swim if you ever care to see the stars or sun again."

They moved out immediately, no longer trying to hide their position, desperate for any breath of air they could get. At one point, Basilio stopped, acting as if he could not go on. Vito did not pause. They were close, so close. He would not die here.

With one last deep breath, he grabbed a handful of Basilio's hair, scrunched up against a piling and catapulted them both forward. He kept a hand in front of him, bracing for impact. But only open waters welcomed him.

Basilio fought against him and they were out of air. Vito rose to the surface, praying for space for one more breath. But when they reached the surface, strong arms grabbed hold of them and hauled them aboard a skiff.

"Couple of drowned rats," Ugo said, hands on hips, his form silhouetted against a canopy of early stars.

"Two more over here," Gaspare said, hauling the guide and Rune over the side, one at a time.

"Very good," Piero said, grinning. "All is as the Lord has seen it."

"He saw us almost drown down there?" Vito asked, panting.

"Most certainly," said the good priest.

ꝏ ꝏ ꝏ

"Nay! Nay!" Daria cried as Abramo, Vincenzo, and their knights disappeared up the stairs. Nico was shouting, trying to pull away, but to no avail.

Crying, she fell back to her knees, glanced over at Ambrogio, weeping in his cell, bleeding hand against his chest, and then she cried harder. She shook her head. "Lord, Lord," she whispered through her tears. "I cannot do this any longer. Where are you? Why do you stand by idly and watch this happen?"

Daria felt the shame of her words even as she spoke them—as if she taunted a lion—but her fury drove her onward. How could he heal Nico moments ago, only to see him taken by Abramo? "Where are you?" she said aloud to the ceiling of stone as if addressing heaven itself. "How could you not act now? Why permit this? They are an abomination! An abomination! We are your people, merely trying to serve you! How could you forget us? How could you abandon us?"

She fell to her side and sobbed for a while and soon gave way to fitful sleep. When she awakened, dawn was barely upon them, and she was shivering. She reached up and touched her head. Fever. Her back . . . no doubt there was infection already.

"He is here," Ambrogio said.

Daria pushed herself up to look at him. He still lay across the stones, the manacles at his feet keeping him in place. "What did you say?"

"He is here."

"Who?" she asked in confusion.

"God." Ambrogio turned his head toward her. "You have come too far to give up on your Lord now, Daria."

"But Brogi . . . Because of me, because of the Gifted, you are in chains! And your fingers . . ."

"That is true. But Daria, it will be well. It is already well."

"How? How can you say that?"

Ambrogio sighed heavily. "Time and again, I have painted scenes of God delivering his people. The Scriptures show us, over and over. Two things must happen before he moves. First, the people are often at their very lowest. A place where they know they cannot deliver themselves. Think on it. Moses. David. The disciples."

Daria gave out an unladylike snort. "Mayhap we are in such a place?"

He grimaced through his pain. "Mayhap. But think. What is the second requirement for God to act?"

Daria closed her eyes and thought back through the stories of old. "They asked."

Ambrogio nodded. "God moves when you ask, Daria. Time and again, he has healed, when you but asked it of him. At times it was not immediate, right? Our God is not still; he is a God of action. We saw him come and heal Nico, steal him back from death's door. But have you asked God to free us? Save us?"

"Yes, yes. A thousand times."

He let that settle a moment. "All right, then. In the Scriptures, why does he not choose to move when it makes sense?"

Daria mulled it over.

"Paul himself was imprisoned many times. What did he say about that?"

She remained silent.

"Three years past, I painted the nave of Santo Paulo de Torina. The priest wanted me to paint Paul's sufferings in the nave, and near the front, his victories, to remind all of how God sustains us, sees us through. Think, Daria. Think. What did the man endure?"

"Imprisonment," she said at last. "Stonings, shipwrecks, hunger, nakedness. Pursuit. Torture," she ended in a whisper.

Ambrogio sighed, waiting for her to catch up. "And more. He bragged of those sufferings to the people of Corinth. Bragged of them. Why?"

"Because God's grace was sufficient for him, his power made perfect in weakness," she said, quoting Paul.

"Ah, so you do remember. Well you know the Scriptures of how God's power is perfect in our weakness. Daria, *this* is weakness. This." He paused a moment and lifted his bandaged left hand, his bloody right, staring at them both. "Never have you or I dreamed of being tortured for what we believe, or for our friends," he said, turning toward her. "Never did we imagine losing everything but each other. But we must count it a blessing. Amidei wants nothing more than for you to wallow as you are now. Think, Daria. What else did Paul say about suffering? About boasting in his sufferings?"

" '*Propter quod placeo mihi in infirmitatibus in contumeliis in necessitatibus in persecutionibus in angustiis pro christo cum eniminfirmor tunc potens sum.*' "

" 'That is why, for Christ's sake, I delight in weaknesses, in insults, in hardships, in persecutions, in difficulties. For when I am weak, then I am strong,' " he translated. Ambrogio looked over at her again. "Less of us, more of the Holy. We recede, the Holy swells. We wane, the Holy waxes. Let us rest in our weakness, trust our God. For in that, we force Amidei to face God within us! Amidei sees we have nothing left as humans. He has succeeded in beating you on every human front. Now let him see how our God stands in the gap for you. Let him see that he can never beat the Holy One who lives in you and in me.

"Do not let him twist this in your mind, Daria. It is imperative. Get it straight, right now, and keep it straight. Think of what God did with Paul's life. Think of how Paul's words feed the world, remind us of what we need to glean out of Christ's life! And yet, *God allowed him to suffer*. How did he use his sufferings for good?"

"So that others might know him as one of them."

"Indeed. 'So that Christ's power may rest on me,' " he repeated. He eyed her. "Christ's own power. He has not abandoned us, Daria. He is here. God is here."

It was Daria's turn to nod her assent. "You are right, of course. But Brogi, this is so much more difficult, so much more a trial . . ."

Ambrogio laughed softly. "Well I know the truth of your words. But look at us," he said. "We yet live. We are in the devil's lair, and in poor form, yet we still live. Is that not proof that our God saves? That his angels yet guard us? God still has a task for you. The point, Daria, is what are we doing at this moment? Are we honoring our God or shaming him? Are we using all that he has given us to fend off our enemy? Are we giving him way to hold his own court?"

She remained silent.

"I have watched Amidei for months," he said, staring up at the ceiling. "In Toscana, in Roma, elsewhere we have crossed paths. He is extremely powerful. But it is not because he wields true power; he does as he told you—he finds a person's weakness and then exploits it.

"This is what it means to die to self. God acts not when we think he should at times, but when it is best, when it will yield the greatest harvest—in our hearts, or another's. He moves through our weakness to make us strong, prove that he is alive and well in us. In contrast, Amidei trades on power. He changes tactics if his target proves elusive, but it all boils down to power, control. Vincenzo longed for power, and he gave it to him—in certain measure. Others seek gratification in other measures. Keep in mind, however, that any power Vincenzo believes he now wields, ultimately belongs to Amidei. Amidei *owns* him. As he does anyone who bows to him.

"Amidei called you stubborn . . . it is another reference to how he continues to seek a way to bring you down. He does not believe you will ultimately give in to him—thus his reason for taking Nico with him. Aldo, Beata's deaths. The destruction of my hands . . . all are solely tools to make you bow down to him. You must not falter, Daria. Too much is at stake. He is after you and yours because you put all that he has worked for in danger. You feel weak, appear weak, *but the Christ is alive in you.* Amidei knows this and more than anything, fears you will remember it, too."

Daria sighed and then labored to her feet. She pulled herself up by the bars that separated them and stared in at her friend, wishing she might see him more clearly. "It is I who should be bringing you the Word, encouraging you, telling you of why we are here, why God might allow this."

"Mayhap all those years of painting have actually been my proving ground, my preparation for this moment, to help you."

Daria smiled, seeing the beauty of his logic. "God's strength made perfect in weakness. Bringing you to me when I was weakest. Speaking such strong words of faith, when you are weakest."

"His grace is sufficient, ever sufficient, Daria." He was terribly pale, in undeniable pain. Their conversation had undoubtedly sapped him. But still he forced himself to speak. "Daria, you must know something else. In case something happens to me, I must tell you what Hasani painted upon the wall."

CHAPTER THIRTY-THREE

ROBERTO walked alongside a rowdy group of revelers, some of the last to depart the piazzetta. They were drunk with wine, speaking loudly about the weak and addle-brained guards of the doge, letting the prisoners escape. The guards had waited for the escaped men to emerge along the Canal Grande, but no one appeared. No one thought they would dare to navigate the dark tunnels at rising tide to any other escape point. Either they had found another way out or they had drowned like sewer rats, a guard said to his comrade.

But they did not know the Gifted. Roberto smiled a little, confident he was on the right track. He had lost sight of Gianni and the others in the crowd directly after, and if the doge's guards could not find them among the labyrinth of the underground causeways, how could he?

He tried closing his eyes and uttering a prayer to God, but heard nothing in response. He paused at the corner of a small *campiello,* trying to figure out which way to go. Another group of revelers walked by, musing over the distractions of the evening, and looking forward to another on the morrow, on the dark isle.

Roberto watched the group recede down the street until they disappeared around a corner. The dark isle. The Sorcerer's isle.

Vincenzo would be there, with him.

And if Roberto could not find the Gifted, then he would see justice done himself.

ф ф ф

THERE was barely enough of an evening breeze to beat their way northwest under sail, out to where Gaspare had left a second boat and supplies moored.

Half of the group spilled over into the next, relieved not to remain on the nearly sinking skiff, but it was still tight. "Will this yet be enough room when we rescue Daria?" Gianni asked.

"It will suffice," Gaspare said, leaping aboard to pull up their main sail. He showed Piero how to move the rudder to and fro and told Vito and Ugo how to manage the sails.

"Let us go to the island this night," Gianni said. "Let us rescue Daria and then sail on, to wherever the Lord leads us."

"That is unwise," Piero said. "We shall do as Gaspare suggests. Take our rest on his island this night, then in the morning, go and survey the island where the lady is held captive. The doge will have set up a net for us, beyond the Lido and Giudecca anyway. We cannot escape without the Lord's own plan. Any of you privy to that at this moment?"

It was too dark to see his face, but Gianni did not argue further.

In half an hour, they were docked and made their way into Gaspare's cozy cottage. He stirred the coals and threw some kindling atop them. He took a heavy pot from the hearth, went to a basket he had brought in from the city, and threw in carrots, onions, a whole, plucked chicken, a palmful of salt—a major export from Venezia and in far more ready supply than anywhere Gianni had ever seen—then rosemary. He set it above the flames, now crackling and gaining strength, licking away at the sap that seeped from the pine and oak logs.

Vito, Ugo, Basilio, and Rune sat about the room, plainly exhausted. Piero passed around a jug of wine. Gianni left for wood outside the door and returned, handing the fisherman several split logs.

Gianni knelt, arms on thighs, and studied the flames and the fisherman. "How long have you known you had the gift?"

Gaspare eyed him for a moment, then turned back to his pot, stirring it a bit and laying the spoon to rest across its lip. He remained staring into the flames. "When I was a mite of a boy, I saved my father from drowning."

Gianni waited.

"He lost his footing and went down upon the net. More covered him. He fell in such a way that when he tried to rise, the net was brought back under the ship, and it caught on the rudder." He shook his head as if he hated the memory. "I was a bit younger than Tessa. Not strong enough to wrench the net free. I could barely bring in twenty fish, let alone a full-grown man."

He continued to stare toward the fire, his light-blue eyes even more pale, so close to the flames. Gianni noticed errant, wiry brows that stuck out from his forehead and waited for him to continue. Tessa had drawn near and placed a hand on the fisherman's shoulder.

"But you did," she said.

"Indeed I did, child," he said with a tender smile. His gaze returned to the flames. "I could not pull him up, so I dived in, my knife clenched between my teeth. He was under the ship, still struggling to free himself, and yet not, as if he was giving up."

"Basilio was like that today," Vito put in. "Had to haul his fat behind to the surface or he would've died beneath the piazzetta."

Basilio rolled his eyes, but lifted his cup of wine in silent solute to the younger man.

Vito lifted his cup in response, grinning tiredly.

"So, how did you save him?" Tessa asked the fisherman.

"I do not know," Gaspare said. "I was praying like an altar boy, praying madly for God to come and help me, and all I did was cut away the rope that was tangled in the rudder. My papa did not move then, mayhap too much of the sea in his lungs for him to move. My lungs were bursting, so I broke for the surface, hauled myself into the boat, and then turned and pulled in the nets. I truly do not remember anything more than that. Only that moments later, my papa was in the boat, still covered in nets like a big fish, staring up at me, stunned."

"He lived?" Basilio asked.

"For three decades past that day."

"Quite the catch," Vito muttered.

"There have been other times, twice a year, mayhap thrice, when

God has called upon me to move in his name. Always, it is to do his work. But never have I felt the call upon my heart more strongly than when you, the Gifted, sailed by my isle en route to the lepers. Since then, the Spirit has worked at me, to join you."

"You did not wish to join us," Piero said, drawing a stool near and sitting upon it.

"I live a simple life. It is good to me. I did not care to leave it. And it was not yet time."

Piero nodded, staring into the fire. "I understand."

"But when I went to Murano, Torcello, saw what you were doing, knew the lady's family crest, it became very clear to me. I still struggled against it, but knew I was losing the battle. If the Lord wants something, he's more difficult than a cat after a bowl of milk. He'll niggle at your heels until you pour the milk and sit down to watch him lap it up."

Gianni eyed him with a smile. "It is the truth of it."

"You mentioned the lady's crest," Piero said. "How did it help you know you were to join us?"

Gaspare rose with a grunt and went to the mantle, pulling down a small wooden box. "My mother's," he said, rubbing his fingers lightly over the top. He pulled off the lid and handed it to Piero.

Carved into the lid were two peacocks, each drinking from an urn. The same symbol that was in each church where they had found the glass pieces. The knights rose and gathered around the men and girl at the fire.

"She was always crafting things with which I could amuse myself. I was the only child to live past infancy, so she indulged me." He pulled out a small piece, hidden in his big paw of a hand, and then set it out, then another, one by one. They were figurines, made of clay.

"Talismans?" Rune asked.

"Nay," Gaspare said.

They all leaned closer.

A knight. A priest. A lady. A slave. A girl. And a fisherman.

"There's one more." He pinched it in the corner of the box and lifted it out, setting a female figure beside the fisherman.

"Who is that?" asked Vito.

"The last," Piero said, leaning down with a grunt to take the figure and lift it closer to the fire, studying her features. "The last of the Gifted to come."

☙ ☙ ☙

THE knock came several hours after Gianni's knights had made their escape. Cardinal Boeri rose and opened the door a short distance, then sent it wide to allow in the doge, quickly closing it behind him.

"It appeared exactly as we had hoped. A swelling of the masses and I could do little. The city is in an uproar, some claiming that the prisoners merely vanished."

"But they did not," Cardinal Boeri said, pulling his robe a mite tighter.

"Nay. They went to a tiny island, known only to house fishermen and their families. They appear to be resting there for the night."

"And on the morrow, Amidei has called for his great ceremony."

"Indeed."

"The Gifted will intercede, I know it. They shall be there."

"Why not sail off? Why remain here?" the doge asked.

The cardinal paced. "Because Amidei has something of theirs."

"The Duchess."

"And the pieces to the glass map. They must retrieve both before they are to be away." The cardinal said nothing of the letter. It was better to keep some things to oneself.

"They will have little chance. There will be many on that isle come midnight. Amidei grows in power. How can so few battle against so many?"

Cardinal Boeri smiled and arched a brow. "You would be surprised, my dear doge. We shall allow them to fight their battle and retrieve what they must. We must be prepared to come to their aid, but Amidei must not know it is us. Might we hire some mercenaries who are trustworthy?"

"Already done," said the doge. "Hired men have been watching every move on that isle for weeks. We can use them, should the need arise."

"Excellent."

"Another of my ships brought a Turkish trader to bay yesterday," the doge said. "They were attempting to run some contraband. An entire shipment, in fact. Their intrusions rankle me and the peace of my city. Something must be done!"

"And you tell me this, why?"

"They had a slave aboard. He has asked to see you. He said he is the freed slave of Giulio d'Angelo."

᚜ ᚜ ᚜

"WHAT? What did he paint?" In all the madness of the last days, Daria had never thought to see what had driven Hasani to paint with a stick in his own blood. She had thought it might be a means to cope, not another vision. But now Ambrogio fully had her attention. He had forced himself to his feet, still chained to the ground, but to better see what Hasani had left behind.

"A dragon, with three sheets of parchment behind him, as well as two other objects."

"Lord Amidei. With a portion of the letter? Hasani was trying to tell me something about searching for his letter. That it would show us the way."

"Here . . ." Ambrogio said, leaning and looking as deeply to his left as he could. "Yes, it may be a letter. Difficult to tell, given his instruments."

Daria winced, thinking of her friend, as deeply wounded as she and Ambrogio were now. Where was he? Would she ever be able to find him again? She would, she determined, opening her eyes. She rose and tried to see past Ambrogio to the paintings upon the wall. "What else?"

"The dragon is up on the right. Down a line, to the left, are many churches. Any significance to you?"

"Which churches?"

"Uh, this is San Marco, without a doubt. I can make out Santa Maria Assunta de Torcello and Santa Maria de Murano. These two are more difficult: This one may be Sant' Elena, and this one I haven't seen before."

"The one you haven't seen before," she said lowly, thinking. "Where is it in the placement?"

"Lower left."

"Is there anything else that would tell us where it is?"

"Waves, on three sides. Does that help?"

"It is San Giorgio," she whispered. "Is the next in line San Marco?"

"Indeed." He cast a curious look over his shoulder.

"Then Santa Maria de Murano, Santa Maria Assunta de Torcello?"

"Yes."

"And then the isle with the dragon and the letter?"

"Yes. Daria, what is this?"

"A map."

He looked back to it. "Nay, it would be all wrong. Torcello is—"

"You do not understand. It is Hasani's map. Seven churches. Then here, on the isle of the dragon, Amidei. Three sheets of parchment, which will undoubtedly tell us where we are to go next. Our map. Hasani has painted a map for me, for the Gifted."

"So Amidei has a letter you must obtain?"

"Yes. It's what Hasani was trying to tell me. Amidei has a portion of the letter, our letter. And we must obtain it."

Ambrogio nodded as if this were obvious. "Any ideas how we are to free ourselves and summon the strength to make it out of our cells, let alone take on Amidei, rummage through his belongings, and come up with this mysterious letter?"

"None," she said, leaning her head against the bars. The cool of them felt good against her hot face.

"What do these churches have to do with your quest?"

"We discovered an artifact in each. For what purpose they are to serve, we do not yet know. But they are ancient. Pieces to a glass map, left for us, the Gifted, hundreds of years ago."

Ambrogio's eyes widened in surprise.

She looked away tiredly. "Rest assured, it is only a portion of our story of odd circumstances. One of many signs."

"Tell me," he said. "I am your captive audience."

She laughed. Daria reached up and wiped the sweat from her brow.

"You have the fever?"

"Yes. It is that damnable tick and open wounds. The saltwater did some good, but obviously not enough." She wished for a mouthful of one of her tonics but then shoved the thought tiredly away. "Brogi, we cannot allow Abramo to see Hasani's work. I do not wish to leave him any clues as to our next steps. He'll be more certain than ever which direction we headed, and give chase."

"They have not noticed these?"

"Apparently not. Or they care not."

"Daria, there is something else here."

"What?"

Ambrogio hesitated.

"Brogi."

"A priest. Upon the isle of the dragon. Arms outstretched. Christ-like."

Daria frowned. She could no longer keep her feet, and lowered to her knees, then fell to her side, staring inward to Ambrogio.

"Daria? Daria!"

"I am all right. It is only the fever. Brogi, we need to pray. The Gifted, they will come. We must pray for their safety, Father Piero's safety . . ."

She let her words fall away as footsteps sounded on the stair. Vincenzo appeared, flanked by two maids, each carrying a bucket of warm water, strips of cloth, and a new dress. Daria wearily listened to them unchain the door and enter, feeling so miserable she struggled to care that Vincenzo was there, overseeing the women, seeing Daria in such a humiliating, broken state. She ought to hate him, she thought. Despise him. But still, somewhere, hope lurked. She hated what he was doing, hated what was to become of him, but still longed for his return. His restoration, as Father Piero had helped her define.

"Turn your back, m'lord," said one woman.

"You there, turn away," said the other to Ambrogio.

They cut away the dress from her shoulders, and one set to work, washing and applying salve to each of her wounds. Daria felt each stripe as if she were getting whipped again. But now her head throbbed, her face burning with fever. The other pulled away the decrepit straw tick, swept out the corner, and brought in a pile of fresh hay and a new, clean blanket. Together they washed her arms, legs, and face and slipped a fresh gown over her shoulders. Vincenzo came near then and helped her to the fresh blanket, covering her with another.

"Drink this," he said, offering her a cup.

She took it and threw it in his face. "Be gone, Vincenzo," she said. "I do not want more of your drugs." She laid down, clenching her stomach, intuitively bracing for bodily harm. At what point had she begun to fear Vincenzo as much as Abramo?

Vincenzo reached for a scrap of cloth and wiped his face, staring at her. "It would help you sleep," he said, speaking at last. "You burn with the fever."

"I prefer to burn in fever rather than in hell," she mumbled.

"You will join us on the morrow." He reached out as if to touch her face, but she pulled back. "At the ceremony, you will understand at last, Daria. Then this will be behind us. This will be behind us."

CHAPTER THIRTY-FOUR

PIERO awakened at daybreak the next morning and realized the girl was not beneath her blankets beside the hearth. He sat up. "Tessa?"

No answer came his way.

"Awake," he hissed to the knights, rising to shake each of their shoulders.

In seconds, they were groggy but to their feet.

Gaspare came in with an armful of wood and glanced dolefully around the group.

"Trouble, men?"

"Tessa, where is she?" Vito asked, going to the window.

Gaspare knelt and stirred the coals again, then set some kindling atop as he had the night past. "She is outside praying."

The men relaxed, Basilio and Rune sinking back to their blankets. But Vito met Piero's gaze and followed him and Gianni outside.

The girl stood shivering upon the northernmost point of Gaspare's small isle. In the light of day, they could see that he had extensive gardens and two cows. But the child was not looking upon them, but rather to the east.

The priest and knight padded out and surrounded her. Piero and Vito struggled to see what had drawn her attention. "Tessa?" Vito asked, wrapping a blanket about her shoulders.

"Yes, that is where they are," Gaspare said, joining them on Tessa's other side. "Do not worry, little one. We will soon go to your loved one and take her away from there."

Tessa remained still, as if not hearing him. She looked up at Piero. "They grow in power. Double what we encountered in Siena."

"Double? Any other good news?" Vito asked the child. "Mayhap we get to go through another series of drainways and nearly drown? Or mayhap the Sorcerer will send more poison arrows our way?"

"Vito . . ." Gianni warned, joining them.

"Sorry, Captain. This is just a bit much. Could not the Lord make it a mite easier on his Gifted to see his good work accomplished?"

"Good work is seldom easy," Gaspare put in. "Double what you encountered in Siena?" he asked the girl. "Then we had best prepare well. Come. We must eat, pack, and be on our way." He nodded northward and eyed Gianni, Piero, and Vito. "We'll pretend to be fishermen. They are used to me. They shall think I simply brought others to fish their good waters. Three of you shall hide in the hold and as we make our way past the island, slip over the side and infiltrate the wall, make your way to the prison. Rescue the lady, give us a signal, and we'll come to get you."

"Sounds easy," Vito said with a wry grin. "I've never been much of a fisherman. I volunteer for the over-the-side duty. You, me, and Ugo, Captain?"

"It won't be Basilio," Gianni said, clasping him on the shoulder as they walked back to the cottage. "Rune is a good swimmer as well. But he's also good with the longbow. We could use him from the boats. And he and Basilio are used to fighting side by side. So we shall leave them together. They shall be in one boat, Gaspare and Piero in the other."

The four men paused and mulled over a few more options, but ultimately decided Gianni's first plan was best.

"I shall go with you," Tessa said, taking Gianni's and Vito's hands.

"Nay, child, you must stay where you are safest, in the boats."

She shook her head. "Nay. You promised you would never leave me again. And you need me. I can tell where they are. Give you warning."

Gianni frowned.

"She's right, Captain," Vito said. "Her gift would be well used over there."

"She's a child."

"The Lord knew who she was when he brought her to us," Piero said. "The knight is right. Think. We need brawn to break Daria free, but we also need faith and discernment. The Sorcerer will let loose any weapon he has. You could use the child."

Gianni crossed his arms over his chest and stared down at her. "How well do you swim?"

"A good bit," she said, pulling her head to the side. She was a fairly decent liar. But she had spent her childhood in a famously dry city.

Piero shook his head and pulled her close in an embrace. "How courageous you are, Tessa. You are a wonder."

Gianni remained unconvinced. "We must be stealthy. They cannot hear us or see us. Or they shall pin us with their arrows before we even reach shoreline."

"I know it," Tessa said, lifting her chin in a way he knew she had learned from Daria.

He stared her down. "There can be no shouting, no splashing about."

"I'll get her in, Captain," Vito interceded. "She can hold to my shoulders. You can hold your breath, right, Tess?"

"Yes. I'm good at holding my breath."

Gianni groaned and rolled his eyes. "I hope you all are right. The girl may go with us. But you," he said, turning to tap the priest on the chest, "had better be praying. And you," he said, pointing toward Gaspare, "had better be praying with him."

ぢ ぢ ぢ

THEY beat their way around the isle, pretending to pay no attention to those ashore. But when a knight masquerading as a monk walked alongside an outer walkway, a caged white bird in his hand, Gianni, peering over the edge, nearly sat upright. *It could not be . . .*

It was either a white falcon or a white cockatoo of the South Seas. He had seen such oddities during his days as a knight of the Church. Rare animals, often nearly dead, brought to honor and amuse the powerful.

But then the bird screeched and Gianni knew for certain. It was Bormeo.

Vito rose halfway, recognizing the bird's call. "Stay down!" Gianni hissed. He lay back against the side of the ship, thinking. He could hear the water swish and churn past the wood of the boat as the sail filled with air.

"Almost time," Gaspare said under his breath.

Gianni eyed Vito and Tessa, next to him. "You must move directly after me. Tessa, are you certain you can manage this?"

"Yes," she said.

"You have stowed your knives?" Gianni asked Vito.

"Yes." Each man also carried his sword, strapped from neck to thigh on his chest.

"I have one too," Tessa said.

Gianni grinned. "Good. We will need them all."

"Captain, that bird . . ."

"Bormeo."

"Yes. How did they get him?"

Gianni frowned and shook his head, glancing at Tessa. What treachery was at play? If the mansion in Siena had truly burned down, how had the bird been saved? How was it that he was here, with Amidei and del Buco?

"Be prepared for surprises," he said to them both.

"The moment is ideal," Gaspare said, his head into the wind as if speaking to the sea. "There is a bit of rock; you can hide there, until we distract them."

Taking a deep breath, Gianni tossed the sack of rocks, carefully measured by Gaspare to weigh him down, over the side and then lurched after them. He heard the plunge of Vito and Tessa directly behind him. As planned, he held his breath for as long as possible, hovering just beneath the surface as his boat passed by, and then the second. Another plunge sounded, Ugo most likely, but he could wait no longer. He sliced at the rocks at his feet and pushed upward, breaking the surface as quietly as possible. Seconds later, Vito and Tessa emerged. Then Ugo. The boats, with heavy sails full of brisk morning wind, were already far ahead.

The group studied the sentries above, on the wall, four in all, whose attention was drawn by the boats. They made for the outcropping of rocks that Gaspare had mentioned and sat there in the frigid water, peeking about at the guards. It was well they had not tried to make it to shore. The guards, bored with the fishermen, returned to their posts, studying the water and rocks below them as if they sensed their approach.

Tessa's teeth chattered so loudly, Gianni feared it would be heard by the guards. "Tess . . ."

She shut her mouth abruptly.

"All in all, I find Venezia to be entirely too wet for my liking," Vito said.

Gianni grinned, looking in the direction of the ships, now on the point between the isle and the Giudecca. Beyond the Giudecca was Venezia. Daria had been so close! Did she yet live?

"Come on, make haste." Ugo groaned in Gaspare's direction.

At that moment, Gaspare and Basilio began to yell at one another, gesticulating madly. All of Gianni's knights had donned the simple, hearty clothing of fishermen. Even Piero was in some of the man's old, discarded clothing, with sleeves and legs rolled up.

A guard at the front point laughed and called the other guards in to watch their fisherman defend his turf.

"Move," Gianni said, taking the lead. He went first, then Ugo, then Vito, who was slower with Tessa upon his back. They made shoreline and traveled away from the boats where their compatriots created their distraction, to the far wall. The wall was almost upon the water, at times, forcing them back in, even swimming at one point.

"I hope they keep them occupied a mite longer," Vito said, pulling Tessa out of the sea again.

"We're surely out of time. There. There's the tree Gaspare noticed."

Vito, light on his feet, ran ahead and climbed swiftly into the scrubby oak's branches. Wounded by sea and wind, the tree had but one branch that extended to the fortress wall. In a minute, Vito was up to the top and reached back a hand for Gianni. The bough bent under the weight of both men, but held. Vito leapt to the wall and down, drawing a knife in his hand, but not his sword. Ugo hoisted Tessa up to the branch, and Gianni helped her onto the wall. She jumped down into Vito's waiting arms, and before he even placed her on the ground, Gianni was behind them. The captain unstrapped the sword sheath, then restrapped it at his waist, keeping a watch before and behind them, then up to the tower and to their left.

Ugo jumped to the ground with a grunt.

Tessa stood upright and shivered. And not because of her wet clothes. "He is near. He is in the tower."

"Then let us go this way," Gianni said, heading in the direction the monk had taken Bormeo. "How many?" he asked Vito over his shoulder.

"Ten, by my count. The four perimeter guards, four more near the tower, two at the top."

"Mayhap more inside," Ugo said, pausing at a corner beside Gianni.

"Always the optimist," Vito said. "That's my brother."

Gianni smiled and chanced a glance around the corner. They had to find cover before the guards tired of Gaspare and Basilio's antics and returned to their posts. No doubt Abramo would not look upon their distraction with leniency.

Tessa crouched, her hand to the cobblestones at her feet. She closed her eyes.

"Tess?" Vito asked, crouching with her.

"The Duchess," Tessa said. "She is directly below us."

"Are you certain?" Gianni asked sternly.

But Tessa ignored his gruff tone, only smiled. "I can feel them praying."

"Them?" Ugo asked. "Who else?"

The men shared a long look. "Let us go and find out," Gianni said.

They turned the corner and hurried with soft footfalls to the gate. Rubbing his hands together to urge warmth back into them, Gianni carefully lifted the latch, wincing as it creaked.

"Is that you, Ludovico?" called a voice.

Gianni and Ugo rushed in, leaving Vito behind with Tessa. A scuffle ensued, but they quickly slayed the guard, easing him to the ground with little sound. Ugo hauled him by the feet to an empty room around the corner. He bent and stripped off the man's robe, quickly tossing it over his head and struggling to tie the rope about his waist.

"Here," Tessa said, stepping forward to assist.

"We need to move," Gianni said, checking the wall for guards again.

"We're coming," Vito said. "But if I don't get to don a Father Piero costume before I leave this island, I'm going to be upset. Don't you think I'd make a cutting figure for a priest, Tess? Ugo always gets—"

"Vito," Gianni said, widening his eyes in warning. He brought a finger to his lips and hugged the wall.

Vito was immediately all seriousness, pulling Tessa against the wall with him.

Ugo held two knives at his shoulders, ready to fling them across the open guardhouse.

Another knight entered, gazing at them in surprise.

"Don't watch, Tess," Vito whispered, covering the girl's eyes.

Ugo sent a knife flying and it struck the guard neatly in the throat, cutting off his cry of alarm—and his life. Gianni took Tessa's hand and hauled her out of the guardhouse and down the curving steps to what he assumed was the dungeon or the knights' quarters. All he knew was that Daria was somewhere near . . .

They made their way carefully down the stairs, through a wide, empty room, and down another set of stairs. Gianni glanced at Tessa, looking for any word of warning. The girl was frightened, but not terrified. Was the Sorcerer still behind them, in the tower?

The brothers came up behind them, both in monks' robes now, helping them blend in. All at once, Tessa sucked in her breath. Gianni nodded at the men, and Vito grabbed a handful of Tessa's hair in his right hand, her upper arm in his left.

"Ouch!" she cried. She quieted when two guards came up the stairs and paused, seeing them. They glanced at Vito and Ugo, in hoods now, then back to the girl. Gianni held his head low, hands behind his back as if Ugo held him in chains. They continued to move down the stairs. "Let me go," Tessa yelled, playing it up now.

"Who've you found now?" asked one of the guards.

"The sword of the Lord," Vito said, drawing his blade and impaling one guard as he turned Tessa away with his hand.

Gianni leapt forward and quickly put an end to the second's life. As they had with the first two, they hauled them downward, out of sight, intending to put them in an empty cell. But as they reached the bottom of the stairs and their eyes adjusted to the light of the lone torch, Gianni released the dead man and stumbled forward.

A man in manacles lay chained to the floor, one hand swathed in bandages, the other a bloody mass upon his chest. Gianni's eyes cast left, to the next cell, upon a woman in a thin gown, her back obviously bandaged, but bleeding through. He moved as if on wooden legs, and fell to his knees in front of her cell. "Daria? Daria!" he groaned.

She was curled in a ball, her face toward the wall. She stirred but did not wake.

Gianni glanced over at the man as his head came up and he looked over his shoulder. Gianni rose to his feet. "Am-Ambrogio?"

The man sighed and nodded. "It is I, Captain."

Gianni paced, back and forth. If Ambrogio was here, what had transpired in Siena? Had it all been a lie? The fire? Or had he been captured to lure in Daria? "Quickly, get those knights out of sight, down here," he said to Ugo and Vito, nodding to the third cell, past Daria's. "We need to get our people out of here," he said, rattling the bars, looking up and down their length as if he might tear them from the stone himself.

Tessa knelt at his feet, reaching out to Daria. "Duchess? We're here, m'lady. We're going to get you to safety."

Daria stirred and looked up at the ceiling.

"What happened to her?" Gianni hissed over at Ambrogio.

"She was whipped," he said, meeting his gaze wearily. "She burned with fever through the night."

Gianni scanned every bar of the cells, looking for a weakness, a key, a way to break the chains that held them shut. He lifted the lock. Elban iron. Even his sword could not break it open.

"Gianni, we need to pray," Tessa said. "Gaspare and Father Piero are praying for us right now."

"Yes, yes," he said, but he struggled to still his mind. "Show us, Lord, show us the way. Thank you for getting us here. Now show us the way to free our people. Please Lord Jesus. Give us the way."

"The keys," Tessa said in a whisper. She rose and flew to the dead guards that Vito and Ugo were just depositing in an empty cell. "Over here, Captain!"

Gianni rushed to her and took the ring with three large keys upon it. With trembling hands, he took one, tried it in the lock, then the next. It slid in and clicked with his turn. He slid it down the two long bars and freed the chains, unwinding them from around the bars that held Daria's cell door closed.

She stirred at the sound, turning.

A shout was heard upstairs, and boots scuffled over the stones of the empty room above the stairs. Gianni nodded to the brothers, and Ugo and Vito donned their hoods and hid their knives and swords in the folds of their robes, climbing to meet those approaching as if nothing were wrong.

Gianni turned back to Daria and cradled her head in his lap, stroking her hair and face. "Daria. Daria, I'm so sorry . . ." But she was again unconscious.

Tessa came around to her other side and leaned down. "M'lady, we've come for you."

"And me, I hope," Ambrogio said from the next cell.

"We will free you, man," Gianni said. His eyes went past Ambrogio, to the wall, smeared with blood. What had gone on here? What travesties?

A scuffle sounded above, and it went on for a minute. Swords clashed. Men grunted and coughed. But then it was over. Vito and Ugo rushed down the stairs. "We need to make haste," Ugo said. "There are more bound to come. Gaspare had counted ten on point guard at all times, and up to twenty men on rotational duty."

"Six down, fourteen to go," Vito said.

"Free Ambrogio," Gianni said, nodding to the keys still hanging in Daria's lock. The men hurried to do as he bid, taking him from his chains and hauling him out between them. Gianni gathered Daria in his arms and lifted her.

Her fever was gone, thank God. But she was frightfully weak, blinking in his direction as if not seeing him.

"You must retrieve Agata, in the next bank of cells," Ambrogio said. "And the boy, Nico."

Gianni frowned. "Agata? Agata Scioria? Nico? Quickly, tell me what you must."

"Vincenzo brought them here as captives, to use against Daria."

Gianni gazed down at Daria's face, framed by waves of hair, uncharacteristically loose and unkempt, her full lips parted, cracked with dry heat. Purple bruises lined her throat, about the width of a man's hand . . .

Fury washed through him. Hatred. He had to steady himself against it, remind himself of Piero's words of warning . . . the Sorcerer endeavored to use such feelings for his own good. He must concentrate. Keep his mind on holy things . . . but looking at Daria again, thinking of the old woman, the child brought here . . .

"They said you were all dead," he told Ambrogio. "That you perished in the fire."

Ambrogio shook his head and met Gianni's gaze. "They knew keeping some of us alive was the best way to force Daria to accept their terms. They burned the lady's house. Removed Daria from the guild, sold Hasani back into slavery, whipped her, maimed me before her, tried everything they could to force her to turn. But she would not. Our brave girl. Our brave, brave girl." He looked up as Vito reached to unlock his manacles.

Gianni tried to absorb all of Ambrogio's mad news. Hasani was gone, in the hands of slavers? The Scorias, Lucan, were truly dead?

Ugo and Tessa returned with Agata. She cried out when she saw the men, clasping her hands and thanking her God.

"Captain," Vito said quietly. "We weren't counting on three extra passengers."

"It's two, really," Gianni said. "Nico barely weighs as much as Tess."

"Speaking of which—"

"Yes, we shall need to go in search of him."

"And the letter," Ambrogio said tiredly. "Amidei has both."

Gianni stared hard at Ambrogio.

The artist looked toward his cell. "The blood? That was Hasani's vision. Amidei has a portion of your lost letter. Hasani wanted Daria to find it. He told her it would show the Gifted where to go next."

Gianni drew in a deep breath and let it out in a rush. He glanced down at Daria and up to the ceiling. "So we are to keep you all safe, enter Amidei's lair and steal the letter, and get the child back?" He had been considering abandoning the glass map pieces, praying that they could find some other way.

"That is about the sum of it," Ambrogio said, closing his eyes in sudden agony.

"Your hand?" Gianni asked.

Ambrogio nodded.

Gianni cast about for the best plan. He stared at the brothers. "We will get these people to the boats and then return for the boy and the letter."

Vito and Ugo looked doubtful. "Chances are that if we leave, Captain, we're not getting back on the isle," Ugo said. "If you need to take something with us, it had best be now."

Vito's look told Gianni he agreed.

Gianni leaned against the wall, Daria suddenly heavy in his arms.

"We're but three knights. With two wounded, one woman, a child, and another to save."

"And a bird," Vito said.

"Bormeo will be saved if Bormeo *happens* to be saved," Gianni said fiercely.

Vito put his hands up in surrender. "I'm only thinking that the lady will want her falcon back. She's liable to make us return to save him if we don't save him now . . ."

"Bormeo is last, you understand?" Gianni looked up and bumped his head against the stone walls, as if to force wisdom within. Time was short. He had to think, think! At any moment, the missing guards were bound to be discovered. "We will find a safe place to put Ambrogio, Daria, Agata, and Tess. We will barricade the door and leave Ugo to defend them. Vito and I will go in search of the glass pieces, the letter, and the boy."

Vito caught his eye.

"Yes, yes. And the bird. We'll keep an eye out for the bird."

൪ ൪ ൪

"We should have gone with them," Basilio said, awkwardly tossing a net again.

"There is less risk of exposure if they are fewer in number."

"And fewer to fight off the dark knights, should they discover their intruders."

"We can be there in minutes," Piero said.

"We should be there now."

Piero sighed and glanced over at the other boat, where Rune and Gaspare sat, with feet up on opposite sides of the boat, hats over their eyes, as if napping as they waited for the fish to fill their nets. He knew they were paying as close attention to the fortress isle as he and Basilio were. He sat down and took a loaf of bread from the basket beside him, tried to take a bite as if breaking his fast, but the bread tasted like sawdust in his mouth. Absently, he handed it to Basilio, who sat down across from him, his back to the fortress.

"I cannot just sit here and watch."

"It is well, Basilio. All is going as God has seen it."

"Yes, well, begging your pardon, Father, but I've seen the Lord watch over happenings of late that I wouldn't be able to condone."

Piero eyed him. "Are you saying you do not trust the Lord to see us through this?"

"Nay, nay," the knight said. But his shoulders and chin told Piero he lied.

"You must trust the Lord in all things, my son," the priest said. "In the face of evil, in the midst of your darkest hour, you must proclaim your trust in the God who was, and is, and will be."

Basilio leaned back and studied him. "He asks much, our God."

"More than that. He asks for it all. *Everything.*" He leaned forward and grinned conspiratorially. "But he also *offers* it all. Everything. Anything we could truly care about or wish for. He holds it all. When we know that, truly know that, we accept what is given. We accept what is taken away. We offer our very lives as an offering to him. Regardless of how kings or princes view his justice, we choose to believe that our God is good. In all things."

Basilio looked away and stared at the waves to the west.

Piero reached out and grabbed his forearm, waited for him to look him again in the eye. "I need you to do something for me, Basilio."

"All right," the knight said warily.

"I need you to be my messenger. You are stubborn, but you remember things. I have watched you. When you accept a word as truth, it remains in your heart."

Basilio waited.

"There are times to come when the Gifted will waver. When they will suffer. When they will wander. They will find themselves lost, and need to seek their way to God's path again. But they need to remember, they can do all things through the Christ who strengthens them."

Basilio shifted uneasily. "Why do you speak as if you shall not be with us?"

Piero pressed on. "You will soon see, friend. What was that first thing I wished for you to remember to tell them?"

"We can do all things through the Christ who strengthens us."

"Good. The second thing I want them to know is that God can do what he says he can do. Always."

Basilio shrugged. "That appears self-evident."

"Repeat it."

"God can do what he says he can do."

"Excellent. It seems primary, but it's often the first thing we fail to believe. The next is to trust in the Lord, for he is good."

Basilio began to repeat his words without question, but his brow furrowed with more and more fear, the longer the priest went on.

"Forgive those who do not ask forgiveness . . .

"Love those who are not lovable . . .

Abruptly, the priest shut his mouth and stared at the fortress. Slowly, he rose.

Basilio turned. All but two of the sentries were running away from the wall, toward the tower.

Their friends had been discovered.

CHAPTER THIRTY-FIVE

ABRAMO went to the edge of the parapet, the white falcon atop his arm, no hood over the bird's eyes, a leather strap holding it to his arm. It was a bright and clear day, another respite from the autumn rain. He believed the falcon was taking a liking to him. "Soon, I'll be able to let him loose, watch him fly, knowing he'll return," Abramo said to Vincenzo. "Like the Duchess," he said with a wry grin toward the bird, bending to nuzzle his nose into Bormeo's white feathers.

He lifted the falcon up, letting the wind flow through the bird's feathers, letting him taste the promise of flight again. "Ah, yes, smell that, my friend. Taste it. It will be yours again some day." He glanced toward Vincenzo. "It will be a fine evening for our ceremony. Nothing will impede our faithful from attending. Have you looked in on Daria? How does she fare this morn?"

Vincenzo said nothing, but only turned resolutely back toward the sea.

"What is it?" Abramo asked.

"I know not," Vincenzo said with a frown.

Abramo followed his gaze and stopped where Vincenzo's hovered, over the two fishing boats. He squinted into the sun and noted the same things Vincenzo had.

Two boats where there usually was but one. And two fishermen in each boat, looking so heavy that they dare not bring in their nets. Vincenzo and Abramo looked down over the edge of the tower, catching sight of the lone guard at the point, the others gone. All at once, both men understood why they were ill at ease. Those were no ordinary fishermen.

Abramo turned and pushed the falcon into his cage, hurriedly unstrapping the leather band from his wrist, already running toward the stairs.

Vincenzo looked to the fishermen, saw how two rose up as if alarmed when a guard shouted below. He knew them then, as interlopers, true enemies, recognized it as if in the middle of a dream just before waking. He walked past the cage as Bormeo opened the sloppily latched door and hopped to the edge.

He was only a few paces away and knew he should stop the bird, should firmly latch the cage, but instead turned and walked down the stairs slowly. Below, shouts of alarm could now be heard.

Bormeo stretched his wings, hopped from the edge, and eagerly took flight, climbing sharply into the pale Venetian sky, his leather bonds streaming behind him.

ࣧ ࣧ ࣧ

"Pray for the lady," Gaspare said, his voice carrying over the quiet waters to Piero and Basilio. Beside him, Rune brought his longbow to his feet, calmly placed an arrow in the notch, and pulled it halfway up.

"Rune is preparing for war and the fisherman wants to pray," Basilio muttered.

"He's right. There could be something dreadfully wrong with Daria. We need her to gain some strength, at least enough strength to get them off the island. We know not what she's been through over the last week."

"They can manage. One woman between Vito, Ugo, Gianni."

"If all is as they expected. But if Daria is ailing, or cannot be moved . . ."

"They'll be fine. They're good fighting men. The best."

"But Gaspare is right, something is off . . . Pray with me, Basilio. Pray for the lady."

"Before or after we fend off the attack?" he asked, nodding toward the isle walls. Atop the tower, two archers appeared, their feminine form all too familiar. The archers from Siena, who had narrowly missed bringing them all to death. Those who had taken down Gianni's entire guard of the Vaticana when they dared to chase down the Sorcerer. Basilio shared a look with Rune in the other boat. "Our friends are back, Father. Remember the arrows that nearly killed Rune, Daria?"

"And Gianni," Piero said grimly.

"And Gianni."

"Uh, Father?" Basilio asked, pulling their shields to their chests.

The two women at the top of the tower pulled back their arrows and let them fly, relaxed in their manner, toying with them.

"Yes, Basilio," he said, as an arrow struck beside him and stuck into the splintered wood, tail feathers out.

"While we're praying for the lady, might you pray for us, too?"

"I believe Gaspare is covering us all," Piero said, nodding to their left.

Gaspare stood, meaty hands outstretched toward the isle, head bowed. Rune was shouting at him to get down, but he either ignored or did not hear the knight. Arrows rained down, near him, but never very close.

"Odd," Piero said with a smile. "We know from experience that they are very good shots." He waggled his eyebrows. "I believe our Lord is afoot."

ౘ ౘ ౘ

FOUR men went rushing by. Gianni peeked out from the narrow hallway. Below, they could hear shouts, knew that the dead knights and the escaped prisoners had been discovered.

"We're never going to get the letter and get these people out, Captain," Ugo said. "Mayhap I should try to get them to the docks, while they are still seeking us."

"Nay," Gianni said. "We will stick to the plan. You will make them think that we are all inside the room, trapped, while Vito and I seek out the letter, map pieces, and the boy."

"And the bird," Vito said.

Gianni frowned at him. "We'll return and take the knights that have entrapped you, one at a time. Then, together, we will make our way out and to the docks. With God's blessing, they may not even find you. This way," Gianni grunted, pushing open a door on the first floor of the main tower. He hurried forward, looking one way and then the other, ducking his head into the first doorway and then a second. "In here," he said, pulling his head to the right.

The group hurried in and Agata shut the door, making the sign of the cross in front of it as if locking a door. Gianni knelt and gently set Daria down, careful to ease her to her side. The brutality of beating a woman— a woman!—so savagely! Once again, he recognized the depths of Abramo's darkness. He would repay the Sorcerer for the murders of his fellow knights, the innocents in Siena, for the travesties against his lady. He would make Abramo feel every stripe . . .

Daria groaned and opened her eyes again, this time clearly seeing him.

Gianni smiled and caressed her face, beside himself that she was again conscious. She still burned with a bit of fever, but was it abating?

"Captain . . ." Vito said from the door.

"Gi-Gianni?" Daria asked in wonder.

"Yes, yes," he said, wanting to cover her face in tender kisses. He smiled at her and leaned closer. "We're going to get you to safety, Daria."

"Brogi?"

"Over here," the man answered.

"*Captain,*" Vito said in a whisper, leaning against the wall as two men ran by. Ugo stood on the other side, sword at the ready.

"We have them all, Daria," Gianni whispered. "We're going to find Nico and then we'll get you off this cursed island."

"The letter, we must get Abramo's portion of the letter."

"I understand."

Daria closed her eyes as if to summon some strength and then rose to one arm. "And Bormeo, if you can—please . . ."

Gianni clamped his lips together, feeling Vito's grin from across the room. "We shall do our best, Daria, but I cannot promise it."

"I understand," she said, nodding. She moved as if attempting to stand. "I need to show you the way—"

"Nay," Gianni said, laying a gentle hand upon her shoulder. "We will move more swiftly without you. Please. Stay here and rest. There may come a time ahead that you shall need to move on your own."

She fell back, as if the brief fight within her had already wearied her beyond measure, and stared hungrily into his eyes. She smiled and reached out and cradled his cheek in her hand, looking at him with such a depth of—gratitude? love?—that it took his very breath. "Be careful, Gianni."

"I shall," he said, placing his hand on hers for a second and then pushing abruptly away.

He nodded to Ugo, and together they hauled a heavy table over to the door, then two chairs. The room had but one window, high and narrow. Their only escape would be out the passageway. Gianni paused beside Ugo and placed a hand upon his shoulder. "May the Lord and his angels defend you all," he said.

"And you, Captain," Ugo said.

"We must go," Vito said urgently.

"His quarters," Daria said, meeting Gianni's gaze. "You'll find the letter in his quarters. To the right, through a dining hall with fireplace, up the broad staircase and directly to your right again. Abramo's quarters are on the top level. And Nico, he may be just two floors above us, where they kept me for a time."

"We'll obtain the boy and the letter and be back for you," Gianni said.

"And Bormeo," Vito mouthed to Daria.

Gianni grabbed his arm and pulled him in front of him, then pushed him out the door.

ↂ ↂ ↂ

ABRAMO halted two knights—Ciro and another—running up the prison steps, swords drawn.

"Where are they?" Abramo asked Ciro.

"We know not, m'lord."

"You've searched the entire dungeon?"

"Every cell. Only found some of our own, dead."

"No one has left the island?"

"We think not."

"How many men have been slain?"

"Six, m'lord."

"Guards!" Abramo shouted. Three more immediately rounded the tower. "I want men back to their positions upon the wall." He raised his index finger to each one. "No one leaves this island. Do you understand? No one. You, to the south. You, to the east. You, to the north. You, to the west. If the prisoners escape from your portion of the wall, you shall forfeit your life. Go."

Ciro remained.

"You, come with me. The perimeters will be secured in moments. My girls will keep their escape boats away. So," he said, smiling for the first time, "they must be somewhere within the tower."

It was then he knew. Of course. They were going after the letter and the map. Daria and Gianni had seen the letter in Venezia. And the boy. They would not leave without the child. And if they had gone up, they would be forced to come down. Together, Ciro and Abramo eased into the tower's great hall.

⚜ ⚜ ⚜

In Venezia, Roberto hovered around the docks, listening to groups of sailors speak in the idle way of working men, moving from one to another until he caught wind of what he sought. This group spoke in hushed undertones of the wonders promised to them this eve upon the isle of the Master.

This was the one he wanted.

He leaned against a stack of round bales of cotton cloth, straining to hear. The sailors on the ship he had arrived on had spoken of this isle, but Roberto doubted his chances of hiding in the hold en route to the island, with no cargo aboard. He needed a ship heavy with cargo, one that would move on from the dark island after he disembarked.

This was that ship. With each word that was spoken, he became more sure, eyeing the ship, studying his entry path, mentally timing how long it would take for him to make his way in, what distraction he would need . . .

⚜ ⚜ ⚜

Vito and Gianni slipped out into the hallway, heard the scraping sound of Ugo moving the heavy table, barricading the door behind them. The corridors were eerily quiet. Men shouted outside, but no sound could be heard from left to right.

Gianni pulled his head to the right and they ran on soft steps to the first staircase, up to the large room Daria had mentioned, with fireplace and window at one end, then up another. Gianni pulled his sword in front of him, point down, at the side of one open doorway, and then gestured to Vito, following directly behind him, sword up, ready to strike.

But it was empty.

They proceeded to the next three, with similar results.

In the fourth, Vito paused and reached for a box. "Captain?"

He handed him the broken pair of spectacles.

Gianni shook his head, feeling the impact, knowing these had undoubtedly been used against Daria, part of her torture. Beata, sweet Beata . . .

"Captain?" Vito said. "We must be about it."

He slid the spectacles into his pocket, thinking that one day, Daria might wish to bury them, if she could not bury her beloved friends and servants. He followed Vito out the door; the next room was barricaded. Slowly, they lifted the crude wooden plank that crossed the doorway and eased the door open.

A child hovered in the corner, knees to chest.

"Nico," Vito whispered, lifting his hand to the child. "It is us. We have come to free you. Make haste!"

ↄ ↄ ↄ

THE arrows rained down in steady fashion, just often enough to keep the men aboard the ships from doing anything but move toward the sails and make their way out of range. It was frustrating, moving away from their people rather than toward them, but it was all they could do.

"Why do they tarry?" Rune asked grumpily, sending an arrow flying toward the tower, knowing it was largely hopeless. They were at such range, neither could strike their adversary.

"Something is wrong, different than we anticipated," Piero said, closing his eyes as if his head ached and shaking it, slowly.

"Different?" Basilio asked, hauling sail.

"That is all that I can say," Piero said, opening his eyes to stare at the stocky man. "I know not more, only that things must not be as they expected."

"Surprises are the enemy of victory," Basilio said grimly.

"Nay," Piero said, "lack of faith is the enemy." He stared dolefully at the tower and then over at the other boat. "This does not bode well. Our comrades will not make it out. Come alongside the other boat. We must speak to the others."

Basilio, frowning, did as he bid, hauling sail, tacking until the two fishing vessels were side by side.

"It has not gone as planned," Gaspare said, speaking to Piero.

"Nay," Piero answered.

"They shall not get off the island immediately, and we must find another way in."

"Yes," Piero said.

"I propose we make our way back to Venezia, return on ships bound for the isle this night."

"Let me understand you," Basilio interrupted, frowning, raising a hand toward Gaspare and Piero. "You wish us to leave the isle's shore, so even if our men and the lady get to the edge, we will be absent. And you mean for us to return to a city, a city where we were very nearly hanged just a sunset past."

"Yes," Gaspare said, steadily meeting his gaze.

Basilio looked to Father Piero, who stared back at him with quiet, grim assurance.

Rune waved toward the fortified isle. "They will think we deserted them!"

"The sun reaches high above us," Piero said. He gestured toward the island. "They clearly know us as enemy. The alert has been raised. They will not allow us near, are clearly on the hunt for our Gifted, who must yet elude them. We leave for a time, solely that we might aid their escape as night falls."

"Night?" Basilio coughed.

"Night," Gaspare said. "Under cover of darkness. That is the only way that we might steal from the dark what they believe is theirs."

CHAPTER THIRTY-SIX

THE door lurched and banged against the table, where Ugo stood, bracing against it.

"Over here!" cried a voice outside their door.

Agata gasped, sitting down next to Daria and Tessa as if seeking physical assurance.

"It will be well," Daria said, reaching down to grip the older woman's hand.

Together, they listened as another man joined the first, and both put shoulder to the door.

Ugo glanced in their direction. "I'm sorry, m'lady. I need all of you. Please. Hasten to me, and sit upon the table. They will add heavier men. We must do all we can to be at the ready."

Daria, now stronger than Ambrogio, so recently tortured, went to her friend. Agata went to his other side, helping him to his feet.

The men slammed against the door, pushing the table an inch back. Ugo pushed against it, but the knights outside slid a sword in the crack, keeping it from falling shut again.

The slit in the door seemed to seep cool air in toward them, pulling at them like frigid tendrils. A shout went up outside, the first two knights obviously joined by two others.

Ugo helped Ambrogio atop the table, and the man lay down upon his side, his back to Daria and the others.

The knights outside collided with the door, pushing it another inch forward.

Ugo glanced toward Daria in alarm, and immediately she, Agata, and Tessa sat atop the table.

The next time the door slammed against the table, Ugo was braced, and the remnant of the Gifted's prisoners, wounded, weary, or afraid, clung to the table and prayed.

஢ ஢ ஢

THEY heard them coming, up the stairs.

Vito eyed Gianni across the child's head.

"Stay here," Gianni whispered to Nico. "Stand here in the hallway as if surprised, but do not move. Trust us, child. We shall not let them get to you again."

With that, either knight entered a room on either side of Nico and placed their backs to the side wall, waiting for the enemy's approach.

Nico, nervously eyeing either doorway, listened to the knights move closer. Shouting, stomping. At the very last moment, he fell to the floor, as if he had been struck.

The knights turned the corner and paused, taken aback by the appearance of the boy.

"What are you doing out?" said one, moving forward to reach for the child.

"He was our guide," Vito said, stepping forward and striking out with his sword in one fluid movement, directly over Nico's head and into the enemy's belly.

Gianni moved silently past the first knight as Vito's sword struck, circling his sword above his own head and then coming down in a deadly two-handed strike against the second enemy knight, taking him down with but three quick blows—glancing strikes against the neck and chest, a plunge into the belly.

Vito reached for Nico, white-faced and trembling. "Come, boy," he said. "You wished to be a squire. Show us the way to Amidei's quarters and I shall see you to knighthood myself."

ↄ ↄ ↄ

"Is Amidei out there?" Daria asked Tessa.

The knights outside pounded again against the door. They were building some sort of leveraging system, and with each strike against the door they gained a portion of an inch. It wasn't much, but collectively, in time, they would make their way in. And they were steady about their work. Already they had room for a man's hand to reach through. Ugo stood on the table, sword drawn but resting point down, daggers tucked in his belt, watching their methodical progress.

Tessa went to the side of the table, put her hand to the wall, and closed her eyes a moment. "They are of the dark, but none of them wield even the power of Baron del Buco or Lord Amidei."

Daria internally winced at Tessa's reference to her "Uncle." Wielding the power of the dark . . . *Vincenzo, Vincenzo, what has happened to you?*

"Back to the table, Tess," Ugo said gruffly. "You don't weigh more than a mouse, but we need every stone we can get."

She was climbing atop the table when she suddenly paused, eyes wide with terror. "Now. Now Amidei and the baron are here."

Daria pulled her into her arms, feeling her small heart pound faster than her own. Outside! Just outside!

ↄ ↄ ↄ

ABRAMO and Vincenzo, with Ciro and one remaining knight, walked up the stairs, unhurried, confident that the Gifted had been contained.

They paused in the hallway beside the four knights who worked to gain access into one of the first rooms and studied their progress.

Abramo reached out to the wooden beam that crossed from the door to the far side of the stone hallway, glad for its sturdiness and the ingenuity of his men. "Very good," he said. "I am well pleased with you."

He turned to Ciro and said, "Go outside. There is a high, narrow window. Get to it and find out if they are all inside. Then take three torches and attempt to smoke them out."

"Consider it done, m'lord," said the knight, leaving immediately.

"How many do you believe are within?" Abramo asked another man, nearest the door.

"They are fairly quiet. There are at least two men, a child."

"The Duchess?"

"I thought I heard her voice within, but I cannot be certain."

Abramo thought of the carnage behind him, eight slain knights now discovered in total. It was not the work of one or even two men. There must be more, and . . . his eyes went to the hallway to his left. He grabbed the nearest knight and pulled him near, so he could speak in his ear. "They have left their weakest here, under guard, but they have gone on for the boy and something else I prize. If they return here, you must not let them get to those within, especially the Duchess. Do you understand me? You fight them to the death or I shall kill you myself."

"Yes, m'lord."

ᚖ ᚖ ᚖ

Nico led the way up the stairs to the top of the tower. The stairwell opened up into a spacious room that covered the entire floor, Abramo's quarters. Rich tapestries covered the walls. A massive bed was on one wall, a table and two chairs by the hearth, the embers still smoldering within.

"Captain," Vito said, hurrying to the table. He lifted a box. Daria's. From Siena.

"Look within. See if it contains the letter."

Gianni turned and went to one of Amidei's chests, throwing out fine linens and clothing. He doubted Amidei would keep the letter or map pieces in plain sight.

"Nothing," Vito confirmed. "It appears to simply be the lady's belongings."

"Bring it," Gianni said, shoving down his fury at yet another portion of Daria's life being infiltrated by the enemy. He reached the bottom of the chest and tapped the wooden floor, listening for a hollow space, the common hiding place of nobles for items of import.

"Nothing," he said. His eyes scanned the room. "Behind the tapestries! Nico, assist us. Check every stone! Do it methodically, each one. Miss none."

They rushed to separate tapestries, all aware now that time was growing short.

"Could he have the letter, the glass pieces on his person?" Vito asked, still touching each stone as he spoke, as if feeling for a ripe melon.

"Mayhap."

Vito and Gianni finished the stones behind their tapestries and moved on to the upper portion of Nico's, where the boy could not reach. Nothing.

Gianni sighed and let the tapestry fall behind him. There was one more, above the bed.

They all heard the squeak of the wooden floorboard at the top of the stairs. He nodded to Nico, motioning for him to go to the corner of the room behind them. He and Vito drew their swords, raising them, ready for what was to come.

ↂ ↂ ↂ

I⊤ was Tessa who saw Ciro first. He was looking inside, through the narrow window, studying them all. He shouted to a guard behind him and then looked back to them, smiling.

Daria stared back, feeling hate well up within her. She remembered Father Piero's words, remembered she was not to hate, that hate was what the enemy thrived upon. But it was difficult, so difficult with these men . . . men who had tortured or destroyed her or hers.

Ciro left for a moment and then peered in again, leering at her, taunting her.

"Out, you troll, out!" Daria shouted.

Ciro simply smiled again and turned to speak to another outside.

A moment later, he shoved in a smoldering torch, and then another, and then another, then stuffed the window with a wooden block and other rags, shutting out most of their light. Only dim slivers came from the window, and more from the hallway.

The men outside pounded against the door, gaining another portion of an inch.

"Quickly, stomp on the torches," Ugo said to Tessa, the lightest of them all. "They mean to smoke us out."

She jumped off the table and ran to do as he bid.

In another minute, the block was removed from the window and a female's eyes came into view. They could hear something heavy being dragged to the window, and she appeared again, as if standing on something.

"Amidei's archer!" Daria warned, finally understanding. The tip of an arrow appeared in the window, aimed at Ugo. "Take care!"

ᘒ ᘒ ᘒ

A knight entered Amidei's quarters, with Abramo and Vincenzo directly behind him. Gianni studied them all. He knew from Daria that Vincenzo was an expert swordsman, that Abramo was likely the same. And this knight with them, he seemed lithe on his feet, but sturdy, much like Vito.

"Do you plan more tricks, Sorcerer?" Gianni said, jutting out his chin. "A coward's retreat? Or do you dare to draw a sword?" He looked to Vincenzo. "And what shall you do, Baron, without poison to take me down? Here am I, hale and hearty. Mayhap it will be you that will dare to draw your sword against me."

"You are on my island, knight," Abramo said, slowly drawing his sword, and looking down its shiny blade as if vaguely disinterested. "Your foundation is not so steady here, more like quicksand. You will soon see." He eyed the child behind the men. "Your Gifted will not be able to stand against my men. They will once again be in our prison cells, greater in number, to do with as we wish. We will slay you two, and take the child. The Gifted shall be vanquished. Mine." A small, smug smile crept up his face.

"You do not yet know the power of the One who watches over us," Gianni said, moving his sword toward the Sorcerer. "It is he who will see you vanquished. We will escape your island and be upon his mission. We shall not fail."

"Are you certain of that?" Abramo asked. He glanced out the window, smiling. "How exactly will you make your escape? Your boats appear to have abandoned you."

Gianni frowned, certain he was lying. Father Piero, Gaspare, the knights—they would never leave them behind. Unless they somehow knew that more than Daria was here, that they needed another boat, reinforcements . . .

Abramo scoffed. "You hide your concern well, but I can feel it within you. Doubt. It is powerful, creeping over your mind and heart like a dense fog. Go on, look outside. Know for yourself."

Gianni stared forward, refusing to take his bait. With a roar, he jumped forward, striking the Sorcerer's sword and turning in the same motion to block the other knight's strike. Swords clanged beside him,

Vito meeting Vincenzo's first strike, then jabbing back at him with three quick moves.

✧ ✧ ✧

"BLOCK those arrows!" Ugo said to Tessa. "Quickly, with a chair, anything!"

An arrow came singing through the room, narrowly missing Ugo's chest, cutting open a slice in the armpit of his tunic.

Another followed, grazing Ambrogio's cheek.

"Tessa!" Ugo growled—unable to leave the table or those outside would gain entry—helpless against the barrage to come.

Tessa moved about the room, looking for something suitable to use to block the archer, but everything was atop the table, used for weight. Other than that, the room was bare.

Ugo moved the chairs around to shield the wounded prisoners lying on the table in front of them. The knights pounded against the door, gaining another quarter of an inch every minute. Another arrow came winging its way inward.

Daria sat up, understanding why the archer did not aim in her direction. "She fears striking me," she said. "Amidei still wants me alive."

An arrow came flying toward them, striking the table, directly beneath Ambrogio. "They apparently do not care whether *I* live or die," he said, eyeing the arrow.

"Crouch behind me, Ugo. Agata, you as well. Tess, you stay over there, by the wall where she cannot see you."

"But my weight, m'lady . . . you need me there."

"No, Tess. I need you over there, safe." She moved the chairs in front of Ambrogio, panting at the pain and effort, feeling her back's wounds break open with each movement.

The knights outside pounded again upon the door, gaining a half inch this time.

Daria gasped. "Oh, Gianni. Make haste! Do make haste!"

✧ ✧ ✧

GIANNI charged toward the smaller knight, driving him back and back until he fell upon the ground. He could feel Abramo barreling down upon him and turned at the last second to parry his strike, meeting two others, shoving him back, then turning to drive back the other knight. Vincenzo and Vito still battled back and forth. It appeared Vito had taken a blow to the shoulder, Vincenzo a strike to the thigh.

Gianni knew that if he did not make short work of the other knight, Abramo would have an edge by not wearying. So Gianni met three of Abramo's strikes, sword to sword, then punched him in the face, sending him spinning away. He did not pause. He turned and went after the smaller knight, driving him into a corner, moving as if he intended to go left, then surprising the knight with a blow from the right. The man suffered a mortal blow.

Gianni turned toward Abramo, staring at him with dark eyes. Abramo pulled a cloth from his pocket and dabbed at his dripping lip, slowly looking from bloodstained cloth to Gianni, planning his next move. Behind him, Vincenzo and Vito battled on, but his eyes were solely on Gianni.

"Do you know how long it has been since someone has dared strike me?"

"Apparently, too long," Gianni returned.

"You understand that I must kill you now."

"He's feelin' it, Captain," Vito said, shooting Gianni a grin and a raised brow. "You've gone and ruined his devilish good looks." He raised his arm to parry Vincenzo's next blow and then Vincenzo drove him backward, out of Gianni's peripheral vision.

Abramo came forward hard, anger fueling his fire. He rushed him, striking again and again, driving him back. Gianni pushed him back a few steps and then Abramo drove him backward again. He was as strong as Gianni, as good with a sword. It would take timing and the Lord's own moment to take him down. *Protect me, Lord Jesus.*

Abramo leaned back as if he had spoken aloud. Gianni smiled, remembering Daria's words in Il Campo, how she could keep the dark at bay until they made their escape, when God's angels came down and stood beside her mighty warriors. "Protect me, Lord Jesus," he said aloud. "Bring me your mighty warriors, Father God. Bring them here, into the lair of your enemy, and bring us victory."

His enemy fell back, seeming to have lost his momentum, timing. Gianni easily met his attempts to strike him, silently thanking his Lord, gaining in confidence and strength with each word he prayed. He glanced up at Vito, saw that he had taken another blow to the opposite arm and was obviously tiring. Vincenzo, sensing his edge, moved into a frenzy of strikes, slicing Vito's right forearm, feigning left and then striking from the right, at the last sending Vito's sword skittering away across the floorboards.

Gianni had to get to his friend. Vincenzo was closing in on Vito, as he crab-walked away, narrowly dodging one pierce attempt and then another. But Gianni's attention was again forced to Abramo, coming hard again, gaining strength in Vincenzo's success. They locked, hand to hand, as if joined in a curious dance.

"You can still turn, knight," Abramo said, panting from the exertion. "You have taken down a number of my men today. Come and join us, and you shall be my own captain. Serve me, and you will know the full import of my favor."

"I'd rather perish than ever walk a day in the boots of one of your knights," he spat out, shoving him backward.

" 'Tis a pity," Abramo said. "You force me to decide between killing you now or keeping you alive . . ." He smiled broadly. "Oh yes, I think I shall only wound you," he said, waving his sword to Gianni's upper right, and bringing it down, curiously slow. Too late, Gianni saw the dagger come up from his left. Too late to avoid it, he felt it slice into his belly.

He stumbled backward, hand to his wound, bringing it away from him in stunned disbelief at the bright red upon his hands. He fell and glimpsed Vito, on the ground, Vincenzo's sword tip at his throat.

CHAPTER THIRTY-SEVEN

DARIA thought the archer had given up when one more arrow came through the air and struck Ugo in the shoulder with such force, he fell backward against the wall and then spun sideways, losing his balance and tumbling off the table.

"Ugo!" Daria cried.

Hearing her cry, the knights outside at once put their shoulders to the door and succeeded in opening it to shoulder width. Without pause, they poured inward, one, two, three. All with swords drawn. Ciro entered then, gone from his post outside the small window, with another knight behind him. Then the archer.

Ugo drew his sword, valiantly trying, but Daria could see it was no use.

She stepped in front of him, guarding him from Amidei's knights, and gently placed a hand upon the blade, forcing it down. "Save it, Ugo," she said under her breath. "We will need you later. Do not sacrifice yourself now."

Ciro reached out and took a handful of her hair and pulled her to his side.

Ugo stood straighter, fury etched in his face.

"Ah, the brave knight. I bet it rankles that a man that you once watched dismissed as nothing is now manhandling your lady."

"Ugo," Daria said. "Nay. Do not listen to him. Ugo!"

Blood seeped from the arrow, still lodged in his shoulder. Still he stepped forward, seeming to see nothing, hear nothing, but Ciro's ugly hold upon his charge.

Ciro took a step as well, leaving Daria behind. "Nay," she said, grasping his hand as it left her hair. "Please."

His mouth twisted into a sneer and he stepped toward Ugo as if encouraged by her words rather than discouraged. Ugo attempted to reach for his sword, but could do little more than bend halfway down, his face pale.

Ciro grabbed the arrow at Ugo's shoulder and pushed him back. He stopped and pulled forward, making Ugo gasp and try to follow. Ciro peered over his shoulder. "Didn't go all the way through," he mused, as if informing him. "Pity that, for you," he said, now pushing him again until his back was against the wall.

With his right hand holding Ugo in place, he took hold of the arrow's shaft in his left and slowly twisted it. Ugo cried out in agony.

"Let him be!" Tessa screamed, tears sliding down her cheeks. A man easily held her by the arm, even though she fought to escape. Agata wept. Ambrogio looked upon them, misery in his eyes.

Tessa sucked in her breath and looked to the door in horror. Slowly, Daria's eyes followed the girl's.

And that was when Abramo and Vincenzo arrived, each shoving a bound man forward. Gianni. And Vito.

But while Daria's eyes hovered over the wound at Gianni's belly, all she could think about was where Nico might be.

ॐ ॐ ॐ

THE ship scraped up against the dock, creating a wooden squeak where wet wood rubbed against wet wood. Roberto listened to the squeak for a time, thinking it might drive him to madness, but still he stayed put, wanting the men who had come aboard this ship to become firmly ensconced within their distractions upon the isle before he ventured forward.

He slowly counted to a hundred again, and when no sound but the cries of greetings among men above came to his ears, he slid from his perch in the hold and peeked out from the deck. Other ships were arriving, dumping five to twenty people at a time upon the island's shores. With no more room at the dock, they anchored offshore and came in by rowboat, more as the sun set.

Roberto was glad his sailors had arrived early. Otherwise, he would have been forced to swim ashore. Instead, he pulled out a dark, discarded cape one of the men had left behind, lifting the hood to cover his head. He jumped off the ship and walked down the gangplank to the dock, as if eagerly anticipating reaching the gathering. He never paused, just made his way forward to the fortified island's wall, listening to the armed men, dressed as monks, question each person as they arrived. He knew then that he would have to pull his hood from his head, knew he would have to come up with convincing words for the guards. But on the other hand, who would suspect a child of entering the hold of his enemy?

ⲥⲃ ⲥⲃ ⲥⲃ

THEY had deposited the Gifted within the prison cells, again tying or chaining each of them in separate cells. The first cell, where Hasani and Ambrogio were once held, now contained Gianni, tied with his hands behind his back and on the ground, coming in and out of consciousness, a pool of blood spreading beneath him. Daria was shoved back into her cell, her hands tied before her, and told to stay upon the blanket and rest. Vito was chained in the third cell, and the others were led into the next room to the other bank of cells.

Daria could hear Agata and Tessa weeping, their pitiful voices echoing off the stone walls. She lay down on her side, staring, thinking, hoping against hope that this nightmare would end. She had been so certain . . . A guard watched them for a time, and then was called upstairs to help interview the isle's "guests."

"And so it begins," she muttered. Her rash promise to Abramo flashed through her mind. Would he still come for her? Haul her upstairs to teach her their ways? The very thought of it made her want to retch. Where was Nico? If she refused Amidei, would he be safe? Or was he again a prisoner, high in the tower?

"Of what do they speak, m'lady?" Vito asked.

"Amidei's ceremony of ceremonies. He practices the dark arts upon this isle, and for months he has called his faithful in to worship his lord. Tonight is the culmination."

"I wager he revels in the fact that we're in his dungeon."

She could not summon the strength to respond. She was still trying to breathe, take in the fact that they had not been rescued. In fact, it seemed as if things were more dismal than before, with more of the Gifted captured now than—

"M'lady, Basilio, Rune, Gaspare, and Piero are still out there. Even Nico . . . he escaped as we battled Vincenzo and Amidei. You must cling to hope. Our men, and our God, will see us through this. Find the hope within you. It will bring you strength. Our enemy, he senses your defeat. He will capitalize upon it. Now, more than ever, you must find hope and faith in your heart to battle this monster."

Daria sighed and rose to a sitting position. She shook her head. "I desire it. I do. But Vito—"

"M'lady," Vito said, knowing he was interrupting her. "Remember what Father Piero always tells us . . . our light is brightest when we are surrounded by utter darkness."

"We must be fairly bright at the moment," she said with a sigh.

Vito laughed, and it made her smile. Usually it was he who made her laugh.

"Can you get to the captain? See to his wounds? And I need you to check his coat pocket."

She cast him a puzzled expression.

"It's important. Can you get to him?"

She turned away from Vito and slid across the floor to Gianni, who lay on his side, his back to the bars that separated them. She paused at the bars, holding her breath and watching the man breathe for some time, finding comfort in each rise and fall of his lungs. "Please, Lord Jesus," she whispered. "Give me faith I cannot feel. Do not let him die. You let me heal him once, will you bless us by healing him again?"

"M'lady," Vito said softly. "I'm all for you healing the captain, and I'll join in your prayers, but quick, check his pocket."

She frowned and leaned forward, pushing both arms through the narrow space between the bars, wanting to cry out at the pain in her back. Almost there. Her fingers could grab the edge of a pocket, almost.

A drum began to beat, once every minute, a deep, resonating sound. It was their way, beating at the drum in ever-faster time, until the frenzy upon the taut skin matched their own in their ceremony.

"You can do this, m'lady," Vito said, trying again to pull the manacles from the wall. She had watched him do it a hundred times, could see him even though her back was turned toward him. "Reach for it. It's important."

Daria grimaced and pushed again, uttering a small cry at the pain in her arms and in her back. There. She pinched down on the pocket and pulled backward, smiling. She could feel the odd, hard shape within and quickly dipped into the pocket and pulled out Beata's shattered glasses.

"Oh!" she cried, dropping them to the floor as if they were a giant spider.

"M'lady, quick," Vito said. "I know this must be difficult, but please . . . pick them up. There's someone coming! Hide them within your skirts and get away from the captain!"

She did as he bid, sliding backward toward the wall just as the guard returned to look in upon them all. After a cursory look, he left again. For all appearances, they looked defeated or unconscious.

As soon as he was gone, Daria moved back to the cell wall and did what Vito had obviously been thinking, cutting loose Gianni's bonds with the edge of the broken glass.

"Not all the way through," he warned.

She nodded, understanding. It needed to appear as if he were still bound. Just loose enough that he could use his hands when ready.

"There. I think they are ready."

"Good. Now keep the glass in a place where you can easily hide it. They are coming for you tonight, are they not?"

She nodded, not daring to look at him. She didn't want him to see her sudden, shameful tears.

"M'lady," Vito said quietly, more serious than she had ever heard him. "God has not seen you through to this day to see you sacrificed on the enemy's altar. He is here. You have been savagely beaten, seen things no genteel lady should ever be subjected to. But it is as it is. We must accept it and keep our eyes on where our Lord wishes us to take the next step. It is you, Gianni, Father Piero, the others who have taught me this. Let your own words and life speak to you now."

Daria nodded and sighed, looking up to the ceiling with a smile and then over to Vito. "You are right, of course. I am thankful for you, Vito, walking alongside us this day."

"Good. Now go about your holy business. See if the Lord will answer your prayer and heal Gianni. Because I mean for us to find a way out of here and for you to heal my brother as well."

Daria shook her head. "I do not know if he means for me to heal Gianni . . ."

"Just try, m'lady, *try*."

♛ ♛ ♛

THE men returned to the dark isle with surprising ease, a part of a larger group that surged upon the isle at once. The guards, overwhelmed by the crowds, took to stopping every other man. When they reached the gates, a guard laid a hand upon Gaspare's arm. Basilio was beside him. Rune and Piero were directly behind. Rune's hand went to his sword, but Piero lifted his hand. They had prayed for hours. The Lord was with them. They could not fail.

"The Lord wishes us to pass," Gaspare said lowly, staring into the guard's eyes.

"What our master wishes, he receives," the guard said in a monotone, waving them through. The men proceeded forward, trying not to appear rushed.

"That was fantastic," Basilio said, thumping Gaspare on the back when they were twenty paces away. "Can you always do that?"

"When the Lord wishes. If I speak the truth, others who speak the truth hear it as truth. Others who have succumbed to the father of lies hear their own perverted version, but it is always as the Father wishes. I call it 'safe passage.' It gets me to where I want to go, where my Lord wants me to go. Time and time again."

"But only if your direction coincides with the Lord's?"

"Right."

"Well, at least we know the Lord is well aware of this mad plan," Basilio said.

"Have no doubt, Basilio," Piero said. "The Lord is always and evermore within our plans if we pay attention to how he speaks to our hearts and minds."

"You shall have to teach me how to do that, Father."

"Your Father in heaven teaches you how to do that, my son."

Basilio hesitated and let them take a step forward before following.

cho cho cho

DARIA sliced the last of the rope binding her hands and tossed it to the side, keeping it close enough that she could rewrap her wrists when the guard came. She said a prayer of thanks that this time the guards had opted to tie them with hemp and not lock them into the dreaded iron manacles.

She knelt beside the cell wall and reached through to Gianni, feeling the heat of his wound as if it were a small fire. She closed her eyes and felt across his chest, ascertaining how much he bled within. It appeared fairly contained. But had Abramo's blade been poisoned, like the arrows that had pierced them in Siena's streets? Possibly the arrow that had pierced Ugo?

Daria began to pray, begging for the blessing of healing upon Gianni, begging her Savior and Creator to save and knit back together Gianni from within. She struggled to concentrate, believe her own words, feeling healing edge close and then ease away, every time she was drawn into doubt or the wounds upon her back reminded her of the dark's power.

Only on the light, only on the light, only on the light, she chanted within, concentrating on Ambrogio's paintings she could still see in her mind's eye—images of Jesus as a babe in Mary's arms, Jesus calming the storm, Jesus healing, Jesus with his disciples, Jesus with children, Jesus upon the cross, Jesus in heaven. One after the other, the images washed through her mind, healing her even as she pressed down upon Gianni's wound as if she were cauterizing the wound with a hot iron, *from the inside out,* she prayed, *from the inside out. I am nothing, you are all. I am weakness, you are strength. Heal us, Lord God, heal us all. Make your holy power known, here in this dark place. I believe, I believe, I believe . . .*

Again, she was pushed backward, falling to her back, but the first thing she noticed, lying there, staring up at her prison ceiling, was that her back no longer ached. She moved a bit, first left, then right, thinking something was wrong, that she had lost sensation. But then her eyes sprang open. God had healed her, healed her back! She rose, moving without pain for the first time in days. She grinned and glanced at Gianni, struggling to rise, and Vito, behind her. "Vito, he has done it! Not only Gianni, but me as well!"

๛ ๛ ๛

ABRAMO stilled in his preparations. He rose from his dark altar and went to the window, studying the flow of people still arriving. He knew there would be many this eve, the night in which his dark power would surge, now that the Gifted were firmly in hand. But something was off kilter . . .

His eyes scanned the crowd gathering at the front of the isle where torches blazed. They would not hide this night. This night, they made their practices public, unafraid. He had sufficient hold over Venezia's powerful. He could be brazen. Audacious. Free. They feared him. They all feared him.

The thought should have brought satisfaction. Instead, he could not keep his eyes from the crowd, populated heavily by people in hoods and capes. With a shake of his head, he convinced himself that it was merely the remnant of the Gifted within his dungeon that disturbed him.

He glanced to the western sky, knew that the sun was soon firmly gone. The night, this night, was his. Daria was his. The Gifted would be forced to choose; join them or die, one after another. He reached up and felt his bruised cheek, fury building in his chest that the knight had dared to strike him. He would pay for that, pay for it in excruciating ways . . . after he suffered the ultimate price: watching his lady taken by his enemy.

His eyes went to the sea again, becoming uncommonly still. There was the scent of a storm on the wind. A storm would be lovely. His eyes returned to the sea, remembering the fishing boats, the Gifted's intended escape route. And then he knew what niggled at him.

He went to the tapestry behind his bed, to the stone that moved, the one Gianni had been trying to find. They were all in the dungeon. It could not be.

Abramo slid aside the stone.

"Guards!" he screamed, rushing down the stairs. *"Guards!"*

CHAPTER THIRTY-EIGHT

FATHER Piero and Basilio were preparing to split off from Rune and Gaspare, each heading in separate directions to seek out the Gifted, when they heard Amidei shouting. They moved off, as if heading toward the front of the isle with the others, but as soon as the knights ran to see what their master bid, they turned and followed.

They split up in twos, so as not to be so apparent, sidling in to hear.

Glancing up, Basilio noted the archers and quietly waved to his comrades to move so they could not be seen from above. The archers would be a serious threat only if they identified their enemy. He and Piero moved behind a stack of crates. A young boy, hiding there, gasped.

The child moved and his face was illuminated by a brief shaft of torchlight. He hurried away. Piero turned. He knew that child . . . "Roberto?" he whispered.

The boy froze and then slowly turned. He came to the priest then, limping, rushing, throwing his arms around his waist and hugging him tight. Piero wanted to kneel and find out how the child had come to them, and why, but Amidei emerged from the tower building, directly to their right. Piero pulled Roberto back into the shadows behind the crates, next to Basilio, becoming utterly still.

"The boy has infiltrated my quarters and stolen my treasure. Search every person on the isle. Be certain that they are already known to you, or are known by another. Bring any suspicious person before me to be seen." Abramo turned to a large man. Ciro. "Alert the guards at the gate and those at the wall. Then be certain that nothing is awry with our prisoners. No one is to leave this island without me seeing their face, you understand? The boy will attempt to free the Duchess and the others. Kill any but the woman if they attempt it."

"Yes, m'lord." The big knight moved off to do as he bid. Then Vincenzo rounded the corner, leaning to speak to Abramo in more private fashion. Piero, Basilio, and Roberto held their breath.

"He has the letter?" Vincenzo whispered.

"For the moment."

"And the glass pieces?"

"For the moment," Amidei hissed, waving a hand to cut him off and taking a step forward, pacing. "I told you we should have hunted him down immediately."

"Master, we searched the castle tower, everywhere we could think to look. He is clever, that one. I was certain that he had somehow escaped the island."

"He will wish he had. Mayhap he is not alone."

"The other knights. You think they've dared return?"

"Possibly. If we do not soon find the interlopers, we shall have a small ceremony that will whet our people's appetites for something more. Then we will turn our followers loose." Abramo suddenly smiled. "Let the Gifted try to evade a crowd this large, all scurrying across our isle in search of my prizes. We will find the remaining interlopers and throw them into cells beside their comrades. It is good," he murmured. "This. How else would we be certain that we had them all? Once and for all, the Gifted will be vanquished. Then there will be nothing to stop our spread across Italia and beyond."

Ciro returned, panting. "Master. All guards are aware of your orders. And the prisoners appear as we left them."

Abramo lifted his nose, as if smelling the storm on the wind. The torches flickered and flowed. He smiled again. "Yes. It is all as it should be. Come. We will force the boy out in the open."

"How?" Vincenzo said aloud, as Abramo turned to go.

"By bringing forth the Duchess," Abramo said. "She offered herself in exchange for the child."

"You do not intend to kill Daria—"

"Nay. She will experience nothing but the wonders of our ceremony. But when the boy appears, which he will, valiantly trying to come to the aid of his lady, we will take him. And as it was in Roma, as it was in Siena, it shall be here in Venezia." He rubbed his hands together in eager anticipation, and they set off toward the next building.

Father Piero knelt by the boy and whispered, "Roberto, of what boy do they speak? You? Do you have the letter?"

"Nay," he said, obviously confused.

Piero took him by the shoulders. "Why are you here? This is very dangerous . . ."

"I came to find you!" the boy whispered back. "They killed them, Father. Killed them and burned the mansion."

Piero's frown deepened. "Who? Who did it, Nico?"

"It was the baron! He killed the Sciorias and burned the mansion in Siena! It's gone, all gone." The child shook his head miserably.

Piero stood, trying to sort out the puzzle. The baron? A murder? Had he fallen so far? Tied himself to Amidei forever? He brought his fingers to his forehead, as if trying to press out the correct answers. The boy . . . the boy. "Roberto, could Nico have been taken out of the mansion before it was burned?"

Roberto shook his head and blinked heavily, as if thinking back. "I know not . . ."

"Did you see the Sciorias? Did you see all of them? Were they all dead?"

Roberto continued to shake his head, as if in a fog.

"Roberto!" Piero said, giving him a slight shake.

The boy's eyes met his. "I only saw Aldo . . . thought I saw Beata. But it was so hot, Father, I could not reach them. I tried, I tried to get to them, drag them out, but I couldn't!"

Piero pulled him toward him for an embrace and glanced up at Basilio. "It is why they delayed, why our people didn't get Daria off the island and back to us as planned."

"They're here? In the dungeon?"

"Yes. At least everyone but Nico. He's somewhere about, hidden."

"Father, how will we get them all off the isle? If you're right, and del

Buco brought back Ambrogio, Agata, Nico . . . And if our knights, the lady, any of them are injured—"

"We must not hesitate," Piero said. "Our Lord sees us. We must simply go where he bids and he will see us through."

They joined Rune and Gaspare, and quickly told them what they knew. "Strike and withdraw, strike and withdraw," Rune said. "We shall remove our enemy one at a time. We are far too outnumbered to do anything else."

"We begin with the dungeon guards?" Piero said. "Trap Amidei, Vincenzo, and Ciro down in the dungeon?"

"Nay," Gaspare said. Even in the shadows, Piero could feel the grief emanating from him like heat from a stone. "Our only hope is that we allow them to take the lady. They will be distracted by her, convinced that all is as it should be. We can get the others to safety, then return for her. If we trap or harm the leaders, we risk an islandwide alarm. Do that, and we shall all perish."

⚓ ⚓ ⚓

THE three men, Amidei, Vincenzo, and Ciro, moved through the guard tower and down the stairs to the dungeon. The wind was picking up now, in time with the drumbeat, now six strong. Amidei was certain that even with the wind, the drumbeat would be carried across the water to nearby islands, mayhap even Venezia herself, calling more of his faithful forward. *Come, my children, come and worship me.*

He scoffed at the idea of the Christian God. Who reigned here, on his island? Who would reign, in time, throughout Italia? Throughout the world? The Gifted's God was gone, absent, driven out. Amidei's territory stretched before him to be taken.

Ciro paused behind them and Abramo pulled up short, Vincenzo beside him. "What is it?" he asked, looking up at the knight, eight steps above him.

"Heard a voice," Ciro said quietly, pulling his head back toward the guardhouse.

"Go," Abramo said. He looked to Vincenzo, and the baron reluctantly turned and followed him out.

⚓ ⚓ ⚓

GIANNI stood, hands clenched at his side, as Amidei walked down the stairs. The Sorcerer stopped, obviously surprised to see him alive, let alone standing and free of his bonds. He let out a humorless scoff and gave his head a slight shake, raising an eyebrow. "I must say, I will miss these skirmishes, Captain," he said.

He walked over to Daria's cell and looked in at her, halfway back, standing as well, hand to the cell wall as if reaching out to Gianni. He looked back and forth between them, then smiled. "Bittersweet, is it?"

"Of what do you speak?"

"So newly reunited, and yet already over. I have come to claim your lady, de Capezzana."

Daria looked away, as if caught.

Abramo brought out his keys and slowly turned to the right one, watching Daria as he slid the key into the lock, turned it, then slid it off the chains.

Gianni strode to the cell wall and clenched a hand around two bars. "Daria . . . of what does he speak?"

Abramo entered the cell and Daria raised her chin.

"Stay away from her," Vito said.

Abramo glanced over at the other knight, still hanging from his chains in the third cell, then back to Daria. He lifted a hand to her, as if in invitation. "Come. It is time."

"Daria . . ." Gianni said.

"You have given me your word. Or shall I go and fetch the boy?"

Daria crossed her arms and tried to pass by him, ignoring his hand, but he caught her arm, then moved her back and forth, studying her from head to toe.

Wonder pervaded his face. "My queen. You healed *yourself?*"

"My Lord and my God healed me," she said through narrowed eyes.

"Magnificent," he whispered, his face alight in a smile. He suddenly turned her around toward Gianni, one arm across her chest, the other across her waist. "Tell me, knight of the Church. As one devoted to this woman," he said, lifting his left hand to run a finger slowly down Daria's temple, cheek, and neck when she tried to move away from his touch. "What would you do, Sir de Capezzana, if I told you I wouldn't make her suffer in our ceremony? Might you join us?"

"Our God does not negotiate," Gianni said in measured words. "You are for him or against him." He spoke to Abramo, but his eyes could not stay away from Daria.

"Your lady traded herself for the boy," Abramo said. "Would you trade yourself for the lady?"

"Yes," Gianni said, without hesitation, his lips set in a grim line. "Take me and leave her behind."

Abramo smiled. "So devoted to one another, you Gifted. You really must learn that one can accomplish more by serving oneself. My men shall be back for you, Sir Gianni. They shall make you watch. And before this night is over, you shall both claim me as your new master."

ひ ひ ひ

VINCENZO left the guardhouse and, with sword drawn, searched the immediate grounds around the guardhouse. Abramo had been training Vincenzo, teaching him the dark arts. He closed his eyes, reaching out in his mind in an ever-broadening circle, as if he could feel his enemies with his eyes, know their shape. There was something odd on the island; not all was as it should be. Where were they?

"There are intruders here," he said to Ciro. He closed his eyes and tried to sense where they might be. There. To the right of the tower doorway.

Vincenzo set off, sword low but with both hands in strike position.

He motioned to Ciro to go wide, to the right, come around behind the stack of crates and meet him in attack. The giant knight set off immediately.

He set one foot in front of the other, sidling inward at a diagonal, careful not to make a sound. He strained to hear anything, studied the cracks between the crates. There. Someone was there. More than one?

Vincenzo glanced up and saw Ciro moving closer from the back. With but five steps to go, they let out roars, designed to frighten their enemy, and rushed the crates.

A woman screamed and whirled, pushing herself behind a man. Both were half-dressed.

Vincenzo frowned and looked about, frowned more deeply when he saw Abramo approach, holding Daria by the arm. Abramo glanced at the couple and then back to Vincenzo and grinned. "You shall have a busy night if you are in search of every couple on this island." He motioned for the two revelers to move back toward the group at the front of the island.

"They are here, Abramo," Vincenzo said tonelessly as the couple scurried away.

"It is her we sense," he said, leaning his head toward Daria, "and the others, down below."

"Master, I sensed them here, thought they were here, behind the crates—"

Abramo smiled patronizingly, rankling Vincenzo. "You have come far. But I have much yet to teach you, my friend. Do not further tax yourself."

"What of the knights? Could they be here?"

Abramo studied Vincenzo, watching him as he glanced at Daria, who refused to look at him. "Be at ease, friend. Our enemies are shaken, weak, or in chains. Mark my words. Once Daria becomes ours this night, the Gifted will crumble. If any remain here, they shall join us."

He turned to two women behind him, with two guards behind them. "Take the lady to my quarters and prepare her for the ceremony. Do not let her out of your sight, even for a moment." He pulled Daria up before him, yanking on her hair and forcing her head up.

Slowly, she lifted defiant eyes and he dropped his hand. "Where is Nico? You promised to free him in exchange for me."

"And I shall keep my word. As soon as he is found, he will be free. But first, I will get something he has taken from me."

Daria's eyes widened and then narrowed in hatred as she realized he did not have Nico to trade. He had tricked her. She writhed, tried to loosen his grip on her.

Abramo smiled and held her easily. "Good. Still some fight within you. It is just as I wanted." He leaned closer and said softly, "Dare to escape my guards and leave this island and I will make your comrades suffer in ways you have not yet observed."

Daria panted with fury, staring up at Abramo with a mixture of terror and hatred.

Vincenzo clenched his fists. This was not as it was supposed to be. They were supposed to have brought her along, made her one of them. She was to have come to them willingly. This, this, could not end well.

They had not convinced her, broken her, healed her in their ways. There was a new strength within her. Defiance, not compliance.

But Abramo was already handing her off to the two women behind him. "Take your time in your preparations for our ceremony, m'lady." He glanced at the women. "Anoint her with oils; leave down her hair. Her gown is upon my bed. I will be up shortly to watch over the final preparations myself."

Chapter Thirty-nine

THEY moved off around the tower and Gaspare and Piero released Rune and Basilio. Both men shook with fury, finding it nearly impossible to see their lady manhandled by their enemies. Piero felt it deep within him too, like a tear within his belly. But it was the way of wisdom.

The drums beat faster now, in tandem with the wind.

Rune shook his head and rubbed his hair and then his face, as if trying to wipe away the memory of what they had just seen. Basilio whirled upon Piero, fury etching his face. "We cannot allow it. We cannot."

"Nor do we intend to, my friend," Piero said, reaching out to lay a gentle hand upon his shoulder. "But we did not have a chance of freeing the lady. Her only hope is that we free her people. Amidei shall use them against her if we do not. And you just saw it for yourself—the idea of conquering Daria has dissuaded Amidei from pursuing us. It is God's own plan."

Basilio moved away, out from under the priest's hand. He did not like God's plan, but he would abide by it. He glanced up suddenly and pointed with his chin.

Piero glanced over his shoulder, noted the western wall guard was moving away from them, and eased forward. But then he spied a child, not five steps away. The boy was staring at the guardhouse, kneeling behind a barrier.

"Nico?" Piero whispered.

The child whirled, letting out a small cry, and Piero dropped beside him, covering his mouth. A guard peeked out, stared for a long moment, but they were out of sight. "Nico? Nico, child, it's me. Father Piero. You are all right." He pulled the child into his arms and rocked him slightly as the boy let out a gasp mixed with a sob.

The child wrapped both fists in Piero's robes, clinging to him. "Father, I was so frightened. I have the letter, Father. I have Amidei's letter! And something else. Two pieces of heavy glass, like none I've ever seen before."

Piero leaned back and tried to peer into the child's eyes. But it was much too dark. "How did you manage that?"

"He hid it. In his room. Gianni and Vito were looking for it. As the men battled, I found it and then ran. I cannot let them catch me, Father. I almost died, and the lady healed me and—" He broke off in a cry of fear, suddenly aware that he was no longer alone. Help was here.

Piero hugged the boy again, aching for the agony he had undoubtedly suffered at the hands of Amidei. But he had found the letter! The rest of the map! The Gifted could move on! Surely it would show them where they were to go next. "I am so proud of you, my son. You are very courageous." *Father, we are surrounded by our enemies. They shall kill us if we are found. Show us the way out. Help me get your people to safety. Make a path, Lord Jesus. Be our protector—*

"Father?" Basilio said, suddenly beside them. "Nico?" he said in wonder.

"It is him," Piero grinned. "And he has what we need."

"The letter of the Gifted? And the glass?"

"Yes. It is why our people had to brave this island." He reached out to the child. "Give me the letter, my son. I shall keep it safe and you will be better off without it."

Nico reached inside his tunic and handed him the leather satchel.

Piero looked at Basilio. "We have the boys, the letter. Let us go and free the others, then Daria."

ಈ ಈ ಈ

DARIA pretended to stumble as they entered, risking her move when there was but one woman in front of her, inside the room. One arm went out to catch herself, and with her right, she moved the piece of glass into her mouth.

"M'lady!" cried the woman behind her, drawing the first woman's attention. Both rushed to help her up.

The glass cut her cheek inside and she swallowed blood, but Daria moved the edge to her teeth, holding it in place so it could do no further damage. She pulled her arms away from the women as if offended by their touch.

"See to her bath," said a guard. The two men took up positions on either side of the doorway.

They led Daria toward a steaming tub. She was grateful for the screen that shielded her from the guards, and grimly remembered the contessa's screen, Abramo in the room . . . Her heart pounded in terror and she fought to find her faith within her, trust in her God, belief that he could save her now, in spite of how grim it appeared.

Daria allowed them to undress her and slipped into the waters, madly praying for God to make a way for her to escape. She went under the water, calling out to her Savior. *Jesus, Jesus, Jesus,* she chanted, unable to form even a phrase or plea. *Jesus, Jesus, Jesus.*

It was as if she fought to break free of the dark, clinging to her from all sides, suffocating her. *Lord of Light, Lord of Light, Lord of Light . . .*

You are not forgotten.

She rose and submitted to the women lathering her hair with fragrant soap. They eased her forward and paused, wondering over the scars upon her back, already healed over as if the scabs had come and gone, but then moved on to washing her.

Daria chafed at the humiliation, fought back against the dark that clouded her mind and heart. *I am not forgotten. I am not forgotten. I am not forgotten,* she told herself, fighting to hear her Father's tone, his reassurance, as if he were wrapping his arms around her.

👑 👑 👑

FATHER Piero took Nico and Roberto by the arms and approached the guardhouse. The two guards emerged and looked him up and down, then at the boys.

"Little old to be on the Master's guard, aren't you?" said one to Piero. He reached forward and pulled back his hood.

"Your hair—doesn't this one look the part?" the guard said to the other. "I suddenly feel as if I'm back in church!"

"I brought these boys," Piero said. "Found them hiding. The Master has searched the entire isle for a child, has he not? It has to be one of these two."

The second guard squinted his eyes as if thinking, then pulled his head to the side, saying, "We'll keep them down here," leading the way to the dungeon. After they took three steps, Piero grabbed the boys and hauled them to the right, around a table, just as Rune took the back guard down with a quick jab of his sword. The first guard whirled, pulling his sword, but Basilio was already striking, killing him quickly and silently.

"We will return," Piero said with a curt nod to the knights.

"We will not allow anyone through, Father," Basilio said.

The men moved down the steps, with Nico guiding them, keys in hand. Gaspare and Piero carried the slain guards' swords.

"Thank God in heaven," Gianni said, stopping his pacing and moving to the cell door. "Quickly, man, quickly. They have Lady Daria."

Piero tried one key and then the next. It slid into the lock, he turned it and released the lock from the tangle of chains. Gianni paused in the open doorway when Father Piero did not react to his words, staring at the priest. "You allowed it? You allowed them to take her?"

"Think as a tactician," Gaspare said, stepping up behind Piero. "Our only hope to get as many of you out alive as possible was to allow it, get our injured to safety, then go and free the lady."

"I tried a similar plan," Gianni said, stepping forward, facing the old fisherman. Gaspare moved on to free Vito, and Piero moved into the next cell block to see to Agata and Ambrogio. "It ended with us all in chains."

"Call upon your great faith," Gaspare urged Gianni, handing him a sword. "You are allowing your fear to cloud your judgment. Fear, confusion is not of our God. It is of the enemy. Search your heart and you shall know that this is the way we are to go, regardless of how your own plan came to resolution."

Vito emerged from his cell, shaking his hands, wincing as blood returned to them. "He's right, Captain. This way we get our wounded to a ship and we're back together. What of Basilio and Rune?"

"Up in the guardhouse," Gaspare said.

Piero emerged, with his arm about Ambrogio's waist. Agata clung to the priest's arm and rushed to Nico and Roberto, weeping, when she saw the boys. Ugo trailed behind, an arrow still sticking out of his shoulder.

Gianni sighed and ran a hand through his hair. He strode to the window. The wind was whistling now, and they could all hear the waves crashing upon the beach in tandem with the quickening pace of the drum. "If we do not soon set sail, we shall be trapped upon this isle. Do you smell the rain on the wind?"

Gaspare joined him there, looking out to the angry seas. "It will be a fierce one. We need to abandon our two smaller vessels and take one of the larger ones that has been moored. We will fare better in a larger vessel, working the sea together."

"All right," Gianni said, giving in to the wisdom of the plan. "We will take down the southern wall guard and ease Ugo, Agata, Ambrogio, and the children down to the rocks below. Gaspare, you must get them all to the biggest ship and prepare to set sail. We will distract the eastern wall guard so you can get by, grab a skiff, and get to the ship. If we kill him, it will cause an alarm. Best to sneak by."

"Our God will see to us. You see to the lady," Gaspare said.

Gianni gave him a long look, then glanced at Vito and Piero. "I want you with them."

"Nay," said the priest. "I am to go with you."

"I want to go with you as well," Tessa said, stepping forward.

"Nay!" Gianni said, obviously more fiercely than he had intended.

"Captain," Gaspare said, reaching out a hand of peace. "I shall get your wounded and weak to the ship and prepare to set sail. I will do as much as I can to hold her there, ready for you. But make the most of what God has provided. He has not brought the Gifted together to allow you to be vanquished. You need each of us. There is still much to do, ahead. Reach within. Find your faith, beyond the fear, deeper than the fear. What does your God tell you? How does he ask you to face the Leviathan?"

Gianni pulled his head back, studying him. Then he turned, placed a hand against the stone wall, and bowed his head, one hand over his face. It took only seconds. "It will be as you say," he said to Gaspare. He stared at Piero and Tessa. "Piero, you shall remain at my side, at all times. Tessa, you will be beside Vito. Understood?"

Both nodded eagerly.

"I know we are short on time," Piero said. "But please. Come together for a moment." They gathered in a small circle.

"Lord God in heaven," Piero prayed, "we need you to be present here, in the midst of so much darkness. Thank you for bringing us together, for making a way. We ask for your protection. Please get our people past the guards and to the ship. Hide us, Lord, from your enemies present here. Help us get to Daria and get her to safety. Show us where we are to go next. Guide us, Holy One. Guide us. Amen."

"Amen," said the rest.

Piero put his hand in the middle. "If God is for us . . ."

The others placed their hands atop his. "Who can be against us?"

CHAPTER FORTY

DARIA raised her arms and allowed the silk gown to fall down past her shoulders and cling. The women yanked it down, pulling it into place. It did not escape Daria's notice that the gown was one she might have worn for a betrothal ceremony, that Abramo intended to make her his bride this night. She began to pant with fear and closed her eyes, fighting to remember her Lord's words to her heart. *I am not forgotten. I am not forgotten. I am not forgotten.*

The women sat her down upon a stool and began combing out her long hair. Daria could feel the damp seep through her gown to her back all the way down to her waist. Damp tendrils coiled at her neck and upon her bare shoulders. On and on they tugged and yanked, pulling her head back until all the tangles were free.

The women seemed to move in tandem with the beating drums outside, and began to breathe in an odd manner, as if asleep and dreaming. Daria wished she could recoil, draw away from them, but there was nowhere to go. At some point, her Lord would show her the way. He had not forgotten her.

Abramo entered then. Daria eyed him over her shoulder and then turned away, staring resolutely forward.

He took the comb from one of the women. "Very good. Very, very good." He put the comb to Daria's scalp and drew it downward, slowly.

"You may leave for the ceremony," he said to the women. "Baron del Buco and Ciro are already seeing to the preliminaries."

The guards moved to outside the door and shut it after the women came out. Daria closed her eyes, wondering if this was the time for her to move, to strike out with the glass hidden in her mouth. She bit down on the ragged edge, taking the discomfort as strength. He combed her hair, placing one section in front of her shoulder, allowing his hand to brush past her breast.

Daria fought the desire to rise and strike. It wasn't the time, wasn't the time . . .

Apparently satisfied with her hair, he turned and then placed a slender band of gold atop her hair. It came down across her forehead and fit snugly around the crown of her head. He moved away for a moment, to a box in the corner, and slowly pulled out several strands of green beads and then returned to her. She remained still as he went behind her again and fastened them around her neck and lifted her heavy hair through, settling it back down as he saw fit. "They are bronze, my queen," he whispered in her ear. "A thousand years old. Legend has it they once belonged to a Roman empress." He walked around her and looked her up and down. "As perfect upon your slender neck as I had hoped."

He reached into his pocket and pulled out a massive gold ring, with a beetle captured in amber. He reached for her hand and slid it on her middle finger. "Egyptian," he mused, with one eyebrow raised in delight, lifting her hand to the light. "The Egyptians believed the beetle was the symbol of power. This belonged to one who wielded quite a bit of it. The pharaoh's queen, perhaps? Come," he said, pulling her up.

Seeing no other option, wanting him to believe she was finally acquiescing, would give him no fight, she took his hand and rose. He led her to the shuttered windows, where the shutters were banging against their fastenings, eager to be loose.

Abramo took a step forward, unlatched the shutters, and then opened them wide. The wind flooded inward, blowing back his jacket, making it appear as a cape. He looked back at her with a grin, his face flickering in the windblown candlelight. Again, he offered his hand and then pulled her in front of him, his arms again around her chest and belly, already claiming her.

Below them, torches blew their flames horizontally in the wind. The drumbeat was fast and deep, six strong now. Women and men danced and writhed below them . . . Daria shut her eyes to it, pretending to lift her face to the wind, relish it as he did.

"Ah yes, smell of it, Daria," he said. "Feel the power of the earth upon your face. Feel the fury and strength of the sea." He leaned down to kiss her neck, bestowing another and yet another with each phrase. "I shall show you the way. The way to harness that power. You have only begun to learn what I shall teach you. Together, we shall rule. You will know glory . . . and pleasure that only the court of the gods can rival." Daria swallowed hard, struggling to not wrench away. His lips felt as appealing as wet worms upon her skin, making her feel like retching. Was now the time?

Hold. You are not forgotten. Hold, hold, hold . . .

👒 👒 👒

GASPARE practically carried Ambrogio across the rocks. Without the use of his hands, their path was treacherous. Nico, Roberto, and Agata behind them. Ugo trailing last. All at once Gaspare clung to the wall, bringing Ambrogio back so suddenly and hard that the man let out a small cry.

"Forgive me, man," Gaspare said. He dared to move his head forward and peek around the slight curve in the wall. As he feared, the guard had glanced back in their direction. He raised his torch, the flame blowing in their direction, trying to peer among the shadows, and Gaspare tried to settle his heart and mind.

"Use his sinful heart to his disadvantage, Lord God on high," Gaspare whispered. "Cloud his vision. Distract him from us. Bring us safe passage. In Jesus' holy name, amen." He dared to peek around the edge of the wall again and pulled his head back, grinning.

"What do you find humorous?" Ambrogio mumbled, closing his eyes and leaning his head back.

"Our Lord has made a way," he said. He moved forward. The guard was only thirty feet away, then twenty, then ten.

Gaspare drew reassurance more from his Lord than from the reach of man. God never failed him. Never. And his Lord wanted the Gifted off this cursed isle; he was certain of it.

He looked up and studied the guard. His back was to them, and he stared forward, toward the frenzied ceremony, the flickering torches, the frantic drumbeat, as if once again entranced.

Gaspare shifted Ambrogio upon his back and crept over the rocks, finding one secure foothold and then another. *Protect us, Holy One. Protect us,* he prayed silently. *Guard us, shield us, bring us to safety.*

do do do

"You are trembling," Amidei said, turning Daria around to face him. "And oddly silent." He studied her face, tracing her lips slowly, seductively.

Desperate to keep her weapon a secret, she bowed her head as if about to cry, pulling away from his hand, and then went into a deep curtsey, her hands in his.

Abramo sighed in pleasure, taking her motion as true submission. "Ah, Daria, Daria, you have no idea how happy I will make you. At my side, you shall submit to no other but me and our dark lord. You shall be like a goddess upon this earth. No delicacy shall be out of your reach; only the finest silks will be upon your skin. I shall buy you a treasure chest of jewels. You will know every pleasure available to us and never fear again. Rise, rise, my goddess."

Now was the time. She felt as if the angels were there with her, urging her on, telling her not to fear.

A thud sounded at the door, and then the soft, sickening sounds of a fist against flesh. More footsteps sounded upon the wooden floor, more fighting ensued, and then all was silent. Abramo reached for his dagger and pulled her forward by one hand, his eyes upon the door. Daria turned her head away, spitting the glass into her left hand.

The door came crashing in and Gianni and Vito were once more inside Amidei's quarters, swords drawn. Tessa peered inward.

Abramo glanced to the window. Outside, more drums had joined the first six and added to the wind and the frenzy of his people; no one would hear any of them, even if they shouted. He pulled Daria in front of him, dagger to her throat.

"She is mine. She has promised me her allegiance."

Gianni eyed Daria. "I very much doubt that." Vito moved to the right as he moved to the left.

The girl entered the room and peeked around Gianni. "He is afraid."

"I fear no one. It is you who should be quaking. You cannot escape this island alive. Be foolish no longer. Turn to us. Become one with us. We are power. We are glory."

"Nay," Gianni said, shaking his head slowly. "Only to God shall we give glory and honor. He wields all true power. The rest is but temporary."

Abramo lifted the dagger to its edge, against Daria's throat. "You shall have to kill your lady to kill me."

Daria motioned with her eyes to Gianni, down to her left, her hand. In a moment, Gianni knew what she was about to do, gave her a nod. Daria lifted up and slashed Abramo's hand. He cried out and instantly dropped the dagger. She whirled as her knights flanked her, but she was not done. She struck upward again, gashing his cheek, his eye, making him scream with pain.

"Captain," said Piero urgently from the door. "There are others approaching."

Gianni grimaced. "You must hold them at bay!" he cried, lifting his sword, intent on ending Amidei's reign, once and forever. But his blade met only air.

"Gianni!" Tessa cried, pointing to the stairwell.

He whirled, seeing the edge of Amidei's coat as he stumbled up the stairs to the tower, dripping blood.

Gianni swallowed a cry of rage and frustration and moved to follow.

Daria reached out a hand to stay him. "Come. Let us be away," she said quietly.

"He is wounded. I must kill him now."

"We must flee and get the others to safety before we battle the dark lord again. Come, come, Gianni. If we move now, we might all escape with our lives. We are about the Lord's business. He will see to Amidei's end when the time is right."

"Captain!" cried Piero, meeting the first knight's strike with his own small sword.

Vincenzo moved past them and entered the room. Behind him, Ciro took three jabs at the priest and sent his sword skittering away.

❧ ❧ ❧

GASPARE rowed harder than he had ever rowed in his life. The waves were already so high that they threatened to capsize their small boat. The boys were bailing with their cupped hands, their knees disappearing into the dark waters. Gaspare looked over his shoulder and could barely make out the silhouette of the ship.

She was larger than anything he had sailed before, capable of holding twenty men. He squinted against the dry wind, wondering that the heavy clouds had not yet unleashed their weight in rain. Had he chosen wrongly? Was this the ship they were meant to take?

He groaned against the oars, hauling backward. There was nothing for it. God would have to make it right, somehow. But how was he to set sail, in a fierce storm, with no one but an old woman and two boys to help him? He tried to see Ambrogio, at the end of the boat. It appeared he was almost unconscious again, huddled over his useless hands. Ugo had but one good arm and had lost a fair amount of blood himself.

"Lord God, you've gotten us this far. Get us a bit farther, would you?" He pulled and pulled and pulled, pushing his feet against a cross-beam in the floor of the boat. In another few minutes, they were close to the ship, very close. "Get to the ropes!" Gaspare cried to the boys.

Tentatively, they moved to the hanging climbing net and reached. The waves pulled them away, then tantalizingly close, then away again. The waves were building, the ship herself rocking in haphazard fashion. If she rocked the wrong way, she'd capsize them all . . .

Gaspare roared against the wind. "Please, Lord Jesus, please. Just get us aboard the ship. Get us to safety. Give me strength, give me strength, give me strength!"

⚓ ⚓ ⚓

PIERO went down to the ground and Ciro immediately moved to deal a fatal blow. Vito ran as fast as he could, narrowly stopping the giant's downward plunge. The priest scurried backward and regained his feet.

"Daria," Gianni said softly. "Take Tess and Piero and make your escape. We'll join you shortly."

Daria moved to the door, but paused, eyeing Vincenzo. "Turn from him, Vincenzo. Amidei is evil. You have pledged your life to the devil himself. You have done unspeakable things. But God still reaches for you. You can find your way back."

"Save your breath, Daria," Vincenzo muttered, staring at Gianni.

"He is a false lord," Daria tried again. "He has fled to the tower rather than stand and face us. He will share nothing of consequence with you. Please. Come with us. Find peace. Find honor in the holy."

Vincenzo feigned right and then whirled to his left, bringing down his sword as if to strike Daria, cutting off her words. Gianni narrowly blocked it and was hard-pressed to push him back, given his downward momentum. Vincenzo stared at her across the locked blades, his teeth clenching in effort. "You are dead to me, Daria. Be gone from this place and never return."

Daria studied him a second longer, and then Gianni pushed him backward. Her heart was in her throat. Vincenzo's words were brutal, stealing her very breath. But had that been hesitation in his eyes? Was he giving her permission to leave?

Ciro and Vito exchanged blows, the larger knight having the edge of brute strength, Vito having an edge in agility and speed. Vincenzo turned from her and made three elegant moves against Gianni, driving him backward.

Piero grabbed Daria's hand. "Come, daughter." She hesitated. "Daria, we must be away." Tessa joined the priest, hauling on her arm.

That was when the first shudder went through the tower, knocking Daria and Piero to the ground, as well as Vito and Vincenzo.

Piero looked at Daria. "It is the Sorcerer. He means to take down the tower and kill us all."

"But he is atop it. It will mean his own death!"

"All he can see is his hatred. His dark lord wants us dead, if we cannot be turned. We must be away from here!" He got to his feet and pulled Tessa forward as another shudder went through the tower. Dimly, they could hear Abramo's screaming incantations above the whine of the wind.

"Gianni!" Daria cried.

"We shall be along! Go, Daria!"

Daria turned and fled down the stairs with Tessa and Piero.

They stumbled out of the tower and met the western wall guard. He leapt to the ground from the wall, sword drawn. Piero pulled his own small sword and said, "Daria, take Tessa to the end of the pier. Ready a boat for us. No matter what, do not return here. Swim to the ship if need be. Do you understand me? *Do not return.*"

"Yes," she said, and pulled Tessa along the dark pier. Waves were cresting over the edge of it. Boats crashed together in the high seas, nearly all escaping their moorings. The wind was so strong, Tessa and Daria had to lean against it. The lagoon, long protected from the ravages of the sea, was boiling up, as if to unleash Abramo's fury upon them. She turned back to glance at the tower, then shied away, pulling Tessa to her, when a bolt of lightning came down from the sky and struck the tower. In that instant, she could see Abramo, hands raised to the sky.

He did not want them to reach the ship . . . and if they did . . . would they escape the island merely to perish at sea?

CHAPTER FORTY-ONE

VINCENZO pushed Gianni to the wall. Gianni had the strength of a man in his prime, but Vincenzo benefited from years of sparring, the idle activity of all Toscana nobility. Again, Gianni narrowly kept his blade away from his throat and held it there. "If you love her, be away from here," Vincenzo said so low that Gianni could barely make out his words.

Behind him, Vito and Ciro continued to spar.

Gianni frowned. "It was you who captured her, kidnapped her, brought her here," he returned, driving the man back and making three quick strikes, all of which Vincenzo blocked. Was it his imagination or did Vincenzo question his path?

He studied the baron as they parried back and forth. His cheek worked in frustration, his eyes shifted as if thinking, his eyebrows lowered in grief more than anger. "He does not yet own you, Baron," Gianni said.

Vincenzo's eyes met his and became hard. He drove forward, succeeding in nicking Gianni at the chest and the arm.

Gianni became equally angry. "My God is a forgiving God. So if you turn to him, you shall find rest. But I am not nearly as forgiving." He drove forward, nicking Vincenzo on the chin. "That is for my lady, the one you should have protected, not attacked." He drove forward again, striking him across the thigh this time. "That is for me, whom you watched imprisoned."

Vincenzo stumbled backward, one leg now weak. He tried to block one of Gianni's last blows, but it caught him at an angle that sent a shudder through his hand. The sword went to the ground with a *clang*. He reached for it, saw it was hopeless, then turned to look Gianni in the eye. Gianni pressed the point of his sword to his throat, wishing he could kill the man. But something stopped him. "This is for my Lord God on high, who wishes you to spend eternity with him rather than in the miseries of hell. It is only because of him that I spare your life once more and give you the chance at redemption. Choose wisely, Baron." He pressed forward slightly, then released and turned, striking Ciro's back just as he was striking downward toward Vito.

Ciro let out a heavy *whoosh* of air. His armor had protected him from evisceration, but the strength of the blow had stolen his breath, sending him to his knees.

The castle tower again shuddered. Stones visibly moved upon those beneath them, shifting, sending rivulets of dust and gravel to the floor. Gianni grabbed Vito and hauled him toward the stairs.

ↄ ↄ ↄ

ABRAMO leaned over the tower wall and saw Piero facing off with his guard while Daria and the girl moved to the pier. "Nay!" he screamed. He had seen Vincenzo and Ciro enter, had been confident that they would keep the Gifted within his tower, within until he could bury them all. It mattered not that he might die in the collapse, only that the Gifted would perish. His lord demanded it, screamed at him to stop them, kill them.

He looked to his people, who had stilled and stared up at him, where he brought down one lightning bolt after another. He sought out his archers, his faithful women, and motioned them around the tower. They paused only to gather their weapons and do as he bid, then took off toward the tower at a dead run, capes pressed against their slender forms. They would kill those that had escaped. He would see to the others still below him.

ↄ ↄ ↄ

"WHY are we not hoisting the anchor?" Roberto shouted at Gaspare.

Gaspare squinted toward the flickering torches on the isle, at the madly bobbing boat at the end of the pier. Two were aboard. It had to be a couple of the Gifted, waiting for the others. The waves had gained height and strength. If the boat simply was released from the pier, it would come very close to them.

Suddenly Gaspare could see the wisdom of his Lord's plan.

Nico neared, and even Agata. She looked surprisingly strong and brave in the wind, her gray hair streaming behind her. She stood with one foot in front of the other, bracing against the storm, chin raised. Ugo stood beyond her, facing him as well, a broken arrow shaft still protruding from his shoulder.

"Our Lord sees this storm, knows our needs. He is Lord of all. We stand at the ready, waiting for our people to come to us. Then we will weigh anchor and lift but one sail. The storm itself will take us to safety. You, Nico, and Roberto, will climb the main mast and sit on that first beam. You shall release the lower sail at my direction and keep an eye out for our people and any of our enemies."

He turned to Ugo and Agata. "You two will need to help me weigh anchor. With this wind's pull, it will be plenty to manage. Let me show you how. You will need to show the knights, when they join us."

They did as he asked, listening intently to his instructions.

"What do we do now?" Nico asked.

"We pray, child. We pray."

ፙ ፙ ፙ

DARIA blinked, wondering if she had truly seen the tower come down, heard the roar of cascading stones and women's screams above the storm. Was that Gianni, fighting back the western wall guard? Vito moving past him? It was impossible to make out.

She glanced to the right and saw the mass of people moving in their direction. Nay, nay, nay, she chanted under her breath, shaking her head. She caught sight of one of Abramo's deadly archers creeping forward.

An arrow flew, but not from the woman's bow. It struck Abramo's archer in the shoulder and she fell back. Daria's eyes moved back to the left, to find its source. Rune!

He and Basilio could not come to Gianni and Piero's aid, separated by a group. She saw Gianni motion sternly but could make out no sound other than the crashing of the waves upon the rocks, the howl of the wind. Vito broke away and ran down the pier.

Rune and Basilio flew over the edge of the wall, waist-deep in water, and then climbed on top of the pier, running, hunched over, toward Daria's waiting boat. All three knights reached the end about the same time.

Still, Piero and Gianni held the enemy at bay at the mouth of the pier.

Daria tore her eyes from them and moved with Tessa to the back of the boat as Vito made his way back to them. "You left the priest to fight?" Daria asked.

"Captain's orders," he said.

Basilio and Rune hopped aboard and let out some rope to keep the boat from capsizing against the pier.

"Come on, Captain!" Vito cried.

Daria then saw what he had seen. Their enemies, moving over the wall as Basilio and Rune had done, edging closer to Piero and Gianni, threatening to cut them off from their escape route.

An arrow flew toward Piero and Gianni, and skittered across the pier.

A massive wave struck, nearly pulling the boat under the next. Across from them, a boat came up and over the pier, landing upside-down.

Gianni and Piero finally broke away, running as fast as they could toward their waiting boat, the enemy in pursuit, streaming onto the dock, screaming together in a horrible, grating sound that even surmounted the wind and waves.

"Get ready," Rune said, already at the oars. "Get ready to let go of the rope on my say," he said. "M'lady, where is Gaspare's ship?"

"Behind us! Downwind!" Daria yelled back.

"Make way!" Vito said. "They're going to have to jump in!"

Gianni and Piero did not pause. They came at a dead run, Gianni allowing the priest to go before him, protecting him. Arrows flew at them but missed, one after the other, hampered by the fierce winds.

"Now!" cried Rune, and the rope was released. In a breath, they were three feet away.

Piero came flying toward them. Basilio and Rune caught him, put him behind them, then reached for Gianni. Rune pulled back on his oars.

They were now five feet from the dock. Gianni came flying through the air, landing hard in the front of the boat. They all heard the terrible crack of wood, even above the wind.

Those of the dark lord streamed to the end of the pier, three of them carrying torches. And it was then that Daria saw the problem. They were heading downwind, swiftly placing some distance between themselves and their enemies. But there was also nothing to hamper the archer's deadly aim.

"Get down!" Daria screamed, rising. "Gianni! Beware!"

But then she could see Gianni was caught, his foot trapped in the broken wood of the boat, knew that he would be hit. She tried to scramble forward. "Gianni!" she screamed. Vito held her back, forcing her down. Rune kept pulling back on the oars. Giant waves seemed to form walls of protection for moments of time and Daria hoped, hoped against hope.

Piero rose then to face the enemy, and moved in front of Gianni, struggling to keep his balance, arms out, protecting his friend.

He straightened, stiffened, as Gianni tried to turn and pull him down.

Instead, the priest fell back against him.

Tessa screamed, not seeing the arrow, but feeling it, as they all seemed to. Rune stopped rowing, hand to his chest. Vito released Daria, bringing his hand to his chest, pulling it away, as if thinking he would see blood. Daria felt the pierce of it herself, and looked down to see that she had not been hit.

Gianni faltered, lowering Piero.

And this time, Daria could see the second arrow wing its way across the high seas, impossibly straight, impossibly true, and slice into Piero's chest.

She fell backward, as did the rest, feeling Piero's arrow as if it had again plunged into their hearts.

CHAPTER FORTY-TWO

TESSA collapsed against her, gasping for breath, hand to her small chest. She panted and looked up at Daria.

What was this madness? Daria gazed forward, at the four knights before them. All sat still, heads to chests, as if wounded. "Piero," Daria found the breath to whisper. "Piero!"

She forced herself to stand, try to make her way through the boat, now calf-deep in water, tried to avoid seeing the enemy, still on the pier, raising their hands in a cheer. Gianni, still stuck, stared at them. "They are giving chase," he said to Rune. "Row, man. We are not wounded. It is the devil's own trick, making us feel what Piero is feeling."

"Or God's," Daria said, kneeling down beside Piero. "We are one. Tied." She could barely see him. Crying, she pulled his head into her lap, out of the water. Unable to see, she reached to touch his lips, then sucked on them, tasting blood. "Nay, nay, nay," she said, weeping. "Nay!" she screamed at the sky. She looked around madly. "Pray for him, every one of you. Beseech our Savior that he will lay his hand on this gentle servant and save him." She looked up again. "Not this, Lord, not this!" she said, rocking and swaying with the boat as she cried.

She could feel Piero's life slipping, the cool edge of death drawing near, surrounding them. "Oh please, Jesus. *Please.* Come and heal this man. *Please.*"

The rain began then, mixing with her tears, washing down her face as she wept, calling out to her God again and again when he did not give her permission to heal.

"Daria!" Gianni's firm voice pulled her out of prayer.

"He's dying, Gianni!" she cried.

He laid a gentle but firm hand on her shoulder. "Daria, look."

She turned and saw the massive ship emerge from the pitch black of the sea. Hope surged through her. If they could get Piero aboard, escape Abramo's people—she looked forward again, noticing the three boats that pursued them—then there was a chance . . .

"Rune . . ." she said.

"Doing what I can, m'lady," he said, straining against the oars. The boat was impossibly slow and sluggish, too laden with people and water.

A rope came from out of the sky and landed heavily in the water beside them. Daria reached for it, nearly falling over the edge, grabbed it, pulled it in toward them. Basilio and Rune took it from her and hauled them toward the ship, hovering about five feet distant from the climbing net.

The waves were monstrous. Gianni eyed their enemies, coming fast. "Go, all of you. To the net. Climb! I will pull free of this and bring Piero with me. You see to setting sail. We cannot let them reach us!"

"Father Piero—"

"Daria, go. I will see to him. I promise."

Rune pulled them closer and Tessa, Daria, and Basilio leapt to the net. Daria slipped and fell into the water. Her skirts were instantly like heavy weights, pulling her back, sucking her backward, toward the dark isle . . .

Vito landed in the water and began climbing on one side of her. He hauled her up several notches. Free of the water, she could climb. She reached the edge and looked back. The next boats were coming fast, were nearly upon them. "Weigh anchor!" she screamed toward Gaspare. "Weigh anchor!"

She looked back. It was so hard to see, especially now in the rain. But flashes of light came across the sea, reflecting from the enemies' torches. The better they could see, the worse it was for the Gifted. Rune tied the rope around Piero's chest.

He nodded to Gianni and then hauled back on his captain, freeing him from the boat. Water gushed in.

"Daria!" Gaspare yelled from the helm. "Help them!" he shouted, nodding toward the boys, trying to haul up the heavy main sail. Vito and Ugo were reaching down, urging Rune and Gianni upward. Basilio hauled on the rope, bringing Piero upward.

"Unfurl the sail!" Vito yelled. "We have them! They are nearly upon us!"

Daria and the boys pulled harder upon the ropes, hauling the heavy sheeting upward and securing it as best as they could.

Those at the anchor turnstile roared and pressed against their bars, working now against the pull of the sail. If they could only get it free . . .

Rune climbed over the edge and reached across his shoulder for his bow. He set the arrows he had left beside him. Three.

Gianni reached the top and fell over the edge, onto the deck, panting.

"Help me," Basilio ground out. "He's stuck!"

Gianni leaned over the edge. "It's the arrows! They're caught on the netting!" He eyed the enemy boat, now alongside them. Five men and an archer were aboard.

"Gaspare!" he shouted over his shoulder, hauling back on Piero's rope.

Three men leapt from the first boat and made it to the net.

The archer stood and took aim. She let it loose and it hurtled toward Piero's chest.

At that moment, the anchor broke free and the boat lurched forward, nearly throwing them all to the decks. Gianni regained his footing and lifted his chin, thanking his Lord for freeing them, praying this newest arrow had missed Piero. The sail was rounding out as Gaspare hauled on the ship's wheel.

Gianni glanced over the edge, noted the distance that was quickly falling between the enemy and their vessel. A man, with clenched hands, shouted in fury toward the sky.

One of the men who had made it to the net fell into the sea when the ship lurched forward. The two men remaining clung and climbed, daggers in their teeth, nearing Piero. Daria joined Gianni at the rail and looked over, then rushed to help her men, trying so desperately to free Piero of his entanglement.

"Cease your pulling," she demanded. "Every pull upon that rope is liable to do further damage to Piero. Please. Go and help Rune take care of the men who still cling to our ship's ropes."

Rune let an arrow fly and hit the nearest one in the shoulder. The man lost his grip and, with a cry of rage, fell to the water below. The other climbed faster, realizing the danger. But when he rounded the edge, he found himself surrounded by three knights. They wounded him and sent him flying overboard.

Gianni looked around, trying to see in the dark, wind, and rain. "Daria?" he cried. "Daria!"

With an inward groan, he peered over the edge of the ship. The waves were so high now, they climbed halfway up the side. It was difficult to keep one's feet aboard ship. Daria clung to the nets beside Piero.

"Daria, get up here! I will see to him!"

She lifted her face. "I can't get the arrows free! Haul on my count!"

Gianni let out a breath of exasperation and waited for her call. *Una, due* . . . On *tre,* he hauled with Vito. The priest slid upward, to the edge of the rail. The men hurried to lift him over and lay him carefully upon the deck. Gianni leaned down and gripped Daria's hand, hauling her upward and then helping her over the rail.

She didn't pause, rushing to Piero's side. "I can't hear anything! Quickly, help me get him belowdecks!"

In the dim, flickering light of the covered lamp beside Gaspare, Gianni could still make out Piero's ghastly gray face. Was he gone already? Grimly, he helped Vito lift the priest and carry him down the steep stairs to the open hold below. They laid him out across several sacks of grain, beside Ambrogio, who stirred and awoke.

Daria went to his head and put her ear to Piero's mouth. "God in heaven be praised, he still has breath. Nico, fetch me a bucket of water. Tess, I need some rags. Can you tear some from your skirts?"

Gianni lit an oil lamp and then another, then leaned back against a post, watching her at work. She still had the gold crown atop her head, slightly askew, and her hair was a mass of curls about her shoulders. He shook his head. In spite of all she had been through, all she endured, still she boasted such strength! He leaned forward. "How may I assist you, m'lady?"

"Please," she said, pausing and raising her large eyes to meet his. "Go above decks and tell me we are free of the enemy, that that danger is passed. That they are a league away—he is still in my head, reaching for me . . ." She closed her eyes and turned her head as if pulling away from an unseen force. "Please. Ask Gaspare how many men he needs to manage the ship in such heavy seas. Then bring the rest down here, especially Ugo, he's wounded too. We need everyone on this ship to pray, pray with everything in them, if we are to watch our God save our beloved priest."

He turned to go and do as she bid.

"Gianni?"

He turned to face her and she was once again leaning over Piero's mouth, listening. "Hurry, Gianni. Amidei still pursues us. Death is trying to steal him from us."

ፈ ፈ ፈ

SHE drew the broken glass from her pocket and cut open the priest's robe, from neck to belly. He looked older without his robe, she thought grimly, taking in his slight chest and the blood streaming from the two arrows. She eased him to his side and cut open the back of his robe as well. One arrow protruded, having made it clean through his chest. The second had stopped somewhere within his chest cavity, perhaps lodged against a rib. Judging by their location, both had probably pierced his lungs.

Daria swallowed hard, trying not to cry, but it was impossible. She gestured toward Gianni, who had rejoined them, and he broke off the head of the arrow with a snap. Such a delicate piece of wood, was an arrow, and yet capable of such deadly impact . . .

"Do you want me to pull it out?" he asked softly, reaching out to grip a crossbeam in order not to fall. The storm was raging outside, the fiercest Gaspare had ever seen in or about the lagoon.

"Nay," she sniffed, "not yet. If we take it out, it may release more blood inside his lungs. We shall need much prayer . . ."

Her voice cracked and Daria looked away, bringing her hand to her eyes.

Gianni lowered down beside her, meeting Ambrogio's worried gaze. He reached out a hand to her shoulder. "Daria, you have suffered much. I wish this were not upon your shoulders at this moment, but Piero needs you."

She looked to him, eyes shiny with tears. He fought the urge to pull her into his arms. "Please . . ." A tear slipped down her cheek. "My heart, my mind is still divided. I cannot concentrate, hear what God is telling me. Tell me he is gone. That Amidei cannot reach us again."

"Nay, nay," he said, reaching out to wipe her cheek. He could not stand it any longer. She shook with fear. He pulled her into his arms. She hesitated at first, and then clung to him. Ambrogio smiled at him in silent approval. Gianni leaned back, hauling Daria into his lap, rocking her, kissing her forehead tenderly. "It is all right, m'lady. It is all right. Shh, it is all right. I think he is dead, buried in his own foul rubble. It is all right—you are safe."

Ugo and Vito stumbled down the stairs, then, eyes wide, looked away from such an intimate scene. They knelt beside Piero, fearing he had died, but Ambrogio calmed them.

"Daria." He waited until she looked up into his eyes. "The only thing that shall claim us this night is this storm, and I do not believe that God wrestled us out of the enemy's lair to allow us to succumb to the seas. He has made a way for us to escape. Amidei shall not reach you again. Any other shall have to kill me before they touch you."

Daria cried and looked down, shaking her head. "Please, Gianni. Do not say such things."

Gently, he lifted her chin. "You cannot think on your fears. You must settle into your belief. You have been wounded, within, again." He swallowed hard, against a sudden lump in his own throat. "But Father Piero . . . our God, Daria, is he not asking you to heal our dear priest?"

She shook her head, more hair tumbling over her shoulder. "I am weak, Gianni."

"And when you are weak, he is strong," Ambrogio said from the other side of Piero. His hand was on the priest's chest, and he steadily watched the man take one belabored breath and then another. "Come, Daria. You must try. He is failing."

"Find it, Daria." Gianni waited for her to meet his gaze again. "You are strong, deep within. Find the Lord's own strength within you. For Piero. For the Gifted. For all of us."

"The priest told me some things, on the boat," Basilio said from a dark corner. "They made no sense at the time . . ."

"What did he say?" Daria asked.

Basilio looked upward, as if trying to see Piero again before him, hear his words again. "That we can do all things through Christ who strengthens us."

Daria nodded. "What else?"

"God can do what he says he can do." He stepped forward, kneeling by the priest. "He knew. He knew! Lady Daria, these words were meant for you, meant for you to remember, to believe . . ."

"Daria . . ." Ambrogio said in a higher-pitched warning.

"What if God does not choose to heal him?" she whispered. "We can do all things through Christ who strengthens us, God can do all he says he can do, but what if it is not his will, right here, right now? I could not bear it!"

"What if he dies and you did not try?" Gianni returned.

"*Daria.*"

She wearily rose then, and rushed to Piero's side, almost stumbling over him when the ship crested a massive wave, then fell. They all gasped as one, as if they had just emerged from under water. Frightened, they looked about, then to the priest.

"He no longer breathes," Ambrogio said softly. "He is gone."

Daria hesitated, her hands hovering over the arrows.

"Concentrate, Daria," Gianni urged. "Cast off Amidei's hand upon your mind, your heart. You are free. God is here. God is here! We will surround you in prayer. Lord God," he said, looking up to the cross-beams and decking of the ship as if he could peer into heaven itself. "Show her. Come and save our Piero. Show Daria what to do." He leveled a gaze at Daria. "Think, Daria. Just as he's shown you before. What is he asking you to do?"

Her beautiful face was stricken, a mass of consternation and confusion. "Our God is not the God of confusion," Basilio said, suddenly with them. "The priest told me that, too, once."

"Fight the confusion, Daria," Ambrogio said urgently. "Reach for him."

She glanced at Piero's face, swiftly becoming blue. " 'The Lord God formed the man from the dust of the ground,' " she whispered, " 'and breathed life into his nostrils the breath of life, and the man became a living being.' "

She looked to the men. "Take the arrows from him. Quickly."

The men moved forward. Daria watched them, unseeing, lost in thought, reaching for her Lord, what he wanted from her, what he was trying to tell her. Another Scripture came to mind. "Jesus said, 'Peace be with you! As the Father has sent me, I am sending you,' " she whispered. "And with that he breathed on them and said, 'Receive the Holy Spirit.' "

She racked her mind, wanting to hit her head against the side of the ship, shake loose what her Lord wanted her to know. She thought of the disciples, how they were weak and fallible, like her, leaving the Christ at his darkest hour. She considered his absolute love for them, and his desire that they reach out to the world, spread the Gospel, whether or not people wished to hear it. "Like your servant, Piero," she whispered.

Daria looked to the men, holding the wounds closed.

"He is dead, m'lady," Ambrogio said, a tear slipping from the corner of his eye. "His wounds were too grave."

Daria looked to her beloved friend's face, so deadly still, and waved Gianni and Vito away, suddenly seeing where her hands were to be placed. She knelt and reached for the thin priest's chest, trying to ignore how frightfully cold he was. "Move through me, sweet Spirit," she said in a moan. "Return this man to us, Lord God on High. Return him to us. You breathed life into him once; do so again. Together we shall serve you, we shall spread your Gospel everywhere we go. People will learn of your light and turn away from darkness. Use us. Use us all, Savior. But please, Lord, we beg you to come and enter this man's body, to knit together his wounds within, sear them as if with a hot branding iron."

She concentrated on his wounds, seeing them cauterized within, felt heat beneath her fingers as if holding a hot stone. "Seal his lungs, Lord God, and suck out the blood that has seeped within them. Fill them with your breath, Holy One. Fill them. Please, Lord Jesus. Please, Lord God on High. Please, Holy Spirit. Come, come, come and be present in this place. Heal our brother, our mentor, our priest. Come, come . . ."

Daria opened her eyes and pulled her hands away, staring at Piero's face. Was it her imagination or had his death mask slackened?

"Ambrogio, does he breathe?"

Ambrogio leaned in and listened. He gave his head a sorrowful shake.

Daria frowned. What was it that her Lord wanted her to do?

" 'The Lord God formed the man from the dust of the ground,' " she whispered again, " 'and breathed life into his nostrils the breath of life, and the man became a living being. The Lord God formed the man from the dust of the ground,' " she repeated, " 'and breathed life into his nostrils the breath of life, and the man became a living being. The Lord God formed the man from the dust of the ground,' " she said yet again, " 'and breathed life into his nostrils the breath of life, and the man became a living being.' "

She moved to the priest's head and closed her eyes. "Lord, breathe in me," she prayed. "Breathe through me, into Piero. Make him live. Make him live, Holy Spirit." She leaned down and covered his lips with her own, breathing a long, steady breath into him.

Daria sat back as Tessa sat up. "Yes, m'lady, do that again," she said, wiping away her tears, her face suddenly wild with hope. "I felt it! I felt it!"

Daria leaned forward again and studied the priest's face, remembering the sound of air coming from his nostrils as she breathed into him. Gently, she pinched his nostrils shut, prayed again, then breathed another long, steady breath again into his lungs. His chest rose with her breath.

His chest fell, but he did not take another breath. He remained a frightful, gray blue. Dimly, Daria thought she should be fearful. But her fear had edged away, replaced by a gentle warmth. The scent of oranges and cloves filled her nostrils. God was present. He was here. Urging her onward. She smiled, once again awash in peace rather than fear. "My Lord and my God," she said. "Come and abide with us. Save him, Father. Save our friend and priest." She leaned forward and again breathed into Piero, and again, and again.

Daria leaned back and waited.

The hold was silent as they all held their breath, hearing not the groaning and creaking of the ship, nor the waves outside, washing past, nor cargo within the hold shifting with each wave. They only listened for Piero, praying for the blessing.

And it was then that Piero took a sudden, gurgling breath and began coughing.

CHAPTER FORTY-THREE

GIANNI awakened in the hold, a few feet from Daria. It was hardly an intimate moment, but among the soft morning light, the gentle waves after the storm, the snores of men, the quick breathing of children, the wet but constant breathing of Piero, he smiled. Never had he felt more glad to greet a morn than this one. He turned to his side, feeling every one of his battles over the last few days, every strained muscle. But his mind was upon Daria. He flanked the men and boys; she flanked Agata and Tessa.

Her hair cascaded over her shoulders and partially over her face. The bruises at her neck and wrist still were purple and green, but already fading. Gianni thought back to last night, when she had hesitated when he pulled her to him, then settled into his arms. He had been reluctant to let her go, to go about her holy work. And she had wanted to stay; he was sure of it.

His eyes flicked to Abramo's crown and necklace, set in a neat pile beside her, destined for sale in trade for much-needed supplies. When the storm had abated, Gaspare came to the hold and scanned every inch until his eyes landed upon the beetle in amber. He picked it up and held it to the light, then glanced at Daria. "M'lady, this ring does not belong among us. It is an evil talisman."

"Dispose of it," she had said, tiredly sinking into her blankets.

Gaspare had left, and returned only after he had flung it as far as he could into the depths.

His eyes returned to hers, watching as they shifted beneath her lids, heavy among the dream realm. Her breathing quickened, as if she were frightened, and Gianni fought the urge to shake her awake, remind her all was well.

He sighed heavily. He knew this stirring within him. The fierce desire to protect, the longing to hold, the wish to always be at her side. He had felt the same as a young man, for a young woman in his village, but a call had already been placed in his heart to serve the Church. He never pursued the woman, knowing she would never be happy outside Toscana. And here he was . . . in love now, with the Duchess. The Duchess of Toscana.

He was in love with Daria d'Angelo. He let the words roll around in his head, trying them on like a new pair of boots.

Admitting it came at a price. This was hardly the time and place to fall in love. He was not suitable for her, far beneath her station. Her previous lover had been Marco Adimari, now one of the Nine of Siena. The Nine!

He shook his head, thinking of how foolish Marco had been to leave her. Now he knew why the man looked at her with such plaintive looks, as if he would do anything to be by her side, once again. He had known Daria, known her as husband, and then left her. And now . . .

Her eyelashes fluttered open, her dark olive eyes slowly focusing upon Gianni. A small smile lifted the corners of her full lips and she did not look away.

He returned her smile, staring into her eyes, wishing she could read the words he longed to say within his gaze.

৬ ৬ ৬

DARIA watched as Gianni broke their intense gaze, turned, and rose. He took his jacket from the hook and went to the stair, paused, glanced back at her as if making sure she was still there, still safe, and then climbed to the upper deck.

She knew the look in his eye. He was in love with her.

Daria turned to her back and stared upward, feeling the gentle rock of the sea beneath her back. Marco had loved her; they had shared a great love. But this, what she felt from Gianni was different, more steady, solid somehow. He knew her to be barren. He knew her weakness. Every one of them. And still he loved her.

Her parents would never have approved the match. He was the seventh son of a Toscana landholder, with no means to pay a dowry. But her parents, her home was gone. She might never return to Siena. Only God knew where they were to go . . . A thought came to her, making her smile. The only opinion that truly mattered was her Lord's. He knew they would be here, together. He knew each of them, through and through. They had both been called as part of the Gifted. Were they also called to something more?

She sighed and rolled to her knees, aching in ways she did not know she could. She wished she could sleep, but forced herself forward, to check on Piero. She crawled over, lifting his covers and checking his wounds, shaking her head at the fact that not only were they already scabbing, but that the priest breathed at all.

She stared at his odd-shaped head, his weak chin, thinking him beautiful, thanking God he lived. She covered him again and rose, thinking she would need to see to God's other wounded warriors this day, once they awakened and she gathered some supplies. Ambrogio desperately needed care, and Ugo . . . even Vito and Gianni had cuts that needed attention. She sighed happily, so glad they were all alive at all, and climbed up the stairs into a bright, clear autumn day at sea.

"Where are we heading, Captain?" she asked.

Both Gaspare and Gianni raised their heads to look at her.

"Southeast," Gaspare said, with a grin. "Off the normal trade routes, out of Amidei's reach, as far as we can go."

"No sign of pursuit?" Daria asked, glancing back to the white, churned-up sea that trailed behind them. No ship was on the horizon.

"Not yet," Gaspare said. He looked at them both with red eyes, under heavy lids. "You understand that this is a temporary respite. If he still lives, Amidei will come. He is but one of our enemies, and now that we have proven to him that we cannot be turned, he will have but one goal."

"As it shows in the illuminations," Daria said. "The dragon will hunt the peacock."

Gaspare took a step forward and put a finger beneath her chin. "But the peacock has proven herself as an eagle. Do not fear, woman, simply be aware."

"Indeed," she said.

He left them then, walking slowly down the stairs.

Gianni took the wheel and looked up at the gently billowed sail, then down at Daria as she took his arm. He smiled down at her. "It's a new day, Daria. Be at ease."

"I shall if you shall," she said, looking up at him from the side.

"Daria, I . . . I hope that one day you might forgive me."

"For what?"

"For allowing it." The muscle in his cheek worked and his eyebrows lowered. "For allowing them to take you."

"You did not allow it, Gianni. You did all you could. You were poisoned. I felt the effects of it myself. It was I who was foolish, taken in by Vincenzo . . . I had so hoped . . ."

"You've lost everyone you've ever loved," he said, his green eyes becoming shadowed with grief for her. He reached out and tucked a strand of hair behind her ear.

"Not everyone, Gianni," she said, looking up at him.

He stared down at her for a long moment, until she could feel the heat of a blush climb her neck and jaw.

He slowly tied the wheel in place and turned back to her. Still she stared up at him, invitation in her huge, olive eyes. Gianni reached for her, settling his hands upon either hip, still silently asking if she was all right, if she was certain . . .

She smiled at him, and he slowly wrapped a strong arm behind her back with his right and lifted a hand to her chin, moving carefully, so carefully, inherently knowing he had to be tender, careful not to frighten her. He lifted his left hand to her cheek and she closed her eyes, leaning into his touch, feeling it as healing. She opened her eyes as he pulled her a bit closer and lifted her lips as he bent to meet hers.

He kissed her softly at first, small, short, searching kisses. Then he took her face in both hands and groaned, kissing her all across her forehead, her eyes, her nose, her chin, then seeking her lips again, this time, with more fervent hunger.

It was he who pulled away and smiled, shaking his head. "Will you never cease to amaze me?"

"I hope not," she said, leaving her hands in his.

A cough pulled them apart. Vito stood against the rail, arms crossed, grinning. "I was wondering when you two would see to the business at hand. Gaspare sent me up. Said you'd need someone at the wheel, distracted as you were." He coughed and grinned, raising his eyebrows. "Appears I arrived in the nick of time." He gestured toward the wheel. "May I? I've always wanted to try my hand at the wheel."

Gianni gestured him forward and Vito took it, raising his face to the morning breeze. Daria stood beside him, then took his arm, reaching up to kiss his cheek.

"M'lady! What was that for? What will my captain think, with him right there and all?"

Gianni grinned over at them.

But Daria stared at Vito. "That was for being such a trusted friend and worthy knight. God has indeed blessed us in bringing you and your brother to the Gifted."

"I do what I can, m'lady. And mayhap I'll earn another kiss when you discover something else."

"Oh yes? What would that be?"

"I found your bird."

Daria took a step away from him. "Bormeo?"

Vito grinned and pointed to the sky. High above, a white falcon circled their ship.

Daria let out a gasp and reached up on tiptoe to kiss him again. "Is it really him? How did he get free?"

"I'm certain I did something. The captain, as much as you think highly of him, I have to say he was not all that eager to go after your bird—"

"Vito," Gianni warned, crossing his arms over his chest with a smile.

"It was I who thought of poor Bormeo, caught by the evil Sorcerer. I knew he was important to you, m'lady, and that we should try to save him, but our captain . . . for some reason, all he could think about was you." He winked at her and leaned closer. "If it doesn't come to fruition, this thing between you and the captain, always know that I'd be happy to serve in his stead."

"Thank you, Vito," she said, trying to swallow her grin. "A lady always needs her admiring servants."

"And I will always remain as such," he said, bowing lowly. "Now, go and fetch your bird, m'lady, before he gives up and thinks you are not aboard this ship after all."

CHAPTER FORTY-FOUR

THREE days later, Piero rose from his bed and came above decks. Nico and Roberto were on either side of him, supporting him, and Tessa hovered behind. They had put into port on a small isle in the Ionian Sea, finally daring to believe that they had outdistanced the Sorcerer. Since funds were scarce, they found an antiquities dealer, traded in the crown and necklace, and then purchased only the most basic of supplies and a peasant's dress for Daria, who was likely to attract attention in the queen's gown Abramo had dressed her in.

That evening, they gathered on the deck of the ship. It was a temperate night, even in the middle of November, this far south. By the light of the lamps, they read aloud Amidei's portion of their letter. The text spoke more of light battling dark, of trusting the Lord when it seemed all had been set against them. Piero looked to Daria and nodded when he finished that portion, silently saluting her.

The Gifted gained strength from the words, and in the margin, they studied the illumination, pictures of the dragon and the peacock, an island fortress and dark storm clouds, surrounded by heavy seas. "The fresco in Torcello," Piero mused. "It showed us on a ship, in the midst of a storm."

"Let us hope we just weathered that one, and do not have another ahead," Vito said.

"There will be other storms," Piero said.

"Yes, yes," Daria said, "can we put that aside for now? I would prefer not to think of storms, at least for another day or two. Father, Hasani spoke of Abramo's letter, of holding it to the light as we did ours. That it would show us the way to go."

Piero pursed his lips and then shuffled the sheets together, holding them to the sunlight. He shook his head and handed them to Gaspare and Gianni. "I do not see any semblance of a map in those three. Certainly, not like in our portion." When they had lifted the three pages of their own in Siena, and held them up to a candle, they could clearly see the coast of Italia and Venezia marked. They had seen it as their own heavenly map.

Gianni and then Gaspare both looked and then shook their heads. All seemed to let out a sigh of disappointment.

"Hasani's vision was untrue?" Daria said.

"I doubt that. We are missing something. Go and fetch the glass pieces," Piero said to Tessa, "all of them."

The girl ran and quickly returned. Piero spread them out. With all seven, now they could clearly see how they interlocked, the small metal prongs joining together. The deep blue was the sea, the tan the land of Italia. It was as they had hoped, another map! There was the great basilica of Roma, of Siena, of Firenze, of Pisa, of Lucca, of Venezia. The golden path atop the glass pieces curved from Roma, to Siena, to Venezia and up and to the left.

"To Avignon," the priest murmured. "This is our next step."

"Uh," Gaspare said, "if that is true, then we are headed in the wrong direction. We must head west and sail up and around toward France."

"Let me be certain I understand the task before us," Vito said, pacing back and forth as if lecturing them. "We're sailing a ship with but one true sailor among us. We harbor escaped prisoners of the doge, a man with the greatest fleet in all the world. According to the illuminations, the dragon will continue to pursue us, and if he lives we have left him maimed and burning in fury. Let us not forget that we, a group not likely to be favored by the Church, now are to go to a city *full* of churchmen. Oh, and at some point, we must free one of our men from slavers. Turkish slavers." He raised his eyebrows and pursed his lips as if considering the odds and then nodded. "I'm in."

Ugo shook his head and the others smiled.

Piero brushed his hands over the glass map. "Our road will not be easy, but we have endured much, learned much. Our God will see us through. Are we all up to the task? Might we see where our God is taking us, what he intends? Do we have the strength to see this through?"

A heavy silence settled among them.

Basilio coughed. "A wise man once told me that we can do all things through Christ. He also said that God can do all he claims."

Gianni clasped the man on the shoulder and leaned forward, lifting his hand between them. "If God is for us . . ."

Vito, Daria, and Gaspare moved at once to place their hands atop his. Then Tessa, the boys, the other knights.

Piero held back, and they all looked to him. He moved inward and smiled at each of them, one at a time, then placed his hand atop theirs. "Oh, my dear Gifted," he said softly, reverently, "God is indeed for us. Who can be against us?"

AUTHOR'S NOTE

As you may have guessed, I took some creative license in spinning this tale. Here are some things to separate fact from fiction . . .

Apollos, a learned Alexandrian Jew, was a contemporary of Priscilla and Aquila, a devoted follower of Saint Paul. They crossed paths in either Ephesus or Corinth. According to Scripture, he preached quite cogently, but had to be set straight on the facts about the Holy Spirit. After that, he was lauded as one of the finest disciples of Christ in Ephesus and beyond. Some (including Martin Luther) believe him to be the author of the Epistle to Hebrews. He is not known to have a prophetic bent, as described within this novel.

Glasswork was first created by the ancient Egyptians (multiple vessels have been discovered in tombs), traveled throughout Mesopotamia, and eventually reached the Phoenicians. The Romans practiced the craft between the first and eighth centuries, and then seemed to lose the art for four hundred years, when Italians relearned the craft from other Northern Europeans. However, the glass map of Christendom depicted within *The Betrayed* is a figment of my imagination.

San Giorgio was destroyed by earthquakes and rebuilt decades later. I placed her remains in the water for dramatic effect.

Saint Mark's body was reportedly stolen from Alexandria in the ninth century and interred in San Marco—the doge's private basilica. It was one of the greatest coups among holy relics (and I think rather scandalous!). The grotto beneath San Marco is purely a fictional device (although the crypt is there). And while there are twin peacocks and a green disc in a nave of San Marco among the mosaic flooring, they are a good distance from the altar and crypt.

There are numerous islands in and around Venezia, and some have history as quarantine islands and monasteries. There is no island, however, where I placed Abramo Amidei's dark fortress, and there was no isle for lepers in 1341.

There was a fierce winter storm in February 1341. It threatened the city herself and became my inspiration for the climactic ending of this novel (although I moved it to November). Legend has it that Saint Mark himself intervened and saved the city from certain destruction.

Thanks for joining me on this adventure!

Lisa T. Bergren
January 2007

READERS GUIDE FOR

The Betrayed

DISCUSSION QUESTIONS

1. Things go from bad to worse for the Gifted, in *The Betrayed*. What was the hardest scene for you to read in this book and why?

2. Have you ever been in a position where you thought it was as bad as it could be, and then it got worse?

3. The author attempted to show each character experiencing a measure of betrayal—Vincenzo feels as if Daria has betrayed him and then betrays her in horrific ways; Gianni feels betrayed when Daria's eye is drawn back to Vincenzo and Marco, even when he warns her; Hasani is betrayed by those who capture him; Basilio and Rune are betrayed by former employers. Have you ever been betrayed? By whom? How did you deal with it?

4. On p.293, Abramo Amidei taunts Daria about God's inaction. What biblical scene did this remind you of? Have you ever wrestled with this question yourself?

5. Have you ever been drawn to or pulled in by evil? In what circumstance? How were you successful (or not) in combating it?

6. Amidei attempts to break Daria *emotionally* (using fear and threats to her friends), *spiritually* (asking questions that are logical and difficult to answer), and *physically* (whipping). If you were in her shoes, which would have been the most difficult attack to endure and why?

7. On p.298, Daria rails against God. Have you ever been furious at God? Told him about it? Do you think he can handle it?

8. If *The Begotten* is largely about healing and love, *The Betrayed* is largely about perseverance and faith. What is it about persevering through a difficult time or experience that can make us more faithful, stronger? Describe your own experience.

9. If you could have one of the Gifted's gifts, which would you ask for, and why? As a reminder, we've seen so far: wisdom, faith, healing, visions, discernment, miraculous powers.

An Interview with Lisa T. Bergren

Q: What inspired you to write this series?

A: I've always loved the epic saga—stories and characters that you can invest yourself in, learn from, experience. In watching the *Lord of the Rings* trilogy on film, I wanted to go after something similar in feel. Classic good vs. evil, heroes and villains, the whole kit and caboodle. When *Publishers Weekly* said, "Disregard *Da Vinci Code* comparisons and think *Lord of the Rings,* but without Hobbits and the allegorical trappings," I took it as a huge pat on the back.

Q: Were you inspired by *The Da Vinci Code* too?

A: I loved the pacing of that book—the mysteries and turns. It was the first novel in many years that I read in under twenty-four hours. But I objected to the conclusions of the author, things I found objectionable to my faith. So . . .yes and no.

Q: Is it hard to keep a cast of characters straight?

A: It's definitely a challenge. But I love the plot twists that so many characters and personalities allow me to write. You have Daria, who has taken over this series (and I didn't see that coming!), what with her highly desirable gift of healing, and the handfasting all gone wrong. Gianni stole my heart with the conflict in his own; Hasani, tall and strong and silent, I find fascinating. Piero is the perfect "wise man" for my cast, a classic fictional archetype, and Tessa surprised me as showing up as a child. And Vito . . . I'm always drawn to the funny sidekicks that break the tension in movies. That's why he's in the mix.

Q: What is with the handfasting? Were Daria and Marco married or not?

A: Research always turns over fabulous elements for any fiction writer. I learned that in that time, particularly among nobles, that they could have a Church-sanctioned "handfasting," basically a dry run at marriage, with the distinct goal of becoming pregnant. If things went well, they went through with a betrothal and the sacrament of marriage. For Daria and Marco, both so desperate for an heir, since they are the last in each of their families, it was vital. It's a tragic element that I think adds depth to the series—to have loved, and yet not been able to continue on together, simply because of the practical needs of the times. A romance novel would have made them choose to stay together, regardless; an epic trilogy allows us to see what happens to them both when a different choice must be made.

Q: Were women really as educated as Daria in this era? Allowed to run businesses?

A: I turned up a few in my research. So there was historical justification to write her that way, especially as the sole heir of the d'Angelo fortune.

Q: What about medical advancements of the time?

A: It was pretty archaic. They were all about the bodily "humors" and somewhat mystical means of healing. But they also made extraordinary use of natural materials—herbs, roots, etc.—to treat ailments. Still, I read an account of an entire leg being transplanted about the time of our series. It didn't work out, but that they even tried is amazing!

Q: How involved was your research?

A: Pretty in-depth. When you come up with a concept for a novel, it seems like it will be easy. You go off of what you know, have read, have

seen—the romantic stuff in the catalog of memory. But then you begin reading, you pick up a massive two volume encyclopedia of Medieval Italian history, you discover discrepancies between the historians, and that the Gifted's society is even significantly different from the Renaissance era a hundred years later. It's really getting to know a world from scratch. The trick in writing a historical supernatural thriller is that you have to weave in enough history to give the reader a sense of the times, but you can't be too absorbed in the detail, because it will detract from the pacing. For instance, I elected not to get into the fact that at the time, each area of Italy spoke a different language, or a significantly different dialect; it was really Dante who unified the languages. So, in honor of the genre, you pick and choose what you use.

Q: Where did Abramo Amidei come from?

A: Not a whole lot more inspiration than Classic Villain here—charming, handsome, but evil to the core. I did quite a bit of research about the cults of the time, dark magic and all that, and his troop emerges from that.

Q: What about the group he leads?

A: Abramo Amidei's followers came out of my research too. There's historical evidence that groups who practiced the dark arts often gave themselves over in orgies, bestiality, really an "anything goes/anything you feel like" mentality. There were black cats on the altar, child sacrifices . . . many horrors. My goal was to hint at it, without bringing it on stage too much. But we need to see how depraved this group is to truly recognize how good and righteous (although imperfect) our Gifted are—to contrast the light against the dark. Abramo Amidei is bent on owning people any which way he can get them—mentally, emotionally, physically, sexually, financially, spiritually. And he's very good at bringing people in on all these fronts until he meets up with the Gifted. Amidei uses his full arsenal in his desire to break apart the Gifted, and in his pursuit to turn Daria, bewitch her, own her. He wishes to own or destroy the Gifted because in defeating his enemy, he becomes stronger yet.

Q: Talk to us about your views of the Catholic Church.

A: My views of the medieval Catholic Church would be widely corroborated by contemporary Catholics. Internally, things were going poorly for the Church at the time, with major corruption that only escalated as decades passed (that which Martin Luther really objected to c.1500—and led to the birth of the Protestant Church). We'll see more "bad guy Catholics" in the next book, as well as many "good guy Catholics," because the Church is a major "character" in book three and I want it to be clear that not all were off the path.

Catholicism, of course, was the *only* Church of the time—so I fervently hope I am not seen as Catholic-bashing; I know many faithful Catholics who are doing Christ's good work in the world! Jesus took issue with the clerics in power during his time; we've seen powerful non-denominational preachers fall in our day—again, it's something we always have to keep an eye on. The devil will always be preying upon those in power, regardless of their religious affiliation.

Q: What happens next for our Gifted?

A: They're heading to Avignon to take on the Church, about to discover the full extent of their call and how they might fulfill prophecy, and they're still pursued by forces of evil. There will be a big, climatic ending. You'll have to read book three to find out if Amidei is a part of that or not!

Q: Did you get to go to France to do research?

A: The South of France, briefly, yes. And a third trip to Italy. I keep reading novels and research material that makes me want to go back *again*. I'm totally in love with Italy and am very concerned that no other country will ever measure up when I explore them (which I hope to do anyway!).

Q: What else is in your book stacks?

A: I just finished *The Memory Keeper's Daughter* and loved how Dunant wove in the storyline of the degenerating properties of a bad decision and

a secret long kept, and I'm looking forward to Hosseini's *A Thousand Splendid Suns,* Mackel's *The Hidden,* Groot's *Madman,* and Morrisey's *In High Places.* I always have a pile of books, tempting me to sit back and read rather than sit down at my computer and write!

଼ ଼ ଼

FOR MORE ON LISA T. BERGREN, please visit her website: www.LisaTawnBergren.com

Look for the other books in the Gifted series!

BOOK ONE

The Begotten

Available now!

BOOK TWO

The Betrayed

Available now!

BOOK THREE

The Blessed

Coming from Berkley in 2008!